Death in Kabul

Alison Belsham is the author of the internationally acclaimed Tattoo Thief trilogy, which has been translated into 15 languages and was a No.1 bestseller in Italy. As well as writing crime, she is collaborating with her brother Nick Higgins on an action thriller series set in Afghanistan. She is a co-founder of the Edinburgh Writers' Forum, providing professional development and networking for writers.

From 2003 to 2007, Nick Higgins worked in Afghanistan as a security advisor on a variety of projects encompassing the UN, private military companies, the US Embassy and others. He has lived in or visited all the locations mentioned, including Lashkar Gah City in Helmand Province, nearly three months in a guest house in downtown Kandahar City, Herat City and Kabul.

Praise for *Death in Kabul*

'A tense, taut and totally authentic thriller that grips from the first page and doesn't let go. *Death in Kabul* immerses you in ⊃o3 Kabul, riven by corruption where danger lurks in every ⌐ey. Be careful whom you trust in this city without mercy'

D. V. Bishop, author of *City of Vengeance*

vividly portrayed murder mystery in a fresh and fascinating ting. With wonderful characters and a great plot, I hope this he first of many from this duo'

Susi Holliday, author of *The Last Resort*

ıthentic, thrilling and brilliantly plotted, *Death in Kabul* is a ⌐cking action thriller that brings the city vividly to life'

Marion Todd, author of *See Them Run*

ich and atmospheric, *Death in Kabul* plunges us directly into ⌐ grubby, noisy streets of the capital and to a murder invest- tion that kept me in its thrall to the end. I loved being a part Mac's world and only hope I get to see him again'

Louisa Scarr, author of *Under a Dark Cloud*

rip-roaring, page-turner of a novel with a truly clever and ginal plot. *Death in Kabul* is a stunning exploration of life in ⊃3 Kabul, and a fantastic start to an exciting new series!'

Sheila Bugler, author of *The Lucky Eight*

ıe of the most authentic thrillers I've read for ages. Drags headfirst into the colourful Kabul underworld, and sends barrelling down its backstreets at a frenetic pace that just ⌐n't let up'

Robert Scragg, author of *End of the Line*

'It's a first class police thriller with a big difference. The investigation whips through shady characters and locales at breakneck pace but the setting removes all the familiar procedural techniques, keeping you on the edge of your seat right to the stunning finale. Explosive stuff!'

D. L. Marshall, author of *Black Run*

'A fast-paced and gripping thriller that conjures up vivid images of deserts and alleyways, stolen artefacts and bloodied sands, where knowledge is currency and murder is committed behind a mirage of lies'

Ian Skewis, author of *A Murder of Crows*

'Superbly plotted – if you like your thrillers brimming with authentic detail and non-stop action, this is for you!'

Margaret Kirk, author of *In the Blood*

'A bumpy ride through mystery, lawlessness and betrayal in mountainous Afghanistan that leaves you constantly looking over your shoulder. *Death in Kabul* throws together an eclectic cast of characters, driven into an unlikely alliance by a shared quest for justice – even if justice means something different for each'

Heleen Kist, author of *In Servitude*

'This exciting and compelling crime thriller is like nothi
I've ever read before. A colourful, visual depiction of life i
Kabul coupled with a fast-paced investigation, this book trul
transports you to somewhere else entirely. *Death in Kabul*
100% one of my books of the year!'

Roxie K

A.BELSHAM & N.HIGGINS

DEATH IN KABUL

CANELO

First published in the United Kingdom in 2022 by

Canelo
Unit 9, 5th Floor
Cargo Works, 1-2 Hatfields
London, SE1 9PG
United Kingdom

A CIP catalogue record for this book is available from the British Library.

Print ISBN 978 1 80032 744 3
Ebook ISBN 978 1 80032 743 6

Look for more great books at www.canelo.co

Printed and bound in Great Britain by Clays Ltd, Elcograf S.p.A.

1

For Baktash, Shariff and many more Afghan friends

Kabul 2003

The Taliban have been overthrown by the NATO-led coalition and Kabul becomes a frontier city where crime and corruption have a stranglehold on the fledgling democracy. Coalition troops, NGO personnel, carpetbaggers and warlords co-exist in an uneasy truce...

Prologue

Davie Marshall looked around and tasted fear at the back of his mouth. The dark silhouette of a Soviet tank loomed before him, and beyond it another and another. Row upon row. The manifestation of superpower aggression, an invading force sent to subjugate. A land grab that would broadcast a message to her enemies, and the wider world: we'll take what we want.

The moon came out from behind a cloud and its pale light showed the place for what it was – Kabul's tank graveyard. Metal hulks, abandoned to the ravages of rust, paint stripped away by the grit-laden wind that tore down from the Hindu Kush and raced towards the city across the vast Shomali Plain. Steel carcasses picked over by street kids and beggars for anything that could be sold in the city's bustling markets. Acres of Soviet detritus stretched as far as the eye could see, telling a story of overconfidence, and of failure. Afghanistan had shown the invaders over ten brutal years that it was not a country to be underestimated. The high hopes of the 1979 invasion had turned to dust, and the Russians had retreated with their tails between their legs in 1989.

Marshall shivered, wondering if this latest incursion would fare any better. By early December, the bitter Afghan winter was already making itself felt. The wind ricocheted through the alleys between the vehicles, rattling broken hatches, moaning through empty gun turrets, disturbing the ghosts of the long-dead Soviet tank crews. He darted behind the nearest wreck, not wanting to reveal himself until he'd got the lay of the land.

He should never have come here alone, and anxiety gnawed at his belly.

But he'd had no choice.

He didn't believe the man he was here to meet would come by himself, any more than he believed that the name he'd been given was real. But if the bloke *was* alone, maybe he could make it out alive. If he could be convincing enough...

Clouds scudded across the moon, cloaking the landscape in shadow once more. He ventured deeper into the graveyard, unsure if he was heading in the right direction, listening for the shrill whistle that would signal his contact's arrival.

Instead, he heard a voice.

'*Salaam alaikum.*'

The whispered greeting came from nowhere and sounded anything but friendly. He tightened his hold on the grip of his 9mm Browning.

He recognised the voice. A torch shone in his eyes, blinding him, and the man spoke in guttural Pashtu. He didn't understand what the man was saying.

'Speak English,' he said, a tremor in his voice giving too much away. He squinted into the light, angry with himself for having lost the element of surprise.

'You came alone?'

Of course, he had. Who the hell was he going to let in on this?

He nodded. 'Yes. You?'

The torch was switched off, but still blinded, he could see nothing.

He heard shuffling on the stony ground. There was more than one of them. That meant trouble. He fought the urge to run, heart pounding.

I should have brought someone to cover my back.

As his eyes grew used to the dark, he stared at the man. He was wearing a black shalwar kameez and had a woollen scarf wrapped around his head and neck. But his eyes glinted in the moonlight and his features were familiar.

'You've got the money?' said Davie.

'I'll get it.' The man paused. 'You need to give me more time.'

Davie took a calculated risk. 'Twenty-four hours. That's all I'll give you. After that...'

'And after that, what will you do?' The voice dripped scorn.

The veiled threat had been a mistake. He put a hand out to steady himself on the hull of the nearest tank. The metal was so cold it burned his fingers, making him gasp. His grip slipped nervously on the Browning.

There was a flash of silver in the moonlight. He had a split second to understand that he wouldn't come away from here alive. The man had never had any intention of paying him off.

He knew too much.

Davie felt the sting of the blade slicing across his windpipe. He breathed in and spluttered, choking. His knees went. A jet of his blood arced across the face of the moon, spattering the ground with the sound of soft-falling rain.

Chapter 1

Saturday, 6 December 2003

Alasdair 'Mac' MacKenzie clambered from the ladder onto the roof of the shipping container, – the shitty metal box he currently called home. Taking care not to spill the mug of black coffee in his right hand, he straightened up and looked to the north, as he did every morning, with a deep breath. Beyond the grounds of the Kabul police training camp and the ragtag of rooftops and minarets, in the far, far distance, the great wall of the Hindu Kush soared to nearly eight thousand metres. Though at this time, just before dawn, it was simply a black mass that blotted out the stars in the lower portion of the sky.

He cradled his coffee mug, warming his hands. The rungs of the ladder had been freezing to the touch – time to get gloves. There was a dusting of frost on the top of the container, and the rest of the camp's buildings glistened with it. The air bit his lungs as he breathed. It was a dry cold here, so different to the freezing damp that seeped into the bones at home on the west coast of Scotland. But no matter how cold it got, he wouldn't stop his morning ritual of coming up here to watch the sun rise.

As faint smudges of light began to show over the east of the city, mosques in every direction started broadcasting the first of the five daily calls to prayer. Most were recorded and blared out of loudspeakers, but some were still sung in the traditional manner by the muezzin.

Mac sat down on a low wooden chair he'd picked up in the Pul-e Khishti bazaar and sipped his coffee, listening to the long, wavering wails calling to the faithful. '*Allahu akbar… ashadu an la ilaha illa Llah…*' It only lasted a few minutes, but the hypnotic, mournful sound haunted him long after the last note had faded away. Then the sun crept over the horizon, painting the Kush a hundred shades of orange, red and gold as it climbed. Three months here, and he'd seriously fallen in love with the country. Which was just as well, given the employment prospects back home… With the bitter coffee grounds gritty on his tongue, he savoured the fact that he had at least another hour before he was expected in class.

He climbed down the ladder attached to the side of the container, slipped his mug inside his door, grabbed a towel and set off across the small walled compound that kept the expat training staff at Camp Julien separated from the Afghan trainees. The staff offices were in a squat breezeblock building that ran along the north side of the compound. Opposite this, his container was one of several staff accommodation units – the dubious privilege of being provided with free on-base boarding. Home sweet home it certainly bloody wasn't.

Meals were provided in the cookhouse in the main part of the camp, where the Afghan cooks had a special way with chicken and rice – the menu varied between chicken and rice, chicken and rice, and sometimes even chicken and rice. Although the camp was ostensibly run by the Canadian Army, they clearly weren't shelling out for the police trainees' food. Thankfully, his assistant, Ginger, who bunked in the container next to his, had obtained a two-ring portable gas cooker, and knocked up dubious alternatives when he was able to find lamb or goat meat at the local market.

Mac knocked on Ginger's door.

'Any chance of an egg banjo, chum?'

Ten minutes later he was sitting on Ginger's only chair, balancing a plate with a couple of egg banjos on his lap. A former para sergeant, Chris 'Ginger' Jameson had introduced Mac to this food of the gods. If an army marched on its stomach, the British Army marched on egg banjos – two slippery fried eggs jammed between slices of rubbery white bread – and virtually impossible to eat without getting yolk down your chin.

He munched on them as he reviewed the morning's lesson plan. Ginger sat opposite him on the low truckle bed, also eating his breakfast. Together, they taught Afghan police trainers peacekeeping and counterinsurgency – Mac's background in anti-terrorism in the Met perfectly complementing Ginger's experience from a decade in the Parachute Regiment.

'More caffeine,' he said, swallowing his final mouthful of yolk-soaked bread.

Ginger obligingly filled his cup from the battered metal espresso pot on the table. The sergeant's bulk filled the small space between them. He was all brawn, which somehow didn't sync with the freckled boyish face and red hair that gave rise to his nickname.

'What are we covering this morning?' said Ginger.

'How to search personnel at VCPs,' said Mac. That stood for vehicle checkpoints, which were generously scattered throughout the city to enable the Afghan police to make any journey take three times longer than it should have. 'I'll run through the theory...' He ignored Ginger's loud snort at this. 'Then we'll demo – you can have a concealed weapon, I'll search you for it.'

'After which we get the Joes to search each other, while we try not to laugh.' Joes was their private shorthand for the students.

'Or I get them all to have a go at searching you?' said Mac with a wicked grin.

'Did I tell you I might have found somewhere that's selling KitKats, and they're not out of date or made somewhere weird?'

'Okay, they search each other.'

–

6

'Right, now I'm going to show you how it's done,' said Mac, in his clearest classroom English. 'Ginger, up against the wall, please.'

The interpreter translated, and fifteen Afghan police captains watched as Ginger assumed the position.

'You get them to lean like this on the side of the vehicle – arms outstretched and legs apart. Then, hook one of your feet behind one of their legs while you search them.' Mac did this, then frisked Ginger's arms, legs and torso.

He knew Ginger wouldn't make it that easy, so when the para made a move for his concealed weapon, Mac was ready for it. This was the point of the hooked foot – he used it to sweep Ginger's leg out from under him and Ginger crashed to the floor.

'Oomph! Fucking hell, Mac.'

Mac laughed and so did the students. He put out a hand to help Ginger up, but then thought better of it. He didn't want to share the indignity of ending up on the floor as well.

One of the Joes stuck up a hand and said something in rapid Dari.

'Mr Mac,' said the interpreter, 'Captain Sadiqi is asking if that's how you searched people in the London police?'

'Um...'

'Yes, do tell us,' said Ginger with a grin, now back on his feet.

'Um... not exactly.' Of course bloody not. Kicking your mark to the ground was strictly against the rules in the Met. But things were different here.

Luckily, he was saved from explaining by a knock on the door. One of the project-management staff stood tentatively on the threshold.

'Got a minute, Mac?'

'I'm teaching, Steve.'

'Yeah, but Phelps wants to see you in his office. Straightaway, he said.' Steve shrugged apologetically.

Mac wondered what could be so urgent. 'Any clues?' He turned to Ginger. 'You can finish the lesson, right?'

Ginger nodded as Steve backed out of the doorway. 'No idea. But he wasn't looking too cheerful.'

'Okay. Let's go.'

He followed Steve across the open training ground at the centre of the camp and through the gate into the staff compound. Egon Phelps ran the training project on the ground for the American company that had the contract, World Training Providers Inc. He was American too, but the staff he employed were a mixture of Brits, Yanks and a few Europeans. All of them had police anti-terrorist or special-forces experience and their remit was to transform the Kabul City Police into a professional force that could provide high-quality professional security throughout the city.

Steve ducked away into his own office as they entered the block, obviously not invited to the meeting.

Mac knocked on Phelps's door.

'Come in.'

He walked in and dropped into a chair in front of the manager's desk.

'This better be important.'

'Mac, I'm going to need you to pass the rest of this course off to your number two,' said Phelps. 'Something's come up.'

Mac wasn't sure he liked the sound of this, but he waited for Phelps to continue.

'Kabul City Police HQ have just been in touch, a Major Jananga.'

'And?' This still didn't tell him why he'd been hauled out of his classroom.

'They think they've got a British soldier,' continued Phelps. Cryptic, as always. The man made need-to-know an artform.

'Got a soldier?'

'They've found a body.'

'Where?' said Mac.

8

'They were called out to the tank graveyard at first light. A couple of kids found him. Throat cut, British uniform.'

'Jesus.' Mac exhaled. If this was true, it would open a right can of worms. 'But what's that got to do with us?'

'Major Jananga, in a frankly off-the-chart moment of self-awareness, has wisely realised that with a British victim, he might be expected to do things a little differently from... um... standard Afghan police practice.' Phelps pulled a face. 'You know as well as I do that the Afghan police are pretty amateur in these things and have no forensic capabilities. Being aware that we use ex-Met police for our training programmes, he's requested someone with "Scotland Yard experience" to assist. I've volunteered you.'

'What the...? No way.' Mac shook his head. 'Scotland Yard? Is he expecting Sherlock fucking Holmes?'

'You were in the Met.'

'Yeah, sure. But I was SO15 – Counter Terrorism.'

'And before that?'

'Three months on a Major Incidents Team, before I transferred. I didn't even see a single murder investigation from end to end. I'm not the guy he's looking for.'

'Yes, but you're the guy we've got. Everyone here is Counter Terrorism – it's what we do, so you've got more experience with murder investigations than the rest of us. And more experience of them than Major Jananga.'

'So just tell 'em it's not our area of expertise.' Mac was determined not to get roped into something that would clearly end up being a giant headache. 'And what about the army? If the victim's a soldier, surely they'll do the investigation?'

'Not their jurisdiction.' Phelps leaned forward across his desk. 'Listen, pal. Our contract's up for renewal in four months. It's worth eight million dollars to the company. So the message from the top is clear – if the Afghan police say, "Jump," we say, "How high?" Got that? You're on the job.'

'What if I fuck it up?'

9

'You won't,' said Phelps, with a grimace. 'Not if you value your job with WTP.'

'You're kidding? I don't really take kindly to threats – and that sounded like one.'

'And I don't really give a shit. Major Jananga's got a reputation for being a straight-up guy, one of the few police officers in the city who's not on the take, so give him the time of day, right?'

'So no choice?' said Mac.

''Fraid not.'

'What have you told him?'

'That you were in the Met for fifteen years and you've got the experience he needs.'

'And nothing about how or why I left the Met?'

'Of course not.' Even Phelps didn't know the full truth of how Mac's career had blown up, and that's how Mac intended to keep it.

He heaved a sigh of resignation. 'When do I start?'

'Right now. His English is fluent, but take your interrupter with you, just in case.' Phelps used the camp slang for interpreter. 'Here's Jananga's number.' He held out a scrap of paper with a number scrawled on it.

'Right.' Mac took the piece of paper. 'I'm going to need a vehicle and a driver if I'm going to do this. A weapon – I'll want to be tooled up at all times. And a budget.'

'For what?'

'Travel, subsistence.' He paused. '*Baksheesh.*' He'd been in the country long enough to understand that everything in Afghanistan had its price.

'Sure. I'll draw some dollars and some Afs for you. Check out a weapon, and take a Land Cruiser from the pool. You can take Pamir to drive.'

Phelps pushed his chair back and stood up, indicating the meeting was over.

Mac headed for the door.

'Okay. Get to it and keep me in the loop. And, whatever you do, don't upset the Brits.'

Now he's demanding the impossible... thought Mac, heading back to his container to get ready. He ran into Ginger as he crossed the yard, the morning's lesson having just finished.

'What was all that about?' said Ginger.

'A fucking clusterfuck,' said Mac. 'Apparently I've got to go play detectives for the Kabul police.'

'Damn!' Ginger's eyebrows nearly hit his hairline. 'What's the crime?'

'A British squaddie, found with his throat cut.'

It seemed mean of Ginger to laugh, but he did, long and hard. 'You'll have your bloody work cut out, then.'

'Yeah, tell me about it. And chicken and rice to look forward to for lunch.'

Chapter 2

Kabul City Police Headquarters was on Harsheef Street in the old town, De Afghanan, some five miles north-east of where Camp Julien lay at the southern reaches of the city. It should have taken half an hour to cover the distance along Darulaman Road to the city centre and then straight down Salang Wat Road, but with Kabul's constant traffic congestion, roadblocks and detours it was closer to an hour's drive.

Mac sat in the front of the Toyota Land Cruiser he'd signed out from the pool, while Ahmed, his interpreter, sat in the back, leaning forward between the two front seats as he kept up a constant stream of Dari chatter. Pamir, their driver, was monosyllabic with his answers, and Mac sensed that he didn't have a lot of time for Ahmed's bluster. The interpreter swore loudly in Mac's ear as Pamir swerved to avoid a couple of potholes and then ran a red light.

'If I'm reading this map right,' said Mac, 'we should be able to cut through that alley over there and come out on Harsheef Street. Then Police HQ is literally a block along.'

Ahmed gave a hollow laugh and jabbed a finger at the Soviet-era map Mac was consulting and shouted something at Pamir. Even though Mac didn't understand what he said, it appeared that he was suggesting a different route.

'Shut it, Ahmed. Let Pamir drive.'

Pamir turned down the alley Mac had suggested, and a minute later they emerged onto Harsheef Street and pushed their way into the traffic, despite shouts of protest and much hooting from an enraged taxi driver they cut up in the process. Acrid clouds of exhaust fumes belched from a truck ahead of them, making Mac cough. The stink of burnt petrol filled the front of the Land Cruiser. At least it covered the stench of the open sewer by the side of the road.

Mac looked around. Harsheef Street was a mixture of cheap office buildings and dismal-looking shops. The traffic was crawling, so Mac was relieved when the truck turned off at the next junction. Pamir closed up the gap before something else could barge in front of them from the side road.

'Left here,' said Mac, a moment later.

The police HQ loomed up in front of them – four floors of 1970s Soviet-style brutalism behind a ten-foot wall of crumbling concrete.

The Land Cruiser stopped at a high gate where a handful of armed, uniformed Afghan policemen milled about, smoking cigarettes and watching the passing traffic through narrowed eyes. One of them tossed a stone at a stray dog sniffing litter at the base of the wall.

Ahmed wound down his window and gestured to one of the policemen.

Mac listened to the exchange in rapid-fire Dari, catching only his own name and the name of the Afghan major he was here to see. Dari, similar to Farsi, was the language spoken by Kabul's non-Pashtun communities, but many of the city's four million inhabitants spoke both Dari and Pashtu. Mac was no linguist, but after several months here he was reasonably confident he could tell which of the two languages was being spoken at any given time, even if he didn't understand what was being said.

Ahmed got out of the car so he could gesticulate better, but the head guard was having none of it.

Mac climbed out too. 'What's the problem?'

Ahmed shrugged. 'He wants us to leave the vehicle out here and hand over any weapons.'

'Not fucking happening,' said Mac, making eye contact with the guard. He was treading familiar ground. Nothing ever ran smoothly – despite the fact that Major Jananga had requested their presence, the message didn't seem to have filtered down to his own men. But there was no way he was handing over the Beretta.

He pulled out his phone. 'Tell the guard I'm calling Major Jananga.'

Ahmed translated, but all Mac got was an insolent stare in return.

'*Baleh?*' The voice at the other end of the line was deep and gruff. It sounded irritated, as if the major had been interrupted.

Mac wasn't going to test his limited Dari vocabulary. He went straight into English. 'Major Jananga? This is Alasdair MacKenzie. We're having a bit of a problem with your gate detail.'

Jananga let out a deep sigh. 'A thousand apologies, Mr MacKenzie. I will come down and sort the bastards out.'

A couple of minutes later and the policemen were standing to attention as a short man appeared on the other side of the gate. He had a dark, heavy stubble, and he wasn't in uniform. The baggy grey trousers and shapeless khaki windcheater gave away nothing, and it was only because the head guard saluted and said his name that Mac realised this was Major Jananga.

The officer barked at the men in Dari, standing in the open gateway. The policeman who'd caused the problem shrank back from him, eyes widening, while his companions gave him side-long glances, distancing themselves from his bad decision. The man put up a feeble argument for a moment, then sounded contrite.

'*Khar nasho, awlad e knalek.*'

'Stop acting like a donkey, you son of an idiot,' Ahmed whispered to Mac, translating what the major was saying.

Then Jananga cuffed the man hard across the side of his head, making him stagger and fall to the ground. Bending down to let out another stream of invective, Jananga gave his subordinate a good hard kick in the ribs. The man let out a loud whine.

'Jesus!' said Mac under his breath.

The major frowned, rubbing his knuckles, then turned towards Mac, looking at him properly for the first time.

'*Salaam alaikum, chutor asti*, Mr MacKenzie?' He extended a hand and Mac shook it.

'*Alaikum a'salaam*,' replied Mac, exhausting the extent of his language skills with the standard greeting. He needed to act as if he hadn't just seen the major give one of his men a beating.

'Please excuse these fools that work here for me.' He let out an exasperated sigh. 'I told them you were coming but nothing seems to sink in.' He tapped his forehead with two fingers and glared at the men again. 'Tell your driver to bring your vehicle into the compound.' His English, although heavily accented, was fluent.

'Thank you, Major.' Mac nodded to Pamir to bring the Land Cruiser through the gate. Then he turned back.

'My information is that you've found the body of a British serviceman?'

Jananga's face clouded as he nodded. 'Please, come up to my office. I'm just about to question the boys who found the body.' He led the way towards the entrance of the building.

Mac quickly turned round. 'Come on, Ahmed.' Then he peered into the Land Cruiser. 'Pamir, stay with the vehicle.'

Another uniformed policeman on the door nodded them in – Jananga obviously didn't need to identify himself or explain his visitors. Inside, the building was drab and cold. Fading paint peeled off the concrete walls, and the floor evidently hadn't been cleaned for weeks. Passing an unmanned reception desk, they headed down a long corridor. Mac could hear the shrill sound of the wind buffeting the corners of the building, and there was a sharp draught coming in somewhere. Jananga opened a door and led them into a dingy stairwell.

'A thousand apologies – the lift isn't working today, and my office is on the top floor.'

Mac wondered if it worked any day. Ahmed, who was a lazy bastard, scowled at the steep staircase that lay ahead of them. Mac didn't waste any sympathy on him, but headed up after the major, taking the steps two at a time.

'Where's the body now?' said Mac as he caught up with Jananga.

'Still where the boys found it, at the tank graveyard. We should go there, before it's removed to the morgue.'

If it really is a Brit, the army will have something to say about that, Mac thought. There was no chance they'd let the body of one of their own go to the Kabul municipal morgue. But he didn't say anything – that wasn't his particular battle to fight.

They reached a doorway – Mac assumed it was to Jananga's office – and the major paused, his hand on the handle.

'I should be addressing you as Detective Inspector, right? That's what your Mr Phelps told me.'

Mac cleared his throat. 'That was my rank when I was in the police, but now I'm a civilian.' He shrugged. 'Just call me Mac.'

Jananga gazed at him without saying anything. Mac hoped there wouldn't be any more questions about his time in the Met. He wasn't quite comfortable being here under false pretences – and if Phelps had told the Kabul police that he was some sort of crack murder detective, they might be in for a disappointment.

They went into a small, square room, which was already crowded with people. In front of a chaotic desk sat two scruffy street kids, maybe nine or ten years old, clearly nervous and unhappy to be at the police headquarters. One was picking at a scab on his elbow, while the other stared fixedly out of the window, determined not to cry. The room smelled of dirty boy and Mac wondered when they'd last had a bath. A bearded man in his mid-thirties, dressed in a grimy shalwar kameez, stood behind them, while a uniformed officer was leaning on a filing cabinet in the corner, picking his teeth with a wooden tooth-pick. He hastily stood to attention when the major entered. The office felt hot compared with the stairwell and corridors – a small gas heater stood purring behind the desk.

There was a quick exchange between the major and his officer, and the officer went to the opposite corner of the room where a large, brass samovar stood on a low table. He started filling small glasses from it, releasing an outpouring of steam which made the hot room feel positively tropical.

Finally, Jananga explained what had happened.

'These two boys, Baktash and Shariff,' he said, pointing to them in turn, 'discovered the body of a man early this morning at the tank graveyard out by the Jalalabad Road. Shariff's father brought them here when they told him about it.'

'I've heard of the place,' said Mac, with a nod. 'What were they doing there?'

Jananga shrugged and spoke to the boys in Pashtu, his voice low and the tone gentle. They'd obviously had a fright and were reluctant to answer. The smaller boy said a few words, staring intently at the threadbare *kilim* on the floor.

'Just playing,' Jananga translated.

The older of the two boys spoke.

'Pretending to be soldiers in the tanks,' said Jananga.

The national pastime of Afghan boys – playing at being the soldiers they would grow up to become.

The man standing behind them, the father, spoke and Jananga translated. 'They were hunting for copper wire that they could sell. They found the body lying behind a burned-out tank and ran home.'

'What made them think he was British?' said Mac.

Jananga spoke to them again. There was a moment's silence. The father grasped one of the boys on the shoulder and said something that Mac took to be a prompt. The boy touched his upper arm and said a few words, amid which Mac heard a reference to 'Englishstan'.

Jananga translated. 'The body was in uniform. He saw the flag of Englandstan on the sleeve of the man's jacket.'

The man spoke again and held out his open hand. On his palm lay a heavy metal disk, about three centimetres in diameter. It was heavily tarnished, almost black, but there was some sort of relief design on the visible face. A metal loop had been soldered to the rim, and a length of tarnished silver chain hung from it. Mac took it from the man and examined it. The design was a crude rendition of a man's profile – a king presumably as he was wearing a crown. He had long straight hair, and a beard. His eye was fierce and his nose sharp. Mac turned it over. In the centre of the reverse side, there was a tiny picture of a seated man holding what looked like a bow and arrow. It was bordered by three rows of writing in a script Mac didn't recognise. There was a length of broken chain attached to it. He looked up at Jananga.

'What is it?'

Jananga shrugged. 'Looks like an ancient *drachm*, but it's certainly fake. The boys found it near to the body. There's so much rubbish up there – it's probably nothing to do with the British soldier.'

Shit! Now it had his prints on it, the father's, the boys', Jananga's… who else had touched it since it had been found?

'But maybe it belonged to the killer,' he said.

Jananga pursed his lips. 'Perhaps it could have been dropped during the attack.'

'Dropped or left. A message, possibly? This wasn't a street attack or a robbery. The soldier went to the tank graveyard at night for a reason – probably to meet someone.'

'But what message?' said Jananga.

Mac shrugged. 'What does the inscription mean?'

He passed it to Jananga, who took it from him and looked at it more closely. 'I can't tell you but, look, the chain is broken.'

He held out the ends of the chain and Mac peered at it. He was right – the final link of one end had been pulled out of shape. There was a clasp attached to the other end, and the link that was soldered to it had snapped in half. But Jananga clearly viewed it as a red herring. Without giving it another glance, he dropped it into the top drawer of his desk.

Not quite the way Mac would have treated potential evidence.

The older boy watched him, wide-eyed, then turned angrily to his father. A stream of harsh Pashtu issued from his mouth. His father scowled and cuffed the boy's ear. Jananga laughed.

'The boy wants it back. As far as he's concerned it's his.'

The father said something apologetically.

'He wanted to sell it in the market.'

'Not this time,' said Mac. 'Please thank the man for bringing it in. It could be important evidence.' He dug into his pocket and held out a five-dollar bill.

The father snatched it and swiftly pocketed it.

Jananga's officer handed out glasses of fetid green liquid that smelled vaguely of mint.

'And they're sure he was dead?' said Mac. 'I take it you've sent someone up there to check?' He sipped the bitter tea and did his best not to grimace.

'Yes, of course we have,' said the major, a brief flash of anger in his eyes. 'We have very little budget, I'm sure you know, and what we do have is often…' He paused, searching for the right words. 'Diverted. To other things. But we would not leave a man lying in the open to die. I sent two of my men up there immediately, and they have confirmed the boys' story. The man is dead.'

Mac's cheeks flushed as he realised how much he'd offended Jananga.

'I'm sorry. My mistake.'

Even though the major was still glaring at him, and making him feel uncomfortable, Mac had to wonder where large chunks of his budget were diverted to. Or maybe he didn't need to wonder. Corruption was a way of life here, spreading its tentacles from the smallest transaction up to the heights of power, with warlords and politicians trading favours that had nothing to do with the good of the country. In Mac's view, it stank.

'Did your men confirm that it was a British uniform?'

The major gave him a curt nod.

There were over a thousand British soldiers based at Camp Souter, to the east of the city. Apparently now there was one less.

'And you've informed the Brits?'

Jananga gave him another pained look. 'We are going to meet them at the site at two o'clock.'

'Right, we'd better get up there, hadn't we?'

Chapter 3

Baz Khan swore softly under her breath as she wound the pale blue hijab around her head and neck. It slipped back, and her fringe drifted forward – not the desired effect at all. Her birth right might be one hundred per cent Tajik, but having been born and brought up in America, wearing a hijab was as alien to her as it would be to a blue-eyed blonde from California. She took a bobby pin from the corner of her mouth and tried to pin the slippery fabric in place over her unruly hair.

There was a knock at the door.

'Miss Basima, your driver's here.'

'Coming,' she called, shrugging into her quilted jacket.

Checking herself in the mirror, she scowled. She had to wear a long tunic, or kurta, over her trousers for modesty whenever she left the guesthouse and it hung down beyond the bottom of the coat. In no way did this look stylish. She thought she might have got used to it after four months in Kabul, but she hadn't.

Her room in the Gandamack Lodge was on the first floor, at the end of a corridor. She was the only woman staying here at the moment, but not the only journalist. Her fellow guests were a mixture of European and American hacks and second-tier contractors whose companies didn't put them up in the smart hotels closer to the centre of town. But it was more fun to stay at the G Lodge. And, of course, there were a few shady-looking individuals who spoke to no one. She didn't care to guess what they might be doing in Kabul but wondered regularly if there was a future story there.

She snuck down the stairs and tried to pass through the lobby as quickly as possible. The last thing she needed was one of her self-appointed team of 'protectors' asking her where she was going. Bob from the *Post* and Carlos from CNN would try to stop her, or insist on accompanying her. But she needed to keep this scoop to herself. This potential scoop, at least.

Thankfully, she managed to get out of the building unhindered. Javid, her occasional driver, was waiting for her in the drive, standing by his ancient Toyota. Baz could see that it used to be red, but this was now virtually hidden under a layer of dirt.

'You ever gonna wash it, Javid-jan?' she said by way of greeting, adding -*jan* as a sign of respect and affection.

'Hello to you, Miss Basima,' he said, with a wide smile as he opened the front passenger door for her. 'Why do that? I drive a mile through the city and it's filthy again.'

She couldn't fault his logic. She climbed in.

'Where we going today, Basima-jan?' he said as he climbed in beside her.

'Where *are* we going today?' she corrected him, acting as his unofficial English teacher. 'Chicken Street.'

'The Chelsea Supermarket?' Javid started the car and pulled out from the front drive of the Gandamack onto Sherpur Square. Chicken Street was only a five-minute drive away, assuming they weren't sent round the houses on a detour.

'Much as I love it,' she said, 'that's not our destination.' It would be if she needed more peanut butter or a tube of toothpaste – the Chelsea Supermarket, with its 'Be Happy All the Time' command above the door, catered exclusively to the needs of Kabul's growing population of westerners. 'Just drop me off at the top end of the street and wait for me there.'

Javid shook his head. 'No, Basima-jan. Let me come with you. Not safe for you to wander up and down Chicken Street alone. You need a *mahram*.' A chaperone, preferably male.

Baz bit back a sharp retort. He meant well, but she'd grown up in Baltimore. She could handle herself.

'It's just Chicken Street, Javid. I have some business I need to attend to.'

Javid knew better than to argue with her, but he was shaking his head as he manoeuvred up to the curb at the corner of Chicken Street and Zargona Road. They were in Kabul's commercial centre and the pavements were teeming with people – mostly men – going about their business. Baz got out of the car and turned back to talk to Javid through the window.

'Stay here. I'll be less than an hour.'

'Yes, Miss Basima.'

Chicken Street, once the city's chicken market, was narrow and overcrowded with shoppers – as well as the Chelsea Super-market, there were shops selling bric-a-brac, household goods, pet birds and second-hand clothes. But the street was best known for its myriad of antique furniture, jewellery and rug emporiums, and these were the focus of Baz's interest. Her day job was reporting on the ongoing political crisis for the *Baltimore Sun* – telling the folk back home about the country where, according to the old Afghan proverb, God goes to weep. But off the books, Basima Khan was working on an exposé of an issue that was close to her heart – the black-market free-for-all on Afghanistan's priceless antiquities. Historic sites were being plundered for artefacts that were then smuggled out of the country and sold to western buyers at exorbitant prices. That money then went straight into the hands of warlords, the Taliban and terrorists. Everyone knew it was happening, but no one seemed to be doing anything about it, and it broke her heart to think of her parents' homeland being stripped of its heritage in this way.

She'd been piecing together what she could on the subject since she'd arrived, finding and nurturing contacts who could give her the information she needed. Now she'd heard that there was a dealer in Chicken Street who could get hold of an original bronze Paiza – a small, engraved bronze tablet that would have been carried by the emissaries of the Mongol emperor Genghis Khan, giving them free passage throughout his vast empire like a medieval passport. The objects were incredibly rare and valuable, and to sell them privately was a crime that Baz was determined to expose. And if it happened to steer a Pulitzer Prize in her direction, well, she wasn't going to bitch about that.

Baz pushed her way through the glut of people that spilled off the pavements and into the road. An open sewer, about a foot wide, ran the length of the street right next to the curb, making its own contribution to the unique smell of the city. Baz had to concentrate on where she was walking to avoid being jostled into it. Even though she kept her head down and her eyes averted, she could sense the stares of men as they took in the combination of kurta and hijab and her American-style jacket, trousers and shoes. An elbow dug into her ribs and she almost stumbled. She knew it was on purpose, and she knew that the Afghan men who behaved like this would never dream of treating their own women in the same way.

Gritting her teeth, she scanned the shop fronts for the store she was searching for.

A hand tugged at her sleeve. '*Baksheesh, khala?*'

A one-armed beggar was crouching on the edge of the pavement. He had a scar that completely disfigured the left-hand side of his face. No doubt a casualty of the country's recent past.

'*Yag dollar? Yag dollar?*'

She pulled away, before digging into her jacket pocket for an American dollar bill among the crumple of notes she kept for just such encounters. She dropped it into his open hand with a slight nod, then carried on walking, his thanks and blessings ringing out behind her.

Halfway down the street, she saw a small shopfront with the name she was looking for. The window was obscured by drapes, but a handwritten sign in English and Dari declared,

'Best rugs, best antiques, best prices'. She leaned forward to peer through a gap in the curtains. Inside she could see high stacks of multi-coloured Belouch rugs, a jumble of wooden furniture and, along one wall, a row of glass-topped jewellery cabinets. She took a deep breath and pushed open the door.

'*Salaam alaikum*,' she said loudly, to make her presence known.

She stepped inside and assumed the role of an interested shopper, lifting the corner of a rug to see the one underneath, then examining a carved stone frog that looked like alabaster but felt like plastic to the touch.

A middle-aged man appeared from a dark doorway at the far end of the narrow gallery that formed the shop floor. He was clean shaven and dressed in western-style clothes – chinos and a checked blazer – but underneath he wore the style of collarless shirt favoured by Afghan men. She wondered if this was a show to put his wealthy foreign customers at ease.

'*Alaikum a'salaam*,' he said. 'How is your day going?' he continued, still speaking in Dari.

'Very well, thank you.' Baz answered him in Dari – her parents had always spoken to her in their native language and she'd only learned to speak English when she'd started pre-school. 'And yours?'

'Allah has favoured me with a customer.' He smiled at her. 'Can I offer you some tea while you're looking around?'

'Please,' she said, with a small bow of her head. If her information was right, this man was denuding the country of its heritage and dealing in stolen goods, but she would need to cultivate his trust over time if she were to get anywhere with her investigation.

She continued to browse, genuinely interested in a shelf laden with bowls, carved animals and eggs fashioned out of lapis lazuli – a dark blue semi-precious stone that came from Badakhshan Province, north-east of Kabul.

'It's beautiful, isn't it?' The man had returned with a tray holding two small glasses of smoky green tea.

Baz took one with a nod of thanks. She sipped it slowly while she carried on looking around.

'Tell me,' she said as she finished the tea, 'do you have any antique lapis pieces? I can see that these ones are all new.'

They went back to the lapis display together.

'You're right,' said the man, giving her face a searching look. 'These ones are for the tourists. But obviously you know about our beautiful stone.' He pulled a set of keys out of his pocket. 'Come.'

All going according to plan!

He led her through the door at the back of the shop and into another, more cavernous room. Baz scanned her surroundings, doing a mental stocktake. There was certainly a difference in what he kept back here – better quality rugs, and she saw a number of objects on display that wouldn't have been out of place in a museum. Of course, there was no sign of the Paiza she was looking for. Such an item would never be out on open display.

'This is lovely,' she said, indicating a small stone carving of a Buddha.

'You have a good eye,' said the man. 'But you're not from Kabul, are you? You speak with an American accent.'

'My parents are from Bagh-e-Bala, near the Poly, but I was born in America.' What she wasn't going to mention to him was that her father used to work at the Kabul Museum, and was now a curator of Afghan antiquities at the Smithsonian. She'd grown up immersed in her country's heritage, and probably knew more about the provenance of his stock than he did.

It hadn't been a casual question – he was probing, which meant he was suspicious. As suspicious of her as she was of him, and both pretending not to be. She was treading a fine line between appearing to know just enough, but not too much. She knew perfectly well he was only being polite to her in the hope that she was going to buy something from him for far more than it was worth.

It galled her to have to do it, but it was precisely the right course of action.

'This is gorgeous,' she said, fingering a string of striking lapis lazuli beads.

'They would do your own beauty justice.'

Oily, just oily, she thought, holding up the necklace in front of a mottled mirror.

'How much are they?'

'Four hundred dollars.' He certainly didn't want to be paid in afghanis.

She put the piece down carefully where she'd found it, with a sigh. 'Ah, that's too much.'

The haggling began and twenty minutes later she left the shop with the necklace in her bag and her purse lighter by two hundred dollars. She'd paid well over the odds, but they'd make a suitable present for her brother's wife when she went home. The main thing was that she'd made progress in her investigation. The shopkeeper had given her his card – Baseer Ghilji – and he was definitely the man she was looking for.

She headed back up Chicken Street lost in thought. She would need to tread carefully if she was to gain his trust enough to get close to the Paiza he apparently had.

Out of nowhere, a man in a brown shalwar kameez and a flat, circular Pakool hat loomed in front of her. She blinked, and stepped to one side to avoid colliding with him. As they passed each other, he stuck out his hand and grabbed at her breast. The pain made her gasp.

With lightning speed, she struck his arm away.

'Fuck you!' she yelled, starting to run. The sudden movement dislodged her hijab. It slipped down to the back of her neck, revealing her tousled, pixie-cut hair.

The man laughed and spat in her direction.

People – men – stopped what they were doing to stare at her as she sprinted to where Javid was waiting with the car. A few of them catcalled and one made a rude gesture, putting his fist to his crotch.

It had happened before, and no doubt it would happen again. Javid had warned her. It was the price she paid as a western woman going out and about on her own, though she wasn't going to let it stop her doing what she wanted.

But suddenly Chicken Street didn't seem quite so benign anymore.

Chapter 4

They drove along the Jalalabad Road in Jananga's aged black SUV, with Pamir following behind. Mac had decided to travel in the police vehicle so he could ask the major more about how he intended to investigate the case as they drove. If the body really was that of an English serviceman, Mac had a feeling it would fall to him to have to build bridges between the Brits and the Kabul police during the subsequent investigation, so he wanted to have all the salient facts.

'I assume we'll be meeting your forensics team at the site?' he said.

The two of them were sitting in the back, with Jananga's driver and a uniformed police officer riding shotgun in the front. Jananga looked across at him askance. 'We are not on an episode of *CSI*, you know,' he said. 'Do you think there are forensic labs full of pathologists in white coats in Kabul?'

His words stung, but then Mac realised that maybe he'd been a little insensitive. The major was clearly running his department on a shoestring, and any expertise at the scene was expected to come from the Scotland Yard import.

They rode in silence for a few minutes.

'Look,' said Jananga, pointing out of the window on Mac's side.

'What?' said Mac, trying to work out what he was being shown.

'There – see that?'

They were passing a stretch of empty ground on the left. In the centre of it, the surface had been hit by something, forming a small crater some three or four feet across. Rocks and gravel were strewn around it.

'It happened yesterday,' said Jananga. 'Some *ahmaq* took a shot at the US embassy. They missed by a mile.' He shook his head with disbelief.

Mac had heard there'd been an attempted rocket attack the previous day – and the US embassy was a little way to the west of where they were now.

'How long do you think it will take, Major, to get your country in order?' said Mac.

'That's what you think will happen?' said Jananga, cocking an eyebrow.

'Isn't that what you hope for?' said Mac.

Jananga threw back his head and laughed. Then he looked at Mac with a broad grin that showed off strong white teeth. 'You westerners will never make order out of our chaos, Mr Mac. Chaos is simply the Afghan way and we won't give it up for the British, or the Americans, or the Russians. Ever.'

Mac must have looked nonplussed, because Jananga laughed again.

'It's a beautiful country, but it's our country,' he said. 'You people will only ever be guests here – and I can only ever be apologising that some of my countrymen make you feel less than welcome.'

Mac was beginning to like Major Jananga. He had a suspicion that, although he'd spoken with a humorous tone, the man really did love his country and wanted to be proud of it. But how that would translate into their working relationship was anyone's guess.

It took them two detours, a roadblock and a gridlock that had to be shifted under the instruction of Jananga's deputy – half an hour longer than it should have – before they reached the emptier stretch of the Jalalabad Road out to the east of the city.

Although Mac had heard of the tank graveyard, he'd never been there. It was an open expanse of barren land where both the Soviets and the Taliban had quite literally dumped their damaged and obsolete tanks and armoured vehicles over the course of years of bitter conflict. 'Where old tanks go to die,' Ginger had said as they'd discussed it over lunch. 'Like the elephant graveyard, but made of metal.' And, despite the grim reason for their visit, Mac was fascinated to see the place. It had once been the site of the main armour workshops for the Russians' Kabul garrison, a natural collection point for damaged tanks that could be mended or stripped for spares.

By the time they turned off the main road it was past two. With four men inside it, the vehicle was stuffy despite the cold outside. Mac took a drink from the bottle of water Jananga's driver had given him when he'd got into the car.

The tank graveyard sloped down, away from the road. Beyond the last lines of tanks, an empty expanse of water-logged mud stretched out until the ground rose up again into a sprouting of small hillocks in the distance. The car bumped over stony ground, jolting Mac in his seat and at one point throwing him sideways against Jananga's shoulder. There was no road and the driver simply cut across the open expanse towards the eastern perimeter, where a mud-spattered white truck was parked crookedly next to the crumpled hull of a T54/55 Soviet battle tank. Two uniformed policemen were leaning against the bonnet, smoking, with their arms wrapped round their bodies against the cold. There was no sign of the British contingent yet – Mac guessed they'd got held up in traffic as well.

As the Surf passed tank after tank, all wrecked and mostly entirely rusted, Mac saw T62s, BRDMs, BMPs, ZSU-23-4s and God knows how many other types, too rotted to recognise. He tried to do an approximate count, but the rows were haphazard, and he couldn't even see the full extent. There had to be hundreds. If they'd come here for any other reason, he'd have taken some time to look around more thoroughly, but there was a dead body waiting for them and Mac needed to see it for himself before he would believe it really was a British soldier – he could think of no reason for a squaddie to be out here alone.

The driver pulled up next to the truck and the two policemen stubbed out their cigarettes. Mac and Jananga got out and went around to them. The wind cut through Mac's WTP-logoed windcheater and the warmth he'd felt in the car dissipated in seconds. It could freeze the balls of a brass monkey.

He looked around the scene with interest. Now was the time to take on the role of the seasoned murder squad detective, and he thought back to his brief moment in the MIT. There was no crime-scene tape, none of the process that would have immediately kicked into play if a dead body had been found in the UK, and no sign of anyone putting on crime-scene suits before going any closer. From an evidential standpoint, it was going to be a fuck up, but somehow he didn't think the Afghan police would be sticklers over chain-of-custody rules.

Jananga was talking to his men. After a moment he turned to Mac.

'Come, he's behind this tank.'

They made their way round the wreckage. The two officers didn't bother to accompany them.

Mac had seen dead bodies before – plenty of them – but never one with its throat slit. The man was lying on the ground, flat on his back. He was certainly in uniform, and it was the sand-coloured camouflage of British desert fatigues, but the whole of the front of his tunic was soaked with blood. There was a gaping wound to his throat and, above it, his face looked ashen, the skin waxy. He had black hair, slightly peppered with the first signs of grey. His dark eyes were open and stared up at the sky. Mac wondered if the stars had been the last thing he saw, or if he'd been looking up into the face of the man who killed him.

Despite the wind, the stench of drying blood was strong enough to make Mac feel nauseated.

'Right,' said Mac, with a sweep of his arm. 'This whole area is a crime scene and needs to be taped off. Put one of your men in control of the perimeter and restrict access to only necessary personnel. And get a couple of them to search the area for evidence of what happened – footprints, blood stains, a weapon, or anything either man could have dropped.'

He'd picked up a compact digital camera from the company stores before heading out. Now he pulled it from his pocket and started taking photos of the scene and the body, as there was no sign of an Afghan police photographer. There was an arc of blood spatter, now soaked into the dirt underneath and to one side of him, and Mac made sure to take a couple of good close-ups of it.

Jananga bent over the body. Mac gritted his teeth and squatted down beside him. From the insignia on the front of the man's jacket, Mac could see that he was a captain, but the name that would have been stitched across the top of his left breast pocket was too obscured by blood to be decipherable. He took a couple of pictures, then pulled a biro out of his own breast pocket and used it to carefully shift the man's blood-soaked collar to one side. His intention was to hook the cord around his neck to gain access to his dog tags.

The heavy, fetid smell of death was overpowering, and Mac fought the urge to retch. The tags weren't there. Just a red mark as if the cord had been dragged across his skin.

Mac stood up, still holding the end of the bloody biro. He didn't want to put it back in his pocket. Jananga took it from him and wiped it on the man's trousers, then handed it back.

'So, he's definitely a British soldier,' said Jananga.

'But no tags.'

'Taken by the killer?'

Mac shrugged. 'Maybe... Or maybe they're somewhere inside his uniform. I take it your men checked him for a weapon?'

'There was nothing on him. Not even any ID.'

33

'Have you sent for a pathologist to assess the body and make an estimate of the time of death?'

Jananga gave him a blank look. 'We only have a couple of pathologists in Kabul – they don't have time to come out to every dead body. We take the body to them, and they look at it in the morgue.'

Everything was run on a shoestring here, and the investigation would suffer as a consequence. On the other hand, it made it less likely that Jananga or anyone else would realise he wasn't as experienced as they'd been led to believe.

Mac grimaced and looked around the desolate landscape, hugging his arms to his chest against the cold. They had to wait here until the British contingent from Camp Souter arrived to view the body. Jananga's men shuffled around attaching lengths of rope between various tanks to create a crime-scene perimeter as instructed. A glint of something flashing a few rows of tanks to the east caught his eye.

'What was that?' he said to Jananga. 'One of your men?'

'I didn't see anything,' said Jananga, shrugging as he looked in the direction in which Mac was pointing.

'And again, see?'

'Yes. I think someone's there.'

'Major,' said Mac, turning to where Jananga was standing next to his deputy. 'Did you send someone out to create a wider perimeter?'

The major shook his head. 'Why would I do that?'

'No matter,' said Mac. 'I thought I saw something. I'm going to check it out.'

Mac pulled out his Beretta for the second time in just a few hours, holding it low by his thigh so as not to draw attention to it in front of Jananga's men. There was no reason to think he'd need it, but he'd look like a fool if he did and got shot as he scrambled to get it out of his holster. Jananga said something to his sergeant, who also drew his weapon and followed.

Mac ducked behind the hull of the nearest tank to them – he wanted to stay low and out of sight to get as close to whoever was there as they could before they were seen. The next time he saw the light flash, he had a clearer view. It was the sun reflecting off the lenses of a pair of binoculars. A man, tall, with short black hair held them to his eyes, obscuring his facial features. He must have seen Mac at the same instance as he immediately ducked down behind an armoured vehicle. There was the scuffle of feet running on gravel and the hiss of a couple of words that Mac didn't understand.

'There's more than one of them,' he said to the deputy, who was peering round the other end of the wrecked tank. 'Come on, let's see what they're up to.'

He felt pretty certain it wasn't just a pair of kids – the binoculars and the man's voice meant they were dealing with adults. Adults who were interested in what was going on up here. Had they seen the body already? Were they involved?

They had to follow by ear as row upon row of tanks and armoured vehicles blocked their view of whoever was running from them. The ground was uneven and in the dark shadows under the hulks of vehicles it was difficult to see stones and potholes. With a yelp of pain, Jananga's sergeant tripped on something and fell headlong onto the stony ground. He swore loudly, but Mac didn't stop. He needed to find out exactly who had been watching them and why.

As he came to the last row of tanks at the top corner of the graveyard, two men broke cover and ran across the open ground beyond. Mac spotted their destination – next to a scrubby-looking birch tree some fifty metres further on he could see a parked motorbike. The man with the binoculars was ahead, almost halfway there. Behind him, a youth was struggling to keep up. Mac could see that one of his legs was slightly twisted, making it hard for him to run hell-for-leather across the uneven ground.

'Stop, police,' yelled Mac, raising his weapon.

The kid didn't even look round, so Mac let a round off into the air and carried on running. If anything, the shot fired made

35

the boy run even faster. The man had reached the motorbike now and was gunning the kickstart pedal with his foot. The engine roared to life and the rider practically skidded over as he spun the bike round on the gravel to turn towards the boy. Mac pounded across the dirt, kicking stones and leaping over larger obstacles, determined to reach the boy before the rider did, even if his chest burst doing it. Panting loudly and waving his weapon in front of him, he was gaining ground. The man on the bike realised what was going to happen – all three of them would collide at the same moment – and he quickly changed course with a sweeping curve, directing his bike now towards the entrance to the tank graveyard below them. Mac realised what he was doing and had a split second to decide. Should he go after the man or continue to chase the kid. The man was putting distance between them fast. Mac's only choice to stop him was to shoot him off the bike – and given that he didn't know if the man was armed, or whether he was actually anything other than an innocent spectator, he lowered his weapon. He could catch the youth, and they would find out from him what the two of them were up to.

'Stop,' he yelled again.

The boy had let out a howl of anger when he realised his friend was deserting him, but he didn't stop running.

As Mac got closer to him, he holstered his weapon and once he was within a matter of feet, he pushed forward to tackle the kid. They fell to the ground together with a thump, both of them winded. Mac grabbed the boy's torso and held onto him to stop him struggling away. The boy swore in guttural Dari, then sank his teeth into Mac's arm.

'For fuck's sake, you little shit,' gasped Mac, tearing his arm out of reach.

They were still rolling in the dirt when Jananga's sergeant arrived. He stood above them, pointing his gun at them both, until finally the kid gave up the fight and allowed himself to be handcuffed. Jananga and a few more of his men arrived and as always in these situations, there was a lot of shouting that Mac didn't understand. He didn't care. The boy was the major's problem now, and Mac was sure he knew how to deal with him. And how to find out the identity of his accomplice and what they'd been doing there.

The distant rumble of tyres over rough ground caught his attention, and he strode back up to where the body was, rubbing his arm where the boy had bitten him. A British Army Land Rover with a machine gun mounted on the back was approaching at speed, churning up a cloud of dust in its wake. Now the fun would begin. Jananga joined him as the boy was put in the back of one of the police vehicles, and they watched as the Land Rover parked up a few metres away from the Surf and a handful of uniformed men spewed forth. The man in charge was wearing a Royal Military Police uniform, and as he came towards them, Mac could see he was a captain. He had an Afghan interpreter with him, and two infantrymen, both carrying SA80 rifles.

'Captain Andrew Holder,' he said officiously once he was in earshot.

'I'm Major Jananga.'

Holder looked askance at Mac. 'Who the fuck are you?' Mac didn't care for his tone.

'DI Alasdair MacKenzie, on secondment to the Kabul police.' He was still slightly breathless from the chase.

The captain didn't seem impressed. 'I had no idea we had British police working out here.' He pointed at Mac's windcheater. 'Or are you actually employed by WTP?'

'He works for me,' snapped Jananga.

'I see,' said Holder. The glance he gave Mac spelled trouble. 'Right, where's the body? If he's one of ours, we need to get him back to Souter asap.'

Jananga tilted his head. 'That won't be possible, Captain.'

'What?'

'You can't take the body,' said Jananga.

37

'This land falls under Afghan police jurisdiction and the body needs to come back to the city morgue.' Mac was making an assumption here, but Jananga nodded in agreement.

Holder's brow furrowed. 'Let's take a look. Then we'll sort this out.'

Mac knew exactly what he meant by sorting it out. Captain Holder had no intention of letting the Kabul police waltz away with the body of a dead British soldier.

They went back to where the dead man lay, and Holder bent down to take a closer look.

'Certainly looks like he's ours. In uniform, but we'll have to wait for proper ID.' He turned round to address one of the hovering soldiers. 'Get on the radio and call an ambulance out here. Let them know they'll be picking up a body.'

'Yes, sir.'

Jananga scowled. 'The body will be coming with me. This is my investigation, Captain.'

'Do you really think you can handle it? What about a pathologist to assess it here? And a crime team to search the site?' Jananga's men were still messing about with the cordon.

'And do you really want to obstruct a murder inquiry?' said Mac.

Holder glared at him.

It didn't matter to Mac that the man's body would go back to Kabul's overcrowded morgue, where it would probably have to share a drawer with a couple of other random bodies, or that all the evidence on it would be compromised and a proper investigation would never materialise. His mission was to keep Jananga happy, and the snotty army captain could fuck off.

'Major, it would clearly make sense for the body to go back to Camp Souter. We can perform a detailed autopsy on-site and give you the results of our investigation.'

'There's no question over the cause of death,' said Jananga.

'Of course,' said Holder. 'But British military regulations will demand—'

Jananga cut him off mid-sentence. 'Captain, you're forgetting that Afghanistan is a sovereign state. You and your army are guests in my country, not occupiers. The murder took place out here, where I'm in charge – not inside your camp.'

Mac had had enough. 'The body comes with us to the city morgue. I'm sure the major can arrange it so an observer can be present for the autopsy.'

'I still don't quite understand your role in all of this,' said Holder.

'You don't need to.'

In the distance, Mac heard the engine roar of approaching vehicles. He looked round and saw an army ambulance tearing towards them, tailed by a black transit van which was steadily gaining on it. The race for the body was on.

When the black van overtook the ambulance, a look of grim satisfaction settled on Jananga's face. 'My team is here.'

'At least don't move the body until my medic has arrived to look at it in situ,' said the captain.

Jananga nodded. 'But I can't delay for long.'

As the van drew up, Mac became aware of a rise in tension. Holder's men were eyeing it cautiously, ready for action if needed.

'Tell your men it's the Afghan police,' he said to Holder.

As the soldiers relaxed, the van and the ambulance drew up close to the other vehicles.

'Okay, Captain, your medic has fifteen minutes to look at the body. Then we take it to the morgue.' Jananga turned to Mac. 'Detective Inspector, you're in charge of the investigation. What do you need?'

Mac ran through the list in his head. A crime-scene team. A police photographer. A forensic pathologist with a good forensics lab. A team of experienced detectives.

'Nothing, Major. I can handle it.'

Chapter 5

For one second only, it looked like Holder was considering removing the body by force. The Afghans at the site probably had more firepower than him, but he seemed arrogant enough to ignore that. Then his face took on a resigned expression. The murder of a British soldier on Afghan soil would already rate as an international incident. A shootout over the body wouldn't be clever.

'Major, would it help if...' He rubbed his finger and thumb together to indicate money.

Mac couldn't believe his ears – Holder was going to try *baksheesh*? Bribery was endemic throughout the country – the greasing of palms and oiling of wheels came as naturally as breathing. Mac was interested to see how Jananga would respond to this.

Not well. He took a step back, brows raised at the affront. 'No, Captain, it wouldn't.' He puffed out his chest. 'I cannot be bought.'

Holder's cheeks suffused with colour. Jananga must have been the only straight policeman on the Afghan force. What Phelps had said about him seemed to be true.

An army medic walked across to them from the ambulance.

For Holder he served as a welcome change of subject. 'Major Jananga, this is Major Oliver, our senior medic.' The British doctor was a tall man with a hooked nose, and the deep tan of someone who wasn't new to the country.

Jananga nodded, then looked towards Mac.

Mac took his cue. 'I'm Alasdair MacKenzie, Major Oliver. I'm running the investigation on behalf of the Afghan police. The body's round here, if you'd follow me.'

Holder cleared his throat. 'I realise that we have to co-operate with the Afghan police over this, but I'm afraid we won't be able recognise your authority over this investigation. We have no proof of who you are or who appointed you.'

'Major Jananga appointed me,' said Mac. He was getting pissed off with this arrogant jobsworth. 'I'm sure he can put it in writing to your CO, but in the meantime, I'm in charge.'

Major Oliver followed the exchange with a look of concern. 'Can we just get on with it, Holder?'

Mac led him to the body and, of course, Holder tagged along.

'You have fifteen minutes,' said Jananga, appearing around the wreckage.

Oliver put down the bag he was carrying and got out a camera. He started taking photos.

'Has the body been moved or in any way disturbed?' he said, as he took shots from a variety of angles.

'No, apart from checking for a weapon,' said Jananga. 'My men were instructed not to touch it.'

Oliver put his camera away and got out a thermometer. He looked up at Jananga.

'Major, if I could arrange for you to attend the post-mortem and undertook to fully share our report with you, would you allow us to take possession of the body? After all, we'll need to repatriate it for burial.'

'We've been through this already,' said Mac. 'The body's coming to the city morgue as soon as you've finished.' He wasn't going to let the army walk all over him.

Jananga's imperceptible nod of approval told him his job was still safe. For now.

The Kabul city morgue was located in the basement of the Afghan Apollo Indian Hospital, a fatigued-looking yellow concrete block on Salang Wat Road. It turned out to be somewhere Mac wished he'd never had to experience. He and Jananga watched the body being unloaded from the black van and carried inside.

The major lit a cigarette and offered one to Mac. 'You might want one of these before we go in.'

Mac declined, leaning against the SUV to soak up the weak rays of late-afternoon sunlight instead. Jananga smoked nervously and rattled off orders into his mobile phone as they waited for the army contingent to catch up with them.

Oliver and Holder arrived a couple of minutes later. Jananga stamped out his cigarette and led them into the building through wide double doors.

The ground floor of the hospital was chaotic and noisy, with staff hurrying back and forth, shouting at each other in multiple languages, and frequently drowned out by the sound of wailing women. It gave Mac the impression they suffered a high fatality rate. Not a place he'd want to be brought to in his hour of need.

The major led them through the centre of the casualty department and out into a corridor where there was a heavy steel door. He pushed it open with his shoulder and as they descended a flight of concrete stairs, the stale disinfectant smell of the ground floor was replaced by something sharper and more rancid that caught at the back of Mac's throat. They were descending to a worse place – the realms of the city's dead.

A neon strip light above their heads buzzed noisily, barely giving off enough of a glow to light their way down a long, empty passage. But Mac didn't want to see into the shadows – the floor he could see was filthy and tacky underfoot. Water dripped from pipes running along the top of the wall and there were drifts of litter against the skirtings. When a rat darted across the corridor ahead of them, it wasn't a surprise.

They went through another metal door, and as Mac stepped into the large room, the stench of decomposition practically knocked him backwards. There were no refrigerated drawers here as there would have been in a UK morgue, but he could see through the open door of a huge cold room. Shrouded bodies were stacked, two or three to a shelf, along its walls, and this was where the stink emanated from. A man emerged, pushing a grimy metal trolley, on which lay a body covered by a tarpaulin – Mac guessed it was their soldier.

The major broke out into rapid-fire Dari, addressing the man as he positioned the gurney underneath the single weak ceiling light.

Behind Mac, Holder had a coughing fit that sounded as if he was about to be sick.

'Jesus,' murmured Oliver.

Jananga turned back to face them. 'This is Hajji Baba, our chief pathologist.'

He was a small man, balding and jowly, his rounded belly covered by a blood-stained leather apron. He nodded to them, smiling, his breath coming in wheezy gasps. It didn't seem like a healthy place to work.

They gathered round the table, Hajji Baba at the top end by the dead man's head. Oliver stood to his left, ready to take notes, while Mac, Holder and Jananga kept slightly more distance between themselves and the cadaver. The room seemed crowded and hot, and the sweet metallic smell of congealed blood wafted into Mac's nostrils.

Baba said something and Jananga translated. 'He's had to cut his clothes off him. The body's already...' He paused, searching for the right words. 'The muscles are stiff already, so he couldn't move the limbs.'

Rigor mortis had set in. Mac wondered what that suggested in terms of the time of death.

Hajji Baba pointed to a trolley against the opposite wall, and Mac saw the dead man's blood-soaked clothes had been laid out as they'd been removed. He went over to take a closer look.

'Is there any ID on these?'

Oliver took a pair of latex gloves out of his pocket and slipped them on. He handed a second pair to Mac, and Mac put them on. Then, together, they inspected the garments.

'Look – D or David Marshall marked in a few of the items. And the rank insignia on his chest indicates he was a captain.'

Mac wrote the name down. 'Was this man missing from your base?' he said, turning to Holder.

Holder shrugged non-committedly. 'There are over one thousand men at Souter, Mr MacKenzie. A head count is underway. When I know more, I'll share it with you.'

Mac doubted it, somehow. 'Let's assume for the time being that that's who he was then.'

He turned back to the pile of clothing, wondering if it could tell him anything else. As the others gathered around the body, Mac turned over Marshall's trousers. The pocket on one side felt heavy.

A loud electrical snap sounded and the light went out, plunging them into darkness. At the same time Mac suddenly noticed the silence as the hum of a distant generator stopped.

'Fuck!' said Hajji Baba, using the English swear word. This was followed by some high-volume shouting.

'It's a power cut,' said Jananga. 'He's calling on his assistants to bring lamps.'

Mac's hand was in the pocket of Marshall's trousers. It closed around something hard and spiky. A set of keys. Unseen, Mac slipped his hand out of Marshall's pocket and into his own. He could work out what they might be keys for later.

They waited uncomfortably in the dark for several minutes, Mac feeling increasingly bilious the longer he had to spend in the stinking charnel house.

At last, flickering light showed out in the passageway, and then two young men ran in, each carrying two lit hurricane lamps, which they placed on the four corners of the gurney.

'For God's sake,' said Oliver. 'You can't do a post-mortem using those.'

Hajji Baba looked at Jananga for an explanation and there was an exchange of words.

'He often does,' said Jananga, with an air of dismissal. 'We'll carry on.'

In the sulphurous, orange light from the lamps, Marshall's naked skin looked grey and the blood in the gaping wound at his neck almost black. His body was completely rigid, making the way he lay on the table look unnatural.

Oliver shouldered Hajji Baba to one side so he could see better. 'The cause of death is clearly this wound in his throat,' he said. 'He appears to have been attacked by someone standing in front of him, probably right-handed, holding the knife backhand, making the cut from his left to right – or the victim's right to left.' He demonstrated by slashing his right arm through the air. 'You'll see that the wound gets progressively deeper from the starting point at the right of the throat to the end of the cut at the left, and death was due to the severance of one of the carotid arteries.'

He bent forward and peered at it more closely.

'The blade was sharp, but not as sharp as it might have been – there's some tearing and dragging of the skin at the margins of the cut. It's possible the edge of the blade was uneven or had a nick out of it.'

'Enough from that to identify a specific blade?' said Mac. He took the chance to get a couple of close-up photos of the wound, the flash of his camera making the gore stand out even more starkly.

'Not with any certainty,' said Oliver.

Hajji Baba came around the side of the table and held up one of Marshall's hands. The pathologist wasn't even wearing gloves, and Mac's gut roiled. The hand was flaked with dried blood, but Baba's interest was his fingernails. He had to bend down to examine them as the rigor prevented him from raising the arm any further. 'No signs of any defensive wounds, or any other superficial injuries,' Jananga translated as Hajji Baba spoke. The pathologist used a metal scraper to remove matter from under the nails and deposit it in a small Perspex pot.

'I'd like to have that sent back to the UK for testing to see if it's just his blood, or if he might have scratched his attacker,' said Oliver.

'Good plan,' said Holder. He looked pale and clammy – he definitely wasn't enjoying the experience.

'How long will that take?' said Mac.

Oliver shrugged. 'Two or three weeks, possibly.'

Mac turned to Jananga. 'Could you get it done faster here?'

Jananga looked at his pathologist and translated for him. The man shook his head and spoke.

'We don't have any DNA testing facilities,' said Jananga. 'But I can't allow evidence to be removed from the country.'

Holder rolled his eyes and gave Oliver a pained look. Mac felt like punching him in the mouth.

'So much for the cause of death,' said Oliver. 'We need to consider the timing – not quite so easy.'

'But the rigor more or less tells you?' said Mac.

'Certainly, rigor gives a good indication. But there are other factors to take into account as well. The temperature last night dipped below freezing for a few hours, which will have delayed the onset of rigor. The peak, which we're seeing now, is generally twelve to twenty-four hours after death – and allowing for a slower onset, that suggests he was killed late last night, rather than earlier today.'

Jananga murmured in his pathologist's ear, who was nodding his head in agreement.

'Hajji Baba wants to turn the body over to check for...' Jananga paused and turned back to the man, who shrugged and said something. 'I haven't the word for it – when the blood sinks...'

'Lividity,' said Oliver.

Jananga repeated it, as if committing it to memory.

Baba and one of his assistants carefully lifted Marshall's body and turned him to lie on his front. Mac darted in to catch one of the hurricane lamps as Marshall's foot almost swiped it off the corner of the gurney. Then the soldier's nose was squashed flat against the surface, making Mac feel an unexpected twinge of sympathy.

The medical men examined the back of the body. Mottled purple patches had appeared on the shoulders, the buttocks and the backs of the calves – the result of blood pooling at the lowest parts.

'The pattern's consistent with how he was found lying, so we can assume that's where he died and that he wasn't moved after death. The bloodstains on the ground around him also suggested this.' Oliver was grim faced. He turned to Baba. 'Time to open him up.'

Mac decided he didn't need to watch this – he doubted Marshall's stomach contents would tell him anything about the crime. He needed to confirm the identity of the body as quickly as possible so he could start to figure out what Marshall might have been doing at such a remote spot, at night, on his own. Or in fact, not on his own – the killer was there with him.

'Major Jananga, can I suggest that we make contact with Captain Marshall's commanding officer?'

Holder's head jerked round at this.

Jananga pointed at the door. They left Oliver working with Hajji Baba, and went outside.

'You'll need to go through me,' said Holder as soon as the three of them were breathing deeply of the fresh cold air in the car park. 'I'm handling this case as far as the army's concerned.'

'Then bloody sort it,' said Mac. 'Or I'll go over your head.'

Holder scowled, but Mac wasn't giving him any choice. He got out his phone.

While he spoke to whoever he needed to talk to, Mac took a stroll to the end of a row of parked cars. Putting a large SUV between himself and the captain, he dug the set of keys out of his pocket and glanced down at them.

Car keys on a fob he recognised. They were for a Toyota Surf. Presumably the vehicle Marshall drove to the tank graveyard.

Chapter 6

An hour later, Holder escorted Mac and Jananga through the checkpoint at Camp Souter's gate with sullen resignation. He snapped at the gate guards who took their details and signed them in.

'Your weapons and your ID,' he said, holding out a hand.

Mac had guessed this was coming.

'No,' said Jananga.

Holder glanced at Mac for support, but he'd done nothing so far to make Mac feel inclined to help him out.

'Major, it's the rules. Non-Army personnel coming onto the base have to surrender weapons and ID to get a visitor's pass.'

'But not the police,' said Jananga. 'My job is always to have my weapon on me.'

'Makes no odds to me,' said Holder, 'but if you want to come in and talk to Marshall's commanding officer, you give 'em up.' He held out his hand again.

Jananga narrowed his eyes, but reluctantly produced his pistol and his police ID. 'You know I will be registering a high-level complaint about this.'

Mac followed suit.

'That's fine. I don't make the rules.' Holder took their weapons and passed them to the sergeant on duty, who logged them in and then handed them each a visitor pass.

Once that was done, Holder walked them through the camp to the separate Military Police compound.

'I'm taking you to see Major Lambert first – my boss. We need to establish some ground rules for this investigation.'

Mac hoped Lambert would be more diplomatic than his subordinate. He could sense Jananga bristling beside him.

'It's our investigation,' said Mac, 'so we'll set the rules. But you're right – we'll need your CO's full co-operation so we can question whoever we need to.'

This was clearly going to be uphill all the way.

Holder led them across to a single-storey wooden building. Its flimsy plywood door was painted black, and a white sign next to it read 'RMP Command'. They went inside and along a corridor, their footsteps echoing noisily on the bare wooden floor. Holder stopped at a door and knocked.

'Enter,' came a voice from the other side.

Holder went in and stood to attention in front of his commanding officer's desk. Mac and Jananga followed him inside.

'Ah, Noddy – these our visitors?'

'Yes, sir. Major Jananga of Kabul Police HQ, and Mr MacK-enzie.'

'Good to meet you, gentlemen. Grab a pew.'

Jananga looked questioningly at Mac.

'A chair,' said Mac.

They both sat down, while Holder remained standing to one side.

Lambert cleared his throat. 'Right, we've done a head count here, and there is indeed a soldier missing from the camp.'

'Captain David Marshall?' said Holder. 'We got the name from the dead man's uniform.'

'He was reported as missing at morning prayers – the day's eight a.m. briefing meeting – apparently. He's a loggy, which means his CO is Lieutenant Colonel Tomlinson.'

Jananga gave Mac another questioning look.

'Royal Logistics Corps – they move stuff around,' said Mac by way of explanation.

'I've asked Tomlinson to join us,' said Lambert. He glanced at his watch. 'He'll be here in five.'

With precise army time-keeping, Lieutenant Colonel Tomlinson appeared, and there was another round of introductions.

'Right, Major, what's all this about?' Tomlinson said to Lambert as he settled on the room's one remaining chair.

'Sir, a body was discovered early this morning out at the tank graveyard on the Jalalabad Road. His throat was cut. We have reason to believe that he was one of your men – Captain David Marshall.'

'Yes, I was informed he was missing,' Tomlinson expressed neither surprise nor sadness at the news. Upper class twat with a stiff upper lip. Mac had never been impressed by them.

'Naturally, we'll need you to come and give us a formal identification of the body,' said Mac.

Tomlinson turned to look at him. 'I'm sorry, Mr…'

'MacKenzie,' supplied Holder.

'MacKenzie. Can you explain to me, who you are and what exactly is your involvement here?' It was as if Holder had primed him.

'DI MacKenzie,' said Jananga, stepping in with perfect timing, 'has been seconded to the Kabul City Police to assist me in this matter.'

'On what basis?'

'On the basis of his long experience as a murder squad detective in the London police. He will be leading this investigation, under my direction.' The lie sounded completely convincing, not least because Jananga himself believed what he was saying.

'I see.' Tomlinson gave a slight nod. 'Seems a little irregular. I'm sure the Military Police can conduct the investigation.'

'You think so?' said Mac. 'Aren't your guys just glorified school prefects? The most they get to investigate is petty pilfering and soldiers breaking curfew. A murder investigation is something completely different, and you need someone with the relevant experience.'

Holder bristled visibly but managed to hold his tongue.

'That would be you?' said Tomlinson.

Mac raised a shoulder. 'That's right, Colonel.'

'Did you know Chief Superintendent Chris Joseph during your time in the Met?'

Sure. He was the tosser who forced me to resign and told me I'd never work in a British police force again as long as I lived.

'Only by reputation.' Mac nodded his head thoughtfully. 'A good man, as I understand it. You know him?'

'We were at school together. I follow his career from afar. Pretty impressive.' Tomlinson returned his nod. Connection made, bridge built. 'So, what do you need from us?'

'Do you have any idea what Marshall might have been doing out at the tank graveyard yesterday evening?' said Mac.

Tomlinson slid a glance across at Jananga, obviously reluctant to speak in front of him.

The situation called for tact – if they were going to assume that just because he was British, Mac was on the same side as them, it might be something he could use to his advantage. But he also needed to show Jananga that his loyalties lay with the Afghan police and not the British Army.

'Forgive me, but this is a murder enquiry. Major Jananga has jurisdiction, as the body was found off camp. You can speak freely in front of him.' *Or at least pretend to.*

'Yes, of course. Major Jananga, I'll give you all the help I can.'

The words sounded hollow to Mac and he wondered just how helpful the British establishment was going to be in this matter.

'There was no weapon found with the body,' said Mac. 'Could you ask your adjutant to check his quarters for any sidearms he had signed out.' The army would need to account for any missing weapon. 'Major Jananga and I will also need to speak to the men in his section in case they can shed any light on his movements.'

'Certainly,' said Tomlinson. 'He would have had a 9mm Browning HiPower, plus ammo. I'll get the details sent across to your office. And the details of his vehicle. Now, I suppose we'd better get this bloody ID over with. Where's the body?'

'In the city morgue at the Indian Hospital.'

Rolling his eyes, Tomlinson stood up to signal the meeting was at an end. His expression was bleak. 'I'd better talk to the Families Officer at home about informing his next of kin. If I remember rightly, Marshall's wife had a baby recently. Poor kid.' Stopping at the door, he added, 'All I can tell you is that there was absolutely no operational reason for Marshall to have been off base last night. Whatever trouble he got into, he got into it on his own. So if it's your investigation, MacKenzie, it's up to you to find out exactly what happened and why one of my best officers had his bloody throat cut.'

-

They took their leave of Lambert on the understanding that Holder would facilitate the interviews with the men and keep them briefed with any information on Marshall's weapon and vehicle.

'Jesus, I could do with a tea,' said Holder as they walked back across the MP compound. 'You?'

'Sure,' said Mac.

'Just give me a minute to check my calls. Wait here.'

'We'll go for a smoke,' said Mac as Holder ducked back towards the MP offices.

Mac got out his Marlboros and offered one to Jananga.

'Thank you, Mr Mac.'

'Just Mac is fine.'

He lit the major's cigarette and then his own, looking around the camp with interest. On the far side of the parade ground, two choppers were powering up on the helipad. Someone was going somewhere interesting. Then a door in the building closest to the MP compound gates opened, and a handful of men, heavily armed, heavily laden and heavily bearded emerged. Mac did a double take.

'Hey, Sharky!' he yelled.

One of the men looked round with a frown and then, on seeing Mac, broke into a grin.

'MacKenzie, fuckin' hell! Is that you?' He broke away from his men and came towards Mac and Jananga. 'What the fuck are you doing out here?'

'What I always do,' said Mac, with an equally big grin. 'Policing. And you?'

Sharky laughed. 'Uh-uh,' he said with a shake of his head. 'I'm not even here and you haven't even seen me.'

'Fair do's, no change there then,' said Mac. He held out a card. 'Here's my number, for when you are here.'

'Gotta go,' said Sharky, grabbing the card. His men were already boarding the two helicopters.

'God speed,' said Mac.

'Who was that man?' said Jananga as Sharky jogged across the training ground.

'Sharky – special forces. I worked with him in London on anti-terrorism.' He didn't want to give out more detail than that.

Noddy reappeared and, five minutes later, they found themselves sitting at a table in the cookhouse. It was late afternoon and the place was practically empty. Holder brought across three chipped china mugs of tea and a plate of chocolate digestives, making Mac realise he hadn't eaten anything since breakfast.

Jananga took a sip from his mug, spluttered and spat tea all over the table. He looked furious, and the string of Afghan phrases that followed the tea out of his mouth were definitely not polite.

Holder looked shocked, and Mac laughed.

'This isn't tea,' said the major, mopping his face on his sleeve. 'You English are uncivilised.'

'Nothing like a good brew,' said Mac. He dumped two heavily laden teaspoons of sugar into his own mug and stirred it.

The major pushed his cup to one side with disgust.

'Something else?' said Mac. He gestured towards the plate of digestives that sat between them.

Jananga took one, still frowning. 'I need to change the taste in my mouth.'

'Fine, when it comes to tea, we'll agree to disagree,' said Holder. 'But we've still got to work together.'

'Saw a gang of Pilgrims heading out by chopper just now,' said Mac, changing the subject. 'What are they up to?' He knew damn well he wouldn't get an answer.

Holder frowned. 'I don't think you did. We don't have any SF ops working out of Souter currently.'

Mac gave a dry laugh. 'Oh, I know what I saw, Captain. I knew one of the men – I'd worked with him before.'

Jananga was following the exchange with interest.

'You're mistaken.' There was a bite of anger in Holder's tone, and Mac knew it was a warning to shut up. 'What next for the investigation? Tell me who you want to talk to.'

'I think we need to talk to last night's gate guards,' said Mac. 'I want to find out exactly when Marshall left the base and whether he was alone.'

Holder fished a small notebook out of his breast pocket and started taking notes.

'Let's build a timeline – and work to fill in the gaps,' continued Mac. 'We know the man is Captain David Marshall, and we have an approximate time of death between midnight and one a.m. this morning. I want to establish his movements for the twenty-four hours leading up to his death.'

While Holder enjoyed his tea and Jananga didn't, Mac made a list of all the details they had so far about the case, drawing up a preliminary timeline.

'According to his roster,' Holder said, 'Marshall was working in the logistics office as usual yesterday.'

'What time would his working day have finished?'

'His shift apparently ended at six.'

Mac added it to his notes. 'So we need to follow his movements after that.'

'The gate guards will have logged what time he left the base. After that, he's going to be harder to trace.'

'Until he shows up dead in the tank graveyard.'

–

By the time they left the cookhouse it was after six, which meant the men on the gate would in theory be the same team who'd worked the previous evening when Marshall had headed out.

Camp Souter was bounded by a high concrete wall, punctuated by numerous sangars – small, squat watch towers positioned to have overlapping arcs of fire so the whole perimeter of the camp could be defended. There was a single gate in and out, Holder explained to them, located at the south-west corner of the camp. Coming from the outside, visitors had to pass through a simple drop-arm barrier, manned by Afghan soldiers armed with rifles and disinterest. Beyond that, the steel main gates were more substantial. The all-powerful British guard commander controlled who came and went, assisted by a vehicle searcher, a person searcher and a dog handler, all of whom were afforded the protection of a constantly manned machine-gun post.

Holder pointed out the guard commander. He was leaning against the sandbags at the back of the machine-gun post, smoking a cigarette.

'Sergeant Vincent, a minute, if you're not too busy.'

The man looked around carefully. 'Might just fit you in, sir.' Then he looked at Jananga, an unspoken question on his face.

Mac did the introductions and explained why they were there.

'Jesus! Someone slit his throat? Why?'

56

'That's what we're trying to find out, Vinny,' said Holder. 'Can we take a look at your log for yesterday evening?'

'Of course.'

Vinny dropped his cigarette on the tarmac, grinding it out with the toe of his boot. He led them around the gun emplacement and into the sentry hut by the side of the gates. Inside the cramped space there was a small desk, half of which was taken up by the most important tools for the job – a primus stove, a kettle, a box of teabags and a couple of dirty mugs. The brew was everything when you had to stand at your post for hours on end through the December night. Jananga shuddered visibly at the sight of it. At the other end of the desk, Mac spotted a written logbook and a motley assortment of pens.

The dog handler, a burly man with lank, greasy hair, was sitting in the post's single chair, behind the desk. He stood up as they came in. His sniffer dog emerged from under the desk. Its eyes went to Jananga and it made a low, grumbling noise at the back of its throat.

'Down, Arthur!'

Mac squinted in the bad light to read the name tag on the man's chest. Granton.

'At ease, Private,' said Holder.

The man sat down again, scratching the dog's ears to settle him.

'Same team on duty last night, Sergeant?' said the captain, turning back to Vinny.

'Yes, sir,' said Vinny. 'Want me to call them over?'

Mac nodded, and a minute later two privates who'd been standing by the gate peered in through the doorway. Meanwhile, Jananga had opened up the logbook and was checking the entries. Mac looked at it over his shoulder.

'So, Captain Marshall left the base at 22.05, according to this. Anyone talk to him?'

'I did, sir,' said one of the two privates.

'And? Did you ask him where he was going?'

'No, sir.'

'Don't your men have to give you a plan when they leave camp?' said Jananga to Holder.

Holder shrugged. 'In theory, Marshall should have logged his intentions with his unit. But…'

Jananga frowned and turned away from him.

'Give me the details of the vehicle,' he said to the private who had spoken. 'And check with his unit what plans he'd given them.'

The man looked taken aback. Mac realised he had no idea who Jananga was and had probably assumed he was an interpreter or driver.

'Private, this is Major Jananga of the Kabul police,' said Holder. 'He's assisting us with our enquiries.'

Jananga stiffened. '*You* are assisting me with *my* enquiries, I think.'

The private looked from one to the other of them. It was an awkward moment and Mac realised he'd get much further questioning the gate guards, and any other camp personnel they had to talk to, if Jananga wasn't with him. The Afghan's presence put them all on their guard.

But Jananga wasn't going to be deterred.

'How often did Captain Marshall leave the camp?'

The private shrugged. 'Most days. His work…' He glanced at Vinny to see whether he should carry on. Vinny gave him a small nod. 'Most days he went out to the airport.'

'Anywhere else?'

'I don't know.'

Jananga looked around at Vinny and the other private.

'We're here to stop unauthorised people coming in,' said Vinny. 'We don't police our own people going out.'

It was time to wrap this up – they were getting nowhere. Mac would have to ask Holder if he could come back and talk to the guys later when Jananga wasn't around.

'Come on,' he said, turning for the door.

Jananga reached out and picked up the logbook. Alarm bells rang in Mac's head. Vinny shot him a warning look – the log book never left the guard hut.

'What are you doing?'

'I need to take this, so I can record all of Captain Marshall's trips off the base. I will have it returned to you quickly.'

'No way, mate,' said Vinny, holding his hand out for the book.

'Major,' snapped Jananga.

'Major Jananga,' said Holder, 'we can't let the logbook off the base. Let me get it copied for you in my office – it'll only take a minute.'

'I'll organise the copies, sir,' said Vinny.

Jananga's eyes narrowed, but he handed the book to Vinny.

'Thank you, Sergeant.'

It took longer than a minute, but not much time passed before Vinny came back and handed a sheaf of copies to Mac.

Outside the guard post, Jananga turned and glared at Holder. 'You and your men are not very co-operative. Please to remember, this my investigation.' Anger made his English falter.

Holder at least had the decency to look embarrassed.

'Sorry, Major. That was my fault. I should have explained who you were in there.'

Jananga nodded, but he didn't look mollified.

'You English might think you know it all, with your superior resources and equipment, but remember, Captain, that David Marshall died in my country – and here in Kabul, you know nothing.'

Chapter 7

It had seemed like a very long day. Mac lay on his bunk, wondering what lengths the company went to to source the most uncomfortable mattresses. It was only by constantly shifting position that he could get any rest at all.

He took a sip of his coffee – bitter, and almost cold now. Grimacing, he once again reviewed the notes he'd made on the investigation into Marshall's death so far. Why was Davie Marshall out at the tank graveyard so late at night? Meeting somebody? There would be no other reason to be skulking around there after dark. A clandestine meeting in the middle of the night suggested an involvement in something that was decidedly shonky. It seemed hard to believe that he was just in the wrong place at the wrong time, and had been mugged.

A knock on the metal door echoed around the container.

'Coming.'

Mac went to the door. It was Ginger.

'There's a Sergeant Vincent on the phone. Wants you to meet him at Souter, outside the gates.'

'When?'

Ginger shrugged. 'Now, I think.'

Mac sat up and reached under the bed for his desert boots.

'How'd he know to ring here?'

This time Ginger smiled. 'Might have something to do with you running around all day in a company jacket. Not too hard to ask around and find a number for the company.'

Right, note to self, dig another jacket out of the trunk.

'Okay, got it. D'you wanna ride shotgun?'

Half an hour later, the Land Cruiser pulled up to the kerb opposite the main gate of Camp Souter, with Ginger at the wheel. A figure emerged from the shadows, which Mac recognised as the sergeant he'd spoken to earlier at the gatehouse. He stretched back to open one of the rear doors and Vinny slipped into the back seat.

'Vinny, isn't it?' he said.

'Yup.'

'I'm Mac, and this is Ginger. What can I do for you?'

'Sorry, Mac, to call you out this late, but I had to wait for a break.'

'Not a problem.'

'It's about Captain Marshall.' Vinny leant forward between the two front seats. He lowered his voice. 'I didn't want to say anything earlier, when you were there with your Afghan major. I wasn't sure I should talk freely in front of him or the fucking Monkey.' By this he was referring to Holder, as a member of the Military Police.

It was just what Mac had suspected.

'So what do you want to tell me?'

'Look, I don't know if this is important or not, but Captain Marshall... apart from when he was working, he used to go out quite a lot. Quite often stayed out all night.'

'Where do you think he went?'

Vinny shrugged. 'I don't know. But when he came back in the morning, sometimes I could smell alcohol on him, through his car window.'

'You mean he came back drunk?'

'Not totally bladdered or anything. But, yeah, sometimes I thought he was a bit pissed.'

Mac pursed his lips and thought about the implications. He probably went out drinking and spent the night in one of Kabul's brothels. It wasn't a crime in itself for a British soldier to visit a brothel or to have a drink or two, but it would be bloody stupid to get caught drunk-driving in Kabul. If he did, it would cost him plenty of *baksheesh*, and if he didn't have a wad of cash on him the consequences wouldn't have been pleasant.

'How often was he doing this?'

Vinny shook his head. 'Maybe a couple of times a week. I wasn't always on duty.'

'No, of course not.'

'But you'll see it from the logbook.'

Mac had made another photocopy of the logbook pages they got from Holder, so Jananga and he would each have a set. However, he hadn't had time to go through them yet.

'Was he always on his own, or did he go out with other officers?'

'Never saw him going out or coming back with anyone else, I don't think. Maybe once or twice with Sergeant Dixon, but that wasn't staying out all night.'

'And he never mentioned where he'd been those times when he'd been out all night?' Mac experienced a growing sense of unease – something untoward had been going on.

'No. Always came through without a word. More often than not he seemed angry or out of sorts.'

'Well, thanks for telling me, Vinny. You did the right thing.'

'I just didn't want to show him up in front of the brass if it wasn't relevant.'

–

When Vinny had gone, Mac and Ginger headed back to Camp Julien. Ginger put a fresh pot of coffee on.

'Something's going on, and I don't feel I'll get to the bottom of it with Jananga in tow,' said Mac, taking the chair as usual. 'I really need a free hand to conduct the investigation without the major tagging along the whole time – it's the only way I'll get the men to talk openly to me.'

'Slight problem, isn't it?' said Ginger, handing him a mug. 'Given that it's Jananga's operation.'

'The things I do for this fucking company!'

—

Mac woke up early the next morning and rehearsed what he was going to say in his head twenty times or more, because he knew Phelps wasn't going to like it.

'Sorry, but it's not going that well with Major Jananga.'

'How do you mean?'

'He's sort of in the way… not really helping much.'

'What's your point, Mac?' Egon Phelps was leaning back in his chair, boots up on the corner of his desk, as he nursed a cup of coffee, but his tone became clipped.

'Just… I get why we had to agree to work with Major Jananga on this investigation. But I'd make a better job of it working on my own, without him looking over my shoulder the whole time. People don't open up in front him, so I'm not getting any useful information.'

'But the murder happened in his jurisdiction. It's actually his investigation.'

'Sure, but he's fucking clueless. I can pass details across to him as I find things out. But when he was with me yesterday, the Brits just clammed up. Then one of the gate guards came to me later and actually told me something that was more relevant.'

'Which was what?'

'That Marshall was in the habit of going out all night and coming back drunk and angry.'

'What was he up to?'

'That's what I need to find out.'

'So get on with it and stop belly-aching to me.'

'Just saying, it would be easier without Jananga tagging along.'

Phelps swung his feet down from the desk and straightened up in his chair.

'You know, Mac, that my hands are tied. It's his case, he's in charge. You do what he says.'

'Well, it's a right fucking pain. You know what sort of hassle you get into, working with the Afghans. It took us half an hour to get into his office to see him. Then we got the Mexican stand-off up at the tank graveyard with the army over who would take the body. It's impossible to work that way.'

'Tough. Major Jananga has a good reputation as a straight cop. This is his country and he knows and understands the politics here – I hear he fought for the Northern Alliance against the Taliban and is connected to the Massoud clan. That's how he got the gig he's in – not because of any amazing track record of police experience. In other words, you're going to have to bite the fricking bullet and work with him.'

Mac frowned. Phelps had laid down the law – he had to work with Jananga. But that didn't mean he had to like it.

Phelps was waiting for him to leave, but a thought had just occurred to him.

'Egon?'

'Yes.'

'Can I have Ginger working for me on the case?'

'Why?'

'He was a para, right? He knows the army, how they do things, who to talk to and speaks the same language... I think it would be useful to have him along. Make up for the hassle of having to live with Jananga.'

'But what about your course? Still a couple of weeks left to run.'

'O'Neill can pick up the slack. He's got some time before his next course starts.'

Phelps considered in silence for a moment. 'Possibly. Maybe. I'll see what I can do.'

Mac added a little extra persuasion. 'I'm getting a strong feeling that Marshall was mixed up in something dirty. He was off base a lot and no one seems to have any idea of what he was up to. I think he was meeting someone up at the tank graveyard. There's no other explanation for being up there in the middle of the night. This might be heading into the Kabul underworld – could get dangerous.'

'So you'd like Ginger as an armed escort?'

'The company wouldn't like to put an employee in unnecessary danger, would it? It would be safer if there were two of us.'

Phelps sighed – he knew he'd been caught out. Then he smiled.

'All right, Mac. I'll talk to O'Neill about taking on some of your course work to free Ginger up for you part-time. But don't abuse it – it's not carte blanche for you two to go riding shotgun with the Kabul police.'

'Thanks.' Mac stood up to leave.

Phelps looked at Mac. 'Don't mess this up. You know how important it is for all of us.'

'I won't.' He left the room. 'Oh, ye of little faith.'

Out in the corridor, he punched the air.

Chapter 8

Dead straight and four lanes wide, the Darulaman Road cut a swathe through the south-west of the city, linking the centre of Kabul to the Darul Aman Palace. The name meant 'the abode of peace', but like so many of the city's landmark buildings, the eighty-year-old structure was a testament to the country's decades of strife. Baz stared out of the car window at its charred ruins – its domes no more than iron skeletons, the roof caved in and the walls pockmarked by bullet holes and rocket fire.

Javid turned to follow her gaze and sighed.

'It was supposed to be our parliament.'

The ground it stood on rose slightly from the road. The outer wall had crumbled and what once must have been gardens were now barren earth.

'I wish I could show you the beautiful places of our city, but everything has been destroyed.'

Baz felt for him. She hated the devastation she saw all around her whenever they drove anywhere. Her parents remembered Kabul as an elegant and cultured place to live. Their hearts would break if they could see it now.

'But at least the museum is being restored,' she said, forcing a note of optimism into her voice.

The National Museum was their destination – a 1930s building of soft grey plasterwork, with a white stucco doorway and white balustrades along the rim of the roof. Baz recognised the building from photographs. It was here that her father had worked, before her parents fled the nascent Communist regime in 1980. Now, the building was obscured in part by scaffolding and the land around it resembled a building site, with piles of bricks, stacks of planks, a concrete mixer, the wreck of an elderly limousine and a rusted container with a cardboard sign declaring 'Site Office' pinned to its door.

Javid pulled up the car in front of the main gates, where two teenage sentries stood, roused from torpor by the new arrival.

Baz checked her hajib in the cracked mirror on the underside of the sun visor. She was here to see a former colleague of her father. She got out of the Toyota and approached the older of the two guards. Javid walked behind her.

'*Salaam alaikum.*'

The lad eyed her suspiciously. A western woman who had the temerity to address him. He clearly wasn't impressed.

He looked straight through her and spoke to Javid in a stream of Dari that was almost too fast for Baz to follow.

She cut in, before Javid could answer.

'I have an appointment with Professor Paghahan.'

It took an intervention by Javid and a fifteen-minute wait before they were finally led into the building. Baz's cheeks burned with anger, while Javid followed sheepishly behind her.

Why was the whole country so goddamned chauvinist?

'I don't need a *mahram* to chaperone me everywhere,' she muttered as they followed the guard down the long, arched corridor that ran through the centre of the building.

Javid shrugged. 'It's our way. Our women are used to it.'

'They shouldn't have to be.' But it wasn't his fault, and there was no point being angry with him.

A man was walking towards them, and she recognised an older version of the photograph her father had emailed her. Grizzled grey replaced a sweep of glossy black hair, and now there were deep trenches at either side of his mouth. She let go of her anger and held out her hand.

'Miss Basima Kahn,' he said with a wide smile, taking her hand in his and briefly shaking it. 'You are the image of your mother, with your father's eyes. And, I understand, his sharp intellect.'

He spoke perfect English, with a slight American accent, and Baz warmed to him immediately.

The guard started to say something, but the professor dismissed him with a wave of his hand.

'I'll wait in the car,' said Javid. He followed the sentry back along the corridor.

'Come,' said Paghahan. 'Let me show you what we're doing.'

'I can speak in Dari,' said Baz.

'Of course.' The old man looked at her conspiratorially. 'But the workers here don't speak English, so I think that will suit us better.'

Baz understood immediately.

They walked on down the central corridor, then the professor led her into one of the side rooms. There was no art and no objects to be seen. Shadows on the walls showed where paintings used to hang, and dark rectangles marked out where the floor under display cases hadn't been regularly polished. A man on a ladder was working to restore the coving, and another man was repairing damage to the limestone tiled floor.

'Was everything stolen?' said Baz. It was a sobering thought.

Paghahan drew a deep breath. 'An awful lot has gone,' he said. 'Once the civil war started, the museum was constantly looted. We lost thirty-five thousand precious coins and count-less works of art.'

'And the Bactrian Gold hoard?'

'That, thankfully, was kept safe in the vaults of the Arg.' The Arg was the Presidential Palace – Baz's father had talked of it often.

They reached a small office space that was clearly temporary. The professor was using a battered table for a desk. It was covered with plans and drawings of the building.

'As the Taliban advanced, we were able to hide more than three thousand objects in central Kabul,' he said, gesturing for her to sit down on one of two hard, wooden chairs. 'But they tricked us. Mullah Omar issued a decree protecting our artefacts, so we started to bring things back here. Then, less than a year later, he reversed the decree. Not only did they destroy the Bamiyan Buddhas, but they trashed a large part of our collection.'

The professor fell silent, overcome by the emotion of what had happened. Baz could remember her father openly crying when he heard about the destruction of priceless pieces that the Taliban deemed heretical – and it was the news of this that had driven her desire to come to Afghanistan as a reporter.

'Now we are rebuilding,' he said. 'We have a museum in exile in Basel, where we're gathering items that were smuggled abroad – those we can recover. Here, we've finally got electricity back and glass in the windows. Priceless objects are being restored. But I don't think we'll ever return this place to its former glory.'

'It must have been heartbreaking for you and your colleagues.'

'It was worse than that. I lost two of my staff when a shell hit the roof in 1993, and another in 1996. And for nearly a decade, I wasn't able to pay them. But they still came to work when they could, around whatever other jobs they had, for the love of it.' He looked across the table at her with rheumy eyes. 'Please share our story with the world. So much of our treasure has been looted and taken abroad. We need museums and auction houses in every country to be vigilant on our behalf.'

'This is why I'm in Afghanistan, Professor Paghahan. My father believes that a black-market supply chain is still shipping artefacts out of the country. I'm determined to uncover it so that your police can put a stop to it.'

The professor made a sound that was half laughter, half cry of despair. 'The police? They're more corrupt than anyone. They'll be helping the gangsters get the stuff out.' He leaned forward with his elbows on the table. 'You should go home,

Basima. This is far too dangerous for a girl who doesn't know the country.'

Baz bristled. Always, *always*, her gender was thrown in her face, with the intent of making her feel inadequate for whatever she wanted to do. But all it did was make her more determined than ever.

'No. My father has been broken by what has happened here. He works every hour Allah grants him to track down Afghanistan's heritage. I can form a link between his work and your work.'

The professor rubbed his eyes and stood up, walking across to the window. Outside, the barren ground played host to a jumble of scaffold poles. An old man, who looked well beyond retirement age, was removing scaffold fixings from them and sorting them into plastic crates. Beyond him was the rusted hulk of an ancient steam train.

Baz came to stand next to him. She spoke, keeping her voice low, not wanting any of the workers in the nearby rooms to hear.

'Do you know of a man called Baseer Ghilji?'

Paghahan's head shot round, his eyes wide with fear.

'No, Basima-jan, you must have nothing to do with him.'

'My father heard that he has a Paiza for sale.'

'What? That can't be right. Such tokens were granted by the Great Khans of Mongolia to officials and favoured merchants. They're rare and priceless, and should by rights be here in the museum.'

'I could get it back for you.'

'It's much too dangerous. Men have died for less valuable objects.'

'I'm American. I can promise him access to the sort of buyer he's looking for.'

Anger flared in the professor's eyes. 'Don't be stupid. Ghilji knows all the buyers in his market. He'll sniff you out in moments.'

'Not so far.'

'Please tell me you haven't already tangled with him – he's a very dangerous man. His associates are even more dangerous.' The professor sounded genuinely distressed.

'So help me. Teach me everything I need to know about the Paiza so I can convince him that I'm a genuine buyer.'

'And then what? Even if I did help you, surely you don't have the money he'll be asking.'

Baz shook her head. 'No, of course not. All I need to do is set up the deal and then the authorities can intervene.'

'No, Basima. The authorities will do nothing – he'll pay them to look the other way. I'm not going to help you get yourself killed. Your father would never forgive me. I'd never forgive myself.' He picked up a string of stone prayer beads, *tasbeh*, from his desk and started clicking them through his fingers.

'Then, Professor Paghahan, I'll just have to do it without your help.'

She strode out of his office, head held high. But inside, she was quaking as she made her way down the vaulted centre of the building.

What was she getting herself into?

She heard footsteps behind her and turned around. The professor stopped and raised his hands in supplication.

'Basima,' he said. 'What are you going to do?'

She walked back to where he was standing.

'I've been to his shop in Chicken Street and spoke with him—'

Paghahan interrupted. 'You didn't give him your real name, did you?'

'No. I didn't give him any name.'

'Good. He would find out that you're a journalist. Use a fake name in all your dealings with him.'

'You're right – to an extent. But my real name will allow him to trace me to my father. That will explain why I have the connections in the antiquities market, and the knowledge to go with it.'

'But your father has a reputation to uphold. He would never be involved in smuggling.'

'I'll tell Ghilji we have a family friend who is sick, who we need to help. That's explanation enough. On the other hand, if I give him a fake name, he'll look me up – and there won't be a realistic history.'

'He's not a stupid man. You need something more convincing than that. Say at least that someone in your family is sick… that your mother has cancer, perhaps.'

Just the thought of it brought Baz up short. She couldn't… wouldn't do that. It would be tempting fate. She shook her head.

'I don't like it either,' said Paghahan. 'You should step back from this whole foolish plan. You're playing with fire.'

'But you want to retrieve the Paiza?'

'It's too dangerous.' The professor looked down at her. 'Do you trust your driver?'

'Yes.'

'Then get him a gun and take him with you everywhere you go.'

Baz gasped. 'But I don't want to put Javid in harm's way.'

'He lives in Kabul, doesn't he?'

Where God comes to cry.

She knew where she could get a gun.

Chapter 9

If Davie Marshall had been getting his hands dirty, the most likely people to know about it were his closest colleagues. Holder had filled Mac in on Marshall's job – he headed up one of the three troops that made up Souter's logistics squadron, and Mac had a list of Marshall's troop in front of him as he, Jananga and Holder sat at a large square table in Holder's office.

The captain, seeming to have become resigned to his role as their chaperone for the investigation, was being more accommodating – tea and information forthcoming, including a photo of Marshall and a copy of his service record. The picture was of the whole troop and was a little blurred, but apparently it was the only one Holder had to hand. He'd even told them to call him Noddy, his nickname in honour of the lead singer of the band Slade, Noddy Holder. Jananga, having declined a brew, was copying the names into his notebook.

Mac made a mental note to refuse any more glasses of the bitter green slops that masqueraded as tea in Jananga's office. He'd always felt obliged to drink it when it was offered, but he'd obviously been far too polite.

'Who do you need to see first?' said Holder, pushing the list back along the table to Mac.

'Marshall's sergeant – Neil Dixon.'

Holder went over to the phone on his desk and instructed someone at the other end to bring Sergeant Dixon to his office.

While they waited, Mac questioned Jananga. 'Catch me up, Major – did you get anything out of that kid we picked up at the tank graveyard?'

Jananga shrugged and let out a sigh before he spoke. 'It was nothing. He was a male prostitute, brought up there by one of his customers. It's a place known for…' He shrugged again.

'Cruising,' supplied Mac. It didn't surprise him.

'Cruising,' said Jananga. Another new word for his English vocabulary.

A minute later, there was a knock at the door and a tall, dark-haired man stepped into Holder's office. He was wearing desert camouflage trousers, army-issue boots and a dark blue sweatshirt with the regimental badge on the chest. He stood to attention in front of Holder.

'Sergeant Dixon, sir. I understand you wanted to see me?'

'Yes, thanks for coming in, Sergeant. Take a seat.'

Dixon sat down along the fourth side of the table, giving Jananga a questioning look. Without a uniform, as far as Dixon was concerned, he could have been an interpreter or one of the various other local workers employed on the base.

'Dixon, this is Major Jananga of the Kabul police, and DI MacKenzie,' said Holder.

Mac saw a wave of tension pass up Dixon's spine. He wondered why.

'You'll know, of course, by now that Davie Marshall was found dead yesterday morning,' the captain continued.

'Major Tomlinson informed the troop last night, sir.'

Tomlinson had agreed to give out as few details as possible at this stage. As far as the men were concerned, Marshall had been found dead in Kabul and that was it. They didn't know where he was found or what had happened to him. But they would quickly draw their own conclusions based on the fact that they were being questioned by an Afghan police major.

'How long have you worked under Captain Marshall?' said Mac.

'Since just before we were deployed out here in the spring. Prior to that, Captain Harvey was our troop commander.'

'Any reason for the change?'

'Not my place to ask questions.' The words didn't sound convincing. The sergeant knew something he wasn't letting on. Was this down to his own reticence, or had the soldiers been briefed by their commanding officer to hold back?

Jananga leant forward with his elbows on the table.

'You worked closely with Captain Marshall? You knew him well?'

Dixon flashed a glance at Holder, and Holder nodded. The sergeant returned his gaze to Jananga.

'I worked with him every day. We got on.'

'You were friends?'

'Not friends, no. He was a Rupert.'

Jananga's eyebrows went up. 'I don't know that word,' he said to Mac.

'Slang,' said Holder. 'Marshall was a commissioned officer – a Rupert. Sergeant Dixon doesn't hold a commission.'

Jananga looked none the wiser, but he scribbled furiously in his book.

Mac took the chance to jump in.

'We understand that Captain Marshall would occasionally be off the base all night. Would that be a normal part of his duties?'

Dixon's nostril's flared momentarily. Mac wondered how much he was sweating inside his top.

'We meet the planes coming into Kabul Airport and unload them, and we load planes going out. Our hours depend on the flight times.'

It didn't answer the question.

'Were you working on Thursday night?' said Holder.

'No, sir. We had a plane land in the afternoon, but it was unloaded by teatime.'

'And there wasn't another one? Or a plane leaving?'

'No, sir.'

'So Marshall wouldn't have been going to the airport late on Thursday evening?'

'Not that I know of, sir.'

Mac decided to try a change of tack. 'Do you know what Captain Marshall did with his time when he was off duty?'

Dixon shrugged. 'Wasn't my business. I think he went out sometimes with the other officers. I saw him in the gym on and off.'

'So you have no idea what he might have been doing out of camp on Thursday night?'

'No. I'm sorry, I can't help you.'

No pause for thought. No expression of regret over what had happened. Mac didn't take to Neil Dixon for reasons he couldn't quite fathom – and it made him wonder if the tosser knew more than he was letting on. And how much of this performance was for Holder's benefit.

'Okay, Sergeant Dixon. You've been very helpful.' *Not*. 'If you think of anything else that might be relevant, please let Captain Holder know.'

'Yes, of course.'

After he'd gone, Holder excused himself for a minute, leaving Mac and Jananga alone.

The major shook his head. 'He hasn't told us something. He knows more.'

'I don't doubt it,' said Mac.

'But you let him go.' It was more accusation than question.

'I don't think he wanted to talk freely in front Holder – there's no trust between the Military Police and the regular soldiers.'

Jananga shrugged. 'I would have dug deeper for the answers.'

Mac ignored the implications. They were questioning British soldiers on a British base – he could hardly use the type of interrogation tactics the Afghan police probably favoured. He wondered if the whole exercise was a waste of time. He was sure he'd do better if he and Ginger could talk to the men without others listening in.

Holder came back into the room.

'Who'd you want next, Mr MacKenzie?'

–

Captain Dev Khatri spoke with a thick Brummy accent.

'I can't believe what's happened,' Khatri said, taking the chair vacated by Dixon a few minutes earlier. 'Where did you find his body?'

'Sorry, that's need-to-know at the moment, I'm afraid,' said Mac.

'Foul play, in other words?'

'We know that Captain Marshall went off the base alone on Thursday evening. Can you shed any light on what he might have been doing?'

'Not specifically on Thursday,' said Khatri. 'But he was a bit of a drinker.' Holder frowned but Khatri carried on talking. 'He used to go into town some nights – the Jungle Bar and places like that. He liked to play poker.' He raised one shoulder in a shrug. 'Gambled a bit.'

This didn't add up with what Tomlinson had said about Marshall being a family man with a wife and a baby back home. But then what went down in Kabul, stayed in Kabul.

Jananga wasn't impressed. 'Was that normal behaviour for a British officer?'

Khatri turned to him. 'Sure. Life on base is restrictive. Guys need to kick back every now and again.'

'And you?' said Jananga. 'Do you drink and gamble too?'

Khatri gave him a level stare, his dark eyes hard as flint. 'This isn't about me, Major Jananga.'

Mac stepped in. 'Captain, do you happen to know why Captain Harvey switched troops? I understand that up until this deployment she was in charge of what's now Marshall's troop.'

Khatri turned back to Mac. 'It had nothing to do with this.'

77

Interesting. *It*. *This*. Mac was getting a scent of something, but it was far from clear what the man was referring to.

'What was it to do with?'

Straightaway, he saw it was a question Khatri didn't want to answer. The captain looked down at his hands in his lap. Mac wondered if it was Jananga's presence that was making him reluctant to talk, but then he noticed the piercing look Khatri was getting from Holder.

'I don't really know a lot about it,' said Khatri finally. 'There was some talk of inappropriate fraternisation.'

Jananga looked blank – this was beyond the scope of his English.

'Between Harvey and one of her men?'

'Like I said, I really don't know. It wasn't connected with David Marshall.'

'You mean the woman captain was having relations with a subordinate?' said Jananga. 'With a man who is now in Marshall's troop?'

Khatri nodded.

'His name, Captain?' said Jananga.

Mac thought the major was barking up the wrong tree. What could Harvey's transfer, or even an illicit affair, have to do with Marshall's murder?

Khatri cleared his throat.

'Sergeant Dixon.'

Chapter 10

After that Khatri had clammed up, and Mac had decided they were wasting their time trying to get anything meaningful out of the soldiers under Holder's watchful eye.

'It's time to dump our army friend,' he said as he and Jananga swept out of Souter in Jananga's Surf. 'Do some investigating on our own.'

'How?' said Jananga. 'Anyone who knows anything is inside the base – and surely we need to talk to the woman.'

Mac stared out of the window as they sped back along the Jalalabad Road towards Police HQ. There was no reason to think this affair had anything to do with Marshall's death, so why should Jananga want to question Captain Harvey?

'You don't agree with me?'

'I doubt she'll have anything for us,' said Mac, putting a note of finality into his voice. 'I'm more interested in what Marshall's vehicle might be able to tell us. It hasn't been recovered yet, so I think it's time for a trip to the tank graveyard to see if we can find it.'

Marshall had been driving an unmarked Toyota Surf when he'd left the camp. If he'd driven up there on his own, it was presumably still somewhere in the vicinity. However, if he'd gone up there with someone else – his killer, possibly – then who knew where it might be now? Mac had yet to admit he'd taken the car keys from Marshall's trouser pocket, and he wasn't going to say anything now. That could wait, depending on whether or not they found the car.

'Yes, good plan,' said Jananga, then issued instructions to his driver in Dari.

With a screech of brakes, the driver executed a U-turn, pushing his way into the traffic travelling in the opposite direction, eliciting a blast on the horn from the driver now behind them. Mac gripped the edge of his seat, and tried to push down the horrific memories that always surfaced when he was in a swerving car. He took a deep breath and wondered whether Jananga's driver had passed a driving test or simply bought his licence.

Once his heart rate had returned to normal, he called Ginger. 'Take Pamir and the Land Cruiser,' he said, 'and meet us up at the entrance to the tank graveyard.'

It didn't take them long to reach their destination. The main road ran dead straight, flanked on either side by row upon row of grimy-walled residential compounds, interspersed with warehouses and small industrial units. It was less than three miles from Souter to the tank graveyard and as they weren't going anywhere near the centre of town, they avoided most of the usual traffic snarl-ups.

The sky was a flat grey, the dull light deadening the landscape. Mac stared out of the window without taking in what he saw, his mind whirring. What the hell had Marshall been doing out at the tank graveyard? Who had he gone there with, or to meet?

He was determined to find the answers.

Jananga offered him a stick of Juicy Fruit gum.

'Thanks, but no,' he said. 'From the Chelsea Supermarket?'

Jananga nodded and smiled as he chewed the gum into submission. 'The best place to go to feed our dirty western habits.'

'Have you always lived in Kabul?'

Jananga's expression became grave. 'I grew up here, but it's the most dangerous city in a dangerous country. The Taliban beheaded my father in 1996, so I took my mother and my brothers back to Charikar, where her family lives.'

'I'm sorry for what happened to your father.' He didn't dare ask why the Taliban had executed him. 'Where's Charikar?'

'To the north. It's at the mouth of the Panjshir Valley, at the base of the Hindu Kush. The Taliban attacked the town a year later, but we were fortunately under the protection of Ahmad Shah Massoud – the Lion of the Panjshir.' Jananga's chest seemed to swell with pride as he spoke of Massoud. 'He beat the Taliban back after a few months of fighting. My mother's sister is married to a Panjshiri, so we were safe.'

'Did the fighting get near you?'

'My mother and younger brothers hid up in the valley. I fought for the Northern Alliance with my older brothers until the Taliban fell. Two of them were killed. I was wounded more than once. But, finally, I was able to return to Kabul and so I joined the police.'

'You've only been a policeman for a couple of years?'

Mac's incredulity must have shown on his face, because Jananga frowned.

'In a country with no stability, we don't have the luxury of time that you have in the west.'

A hundred questions crowded into Mac's mind – about the war, about Jananga's childhood, about his life as a police officer. But they were turning off the Jalalabad Road onto the narrow street they'd taken the day before to reach the tank graveyard. It led north through an area of rundown warehouses and industrial units. Under the Russians it had been the site of the main armour repair shops, which is why the tank graveyard had sprung up here in the first place. The Americans had bombed the repair works heavily, so at least half of the buildings were now burnt-out shells.

The WTP Land Cruiser was pulling into the street behind them, so Jananga instructed his driver to stop, and Jananga and Mac climbed into its back seat.

'Find anything out this morning?' Ginger said. He'd spent the morning going through the rest of the course work with a disgruntled O'Neil.

'Nothing,' said Mac. 'I reckon Holder or Tomlinson had warned them to watch what they said. Closing ranks to protect the reputation of the dead soldier.' Inside, he bubbled with anger and frustration. If they were ever going to get to the bottom of what had happened, they needed Marshall's colleagues to be completely open with anything they knew.

'We should start looking out for the Surf,' said Jananga. 'If he went up to the meeting point on foot, he might have parked it down here.'

All three of them scanned the area they were driving through for signs of the silver Toyota that Marshall had taken out from Souter. There were rows of vehicles parked by some of the intact industrial units, but most were shut up and deserted. Side streets led off in either direction and Mac caught glimpses of loading bays, alleyways and vacant lots where a car could easily be tucked out of sight.

'Should we comb the whole estate?' said Ginger.

Mac thought for a moment. 'No, it makes more sense to carry on up into the graveyard, starting close to where the body was found and work our way out from there.'

'Look for fresh tyre tracks between the tanks,' said Jananga.

Here, at the outer edge of the city, there were signs of a light overnight frost – crystals of ice still glittered in the darkest patches of shade. Mac was glad he'd found an old down jacket to replace the windcheater with the WTP logo. The car lurched over the uneven ground, crunching over loose stones with a noise that roused a pair of large, grey buzzards into flight.

'This place is becoming a nature reserve,' said Jananga. 'Great for our tourist industry.'

Despite his reservations about working with the man, Mac was starting to appreciate his dry sense of humour.

The place where Marshall had met his death was still cordoned off with rope, but there was no one watching over it and the flimsy barrier would hardly have kept anyone out. However, there wasn't another human to be seen and the only sound was the sharp keening of the wind and the rattling of broken tank hatches.

'What a godforsaken place to die.' Mac meant the tank graveyard, but realised he could have been talking about the country as a whole.

Pamir stopped just outside the cordon. Mac got out and swung himself up onto an adjacent tank to stand on top of the turret. Ginger handed him a pair of binoculars, and he raised them to survey the entirety of the tank graveyard. A couple of square miles at least of broken and bloodied tanks, left over from a war of attrition. He could see no sign of Marshall's silver Surf.

Jananga watched him from the ground, lighting a cigarette while he waited.

'Can you see it?' he said, through a billow of smoke.

Mac shook his head and jumped down.

'Pamir,' he said, climbing back into the car, 'take us right along to the far edge of the graveyard and then work back up and down the rows till we reach the entrance – that way, if it's here, we'll have to see it.'

It wasn't quite as simple a request as it sounded. The sloping ground fell away steeply in some places. In others, it was too rutted to drive over, or the tanks had been dumped too close together to pass between. Mac felt his bones being rattled, his teeth jarring, as they drove over stones and potholes. At the end of one row, two wide-eyed boys stared at them out of the gun turret of a T62. One of them half-heartedly threw a stone at the Surf but it missed by a mile. There were huge drifts of rusted metal and smashed armoured vehicles, cracked windscreens glinting in the weak sun.

A pack of dogs appeared suddenly in their path, barking and snarling, then scurried out of the way when Pamir revved the engine and cursed at them out of the window. Mac was relieved that he wasn't searching on foot. There were millions of strays in the city and rabies was relatively common. Jananga made a pistol shape with his hand and a popping sound with his mouth as he fired at them.

There was something otherworldly about the place and Mac wondered how Marshall had felt, coming up here alone in the dead of night.

But still there was no sign of the Toyota they were looking for.

They returned to the road by which they'd come in – and moments later they were back at the industrial estate.

'Okay, Pamir, let's do this area now,' said Mac.

This time they were more successful. Pamir took an immediate left turn and drove them through a row of interlinked units. At the end of the last building, tucked just around the corner, they came across a silver Toyota Surf. The number on the licence plate matched the number of the missing vehicle.

'This is it,' said Mac.

Had Marshall realised when he parked it here that he might never come back to it?

They pulled up and all three got out of the car. They walked around the Surf warily, peering through the windows in case there was anyone inside. Ginger took an under-vehicle inspection mirror out of the Land Cruiser's boot and looked for explosives. Seeing this check always gave Mac a flurry of nerves, only quelled when the all-clear was given.

'Nothing there.'

'Thank you, Ginger,' said Mac.

He dug Marshall's car keys out of the pocket of his jeans.

'You've got the keys?' said Ginger. 'I'm surprised that the army handed them over.'

'They were in Marshall's pocket. I took them from the morgue.'

Jananga snapped to attention with a frown. 'Then you should have given them to me. I will take custody of all evidence for this case.'

'Yeah, sorry.' Only he wasn't. Kabul Police HQ would probably be a black hole as far as evidence was concerned.

Jananga's scowl deepened, but he didn't say anything.

Mac dug a pair of latex gloves out of his pocket, pulled them on and then opened the driver's door. The car interior smelled of stale cigarettes and there was a confetti of ash on the floor of the driver's side. Marshall had clearly been a smoker, and the ashtray was open, crammed with stubs. Mac put the key into the ignition and turned it so he could take note of the mileage.

Jananga, also wearing latex gloves, opened the passenger door and looked through at him.

'Was this Captain Marshall's own car or a shared car?' he asked.

'It was assigned to him when he arrived at Souter, according to Holder,' said Mac.

'Then we should check for fingerprints.'

Mac had been about to do just that, but held his tongue. He didn't need to look like he was playing catch-up. If it had been a pool car, it wouldn't have been worth the bother as there would have been far too many to make sense of.

Jananga had taken a bag from the back of his Surf when they'd swapped to the Land Cruiser. Now he retrieved a fingerprint kit from it and handed it to Mac. It was pretty rudimentary compared with the kits Mac had used in the Met, but it would do the job. He set to work brushing the fine silver powder onto the door handles, the steering wheel, the gear knob and the rest of the controls. Jananga watched from the other side without comment as he lifted the prints. There would be Marshall's, whoever he'd used as a driver, probably at least one or two different interpreters. Mac wasn't at all sure they would tell him anything, but he had to hope that something would turn up at some point or he might as well give up and go home.

'Check the glove box,' he said.

Jananga opened it and extracted various items, which he dropped pointedly into clear plastic evidence bags – sunglasses, chewing gum, a book of matches, a couple of crumpled afghanis and a few American dollars. 'This evidence comes with me.' He pulled out a small, foil-wrapped package and held it up to his nose.

'*Chars.*' Hashish. He placed it into a bag.

Mac glanced up at him. 'Will you check the back seat and the boot?' he said.

'The boot?'

'The trunk,' said Mac, realising that the English Jananga had learned was actually American.

'Sure.'

There wasn't much in the back of the car. A pair of gloves, discarded on the back seat, and half a dozen or so empty plastic water bottles in the footwell. If they were in the UK, these could be sent for DNA testing, but that wasn't going to be an option here.

'We can check them for prints back at Police HQ,' said Mac. 'I don't suppose they'll tell us much.'

The boot was more interesting. Mac checked the outer catch for finger marks, then Jananga opened it. Empty at first sight, Mac scoured the worn black carpeting that lined its base. There was grit and dirt, as one might have expected, but also a scattering of small pieces of straw. Mac carefully picked up as many of them as he could and put them into an evidence bag.

Why straw?

'Look,' said Jananga, pointing into the furthest corner.

Mac bent further into the boot. There was something pale caught in the black fibres of the carpet.

'Ginger, grab the torch from the car.'

A minute later, in the harsh beam of a sturdy black flashlight, Mac could see what it was.

A tiny scrap of hessian sacking.

He picked it up and showed it to Jananga.

'Any thoughts?'

The major shook his head. 'Only that he's moved something in his car. But that's his job, yes?'

Ginger looked down at the triangle of material on Mac's palm. 'It doesn't look familiar army issue. The stuff the loggies bring in comes in wooden crates and gets loaded onto lorries.'

Mac added it to the evidence they'd already collected. But there was no sign of Marshall's Browning.

'Right, let's get this stuff back to town. Can you check all these prints against your fingerprint database, Major?'

Jananga's eyes widened. 'Database? We don't have a database of fingerprints.' He sounded mortified.

Of course they didn't.

'Okay, Ginger. Can you get in touch with Holder and ask him to organise fingerprints for anyone in the camp who had access to Marshall's vehicle? Then at least we'll be able to rule them out. And, if we feel the need, we can request the army to send items back to the UK for DNA testing.' He wondered if he was promising more than the army would deliver.

Jananga frowned at this. 'I don't think we'll need to send evidence out of the country.'

In theory, it was his jurisdiction, but Mac was at a loss as to how he was going to run the case without proper access to fingerprints and forensics.

'Let's just wait and see what the evidence suggests.' He wasn't going to get into an argument over it at this point. 'Right, let's go. Ginger, take the Land Cruiser. I'll follow you in Marshall's car. We'll reconvene at Police HQ.'

For once his plan didn't cause an argument and a moment later, he slid in behind the wheel of Marshall's Surf. He was still wearing his latex gloves – he didn't want to contaminate the car with his own prints and, furthermore, everything was covered in a dusting of the silver fingerprint powder that was worse than glitter for spreading from surface to surface.

As Jananga walked back to his Surf and Ginger got into the Land Cruiser with Pamir, Mac put the vehicle into reverse and eased out of the narrow space it was parked in.

An unexpected crunch under one of the back wheels made him hit the brakes.

Ginger and Jananga both looked round, then hurried towards the car as Mac got out.

'What the hell was that?'

There were slivers of glass and plastic by the nearside rear wheel.

'Pull it forward a little,' said Jananga.

Mac moved the car.

When he got out again, Jananga was picking up the broken pieces and dropping them into an evidence bag.

'Marshall's phone possibly?' he said. It was definitely someone's phone, crushed into a multitude of pieces, its circuit board bent and broken.

'Damn! He must have stashed it on top of the rear tyre,' said Mac.

'Why?' said Ginger.

'To prevent someone from tracking him or because he thought it would be stolen. Or maybe to ensure that anything incriminating was destroyed if it wasn't him that came back to the car... I don't know. But now we've lost anything useful that might have been on it.'

Ginger opened the back of his phone. 'Got Marshall's sim card?' he asked. 'Let's try it in here.'

Mac winkled it out of the buckled sim-card slot and passed it to Ginger. It had to be worth a try. If it worked, they might be able to find out who'd arranged to meet that evening, or at least some more about what he'd been up to. Ginger inserted it into his own phone and switched on. He frowned as he studied the screen, then shook his head.

'Nah, nothing doing. It must be fucked.'

Of course it was.

Mac kicked the tyre that had done the damage. Now what?

Chapter 11

Mac realised the trail to discover Marshall's killer was going cold fast, so he needed to pick up the pace of the investigation. Marshall's vehicle was now impounded in the concrete yard of the Kabul police compound, and the evidence they'd collected from it was logged in.

He spent the morning going over the photocopies of the Souter gate log, and the afternoon listing all the points of evidence they'd gathered so far. But after hours of churning over the facts, the lack of progress was frustrating him. Desperate for a change of scene, he suggested that they head up Foreign Affairs Ministry Road to pay a visit to the Elbow Room Bar and Restaurant. Located in an alley next to the Chinese embassy, a tiny door in a wall led into a spacious bar and restaurant decorated in what Mac liked to think of as Kabul-chic – pistachio green walls, brown velvet sofas and spiky chrome bar stools on which a drunk man could easily do himself an injury.

'Gotta say, this beats teaching the Joes how to wipe their own arses and the endless chicken and rice,' said Ginger as they settled at a small table near the back.

'I'm sure they can oblige on the chicken and rice front,' said Mac.

'Ha fucking ha! A cold beer and a club sandwich will be heaven.'

'Someone knows something,' Mac said, as he and Ginger laid into a couple of bottles of Bud.

'The killer,' said Ginger. 'He knows why he did it.'

The waiter arrived with their sandwiches.

Mac took a giant bite and spoke with his mouth full. 'Someone else. Marshall had been up to no good. Out all night, drinking, meeting someone in a deserted part of the city in the small hours. I think Neil Dixon knows more than he's spilling. He's shifty, nervous about something.'

'So what do you propose we do?'

'It's time to dig deeper. What was the name of that bar he said they all go to?'

'The Jungle Bar.'

'Know it?'

Ginger nodded. 'Sure.'

'Their beer better than this?'

Ginger laughed, finished the rest of his sandwich and motioned to the waiter for the bill. Five minutes later, they were cruising down the Zargona Road and took a right at Shahid Road. Ginger pulled the car up outside a narrow shopfront. The windows were shielded by heavy blinds, and Mac would never have guessed it was a bar. You definitely had to be in the know to come here.

Ginger pushed open the door and Mac followed him in. It was not quite what he expected, but then bars in Kabul never were. Maybe he'd made the mistake of imagining what a bar called the Jungle Bar would be like back home – fake vegetation and plastic snakes, with brightly coloured tropical cocktails. But there was nothing bright or tropical inside this Jungle Bar.

The interior was dark, with drifting banks of smoke almost obscuring the dim lights. Beneath the acrid stench of cigarettes and ashtrays, Mac could smell sweat and just a whiff of hashish. When it came to décor, there wasn't any to speak of. A tiled floor, Formica table-tops, plain walls painted a dull red. There was a handful of punters – all westerners, mostly middle-aged men with weather-beaten faces, nursing beers or whisky, or both. Engineering or energy contractors. On one table, the drinkers were younger, with longer hair and trendier clothes. Sure to be NGO workers – they all had beer, and no whisky chasers.

The barman was tall and blond, and although easily into his fifties, he was wearing a stained wife beater, shorts and flip-flops. His arms sported blurry naval tattoos – hearts and anchors, and a ship in full sail.

'What can I get you guys?' he said. The Australian accent came as no surprise, given the flip-flops.

'Couple of beers,' said Ginger.

Mac looked around. There didn't seem to be any squaddies in, but then he spotted a table just round the end of the bar. Loud English accents and short haircuts – they were definitely soldiers, despite being out in civvies. And there was Dixon, sitting with his back to them.

As Ginger carried their drinks to a nearby table, Mac went over to the soldiers.

'Sergeant Dixon, got a minute?'

A shadow of suspicion crossed Dixon's features, but then he nodded. 'Okay.'

Mac gestured with his head. 'Sit with us.'

Dixon came over to their table. After a couple of curious glances, his companions got back to their banter as one of them got up to get another round.

'Make mine a whisky sour,' called Dixon as the man passed. 'How can I help you?'

His cheeks were flushed and his eyes a little glassy. Mac reckoned he must have been in here some time already.

'I was just wondering where you were last Thursday evening?' said Mac.

Dixon polished off the remains of the beer he'd brought to the table with him.

'Thursday night?' said Dixon, feigning thought. 'In my room probably… or maybe playing pool with a couple of the guys.'

'Playing pool where?'

'In camp.'

'That's odd,' said Mac, feigning surprise. 'Because the log in the gatehouse shows you as being signed out. From eight twenty till gone midnight.'

'Thursday? You sure?'

'That's what it says. Where were you?'

There was long pause and Dixon stared longingly towards the bar. Then he looked back at Mac.

'Ah, Thursday. You're right. I was out.'

Mac raised an eyebrow.

'Me and the lads, I think we were here. Wanted to let off a bit of steam. Sink a few pints. You know how it is.'

Mac knew, but acted like he didn't.

'The lads, eh? Which lads would they be?'

'Benj… Sutton… Tarzan – guys from the troop.' Dixon nodded across towards the table he'd been at.

'Oh, I see.' He paused. 'I can go back and check the log, but I don't remember that you were signed out as part of a group. Maybe I'm wrong.'

'I met them here. They went out earlier than me.'

'Is that so?'

Dixon nodded.

'Captain Harvey was also signed out that evening.'

The surprise on Dixon's face looked entirely genuine. So he hadn't been with Harvey. Then who had she been out with?

'I wasn't with her. That bitch doesn't even give me the time of day anymore.' Which was virtually an admittance that there'd been something between them.

'So if she wasn't seeing you, who was she seeing?'

'Your guess is as good as mine.' He looked away and muttered something that sounded like, 'Regimental bike.'

Ginger leant forwards, bringing his face close to Dixon's.

'Listen, soldier. If you know anything about what went on that evening – with Marshall or with Harvey – you need to come clean. Were you and Marshall fighting over her?'

Dixon blanched, shaking his head. 'No way.'

Mac believed him. A fight over a woman might end in a punch up, and a punch up could go wrong if someone fell and hit their head, but slitting another soldier's throat over a woman? No, that wasn't going to happen. Ginger was barking up the wrong tree. But it wouldn't do any harm to apply a little extra pressure, see what they could shake out of the tree.

'My understanding was that you and her were in a relation-ship.'

Dixon's cheeks went a shade darker. At least he had the decency to blush.

'It was nothing.'

'Enough to make her feel the need to change troops.'

'Look, there was a rumour doing the rounds. It was base-less, but it made life uncomfortable for Harvey, so Colonel Tomlinson agreed with her that a swap would be better for the men.'

'That's all there was to it?'

'That's all.' Dixon's voice was sharp. He was losing his temper, and the alcohol wasn't helping.

'Did she in fact have something going on with Davie Marshall?'

Dixon looked relieved that the spotlight was being turned on somebody else.

'Both of them were signed out on Thursday night,' said Ginger. 'Got any idea where they were?'

'Why don't you ask her?' His tone was still hostile. 'But I doubt she was with Marshall. You're on the wrong track there.'

'Meaning what?'

'Meaning if Marshall was out, it wouldn't have been with a woman. He had a gambling problem. He was in debt. Everyone knew about it – he was always trying to borrow money.'

Mac glanced at Ginger.

Ginger nodded. 'Sure. We played a lot of poker when I was in Ireland, but playing for money was strictly forbidden. Not that that stopped us – the pot could easily get as high as a month's wages.'

'And off base, he could gamble to his heart's content with people who didn't already know he was hocked to the hilt,' said Dixon.

'Who did he owe money to?' said Mac. A slit throat was starting to make more sense.

Dixon tilted his head to one side. 'I don't know, but he was getting in deep. I don't think he had a rat's chance of paying them off – I know he'd asked a couple of the guys for a loan last week, but no one coughed up.'

'Did he admit this to you?'

He nodded. 'One night, when he was drunk. I think he regretted it in the morning.'

'How was he going to get out of it?'

'I suggested that he pay just enough to keep it ticking over, and when we were rotated back home, he'd be able to leave the rest of the debt behind.'

'So he owed someone local?'

'He didn't share that with me.' Dixon was again looking longingly at the bar. 'Listen, there were some shithouse rumours doing the rounds…'

'Yes?' Mac made a head gesture to direct Ginger to the bar.

'Whisky sour?' said Ginger.

Dixon nodded. 'Apparently he'd been bragging that he'd come up with a solution, something about robbing Peter to pay Paul.'

'What does that mean?'

He shrugged. 'His words, not mine. I don't know, but it suggests he was up to something, doesn't it?'

'You don't know any more?'

'I'd like to help, mate. Marshall was a good bloke. But that's all I've got.'

Ginger put a drink down in front of him, and he polished it off in one gulp. Then he went back to his table of friends.

'Thanks,' said Mac, but he was already joining the raucous laughter of his mates.

After he'd gone, Mac sat staring into his recharged glass. What the hell had Davie Marshall been up to? Robbing Peter to pay Paul – was he going to borrow more money? Steal it? Who from? Somehow, he'd got sucked into something he couldn't handle. Now he was dead.

And all Mac had to go on was a bunch of shithouse rumours.

Chapter 12

Baz wasn't looking forward to a return visit to Chicken Street. Not because of the episode with the man who'd tried to grab her – she was getting more and more used to behaviour like this the longer she stayed in Kabul. No, her trepidation was born of what Professor Paghahan had said about Baseer Ghilji.

He's a very dangerous man. His associates are even more dangerous.

Was she getting in over her head? Undoubtedly. But it was what she'd come to Afghanistan for. Ghilji, and men like him, were thieves and lowlifes, stripping the country of its heritage. She'd watched it breaking her father's heart for years. If she could play a small part in bringing them down, then she damn well would.

She knew it was dangerous. She knew the men she was dealing with were ruthless, but as a reporter, she couldn't carry a weapon. However, an armed guard might be sensible. Javid, though, didn't seem that keen when she'd suggested to him that he carry a gun when they went out. However, he'd arrived for work the next day with a battered-looking Soviet Makarov pistol, apparently borrowed from his cousin's cousin. Watching him gingerly stow it in the glove compartment of the car hardly filled her with confidence.

'You do know how to use it, Javid-jan?'

His affronted look told her she shouldn't have asked the question.

'Did I grow up here in Kabul, Basima-jan?'

She got into the passenger seat next to him feeling chastened.

'Where to?' said Javid.

'Chicken Street.'

He frowned at her, but didn't say anything.

When they were parked, Baz got out of the car.

'Will you come with me, Javid, and wait while I see Baseer Ghilji? Bring the gun.'

'And why won't you pay for a proper bodyguard, Miss Basima?' he said, not moving from the driver's seat.

Baz bent down and looked back into the car.

'Who's got five hundred dollars a day to spare? Please, Javid. You won't have to shoot anyone. It's just for appearances, and I'll double what I pay you.'

That settled it. Javid embraced his new role as a gunslinger with fresh enthusiasm.

This time when she walked up Chicken Street, with Javid at her side, she wasn't accosted by any men, and even the beggars kept their pestering to a minimum. Because she was walking in the company of a man. It sickened her that places in the world were still like this.

Heart pounding, Baz opened the door and went into Ghilji's shop. Javid gave her a worried look and took up his position to wait outside.

A western couple were conferring over a couple of rugs, speaking to each other in gutsy Italian. Baseer Ghilji was unfurling another carpet, giving them a well-worn sales patter in English, which they were ignoring. When he saw Baz, he stopped what he was doing and came across to her.

'*Salaam alaikum*,' she said, as Ghilji approached.

'Ah, my American friend,' he said in English. His smile was genuine – Baz could almost see the dollar signs lighting up his eyes. 'What brings you to see me today?'

'I'm drawn back here by all the beautiful pieces you have in your shop,' said Baz, switching the conversation to Dari.

'Be my guest,' said Ghilji, with a sweeping arm gesture. 'You know already, my prize pieces are through here.'

He led her once more to the back room of the shop, and Baz spent several minutes making a show of looking around while he finished serving the other customers out at the front. She picked up a hand-wrought silver pitcher and examined it, then looked at a display of animals carved out of stone – lapis lazuli, jade, alabaster. Much of the stock was the same as the last time she'd been in the shop, but she noted a few new pieces. There was a collection of silver *choora* daggers with ornate bone handles that hadn't been here last time, and the rugs hanging on the wall were different. Ghilji came back.

She fingered one of the daggers. The blade was as sharp as Ghilji's eyes following her around the room.

'Are you looking for anything in particular?' he said.

'For me, no...' She lingered over a glass case of jewellery. 'But I have a friend...'

Ghilji waited for her to continue.

She ignored him and carried on browsing.

'How much is this?' she asked, pointing at an ornate silver headpiece on a stand.

'Ah, the Turkoman wedding headdress. It's exquisite, don't you think?'

'It is.'

Ghilji took it off its stand and brought it across to where the light was better so she could examine it. The polished silver plates glinted in the light and the red and blue sapphires that studded it sparkled. A floral-design silver spike rose from the top of the crown, and there were brightly coloured tassels hanging down on either side. It was beautiful, but it should have been in a museum for everyone to see.

'Is this what your friend is looking for?'

'No,' she said, returning the headdress to the stand.

'Not everything I have is here,' said Ghilji. 'I have a warehouse with more stock. Perhaps if you tell me what your friend is after...'

'He collects coins,' she said. She'd decided not to ask about the Paiza straightaway, but instead build up her credentials with a couple of smaller purchases.

'I see. From a particular time period?'

She turned to face the antiques dealer.

'He collects all sorts, but he has a special interest in Ancient Greek coins, dating back to Alexander the Great.'

Ghilji turned his head slightly to the side. 'Then shouldn't he be looking in Greece?'

'Greek coins from the Achaemenid Persian Empire turn up all over the Middle East and Central Asia. When I told him I would be working here, he asked me to put out feelers.'

'And he trusts you to know what you're looking at?'

'He does.' She hadn't broken eye contact with him. The tension in the air could have been cut with a *choora* dagger.

'Then you'll know that the coins you're looking for sell for thousands of dollars each?'

'He has deep pockets.'

'You didn't tell me your name.'

'Basima… Basima Khan.' Her second name was common enough – it would take him a while to work out the link with her father, but when he did, he'd realise where her knowledge came from. This was the credibility she needed.

'And what work are you doing while you're out here?' This would be part of Ghilji's due diligence. You didn't sell stolen goods or smuggled coins to just anyone.

'I'm a journalist.' She knew it would go against her, but there was no point trying to hide it. He'd discover soon enough through the Kabul grapevine.

Ghilji turned away abruptly.

'I don't think I have the type of coins your friend is looking for.'

'He'll be disappointed,' she said. She walked around him to get back into his line of vision. 'Don't worry, Baseer' – using his first name was a calculated gamble – 'I don't write about the searches I do for my friend. I understand very well your concerns. Journalism is my day job. This is something else.'

He looked her up and down. She bore his gaze without flinching.

'Come, we should have some tea. You can tell me more about your friend. And about how you know enough to act as an agent for him.'

They sat on low *kilim* floor cushions in a small alcove on one side of the room. Ghilji made the tea himself and presented it on a brass tray, accompanied by a plate of *sheer pira*, Afghan sweet-meats made from nuts and semolina. Bizarrely, this reminded Baz of her home in America – they were just like the sweets her mother used to make when she was growing up. Eating them here was a sign of trust and she complimented the antiques dealer on them, and on the tea.

Then Ghilji got stuck in. The next hour was like the verbal equivalent of a game of chess. He asked her ever more searching questions, while she in return gave ever more evasive answers, dropping just enough crumbs of information to keep him satis-fied. Yes, her parents were Afghan. Yes, she'd grown up in America. Yes, she had a degree in fine arts. No, she couldn't give him her friend's name – that was very sensitive. No, she couldn't tell him what she'd already bought, or from whom. She shared some details about her 'friend's' collection. Yes, he was American. No, she couldn't give up details about his parentage. Not that Ghilji would expect her to spill all this information. But he had to ask.

They talked about the Afghan Museum, though she didn't admit to knowing Professor Paghahan. They talked about the quality of Afghan antiques flooding the markets in Europe and America, though she didn't tell him then about her father and his work. He'd find out soon enough, and at that point she'd have to come up with a story that would explain why she was willing to get involved with something that could wreck her father's reputation.

Eventually, Ghilji seemed to have satisfied himself, though she had no idea whether she'd done enough to pass scrutiny.

Until he said, in English, 'Thank you for coming to me, Miss Khan. I will keep an eye out for you, and if I come across any Achaemenid Greek coins, I will get in touch.'

Check mate.

Javid was hovering by the shop door when Ghilji opened it to see her out. The two men nodded at each other – it was only polite, but Baz didn't bother with introductions.

'All okay, Basima-jan?' he said, as they walked away.

'All okay, Javid. All okay.'

But it wasn't until she was back in the car that she allowed herself to breathe a sigh of relief.

Chapter 13

Kabul was awash with currency that was earned fast and spent even faster. Of course, being in a Muslim country meant there were no casinos, no legal gambling establishments. But it was a party city. Hundreds of expat contractors had money to burn and nowhere to spend it. There were certain bars with back rooms where illicit card schools met, and just as many of them had rooms upstairs where girls, brought in from China, would relieve hapless westerners of even more of their dollars.

Mac wasn't a gambler and never had been. Not that he had any moral objections – he didn't care how fools and their money were parted – but spaffing money up the wall just wasn't for him, and he had no idea where he needed to look. Dixon and the rest of the troop were keeping schtum about where Marshall went for his nights on the town. However, there was no doubt in Mac's mind that they knew.

He wanted to talk to Claire Harvey, the previous captain of Marshall's troop, about her relationships with both Marshall and Dixon – but to talk to anyone at Souter, he had to go through Holder.

'I can't see what that's got to do with Marshall's death,' he said over the phone. 'You're not suggesting for one minute that she had anything to do with it?'

'Of course not.' Mac tried, not very successfully, to keep the exasperation out of his voice. 'But if she knew him well, she might be able to shed some light as to what was going on in his life.'

'Hmmm… I'll think about it.'

Holder put the phone down. That was a 'no' then. Mac felt sure Holder had been briefed to obstruct them rather than help them, and that the army would be undertaking its own investigation into the facts surrounding Marshall's death. Fuck them.

'Ginger, any of our fellow instructors got a penchant for gambling?' Ginger was more sociable than Mac and went drinking with his colleagues regularly.

But Ginger shook his head. 'Not that I know of. But these underground gambling places are pretty common knowledge usually. Tip your barman well, and he'll be happy to direct you to the local fleshpots.'

–

The morning had seen little headway and after lunch, Phelps had called Ginger away on some spurious errand. Rather than sit twiddling his thumbs, Mac decided it was time for some active investigation. By three p.m., he was sitting in Jananga's office filling him in on the information they'd got from Dixon the previous evening. The major looked underwhelmed and disapproving.

'We should go back to the Jungle Bar,' said Mac. 'I reckon the barman might know where Marshall gambled.'

Jananga grimaced, but pulled on his jacket. 'Give me one minute to talk to my deputy.'

He went out, leaving Mac alone in his office. Mac looked around, taking in the chaos of the cramped space. How did Jananga work like this? There were files piled high on every flat surface, and the heater and the tea trolley blocked access to the battered steel filing cabinet in the corner. A large map of Kabul hung on one wall, a photo of the president, Hamid Karzai, on another. A clutch of framed photos of smiling children stood on the desk.

Mac listened – Jananga's footsteps had receded down the corridor and there was no sound of his return. He quickly darted behind the desk and pulled open the top drawer. It was crammed with notebooks, pens, keys, a watch with a broken glass, a basic calculator and, under everything else, the *drachm* that the two boys had found in the tank graveyard. This is what he was looking for. Mac pulled an evidence bag out of his pocket, dropped it inside and quickly shut the drawer again as he heard footsteps approaching down the corridor. By the time Jananga opened the door, Mac was back on his chair.

'Come on, let's go,' said the major.

–

Half an hour later, Mac pushed open the door to the bar, and Jananga followed him inside. It was late afternoon and the place was quiet – the lunchtime crowd had gone and the evening drinkers hadn't knocked off work yet.

The barman from the previous evening came out from behind his bar. Still in shorts and, judging by the stains, it was the same vest as the night before.

He stepped towards them.

'Listen, mate,' he said, addressing Jananga, 'you can't be in here. You know that.'

As Muslims, Afghans weren't allowed into the expat drinking holes.

Jananga whipped his police ID out of his jacket pocket and held it up at arm's length, right under the Australian's nose.

The man squinted at it for a second and then backed off. The few drinkers there were turned in their seats to stare at the commotion.

'Right. Fine.' He looked at Mac. 'How can I help you guys?'

Mac pulled out the picture of Davie Marshall that Holder had given him. 'Do you recognise this man?'

'Sure,' said the barman with a shrug. 'He comes in here from time to time, mostly with his army buddies.'

'Do you know his name?'

'No. I wouldn't call him a regular. What's he done?'

'He's dead,' said Mac, putting the picture away and watching the barman's reaction to this news. No shock. But then they were in Kabul. People died every day. Who would be surprised?

'Sorry,' said the man. He sounded sincere enough.

Mac looked around the bar. 'Card school here?'

The man nodded his head towards a door at the far end of the room. 'I got a back room. Sometimes there are card games in there.'

'Marshall – that was his name – liked to play. Had a sizeable debt, apparently. Know anything about that?'

'He didn't run it up here. He wasn't a poker player. I heard he played mah-jong, over at the Lucky Star.'

'Mah-jong?' It sounded unlikely.

'He was a Hong Kong brat. Learned it on his amah's knee.'

'You seem to know a lot about him for someone who wasn't a regular.'

'Alcohol loosens people's tongues.' He shrugged again. 'I'm a good listener.'

No doubt he was. Knowledge was currency in a place like Kabul.

Jananga stepped forward – he'd been quiet up to now, leaving Mac to ask the questions. 'I know the Lucky Star.'

'What is it?' said Mac.

'A Chinese restaurant in the Qali-E-Fatullah area.'

'Whorehouse!' said the barman, with a snort.

'That too,' said Jananga. 'A place where you can buy opium and, now we know, play mah-jong.'

'And somewhere Marshall frequented apparently,' said Mac. He turned back to the barman. 'Thanks, chum, you've been a great help.'

When they were back in the Surf, being driven along Hanzala Mosque Road, Mac turned to Jananga.

'Let's check it out. We know from what Dixon said that Marshall was in debt, and this might be where he ran it up, losing money at the mah-jong tables.'

'But it's not where he was killed,' said Jananga.

'True. But his death was hardly a random mugging. He was out in the tank graveyard for a reason, and the Lucky Star might be able to shine some light on that.'

'It won't be that easy to dig around in there. You go in asking questions and they'll shut their mouths,' said Jananga.

Mac had no doubt Jananga was right, but it was their only lead.

'Just one thing – if you know this Chinese place is a brothel and an opium den, why don't you shut it down?' Phelps had said Jananga was one of the few straight players in the Kabul police – but this, like so many other things in the city, stank of vice and corruption.

Jananga looked out of the window, then scratched the three-day stubble on his chin. It was a while before he spoke.

'There are days when I'm ashamed of my country.'

Mac waited.

'The Lucky Star is in Police District Four.'

'That's not your district?'

'I work from Headquarters.'

'But that makes you senior to the district police.'

Jananga let out a sharp bark of laughter. 'The Lucky Star's protected. The District Four chief has a brother in the NSD.'

Of course he did. The National Security Department was responsible for the country's internal security and they took their protective role very seriously. Drugs, prostitution, gambling – all of it seemed to fall under their protective arm. That was why so many of them, and Kabul's senior police officers, lived in sprawling, swanky villas on the outskirts of town, driving to work every day in something a little more impressive than Jananga's decade-old Toyota Surf.

He was staring out of the window again. This time he didn't turn back. The conversation was over.

A few minutes later, the car pulled up.

'That's it,' said Jananga, pointing to an imposing-looking property some thirty metres further along the road.

The Lucky Star Chinese restaurant was on Street 4, Qala-E-Fatullah. This was another thing Mac couldn't get used to – how many streets were just numbered rather than named, and as each district had its own numbering, there were multiple Street 4s in the city. It was in a residential quarter, just beyond the commercial centre – a gated compound surrounded by a high concrete wall. There was a small, hand-painted sign on the metal gate in Chinese, Dari and Roman characters – Lucky Star Restaurant – with a cloudburst of stars around it.

'Let's take a look,' said Mac.

'Not yet,' said Jananga. 'It's too confrontational for us to go in there asking questions in an official capacity. They won't give us answers and they'll call the District Four police. And if the District Four chief was in there and saw me, we'd be in' – he struggled for the words – 'a whole pile of shit.'

'So how do we play it?'

'I'll have my men stake it out. We need to know if there's a police presence there at all times or not. If it looks safe, you can go in there. Not to ask questions. You'll just act like you're going for a meal, but really wanting to check out the brothel. See what you see.'

'Fair enough,' said Mac.

After all, how hard could it be?

Chapter 14

Bob, of the *Post*, had three kids. 'Ethan – he's ten now – my god, how time flies, I remember when he was a newborn – he's just had his first Little League match and he hit a home run – my god, can you believe it? A home run, first time out! And Brianna is finally riding her bike without training wheels – Wendy sent me a video of it and I'm so proud. Me, huh? The proud dad.' He laughed loudly. 'But, wait, I have to tell you about Gabe – you know, he's the baby. He ate a whole box of Lucky Charms, Chocolate Lucky Charms at that, and he was sick all over the floor. Mr Dinks, our dog, ate it – then he was sick. Oh God, do you believe it?'

Baz did believe it but she didn't give a shit. Perhaps she should remind him of Ethan and Brianna and Wendy and Mr Dinks when he next came banging on her door, drunk, at three in the morning. God, didn't the man have a frickin' off switch? She pushed her half-eaten piece of naan to the far side of her plate. It was too much at breakfast time.

'What? Sorry, Bob, I need to get a story finished.'

She stood up and waved at Javid, who was hovering in the doorway of the G Lodge's dining room. Salvation.

'What're you working on?' said Bob.

'Still the museum piece,' she said, grabbing her bag. 'See you later.'

She scurried away from the table before he could ask her more.

'Good morning, Javid-jan, how are you? How're your wife and your lovely daughters?'

'Good morning, Basima-jan.' His face broke into a wide smile. 'My family is well, thank you. How is your father?'

'He's doing great, thanks. Are you looking for me?' She pulled a face to try to communicate to Javid that the answer to this question should be yes, whether or not he actually was looking for her.

'Miss Basima, a man brought this letter for you.'

He held out a thick white envelope with her name handwritten on it in Dari-Arabic script.

'Thank you, Javid.'

She steered him out of the dining room, away from Bob's flapping ears.

'Who brought it?' she said, once they were clear.

'A man – I didn't know him.'

Baz tore open the envelope and pulled out a folded sheet of the same thick paper. The missive inside was written in English.

> *Dear Miss Khan,*
> *I may have news on the goods you are looking for. Please meet with me this evening at the Lucky Star Chinese Restaurant on Street 4, Qala-E-Fatullah, at 7.00 p.m.*
> *Baseer Ghilji*

'Excellent.'

Javid gave her a questioning look, despite the fact it was none of his business.

'Javid, please bring round the car. We're going to the museum.'

–

Professor Paghahan was delighted to see her, was thrilled to hear that she was well, happy to hear that her parents were well, and reported with much pleasure that he and all his family members were in good health. However, he was less delighted when he heard of her proposed mission.

'Basima, you can't seriously think of going to this rendezvous on your own.'

'I have to. After all, you can't come with me.'

The professor frowned. 'Baseer Ghilji is not to be trusted.'

'I don't trust him,' said Baz. 'But if we're going to locate the Paiza, then I'm going to have to deal with people like him.'

'What would your father say?'

'He doesn't need to know.'

They were sitting in the professor's makeshift office, drinking glasses of green tea. Baz shivered. The building was unheated and the professor worked in a long, green-and-purple-striped *chapan* robe to keep out the cold.

Paghahan shook his head. He looked sad. 'This isn't women's work,' he said.

Baz tamped down her anger. Even the most well-educated of Afghans still held what she considered to be sexist views, but she knew better than most how society shapes what was considered acceptable or not acceptable. Afghanistan was a Muslim country that had just come through five years of ultra-strict, ultra-conservative Taliban rule. During that time, she wouldn't have been able to work at all – the Ministry of Vice and Virtue would have seen to that.

'This is my work, Professor,' she said. 'If you want me to be safe, then help me prepare for the meeting. I need a strategy, and I need to be able to convince Ghilji that I'm a serious buyer.'

'Have you ever seen a Paiza?'

'No – only pictures of one.'

'Come,' said the professor.

He stood up and led her out of his office and along the arched central corridor of the museum. They went upstairs and, at the opposite end of the building to his office, they came to a locked door. The professor pulled a bunch of keys from his trouser pocket and tried several of them in the lock. Finally, the door opened and he ushered Baz into a small room.

If anything, it was colder than Paghahan's office on the floor below – probably because its walls were lined with battered steel storage boxes. Originally painted black, now they were scratched and dusty, apart from where someone had wiped a cloth or a finger across the end of each to reveal a white-painted number.

'What is this?' said Baz.

'It's a collection of artefacts that has just been returned to us from Switzerland,' said the professor. 'There are two Paizas in here somewhere. We originally had five, but three are still missing.'

'Did the Taliban destroy them?'

'No, they were taken during the civil war, before the Taliban took control. Those years, between 1992 and 1996, our collections were very deliberately looted. Certain items were stolen to order and smuggled abroad. But you know about this from your father's work?'

'I do. He's trying to track down the pieces that came to the United States.'

'We believe that the three missing Paizas went to Germany, but we can't be sure. If Ghilji has links to someone who's selling one, it could be that they stayed here after all, *insha' Allah*. Or it could be a Paiza from another source.'

'They're rare, aren't they?'

'Extremely rare, and each one is unique.'

Paghahan was scanning the numbers on the boxes carefully. Halfway round the room, he stopped and heaved one of the crates out of its stack. Baz darted to help him, taking the weight of the box above it so he could release it more easily. Once out, he lowered it gently to the floor. He opened it using a small key from the ring in his pocket.

Baz stood just behind him, peering down over his shoulder. All she could see was a collection of bubble-wrapped packages of varying shapes and sizes. The professor sorted through them quickly – he seemed to know exactly what he was looking for. He fished two of them out, stood up and brought them over to a small table at one end of the space.

'Here,' he said, carefully picking at the sticky tape that secured one of the packages. 'These are our two surviving Paizas. I want you to examine them carefully and memorise what they look like, what they feel like, how heavy they weigh in your hand...'

'Are the missing three just the same as these two?'

Paghahan peeled back the bubble wrap to reveal a small bronze lozenge. It was a flat rectangle shape, about three inches long and an inch across, with rounded corners, worn and tarnished with age. Baz picked it up and studied it carefully. Both sides featured intricate patterns and lines of script in relief.

'Not the same, but similar. One is made of gold, one of silver and another, like this one, is bronze, but with the script inlaid in silver.'

'Do they all say the same?'

The professor opened the other package. The second Paiza was round, with inlaid script on one side and a bas relief of a mythical beast on the other side.

'This script is early Mongol – it's called Phakpa, after the monk who invented it. They all have variations on the same words: 'By the strength of Eternal Heaven, an edict of the khan. He who has not respect shall be guilty.' Each one also carries the name of the bearer, so it couldn't be used by anybody else. This is what makes them totally unique.'

Baz memorised the words, tracking the raised script with the tip of her forefinger. It was extraordinary to think that nearly a thousand years ago, an emissary of one of the great khans of the Mongol Empire could have travelled from Hanchow in China all the way to Constantinople using this small piece of crafted metal to guarantee free passage and safety.

It had a small circular hole at one end. Paghahan watched her trace its outline with her finger.

'That's for a cord or thong to go through,' he said, by way of explanation. 'So the owner could hang it round his neck.'

She could see a small nick in the edge of the circle on the top edge, presumably where the cord had rubbed the metal, day after day. These things had really been used – they weren't just precious objects hoarded in a rich man's palace.

'They're beautiful,' she said, putting the first one down and picking up the second one. 'How much are they worth?'

Paghahan smiled. 'To us here, at the museum, they're priceless. But of course, everything has its price on the black market. In America, a Paiza of the quality of these two would sell for' – he shook his head, searching for a figure – 'maybe upward of a hundred thousand dollars. But it depends who's selling it and who wants to buy it – the values placed on such objects can vary wildly.'

Baz handed the Paiza back to Paghahan, and he placed it back into its cocoon of bubble wrap.

'Thank you, Professor, for showing these to me. At least I know what I'm looking for now.'

Paghahan looked at her with searching eyes. 'Does Ghilji know that you're interested in buying a Paiza?'

'No, not yet. I need to make some smaller purchases first to build up his trust in me. I've asked him to find me some Achaemenid Greek coins, and I think this is what we'll talk about this evening.'

'Coins?' said the professor with a smile. 'Oh boy, I can show you coins. How long have you got?'

Even though the mood was considerably lighter, once the professor had locked up the storeroom, he placed a hand on Baz's forearm.

'You know, you shouldn't do this, Basima-jan. I'm scared for you.'

She looked him square in the eye. He seemed like one of the kindest men she'd ever met. She hated to see him distressed.

'I'll think about what you say, *amu*, I promise.'

But she wouldn't change her mind.

Chapter 15

Wednesday, 10 December 2003

Mac had done plenty of undercover work during his time in SO15, the Met's counter terrorism squad. A lot. And he'd been good at it. But a blunder made by his CSI had led to an important operation going tits up. The blame had been put on him and he'd been forced to resign as a result – for something that absolutely wasn't his fault. He'd sworn he'd never go undercover, anywhere, ever again.

However, this was different, he told himself. The previous day's stake-out of the Lucky Star had passed without incident, and now it was up to him. He was just going in, then out, on a fact-finding mission. Minimal interaction, maximum observation, quick turnaround. He wasn't playing a role, apart from that of nervous ingénue, first time in a brothel. And that wouldn't be too hard. Method acting, he thought they called it, trying to quell his nerves as he approached the entrance.

When he reached it, a sullen young Hazara leaning on a Kalashnikov looked him up and down. His face simmered with acne and his clothes were grimy.

'*Salaam alaikum*,' said Mac. 'This the Lucky Star Restaurant?'

The boy pointed at the sign without answering, then slowly pushed one of the two gates open for Mac to pass through.

Glancing back to where Jananga was watching him from the car, Mac took a deep breath and stepped forward. For some reason he felt like he was Daniel, entering the lions' den.

He wondered how sharp their teeth were, but it was too late to turn back.

A number of the ubiquitous Surfs were parked in line on the gravel in front of the compound, as well as a couple of squat, middle-aged Mercedes. All of them could have done with a wash. There was also a noticeably clean, black Land Cruiser with a surfeit of gleaming chrome. Someone important was in the building, and Mac wondered if it was the District Four chief of police or his NSD brother. As he climbed a couple of steps onto the front terrace, he could hear music coming from inside – a woman singing in Chinese in a thin, reedy voice, interrupted every few seconds by a blast of shortwave radio static.

The front door was slightly ajar, and he went through it. He found himself in a narrow hallway. There was a doorway off to the left, no door in it, but with a sign tacked up on the doorframe showing a pistol with a red cross overlaid and an arrow pointing into the room. He glanced inside. It was lined with battered metal lockers, some open, with the keys in the lock, and some closed, keys missing. This was where he was supposed to leave his weapon before going further – but that wasn't going to happen.

There was no one around, so he took the chance to duck into the room and make sure that his sidearm wasn't showing out under his down jacket. He'd rather break the rules than find himself in hostile territory without a weapon.

Once sorted, he continued down the hall, which ended at a heavy, black door. He pushed it open and was hit by a cloud of warm, steamy air that carried the distinctive smell of Chinese food. He stepped into a large space, lit by small, high windows along one wall and red Chinese paper lanterns hanging from the ceiling. The décor was basic – a bare floor, travel posters for Hong Kong and Beijing tacked to the walls, and in one corner a large rubber plant that seemed to be nearing the end of its life. It was lunchtime, and several of the tables were taken. All the diners were men, all westerners – and they looked interchangeable with the men he'd seen in the Jungle Bar. Along with bowls of rice and noodles, there were platters of dim sum and chicken wings that made Mac's mouth water. Tall glasses of beer gathered condensation in the warm air, while squat bottles of warm Shaoxing rice wine added to the steam.

A small, elegant Chinese woman in a black trouser suit hurried across to him. Her hair was swept back in a tight chignon, and her face was expertly made-up. Her blood-red lips curled into a smile that hadn't an ounce of warmth in it. Mac would have put her age at mid-thirties, but with all the make-up, it was hard to tell.

'Good day. My name is Bao Liang. Do you wish for a table or…?' The woman spoke English straightaway. Most of the expats in Kabul were English or American, and the majority of the rest of them spoke English, wherever they came from. It was the lingua franca of international contractors and NGOs.

Mac answered her quickly – 'I'd like to eat, please.' He didn't want the woman to think he wanted anything else that was on offer.

She showed him to an empty table and he sat down. Then she barked instructions at a skinny Chinese woman in a ruby cheongsam. The woman hurried across to him with a laminated menu card.

'My name Mayleen. I get you drink? Beer? Cocktail?'

'Beer, please.'

Mac looked around, checking out each table, between studying the menu. He didn't recognise any of the men and none of them looked like squaddies. On the table next to him, two muscle-bound men in matching polo shirts sporting a construction company logo were chattering in Polish as they worked their way through what looked like enough food to feed a family of seven. Beyond them, a sharp-faced Viking with blond hair and flint eyes was talking angrily into his mobile phone. He raised a finger in the air, and the older woman rushed over to him and placed a tumbler of whisky in front of him. A regular, obviously.

The woman called Mayleen brought his beer, and Mac ordered a bowl of Singapore noodles. He thought of Jananga waiting outside in the car and felt a little guilty.

'You want to stay a bit after you eaten?' said Mayleen.

She was standing with one hip thrust out, and there was no mistaking what she meant.

'Maybe,' said Mac, forcing himself to smile at her.

She smiled back, and Mac felt like shit. She was pushing thirty, and she looked tired, unwashed and unhealthy. Mac took a sip of his beer and still she stood by the table. Was he supposed to buy her a drink? He got out his phone and started scrolling through his contacts. He hoped the message was clear – the conversation was over.

When she'd gone, he looked around the room again. It didn't tell him anything about whether Davie Marshall had come here to play mah-jong.

Bao Liang stood behind the bar, scanning her patrons for any signs that they wanted something. Every few minutes she barked orders at Mayleen and a number of other girls that came in and out from the kitchen with food, or fetched drinks from behind the bar. At one point a younger girl came in and went behind the bar to greet Bao Liang with a hug. The madame looked down at her fondly, brushing a strand of black hair from her forehead, before sending her away. She looked clean and well fed compared to the other girls. The proprietor's daughter, perhaps?

When the staff were busy dealing with other diners, he stood up and glanced at the bar that ran along one side of the room. At the far end, there was an unmarked door. Trying to look as if he knew where he was going, he went towards it. His heart pounded hard, but nobody challenged him. Nobody was even taking any notice of him. It was time to take a look around, see if he could see any signs of the illegal gambling den.

He went through and found himself in a dim corridor that ran towards the back of the building. The walls were painted bright turquoise, but the paintwork was old and marred by scuff marks. Halfway along, it became wider and there was a stairwell, uncarpeted concrete stairs leading up, he supposed, to the girls' rooms.

He went past the stairs and turned a corner. A glass door looked out onto a square courtyard, paved and set with tables for when the weather was warmer. Beyond it, there were a couple of wooden doors on each side of the corridor. The first one he came to had a stick picture of a man painted on the door – the toilet. The next one, just opposite, was plain. He stood close to it and listened. There were male voices coming from inside, talking in Chinese, as fast and aggressive as machine-gun fire. And, there, in the pauses between speech, the clickety-clack of mah-jong tiles being lined up and played on a wooden table.

A man shouted in triumph and the others laughed. Then one of them sounded angry. The tiles clacked again.

Mac eased the door open an inch and peered into the smoky atmosphere. There were eight men, playing at two tables. The tiles were arranged in lines in front of them, piles of American dollars at the corners of the table, weighted by glasses of beer or rice wine. One of the men glanced up, his face registering surprise as he saw the stranger. Mac stepped back and quickly pulled the door shut behind him. He could hardly picture Davie Marshall in there, playing that fast and complex game, but then he hadn't known the man, had he?

'Can I help you?'

The voice behind him had a Scandinavian accent.

He turned around quickly to find the blond Viking from the dining room. He was leaning nonchalantly on the wall, as if he'd been watching Mac for a while. Now the man was standing, Mac could see he was exceptionally tall, several inches over six foot. The creases round his sharp blue eyes suggested middle age, but his musculature didn't.

'I was looking for the toilet,' said Mac.

The man's eyes narrowed and he jerked a thumb towards the door with the sign.

'It's difficult to find, I think.'

'Yes, couldn't have got here without your help, chum.'

He ducked into the toilet before the man had time to answer. It was dirty and it stank, but he waited for several minutes before flushing it and making his way quickly back to his table.

Mayleen seemed to have been watching for him, and immediately brought him a dish of steaming noodles. Mac thanked her and picked up the plastic chopsticks next to the bowl. There was no sign of the Viking, though his jacket still hung on the back of the chair where he'd been sitting. Mac tucked into the food, wondering what else he could find out.

He decided to take a chance and, when he finished the noodles, he looked around to check that the maître d' was nowhere in sight. Satisfied, he beckoned Mayleen across to his table. He pulled the picture of Davie Marshall out of his pocket. It had been a shot of the whole troop, and Mac had trimmed it down a little to centre on Marshall.

'Do you know this man?' he said.

Her eyes widened, and she looked around, checking for her boss no doubt. Then her gaze fell to the picture.

'No.'

'Are you sure? I think he came here often.'

She didn't bother to look again. 'Maybe, I see him here, once or twice.'

'Was he here last Thursday evening?'

She shook her head. But then she snatched the picture from Mac's hand and studied it once more.

'He wasn't here Thursday. But' – she held out the picture, one finger indicating another man, just behind Marshall's shoulder – 'he was.'

Mac took the picture from her and looked where she'd pointed.

It was Neil Dixon.

Chapter 16

Baz unpinned and pulled off her hijab with a sigh of relief as soon as she realised that everyone dining in the Lucky Star was western. Some stupid punk had smacked into her on the way into the Lucky Star as if he couldn't get out fast enough. He'd dislodged her hair covering with his elbow and, though he'd apologised profusely in a soft Scottish accent, she'd rather he'd just watched where he was going.

She looked around the restaurant, and it quickly dawned on her that every diner here was male – the only other women in the joint were the waitresses. Some of the men stared at her as she tucked her hijab into her bag and took a stool at the bar. She didn't dare ask for a table – she wouldn't want Baseer Ghilji to think she was expecting to have dinner with him.

'You want drink?' The woman behind the bar was Chinese and her look was hostile.

'Orange juice, please,' said Baz.

The woman took a jug of juice from the fridge and set a glass on the bar. But before she poured, she gave Baz another look.

'You meeting somebody here?'

'Yes.'

Was she expected to give the woman a name?

The woman waited, her hand still on the handle of the jug. 'Baseer Ghilji.'

The name changed everything. 'Ah, Mr Ghilji.'

The juice was poured and the glass set down in front of her with a folded paper napkin at its side.

'Thank you,' said Baz. She took a sip. It was fresh and delicious, but that notwithstanding, she hoped she wouldn't be kept waiting too long. There was something about the atmosphere she didn't quite like. And nor did she like the way some of the men were staring at the young Chinese girls waiting the tables. The fact that a minute later, one of the men got up and led a girl out by the hand confirmed her suspicion.

The Lucky Star was not simply a restaurant.

The thought of it made her feel dirty, and resentful that Ghilji should have expected her to come to a place like this. She glanced at her watch. He was already ten minutes late, and while she knew that Afghans were a little more casual over punctuality than Americans, she wasn't going to wait much longer.

His timing was too perfect. Just as she started to slip down from her stool, he appeared in the doorway. She wondered if he'd been watching, waiting for as long as he could to increase her discomfort.

'Miss Khan,' he said, sweeping across the dining room towards her. 'It's good to see you again. Has Allah been benevolent to you and your family since I saw you last?'

He spoke to her in Dari, using a typically formal greeting. Was he testing her? Checking out that she knew the ways of her countrymen?

'Mr Ghilji, I'm very well, thank you, and my family is too.'

He joined her at the bar, and the Chinese woman didn't need to ask him what he wanted to drink. She poured a generous measure of Johnny Walker into a tumbler and slid it across to him. They were both breaking the law – him for drinking in a foreigners' bar, her for serving him – but who in here was going to tell the police?

'Thank you, Bao,' he said. 'Let me get you another drink,' he added, nodding towards Baz's almost empty glass.

'Thank you. Just an orange juice would be fine.'

He ignored her and pointed to the whisky bottle. 'If we're going to do business together, Basima-jan, then we need to share a toast to it.'

She didn't care for the fact that he'd swapped to using her first name without being invited to. And she didn't like that he was putting pressure on her to drink alcohol. She didn't drink often and never with strangers. This whole experience was making her feel distinctly uncomfortable, no doubt by design.

He raised his glass and waited. She lifted hers and tapped the rim of it against his.

'To our mutual success,' he said, and took a gulp.

'Yes.' She let a tiny sip of whisky pass between her lips. It was disgusting, burning her tongue and sending fumes up her nose. It was all she could do not to pull a face. She quickly put her glass down.

'What have you got for me?' she said. 'Have you located some of the Greek coins we spoke about?' There was no point wasting more time on small talk.

Ghilji finished his drink and smacked his lips.

'I've an associate, Basima-jan, who might be able to help. He wishes to meet you before doing business with you.'

So that's what this was all about.

'Of course,' she said, giving him a slight nod. 'Is he coming here?'

'I've told him of our meeting. He should be here soon.'

'What's his name?'

Ghilji looked worried and didn't answer her question immediately. Was he nervous of the contact? That was interesting. She took a sip of her orange juice.

'He'll tell you his name if he wants you to know it.'

Baz watched him over the rim of her glass. There was something shifty in the way he glanced around the room.

'Will he be able to help me locate what I'm looking for?'

'He has a great knowledge of Afghan antiquities and many connections in the market. I'm certain that if such coins are available anywhere, he'll be able to lead you to them.'

'For a price?'

Ghilji raised one shoulder as a small smile played across his lips. 'Everything in Afghanistan comes with a price,' he said. 'Surely you know that much now.'

She nodded. 'I do. I just wonder what your friend's price will be.'

'That is something to be negotiated.'

They sat in silence for a few minutes.

Baz looked around, but there was no sign of anyone coming to join them.

'He said he'd be here, did he?'

Ghilji gave her an unpleasant look. 'He's a busy man.'

'I'm a busy woman. I can't sit and wait here for him all day.'

'Of course, that's up to you. But you are the one who wants to buy.'

Baz gestured to the Chinese woman for another orange juice. She assumed Ghilji would pick up the tab.

The door into the restaurant opened and both their heads turned, but it was a couple of Americans talking excitedly about an engineering contract. Ghilji's face registered disappointment.

They waited again. Baz finished her orange juice, and slipped off the stool.

'I'm sorry, Baseer-jan. I have to go.'

Behind her, she heard the door open again. Ghilji's attention was caught, so she turned round. A young man came into the bar. His black hair was cut razor short and he was clean-shaven. Baz guessed from his wide face, Asian-shaped eyes and rough-spun shalwar kameez that he was a Hazara – a member of Kabul's third largest ethnic group, descended from the mountain tribes of Hazarajat. Every other tribe in the country looked down on the Hazara and they suffered persecution heaped on every manner of indignity, not least for being Shia Muslims in a majority Sunni population.

The man nodded at Ghilji and as he came towards them, Baz realised he was exceptionally tall for an Afghan – nudging six foot – and very well-muscled.

'*Salaam alaikum…*'

The two men exchanged hurried greetings. Baz waited to be introduced, but both men ignored her, embarking on a conversation in rapid Pashtu. Baz tried to hear what was being said, while wondering why they weren't talking Dari, which would have been the Hazara's mother tongue. Ghilji knew she spoke Dari, but he didn't know she also spoke Pashtu.

The Hazara spoke with an accent that made it hard to pick up what he was saying, but she caught a couple of snippets – *not coming… other plan… her father, Mehrab Khan*. The reference to her father made Ghilji raise his eyebrows, but that was nothing compared to the shockwave that thudded through Baz. They certainly hadn't wasted any time in investigating who she was. She fought to keep her expression neutral as the conversation continued.

Finally, the Hazara asked a question that Ghilji couldn't answer, so she took her chance to jump in.

'Baseer-jan, is this your colleague who knows so much about Afghan antiquities? Please, introduce me to him.'

The Hazara stared around at her as if he'd forgotten her presence while he'd been talking. There was something chilling about the way he looked at her, making Baz tug nervously at the neckline of her cardigan.

'This is not the man I asked you here to see. My colleague can no longer make our meeting.'

'So who's this?' said Baz, nodding at the tall man who still loomed over them.

'No one you need concern yourself with,' said Ghilji sharply.

'I see.' But she didn't. The Hazara had mentioned her father by name, and in her book, that meant she had a legitimate interest in who he might be.

'He just came to tell me that my associate has been delayed with an important meeting that's running late. We'll have to reschedule for another day.'

'Maybe,' said Baz. She suspected they were giving her the run around. She pulled her hijab out of her bag in preparation for her departure.

Ghilji's expression sharpened. 'My colleague has a question for you.'

'Yes?'

'He would like to know whether your father is aware of what you're up to out here. He thinks that Mehrab Khan, so famous for hunting down antiquity smugglers – that is your father, isn't it? – would take a very dim view of such activities.'

The Hazara smiled at her in a way that was anything but friendly.

'Miss Khan?' prompted Ghilji.

'Yes, Mehrab Khan is my father.' She sat up straighter and took a deep breath. 'And, no, he doesn't know what I'm doing.'

'Really?' Ghilji evidently didn't believe her. 'Here you are, a journalist, with contacts in the antiquities world, sniffing around to buy coins from the Achaemenid Persian Empire. Do you think we were born yesterday, Miss Khan?'

A cold sweat broke out on the back of Baz's neck and she had to push her hands against the tops of her thighs to stop them from shaking.

'I have a reason for doing this.'

'Please share it,' said Ghilji.

'I need money. More money than I can earn, and I need it fast.' She shut her mouth and held his gaze. 'But I also have questions about your nameless associate.'

Ghilji shrugged.

'What's his name?'

'He'll tell you himself, when you meet him.'

His lack of an answer hardly surprised her.

'Does he have some coins for me to see? If so, where did they come from?'

'You're not that stupid to think that he would divulge his source?'

'If they have no provenance, I expect to see that reflected in the price.'

'The price will be whatever he sets it at.'

'Don't think you can rip me off, Baseer. I grew up around this stuff. I think you'll find that I have a very discerning eye and access to some extremely well-informed buyers.' She was making it up as she went along now, and it brought a rush of adrenalin to her muscles.

'I'm sure, Basima. We will fix an appointment for you to see the merchandise. But before you go, tell me one thing – why does a young woman like you, with a good job and a good education, need money so fast?'

Baz looked down at the floor and composed her face. She'd loved acting as a child – now she was facing her most important performance ever. Everything hung on convincing him of something terrible. When she looked up, unshed tears trembled on her lashes.

'My mother's dying of cancer. We need money for her treatment. There's a new technique for the cancer she has, but her insurance won't cover it. And it's her only hope.'

She raised her face further to look him in the eye. A steady stare, while inside she felt like curling up into a ball and crying.

Baseer Ghilji believed her. The Hazara wore an expression that said he didn't. But she wasn't even sure if he spoke English or not.

Two minutes later, she left the Lucky Star, hurrying through the front of the compound to where she'd left Javid parked out on the street. The meeting had left her feeling shaken, and a little frightened about what she'd got herself into. Were they trying to play her? Of course they were. Had she been convincing enough? Lying about something, someone, so special to her sickened her. She felt dirty, and wished she could have found another way of playing it out. Lost in thought, she made her way to the gate.

A crunch on the gravel behind her. Then, before she could turn to look, an arm snaked round her from behind, and a hand

126

clamped over her mouth. She felt herself being dragged around the corner of the building. Out of sight from the street and into the dark shadows.

Fear lanced through her. Had she misjudged the whole thing?

Chapter 17

Wednesday, 10 December 2003

The rain turned to sleet as it got dark, an insistent patter on the windscreen of Jananga's Surf. After leaving the Lucky Star, they'd driven back to Camp Julien to pick up Ginger and now they were heading straight for the Jungle Bar. It was time to catch up with Neil Dixon again, and, given Holder's endless stonewalling, they'd decided they'd approach him off base.

'He claimed he spent Thursday night in the Jungle Bar, but the girl in the red dress said he was at the Lucky Star,' said Mac.

'Maybe he went to both,' said Ginger.

'But then why didn't he tell you about the Lucky Star?' said Jananga.

'Someone must know what was going on with Marshall,' said Mac. 'I mean, if he owed enough money to get himself killed, he must have been in a bad way.'

'You should talk maybe to his wife?'

Jananga could be right. It had crossed Mac's mind too, but even if he could get a number for her, he wasn't sure.

He shrugged. 'We have a saying – what happens in Kabul stays in Kabul.'

'Meaning?'

'The men won't talk about what happens on a tour of duty. If she knows nothing about it, I don't want to dump it on her. She's home in England with a four-month-old baby that Marshall never met. I'd rather find out what was going on from someone here.'

Marshall's wife probably had no idea what he got up to while he was out here, and Mac didn't want to be the one that burst her bubble. He knew first-hand the sort of shame gambling brought down on a family – his mother's brother had lost all his money and more on the horses and it had broken her heart.

Jananga nodded. 'You're right. It would be cruel. But she'll want to know who killed him and why he died.'

'So let's find out for her.'

'Then we should grab Dixon and take him to Police HQ. I could make him talk.'

I bet you could. Mac was under no illusions as to the methods Jananga would use to extract information from witnesses.

Mac cocked his head, thinking it through. 'But we can't take him to Police HQ. That would cause an international incident. Me and Ginger can just pull him into a dark corner out on the street, suggest that he's a little more helpful with our enquiries...'

The sleet had turned to heavy rain as they parked up opposite the bar.

'If he turns up, we'll let him go in and then wait to grab him on his way out,' said Mac. 'He'll be less resistant with a few drinks inside him.'

Sure enough, half an hour later, Dixon emerged from a dark-coloured Toyota Surf and sent the driver away. He ducked into the bar without looking around the street – why should he? He had no reason to suspect there was anyone watching for him.

They waited in the Land Cruiser, all three chain-smoking, until the rain blowing in through the windows forced them to quit.

Two hours passed. Then another.

'He's going to be bladdered,' said Ginger.

'Go grab us some bolani,' said Mac, pulling a handful of afghanis out of his trouser pocket and passing them to Ginger in the back seat.

'Best place round here – go down the road till you get to the roundabout with Sulh Road. There's a cart usually on the

129

corner. They're nearly as good as my mother's.' Jananga pointed Ginger in the direction he was talking about and Ginger got out of the car.

Five minutes later he was back, clutching three paper-wrapped flatbreads filled with a fragrant mix of potatoes, spring onion, coriander and spices.

Mac closed his eyes and took a deep breath before sinking his teeth into one of them. Crispy on the outside, succulent on the inside...

'That's him,' said Ginger, through his own mouthful of bread. 'Just coming out.'

'Fuck! His timing!'

'Of course,' said Jananga, with a dry laugh.

Ginger and Mac folded their bolani back into the paper wrappers and got out of the car. Jananga carried on eating noisily – it had been agreed that it wouldn't look good for him to accost Dixon on the street, so he was just going to observe from a distance.

Dixon was with three other men, heading towards a Surf, probably the same one that had dropped him off, idling by the kerb a little way up the road. Mac and Ginger picked up their pace to catch up with him.

'Sergeant Dixon? A quick word, if you don't mind?'

Dixon turned round, maybe a little unsteady on his feet. 'What the fuck? You again?'

'A chat,' said Ginger. 'It'll only take a moment.'

Dixon's pals had stopped and turned around too now.

'What's up?' said one of them, a short, barrel-chested man with a ruddy complexion.

'Nothing that involves you, chum,' said Mac. 'Neil, a moment.' He said it in a tone that brooked no argument.

'S'okay, guys. Just wait for me in the car, yeah?'

The three men looked puzzled, but did as he asked.

'Good,' said Mac. 'I'm glad you can see the sense in co-operating with us.'

He fell into step with Dixon, and Ginger did the same on the other side. They marched him quickly into the mouth of a nearby alley – they didn't need to do this in front of a live audience.

'Hey!' said Dixon. His voice betrayed his nerves.

'Have a good night, did you?' said Mac.

'Not bad.'

'On your way home now, or going to the Lucky Star again?' said Ginger, on his other side.

Dixon looked from one to the other of them. 'What's this about?'

Mac turned back to face him. 'When I asked you where you were on Thursday night, you told us you were at the Jungle Bar.'

'Sure. I was.'

'But we've found a witness who says you were at the Lucky Star.'

If Dixon's surprise was feigned, he was a good actor. 'But…'

'Come on, Sergeant. Come clean. We're investigating a murder.'

They stood in the icy rain and waited while Neil Dixon worked out his story. Finally, he spoke.

'There's a girl I see there.' He shrugged. 'Just occasionally. You're right. I was there on Thursday.'

'With Marshall?'

Dixon shook his head.

Mac had taken enough of Dixon giving him the run around. Could he justify what he was about to do? He thought of Davie Marshall's baby, and decided that he could.

He leaned back a bit and gave Ginger a nod that Dixon didn't see. Then he dropped back by half a step and threw an arm around Dixon's neck from behind. Ginger stood in front of them, blocking the view of what was happening from the road and forming a barrier in case Dixon tried to get away.

'Listen, you little shit,' said Mac through gritted teeth. He slammed Dixon up against the wall of the alley. 'Fucking spill what you know. There's a fresh widow with a newborn, grieving for him. I mean to find out who did this, so if you've got anything, give it up.'

Dixon spluttered – Mac's forearm was applying pressure across his windpipe. Mac eased the amount of force.

'Honestly, I don't know anything. He wasn't at the Lucky last Thursday – at least, I didn't see him.'

'But we know he went there – regularly. He played mahjong in the back room. Everyone knew he owed money.'

'I've seen him there once or twice. I know he went there to gamble, but I don't know how well he did.'

'Don't lie to me, Dixon, or you'll be looking over your shoulder for me for the rest of this tour.'

There was a long silence before Dixon spoke. Mac started to apply more pressure on his neck again. Dixon put up a hand and tried to speak.

'Look… if he was still alive, I wouldn't say anything…'

'I understand that, Sergeant.'

'One time I was there, I heard shouting coming from the back room. Real angry shouting, not just one of the usual disagreements during the game. And I heard Davie's voice. He was scared.'

'Scared of what?'

'I don't know. They were talking in Cantonese.'

'He could speak Chinese?' said Ginger.

Dixon glanced at him. 'He was brought up in Hong Kong.'

'What did you do?' said Mac.

'Nothing. It was none of my business. But…'

'But what?'

'After that, he was out of sorts for days. Not talking to anyone at work, skulking off on his own. Surreptitious phone calls. There was something going on.'

'You don't know what he was involved in?'

Dixon shrugged. 'Could be anything. Moving drugs. Weapons. If he owed those guys money, that would give them all sorts of leverage…'

Mac didn't need Dixon to explain it. Being leader of a logistics troop put Marshall in a privileged position and there were always people who would try and take advantage of that. The only question in Mac's mind was whether Dixon had told them everything he knew. He somehow doubted it.

'And you had nothing to do with it?'

'I'm not that fucking stupid.'

Mac let go of him and stepped back. He noticed Jananga lurking in the shadows.

'Don't play me for a fool, Dixon, or you'll regret it. Now fuck off. I don't want to see you again unless you've got something useful to tell me.'

Dixon took a deep breath, tugged his windproof down where it had ridden up his back, and scurried away as Ginger moved out of the way to let him pass.

Mac looked at the major.

'He knows more, doesn't he?'

'I say it again,' said Jananga, with a shrug, 'you should let me take him down to Police HQ.'

This time Mac knew he wasn't joking.

Chapter 18

It was a struggle to breathe through the man's hand, and it totally prevented Baz from crying for help. Her feet skidded out from under her on the stony ground as he dragged her around the corner of the building. That meant all her weight was tugging, pressing her neck harder against the man's left forearm, while his right hand clamped itself even tighter over her face.

Jesus H Christ!

She wasn't praying – not her god – she was trying desperately to work out what she should do. She flexed her jaw to try and bite the hand, but the palm was flat over her lips, so her teeth met nothing. She kicked back with her feet, hoping that if she tripped her assailant up, he would have to let go of her. She hit one of his legs but it was solid and steady. He grunted in response to the impact, but didn't miss a step.

The big Hazara? But why?

Between the side of the building and the compound wall it was almost completely dark. A high window cast a small rectangle of golden light, but the man was careful to avoid it, and pushed her up against the cold bricks. He panted with the exertion and leaned his body in to stop her moving.

Was he going to rape her?

She struggled harder.

'Whoa, hold up.' American. Not just an Afghan talking with an American accent, but a proper, born-and-bred American voice. 'I'm not going to hurt you.'

It wasn't the Hazara.

Whoever it was, he didn't take his hand away from her mouth, so she couldn't express her disbelief. She kicked him in the shins instead.

'Goddamnit!'

They stood locked together for what must have been less than a minute, though to Baz it felt like an eternity. She stopped struggling, exhausted by her efforts to get away. Breathing hard through her nose, Baz detected a familiar smell on the man's hand. Tobacco and something more. Weed.

Finally, he spoke again. 'I'm not going to hurt you, sister. I just wanna talk to you.'

Baz grunted.

'Sorry to do it like this but I don't need the guys inside knowing.' He paused. 'If I take my hand away, will you keep quiet?'

She didn't believe anything he said, but she nodded.

He took his hand away from her mouth and she screamed as loud as she could.

'Man!' He sounded frustrated rather than angry as he clapped his hand back over her face. 'You bitch.'

She frantically shook her head this way and that to stop him, but he was much larger than her and twice as strong. He was standing in front of her now, a big guy with tangled shoulder length hair, and an unkempt beard that reached almost to his chest. Despite the fact it was night time, he was wearing a pair of wraparound Oakleys. Another jolt of fear shot through her – the guy could do anything to her back here and Javid would be none the wiser.

'Okay, you're forcing me to do this the hard way.' He had one hand over her face, the other at her throat. She was completely immobilised by his weight, leaning against her and pinning her to the wall of the building. She could smell his sweat. 'The man you were talking to is Baseer Ghilji.'

'I know.' Her attempt to speak was muffled by his hand.

'He's notorious for dealing in stolen antiquities.'

'I know.' She thought he must understand what she was trying to say.

'He's extremely dangerous – brutal to anyone who betrays him.'

She hadn't known this, but it didn't surprise her. There was big money involved.

'He knows your name is Basima Khan and that you're a reporter.'

Baz rolled her eyes. Who was this lummox that felt the need to kidnap her and involve himself in things that were none of his business?

She tugged on his arm. *I'll be quiet.*

He gingerly moved his hand from her mouth. This time she didn't scream.

She stood in front of him and looked him up and down now. Despite the cold, he was just sporting a T-shirt – a Screamin' Jay Hawkins tour T-shirt, of all things – faded jeans and a pair of heavy-duty biker boots. They stared at each other, then she slapped him as hard as she could on his left cheek.

'Ow!' He put a hand to his face.

'Don't you ever pull a move like that on me again.' She was furious. 'Now, who the fuck are you?'

'A friend.' Still rubbing his jaw. Her hand hurt, too, but of course she pretended it didn't.

'Yeah? Well, friends usually tell other friends their name.'

'My name doesn't matter.'

'I know who Ghilji is. He knows who I am because I told him my name. But what I don't know is who you are, or why you've assaulted me. Or why I should listen to anything you say.'

'Those men are dangerous and if you become an inconvenience to them, your life will count for nothing. Ghilji's Hazara friend would as soon snap your neck as smile at you.'

'But what business is it of yours?'

'As a fellow countryman, I'm doing you a favour.'

'Oh, please.' Incredulity had got the better of fear. 'Now, I'd appreciate it if you'd let go of me. My driver's waiting for me.'

'The guy in the red Surf who doesn't know one end of a gun from the other?'

At least he had the decency to step back from her. She could see his face better now. A square jaw under the beard, generous mouth, straight nose. A receding hairline heightened his brow. His lips parted and she could see that one of his front teeth had a corner chipped off.

Baz straightened her crumpled clothing, breathing hard.

'If you want me to listen to what you've got to say, tell me your name.'

'Logan.'

Cha-ching.

'I know who you are.' Mercenary. Arms dealer. Bounty hunter. Ex-Green Beret. Psycho. Nut job. Close pals with Ismail Khan, the rogue governor of Herat. She'd heard the stories about him during rounds of late-night drinking at the G Lodge. 'What are you doing here?'

'Apart from looking out for idiots like you? I have a friend here.'

Stupid question. She should have realised.

'So, Mr Logan, what's your take-home for me?'

'Don't come back here. Ghilji is a bastard. He and his pals treat Bao Liang's girls like dirt.'

'Bao Liang?'

'My friend. She runs the Lucky Star.'

'Why does she let them in, if they treat her girls so badly?'

'It's complicated.'

'It always is. But I'm not giving up my investigation.'

'Which is?'

'The smuggling of ancient artefacts out of the country.'

'Way too dangerous, lady. You need to back off.'

'Listen, Logan, I don't come around here and tell you your business, so butt the hell out of mine. If you're not going to help me, I'm not really interested in what you've got to say.'

'I don't want to help you end up dead in a ditch.'

'That's fine then – because I'm sure I can manage it on my own.'

She pushed past him and strode across the front of the compound to the gate.

'Don't come back here,' he called after her.

Her heart was hammering in her chest as she climbed into the Surf, and it continued for the whole drive home. And when she helped herself to a brandy in the G Lodge's empty bar half an hour later, her hands were still shaking.

Chapter 19

Mac spotted Jananga coming out of the cell block on the far side of the police compound as he got out of his vehicle. There were no more problems at the gates. Mac had come here so they could discuss progress in the case so far, and where they should take the investigation next.

The major waved at him and they met by the door, hurrying to get out of the steadily falling rain.

'Good day to you, Mr MacKenzie,' said Jananga, with a smile.

'*Salaam alaikum*,' said Mac.

'Excellent – we'll have you speaking like one of us yet.' He seemed to be in a particularly good mood.

Mac hoped it didn't have anything to do with the spatter of fresh blood across the front of his shirt.

'Something on your cheek, Major.'

Jananga wiped his cheek with his hand and looked at it. More blood. 'Thank you,' he said, wiping it on his trousers. 'We brought in a man this morning who had beaten his daughter to death because he caught her studying. He is, as your English police put it, helping us with our enquiries.'

Mac bet he was being very helpful now.

Jananga led the way upstairs.

Inside, his office smelt of wet wool, or more precisely, wet dog. There was no dog in the room – a wet jacket hanging on the back of the door was the culprit. It belonged to Jananga's deputy, who was already busy making tea. Outside, the rain beat against the window. Steam rose from the tea glasses that stood on a small brass tray at the end of the desk and heat from the gas heater precipitated as moisture on any cold surface.

The tea was as bitter as ever, but Mac was still too polite to turn it down. He took a sip and grimaced. He watched as Jananga took a boiled sweet from a small dish of them on the tray. Perhaps this was the trick to making it more palatable.

'Who owns the Lucky Star?' said Mac. It seemed clear to Mac that they needed to find out exactly how much money Marshall owed to whom if they were to find his killer.

'It's managed by a Chinese woman, Bao Liang, but she's not the owner.'

'So who is?'

Jananga sipped his tea with a shrug. 'These things are hard to trace – so many records have been lost and destroyed. Too many shadows for individuals to hide behind.'

A mobile lying on Jananga's desk rang. His deputy picked it up, listened for a moment then held it out to Jananga. After a hurried conversation in Pashtu, the major disconnected and nodded to the sergeant, who left the room.

Mac didn't feel it was his place to ask what was going on as he watched Jananga hurriedly finish his glass of tea, then stand up.

'Come with me,' he said.

'Where are we going?' said Mac, following him along the corridor towards the stairs.

'I put a couple of men to watch the Lucky Star. Bao Liang has a lover, an American mercenary called Logan. We know who he is – he's a bounty hunter. He makes his money tracking down wanted Talibs and handing them over to the CIA.'

Mac was intrigued. Afghanistan was like the Wild West, but with automatic weapons. Private military contractors, private militia, bounty hunters... it was debatable if any of them contributed towards peace and stability of the region, but he could see what appealed about it – living out their boyhood dreams of being action heroes. It was just that most of them weren't really hero material.

They clattered down the stairs.

'And?'

'We've found out that he stays at the Mustafa Hotel. We should go and talk to him.'

'You think he'll give us anything?'

Jananga gave a wry laugh. 'Maybe he won't, but I can be very persuasive.'

'He's American.' Mac frowned. 'You won't be able to use your usual methods on him. Not with the CIA keeping an eye on him.'

Jananga clapped his hands. 'You always think the worst of us, don't you, Mr MacKenzie?'

It was a rhetorical question, but Mac felt his cheeks going red.

'I guess that if he knows anything about Marshall he'll tell us, because whatever Marshall got drawn into, I don't imagine Logan is part of it. Gambling's not his business, and he'll want to get rid of us.'

They left the office block and walked across the police compound to where his driver was waiting in the Surf. They climbed into the back and Jananga gave the driver instructions to go to the Mustafa Hotel on Shir Ali Khan Road. It was mid-afternoon, so in theory the rush hour hadn't started yet, but as usual the traffic was snarled up and the rain wasn't helping.

'What else do you know about him?' said Mac as they watched a set of traffic lights turn from red to green, then back to red again, without any forward progress.

'Nothing at all. He has no police record, and in any case, the authorities here tolerate anyone who brings in Talibs from the wanted list. It saves the security forces a job. You know, Mr MacKenzie, we are a poor country and we have to be pragmatic.'

'Mac. Why don't you call me Mac?'

'Good. Thank you, Mac.'

It took them twice as long as it should have, but finally Mac found himself pulling open the glass door and walking into the Mustafa's pink-and-white tiled lobby. There was a small café bar off to one side, which Mac had been to a couple of times before. The place was popular with journalists and expat contractors – it was cheaper and significantly more basic than the Intercontinental, but boasted a more central location.

The untidy desk that served as a reception was deserted. Mac looked around for a bell, but there didn't seem to be one.

'Hey,' he called in the direction of the bar. 'Can we get some help here?'

A small Afghan man came out into the reception area.

'*Salaam alaikum*,' said Mac. 'We're looking for an American who stays here…'

The man ignored him and started talking to Jananga in rapid-fire Dari. Jananga frowned and interrupted him, and Mac heard Logan's name mentioned, and then the man said something louder. It seemed to be developing into an argument and it was getting them nowhere.

'Yo, Firuz, who's that taking my name in vain?' A voice from the bar, American accent.

Mac looked round the corner to be confronted by a giant scarecrow of a man, getting up from one of the Formica tables.

'You Logan?'

'Who the fuck are you?'

Jananga abandoned his conversation with Firuz and held out his police ID. 'Major Jananga, Kabul Central Police. Please, we need to talk with you.'

Logan looked at Jananga as if he was a piece of dogshit on the bottom of his shoe.

'Don't talk to no popo.' Arms crossed over his chest, chin jutting out, all attitude. He stank of dope – a stoner through and through.

'Listen, chum,' said Mac, 'I'm looking into the death of a British soldier, throat slit, left in the tank graveyard. We think he had links to the Lucky Star.'

'And that would concern me?'

Jananga was beginning to lose his cool. 'Mr Logan, we know you spend time at the Lucky Star.'

Logan narrowed his eyes, looking down at the major from his superior height.

'Jesus,' said Mac. 'No one's accusing you of anything. We want some intelligence.'

Logan gave a slight nod. 'Okay, sit with me.'

They went back to the table he'd got up from and sat down. Firuz melted away behind the bar.

'I probably won't have much for you, but first, who are you?' He was looking at Mac.

'DI Alasdair MacKenzie – Mac. UK police, but seconded onto this investigation.'

'Why?'

'Request for help from the Kabul police.'

'The army good with that?'

'No.' Mac shook his head. 'They hate me.'

Logan grinned. 'Okay, ask what you gotta ask.'

'You spend a lot of your time at the Lucky Star, don't you?' said Jananga.

'That's hardly a crime.'

'No, it's not.' Mac glanced at Jananga. If he rubbed the American up the wrong way, they'd get nowhere. 'The dead man was a Captain Davie Marshall. He was found dead last Saturday morning. We believe he used to gamble at the Lucky Star. Did you know him?'

'I don't know,' said Logan, with a wave of one hand. 'I don't make a habit of studying the clientele.'

Mac dug the photo of Marshall out of the back pocket of his jeans. It was getting a bit crumpled, but it was still clear enough. He handed it to Logan, who barely glanced at it.

'No, I don't recognise him.'

'He played mah-jong regularly.'

'Not a game I play.'

The guy was clamming up, which made Mac wonder if he knew something after all, but didn't want to discuss it. Anyway, it didn't seem like he was going to be of help. They were wasting their time.

'My understanding is that Davie Marshall was in hock for more than he could pay. If I can find out who he owed the money to, I might get a handle on who killed him.'

Logan didn't answer. Then he looked at Jananga.

'You ready to go up against Colonel Sarwani, the District Four chief of police? The Lucky Star falls under his protection.'

Jananga grunted. The sound was non-committal.

Logan turned back to Mac. 'Sure, I spend time at the Lucky Star. Bao Liang, the manager, is my partner. I look out for her and her daughter, Xiaoli. But I don't ask her about her business and she doesn't ask me about mine. I can't help you.'

Mac's frustration flipped to anger. *Can't or won't?*

'Christ, man. Marshall's throat was slit and his wife's just had a baby that he never got to meet. See no evil, speak no evil just doesn't cut it.'

Logan's eyes widened. 'Doesn't cut it? Who the hell do you think you are? I don't owe you anything.'

Jananga put a hand on Mac's upper arm to calm him. Mac took a deep breath.

'We'll go now,' Jananga said. 'But if you think of anything I can do for you...'

Logan nodded. He understood. Mac did too – Kabul was a city where favours were done and money changed hands. Information came at a cost.

Logan stood up and rolled his shoulders.

Mac handed him his WTP card. 'Call me if you change your mind about helping.'

Logan took the card, read it, then stuck it in the back pocket of his jeans.

'There was a woman,' he said. 'An American journalist, sniffing around the Lucky Star. You might track her down.'

'Do you know her name or what she was snooping for?' said Mac.

'No.'

He walked out of the bar, leaving Mac with the feeling there was still plenty more he could have told them.

Chapter 20

Mac sat in his office, fingering the *drachm* that had been found at the murder site. What was its significance, if it had any? It looked pretty ancient to him, so if it was a fake, whoever made it had gone to a lot of trouble to age it. Could it be the real deal? The speck of blood on it told them nothing. They would need a DNA test to confirm whether it was Marshall's or someone else's, and there was no chance of that. He put it back in its evidence bag and locked it in the desk drawer. They might never know how it had come to be there, but he was determined to find out how Davie Marshall's body had ended up in the same spot.

His mobile buzzed, vibrating on the wooden desktop.

He didn't recognise the number. 'MacKenzie.'

'Hey, brah, wondered if you wanted to talk to me without your Afghan minder?' The accent was American.

'Logan? Where are you?'

'At the Mustafa.'

He disconnected, leaving Mac staring at the phone. So Logan did have something to share – something he hadn't wanted to divulge in front of Jananga.

It was just getting dark outside, and the rain had turned to snow, though it wasn't settling on the wet ground. Pamir didn't look too impressed with the idea of taking the car out, but Mac ignored his gripes.

'But, Mr Mac, the snow will impede us.'

'No, Pamir, we'll be fine.'

The traffic wasn't though, so Mac jumped out of the Land Cruiser a couple of blocks from the hotel, frustrated by being stuck in a gridlock. By the time he reached the Mustafa Hotel, the wet snow had plastered his hair to his head and was soaking through the shoulders of his jacket.

As he went inside, Logan emerged from the bar clutching half a dozen beer bottles against his chest.

'Come on,' he said. 'We'll talk in my room.'

They took the stairs to the third floor. Even when buildings had working lifts, the city's frequent power cuts made them a risky prospect. Logan passed the bottles to Mac and dug into his pocket for his room key.

Mac followed him inside. The space was small and seemed even smaller because of the mess. It was hard to imagine that this man had spent years in the military. Clothes were jumbled on the floor and on the bed, and there were empty beer bottles and overflowing ashtrays on every flat surface. Mac noticed that the ashtray's contents were not manufactured cigarette butts, and a heavy smell of dope pervaded the room. At the furthest point from the door, there was a padlocked trunk – possibly where Logan would stash his weapons – though it was hard to miss the big semi-automatic Colt handgun tossed casually on the bedside table. A threadbare bazaar rug on the floor and a garish green bedspread gave the room a psychedelic vibe, and there were posters for obscure bands tacked up on the wall.

Logan pointed at a single plastic chair, angled to take the view through a glass door to a balcony. Mac put the beer bottles down on a small dressing table, nudging the empties to make space, then sat down. Logan used his keyring to pop the caps off two of the bottles and handed one to Mac. It was cold and it tasted good, but Mac knew he should limit himself to a single drink. This wasn't a social visit.

'You smoke?' He pulled a neatly rolled joint out of the breast pocket of his shirt.

'No, but you go ahead.' Maybe it would loosen his tongue. He took a long draught from his beer bottle. 'So what did you want to talk about?' he said as Logan dropped down onto the bed and lit up.

'Your accent – Scottish, isn't it?'

'Aye.' It was hardly rocket science.

'My grandma was Scottish. Born in Glasgow. Where are you from?'

'You wouldn't know it. A tiny village on the West Coast, Ardshellach. My parents are farmers.'

'Mine too. I was brought up in Aurelia, population nine hundred and ninety-three.'

'Which state?'

'Iowa.'

Maybe they had more in common than they'd realised. But that wasn't why Mac was here.

'So…?'

'You don't fool me for a moment.' The mood in the room changed in an instant.

'I don't know what you mean.'

'British police? That's bull. Since when have the UK police been operational in Kabul? Since never.'

Mac held up both hands. 'Fair cop. I'm ex-Met police, on a contract to train the Kabul force. They knew I had experience and asked for help – and my bosses gave me no choice.'

'Knew it.' Logan practically high-fived himself.

'But makes no difference. I still need to find out what Marshall was up to that got him killed. So, d'you think you can help?'

Logan nodded and flicked ash from his joint into an already full ashtray. 'Maybe I can. I recognised you,' he said. 'You were in the Lucky Star the other evening, weren't you?'

'One of the dead man's colleagues told me he spent time there.'

'Marshall, right? The Brit with the amulet.'

'What amulet?' said Mac. He played ignorant, but Logan must have meant the *drachm*, and this was suddenly more interesting.

'He wore an ancient coin on a chain round his neck. Claimed it brought him luck at mah-jong.' He drank some beer. 'Dumbass. He lost nearly every time he played. They made sure of that.'

'Who?'

'The guys he played against. They were a clique of Chinese. He was a stranger.'

'Where'd he get the amulet from?'

Logan shrugged, exhaling a cloud of THC-laden smoke. 'Wherever. But it didn't work. He owed a lot – and those bastards don't let you forget it. They would have suckered him into something, you can bet on it. There's a lot of shady dealing goes on at the Lucky Star. I stay out of it – but if he owed them money, he might not have been able to.'

'Who precisely are "those bastards"?'

Logan shook his head, holding down a lungful of smoke.

'Would Bao Liang talk to me?'

'You're fucking kidding me? Her life wouldn't be worth living if she spilled on her clientele.'

'Who owns the Lucky Star?'

Logan shrugged. 'Don't know his name. Some guy, lives in Dubai. He's a nasty piece of work you should steer well clear of.'

Mac wasn't sure whether to believe him, but there was no point in pressing it.

'You know who you should talk to?' said Logan, pointing at the row of beer bottles.

Mac tossed him another one. 'No, tell me.'

'That girl reporter who was sniffing around the Lucky.'

'But you don't know her name.'

'Maybe I do. If you can make it worth my while.'

And now Mac realised the point of his being here. Logan wanted something from him, and he would trade the information to get it.

'Money?' He knew it wasn't.

Logan shook his head. 'I make plenty doing what I do.'

'What then? I can't think of anything I can do for you.'

'Don't worry, I can. You've got an in at Kabul Police HQ. There's bound to come a point when that would be useful to me.'

Mac shrugged. 'I think you'll find my sphere of influence is strictly limited.'

'We'll see. Anyway, the girl's name is Basima Khan.'

'What else do you know?'

'She was at the Lucky trying to set up a deal to buy antique coins.'

Kerching!

'What's that got to do with Marshall?'

'Maybe nothing. But she might be able to shed some light on Marshall's amulet – she seems to know something about antiquities.'

'She's an Afghan?'

'She's as American as I am. But her parents are Afghan.'

'You seem to know a lot about her.'

'Bao Liang's no fool. She keeps an eye on everything that goes on under her roof.'

'And you couldn't have shared all of this with us earlier?'

'I try and steer clear of characters like Major Jananga, keep my dealings with the Af police to a minimum.'

'And your business out here?'

'Is none of your business.'

'I heard you were a merc. Strikes me you're something of a cowboy, Mr Logan.'

'You do what you gotta do when you're working in the Wild West. We all got a story as to how we ended up working out here and why we can't go home.' He studied Mac as he stubbed out his roach. 'I wonder what your story is, Mr Mac?'

Mac didn't trust him. And there was no way he was trading war stories with the guy.

'So where does this Basima Khan stay?'

Logan took a swig of beer and put down his empty bottle with a note of finality.

'I don't know, but I'm sure your major can find out.'

It was time for Mac to leave.

–

Logan was right. Jananga made a quick call to the Ministry of Foreign Affairs to find out that a Miss Basima Khan, accredited to the *Baltimore Sun*, was registered as working in the country. Residence: the Gandamack Lodge, Sherpur Square.

'I'll meet you there,' said Mac, when Jananga shared the information.

As they had to detour via the camp to pick up the *drachm*, Jananga beat Mac and Pamir to the Gandamack's imposing steel gates. He was parked outside, waiting in his Surf, when they arrived.

There were two armed guards on the gate and they were adamant that they would only let westerners in until Jananga pulled out his police ID. The usual battery of fast-spoken Dari ensued until, with a scowl, one of the guards opened the gate.

It was dark now, and although the sleet had turned to rain, it was still freezing. Mac shivered as they passed through the narrow gap and then waited for a second set of gates to be opened. He didn't know what to expect – although he'd heard of the legendary Gandamack, he'd never had occasion to visit it. However, he knew it was home-from-home to numerous western journalists and ex-pat workers. Nothing luxurious, apparently, but somewhere where they could feel safe.

With a loud creaking, the second gate opened and then they were walking through a large, lush garden. Hundreds of coloured fairy lights were reflected in thousands of raindrops. Everything glittered and it was as if they'd entered another dimension. Kabul on acid.

There were tables and chairs out in the garden and on a small, lit veranda, though the weather meant that no one was dining outside.

Mac could hear sounds coming from inside, bar sounds – the clinking of glasses, laughter, male voices speaking English with American accents. He went up the steps to the veranda and pushed open the door. Heat and noise enveloped them. They were in a busy dining room and the smell and sight of the food made Mac's mouth water. He looked around for someone in charge and caught the eye of a middle-aged waiter.

The man came towards them, shaking his head as he looked Jananga up and down. As an Afghan, he couldn't come into a bar or restaurant that served alcohol. The waiter said something in Dari and frowned.

But Jananga had anticipated this and simply held out his police ID.

'We're looking for Basima Khan,' said Mac. 'Do you know if she's here.'

The waiter's bravado had evaporated as soon as he learned who Jananga was, and now he blustered in English. 'Wait, I get the boss.'

The owner of the Gandamack Lodge was a genial Englishman dressed in a pale blue shirt and chinos. Though his hair was receding and his jowls sagged with middle age, his face wore an expression of keen intelligence.

'Good evening, gentlemen, to what do I owe the pleasure?'

Jananga looked perplexed by his turn of phrase.

'Do you have an American reporter staying here – Basima Khan?' said Mac.

The man glanced down at the card Jananga was still holding out.

'Mmm… Kabul's finest. And you?'

'DI Alasdair MacKenzie, British police.' The lie tripped easily off his tongue.

If the man was surprised to see the British and Afghan police working together, he didn't show it.

'Don't tell me our sweet Baz is a wanted woman?'

'Not at all,' said Mac. 'We just need to ask her a few questions about something she's working on.'

'Okay, why don't you take a seat and I'll see if she's around.'

They sat at an empty table and the waiter brought them orange juice. Mac breathed a sigh of relief – he'd had more green tea than he could stomach lately. Within five minutes, a young woman with short-cropped black hair, a white T-shirt and tight Levis appeared. She took the table's third chair.

'I'm Baz Khan. How can I help you?' Her dark brown eyes scanned their faces, then lit up. 'You?' She was looking at Mac.

'Do I know you already?' he said.

She grimaced. 'You nearly knocked me flying coming out of the Lucky Star yesterday afternoon.'

'What?'

'Sure. I was wearing a hijab – that's why you don't recognise me.'

Mac remembered. The small woman he'd bumped into as he came out of the restaurant.

'Oh God, I'm so sorry.' Did she think he was there to visit a prostitute? 'I was just there as part of an investigation.'

She didn't look like she believed him. 'So what's this all about?'

She looked different without the hijab and Mac would never have recognised her. He guessed she was in her early twenties. Her gaze was direct and her voice confident – and despite her Afghan looks, her accent was pure American. He made the introductions, then pulled the bag containing the *drachm* out of his pocket.

'What can you tell me about this?'

'You have it? You took it from my desk?' snarled Jananga.

Shit. Mac had forgotten to mention his petty pilfering to Jananga. He shrugged. 'I wanted to take a closer look at it.'

Jananga scowled at him as he handed it to Baz Khan. She took it from him and examined it, turning it this way and that to catch the light.

'Where did you get this?' she said.

'The man who owned it was a British soldier. He was murdered a week ago and we think he had links to the Lucky Star Chinese restaurant. I understand you visited the place recently.'

The girl's eyes widened. 'Who told you that?'

Mac took the *drachm* from her and put it back in the bag. 'Miss Khan, I'm investigating the murder of a British serviceman…'

She ignored him and, turning to Jananga, she started to speak in Dari. The major answered her, mentioning Logan by name. Mac waited through a couple more exchanges but his patience was wearing thin. He drummed his fingers on the table.

Finally, Basima Khan turned back to him. 'That coin is a *drachm*. It's old and probably valuable. I'd like to show it to Professor Paghahan at the museum. I have a feeling where it might have come from but he'll probably be able to confirm it.'

'And?' said Mac.

'The men I met with at the Lucky Star are smugglers. I'm investigating the black market in antiquities, but I'm sure they also deal in drugs, weapons, people trafficking, and most likely have links to the Taliban and other warlords… whatever pays. They're dangerous. If your guy was mixed up with them, I'm not surprised he wound up dead.'

'So what's your involvement with them?' *And what's stopping you from winding up dead, too?*

'My father's on the commission that's working to return Afghan antiquities to where they belong – in the National Museum. I'm looking into it on his behalf.'

She said it with huge self-assurance, but somehow Mac couldn't quite take her at her word. After all, what father would send his daughter into a war zone to hunt down the sort of men she'd just described?

He looked across at Jananga. The major's eyes narrowed, almost imperceptibly – he didn't believe her either. Basima launched into Dari again and he cursed himself for not bringing his interrupter. Fed up, he cut into their conversation.

'It sounds pretty dangerous to me. And your father sent you out here to do that?'

Basima stopped mid-sentence and stared at him, her nostrils flared and her eyes burning with anger.

'He didn't send me. I volunteered. I feel as strongly about the problem as he does.'

'So you're not just another reporter, chasing fame and glory?'

She stood up and looked around for the Englishman. 'Peter, show these clowns out. We're done.'

Mac cursed himself. God, he was an idiot. They'd maybe been getting somewhere, and he'd needled her into a temper tantrum.

Stupid.

Chapter 21

'I suppose you can't help being a jerk?' It was Baz's response when he'd phoned her after he got back to Camp Julien on Thursday evening. But the tone of her voice had been full of humour.

'I can't,' he confirmed. 'I didn't mean to sound critical of your dad, or anything...'

'No, I get it.' She became serious. 'But you've got to understand, when your country is as fractured as ours is, your heritage sometimes seems like all you've got to cling on to.'

'So, can you tell me a little more about the *drachm* Davie Marshall was wearing when he died?'

'Not a lot, but I know a man who can.'

She'd agreed to take him to meet with Professor Paghahan at the museum, and she promised to call him back when she'd sorted out a time.

He hadn't heard from her on Friday, not surprisingly as it was the holy day. But today was Saturday and the message had come through to pick her up after breakfast. Now, as they drove down Darulaman Road in Mac's Land Cruiser, she was filling him in on what she'd dug up so far about Baseer Ghilji, which wasn't very much.

'Ghilji – a man with a chequered career. He's got a degree in law from the University of Damascus, but I can't find any record of him having ever practised as a lawyer. He doesn't seem to have had the shop in Chicken Street for very long...'

'I checked in with Jananga,' said Mac. 'He said he'd put out feelers to see whose palm Ghilji might be greasing. Apparently Chicken Street is in Police District Four, and that means he'll be paying Colonel Sarwani to keep his shop safe. He seems to be the common thread.'

'He'll also need contacts at the Ministry of Information and Culture,' said Baz. 'Part of their remit is to prevent antiquities from leaving the country. On the surface he'll be co-operating with this, but of course he can make far more money selling objects abroad, so he'll be paying someone in the ministry to not take too close an interest in his activities.'

They pulled up in front of the museum and left Pamir waiting in the car. The boy soldiers at the gate recognised Baz now and waved them through without checking their ID. Professor Paghahan met them as they walked down the central corridor. Baz introduced Mac and they followed him into his office.

'I understand you have something to show me?' said the professor.

Mac passed him the *drachm*, still in its evidence bag.

Paghahan looked at it through the polythene, then looked up at Mac. 'Can I take it out?'

'Go ahead,' said Mac. Any useful finger-mark evidence would be long obliterated, given how many people had handled it.

Paghahan studied it for a moment and then reached for a magnifying glass that was lying on his desk. He held it directly under his desk lamp and looked at it through the glass.

'It's genuine, certainly,' he said to Baz, 'and you were right about its age. It's an astonishing piece of work.'

'What can you tell us about it?' said Mac.

'It's a Persian *drachm*, a common enough piece of Parthian coinage.' The professor angled it in the light. 'It's made of silver.'

Baz said something in Dari and Mac put up a hand. 'English,' he said.

'I was asking if it's an Afghan piece. Its provenance could be important.'

'It dates back to approximately AD 100,' said Paghahan. 'It would have been issued by the Parthian Empire, which stretched from the Euphrates to the Indus. It certainly covered Afghanistan, but there's no way of pinpointing precisely where the coin was minted. You're going to need to know where it was found.'

'But we might never find that out,' said Baz. 'It could have been bought and sold a dozen times before it came into Marshall's possession – or it could have been in a private collection for decades.'

'One thing I'm sure of,' said Paghahan. 'He wouldn't have picked this up in the bazaar. This is a valuable coin, worth more than a thousand dollars.'

'Seriously?' said Mac.

The professor nodded.

'But if that's the case, he could have used it to pay off his debts. Or some of them.' They still had no idea how much Marshall owed.

There was silence for a moment. It didn't seem to make sense.

Baz's face lit up. 'Only if he could sell it. And who could he sell it to? Probably only the people to whom he owed the money and they wouldn't give him the full value for it.'

'His killer could have taken it in lieu of the debt,' said Mac.

'But only if he knew about it,' said the professor. 'If Marshall wore it round his neck, it could stay hidden in his clothing.'

'So you think the kid might have been lying about having found it on the ground?' said Baz.

'Little toe rags picked over him like vultures.' It turned Mac's stomach to think about it. They might be children, but there was certainly no place for innocence here.

'I'm thinking then that he must have stolen the *drachm*,' said Paghahan. 'That might have been enough to get him killed.'

'But if that was the case, the killer would have searched his body for it.'

They debated what could have happened or what might have been for several more minutes. It was becoming clearer that Davie Marshall had got himself into something way over his head, and that he'd paid the ultimate price – but the question they were facing was who had extracted it? And why exactly?

The professor carefully placed the silver coin back into the evidence bag and then placed the bag on one of the shelves behind his desk. Mac glanced at Baz, open-mouthed, but she was saying something in Dari.

'Professor!' He cut across whatever Baz was saying, and held out his hand. 'The evidence bag, please.'

Professor Paghahan clearly knew this was coming, and his face took on a serious expression.

'As Director of the Afghan National Museum, I have the right to confiscate objects of national interest.'

Mac stood up too. 'But you said yourself that you couldn't tell where it was found – it might not have come from Afghanistan at all.'

'It's Bactrian, and that makes it of interest to us – it's an important part of our heritage.'

This was all beside the point. 'Professor, it's a critical piece of evidence in a murder investigation. I'm sure it can be presented to the museum once the investigation is over, but for now, I need to keep it to maintain the chain of evidence.'

Baz started to speak, and Mac was hardly surprised when the language switched to Dari. They argued with increasing volume, but he couldn't tell who was winning.

'Enough!' He raised his voice louder than theirs. 'Professor, please give me the *drachm*.' He made a move as if to come around the desk.

The professor stood up defensively.

'Mr MacKenzie, please remember you are a visitor in our country.'

'So was Davie Marshall. And now he's dead. I'm going to see to it that he gets justice.'

The professor picked up his phone. 'I'm calling security. I think you should leave the museum.'

There was no point getting into a physical fight, so Mac sullenly allowed himself to be escorted out of the building by the teenage security guards.

'Give me a moment,' said Baz as he was marched out. She ducked back into the professor's office.

Mac swore under his breath. He couldn't believe he'd allowed a crucial piece of evidence to be hijacked in this way. And now he was going to have to tell Jananga that he'd lost it.

'Fuck!' said Mac, kicking the tyre of the Land Cruiser once he was outside the gates. The man had no right to do that.

He sat in the car waiting for Baz in a fury. If the *drachm* was pertinent to the case, and if the case ever came to trial in a British court, he'd have to stand up and say he'd fucked up. He'd let go of a vital piece of evidence.

Five minutes later, the car door swung open and Baz climbed into the back next to him.

'I tried…' she said, with a shrug.

'He insisted on keeping it? What a dick.'

'You know what? You really are an A-grade asshole. You have no idea what that man's been through trying to protect this country's heritage.'

Mac stared straight ahead. 'Let's go, Pamir. Drop Miss Khan at the Gandamack, then take me to Police HQ.'

He might as well get his confession over with as quickly as possible.

Chapter 22

Mac was still fuming when he reached Jananga's office. Jananga, on the other hand, seemed quite cheerful. He had apparently spent the morning extracting information from a number of the inmates in his cell block.

'Good work, results achieved. Time for tea,' he said, with a grin.

'Not for me, thanks,' said Mac.

'Something is bothering you?' Jananga waved a hand towards one of the spare chairs opposite his desk.

Mac sat down and looked Jananga square in the eye. 'I lost the *drachm*. I'm sorry.'

'You lost it, Mac-jan? How could this happen? You've searched for it?' He frowned.

'No, it's not lost. Professor Paghahan at the National Museum has it. Basima Khan took me to see him – we thought he could tell us about the piece.'

Jananga looked relieved. 'So, it's not lost.'

'Yes, but he won't give it back. He says it's part of the country's national heritage.'

'Ha, he could be right. But it's my evidence. Don't worry about a thing, Mr Mac. I'll send my boys down to retrieve it from him. He'll give it up to me.'

Mac didn't doubt it for a moment, but it was still embarrassing to have found himself in this position. 'Thanks.'

Jananga made a call and Mac heard him mention Paghahan. When he finished, he turned back to Mac with a shrug. 'Just be more careful with my evidence in future, yes?'

'Yes, of course.' Mac's cheeks were burning, so he was relieved when Jananga's deputy stuck his head around the door and said something. Mac picked up the name Holder and Jananga frowned.

'I should give Captain Holder an update. It would be a good thing for you to come too.'

'Of course,' said Mac. It was the last thing he wanted to do now, but he had his orders. *If Jananga said jump…*

–

An hour later, less their weapons and their ID, they were ushered into Holder's office. Once the greetings were over, he told them to sit down.

'You've got progress to report?' he said. He didn't sound hopeful.

'Not as much as we'd like, Captain,' said Mac. 'But we have good reason to believe that Davie Marshall was possibly being blackmailed over gambling debts.'

'Blackmailed? If he couldn't pay his debts, how could he pay blackmail?'

'Not with money, Captain,' said Jananga. 'But I think his work at the airport put him in an interesting position.'

Holder shook his head. 'If you're suggesting what I think you are, I'd have to say you're wide of the mark.'

'We suspect the people he owed money to are involved in antiquities smuggling,' said Mac. 'Who's better placed than a British loggy to get things surreptitiously flown out of the country?'

Holder scowled. 'That's quite an accusation, Mr MacKenzie. I take it you've got some evidence to back that up?'

'Not yet. We've just made the connection between Marshall and a Chinese restaurant in District Four called the Lucky Star. He was apparently running up debts there playing mah-jong.'

Holder turned to Jananga. 'Can you get this place shut down?'

It was clear to Mac that Holder really didn't have a clue about how things worked in the Afghan capital, and what a tricky question this was for Jananga.

'I would need to co-ordinate that with the police chief in District Four,' said Jananga. That was one way of putting it. If by 'co-ordinate' Jananga meant start a turf war. 'But I think first we need to investigate a little deeper to see exactly what was going on.'

Holder sat in silence, digesting the information they'd given him so far.

'This sounds like a lot of supposition.'

'Supposition?' said Jananga.

'Captain Holder doesn't believe us,' said Mac. 'I think we're done here.' He stood up.

'Wait,' said Holder, without getting up from his desk. 'If Marshall was up to something, stands to reason some of his colleagues would have known about it. He wasn't operating in a vacuum.'

'We've spoken to his sergeant a couple of times – Dixon – but he didn't give us much.'

Jananga rolled his eyes. 'We could have got more from him…'

Mac shook his head, and thankfully Holder ignored the comment.

'He'd want to keep the circle of people in the know as tight as possible,' said Mac. 'But he'd need a reliable contact back home. If he was loading drugs or money or antiques onto the planes at this end, someone had to be offloading them at the other end.'

'I could get on to the RAF Special Investigations Branch at Lyneham,' said Holder.

'Yeah, but whoever it was will have gone to ground as soon as they heard Marshall was dead.'

'Fair point, but I'll ask SIB to have a nose around – they might have had some suspicions anyway.'

'Thank you, Captain.' Holder was finally co-operating with them. Hallelujah!

Holder looked tired. 'Look, it probably won't give us any insight into who killed Marshall, but it might confirm your suspicions about him. Major Jananga, got anything to add?'

'I will put my men to watch the Lucky Star. We'll make a list of who visits often and start looking into their activities.'

Holder nodded his approval, but Mac wasn't convinced it was enough. They'd just end up with a list of punters. Not that he had a better idea at that particular moment. The meeting was over, and they agreed to check back with Holder in a couple of days.

'You might have something from Lyneham by then,' said Mac. 'And we'll have a list of names from the Lucky Star.'

Although Mac had come across to Souter with Jananga in the police Surf, he'd instructed Pamir to follow in the Land Cruiser and to wait for him just outside the gate. As they left the camp, Jananga's driver pulled up so Mac could transfer to his own vehicle.

Jananga raised a hand as Mac was about to open the passenger door. 'Wait.' He nodded his head in the direction of the pavement opposite the Land Cruiser.

'What is it?' said Mac.

The major shook his head. 'Someone is watching your car.'

Mac couldn't see anything untoward. 'You sure?'

'Of course, he's gone now. He ran off as he saw us stopping. Gone to report to whoever's paying him. He'll earn a couple of dollars and feed his family for a couple of days.'

'A dicker.'

Jananga looked puzzled.

'A guy paid to watch.'

Mac looked up and down the road, but there was no sign of anybody. It wasn't unusual. There was always someone who had an interest in who was going where, with whom. And they always scarpered before you could ask them any questions.

'I think he was watching for you,' said Jananga.

Mac doubted it. After all, what would be the point of that?

–

When he got back to Camp Julien, Mac headed for his container. It was cold and it smelled stale. A long evening stretched out in front of him. He mulled over the case and he had to admit he wasn't getting anywhere with it. He lay on his bed and stared at the metal ceiling, then closed his eyes. The Lucky Star. Not so lucky for Marshall. The amulet. Could they trust the professor? Baz did. But what had led her to the Lucky Star? Did all roads lead to the Chinese brothel?

He sat up. He wanted some answers from Baz Kahn. He might have pissed her off by arguing with the professor over the amulet, but they had a shared interest in what was going on. Maybe it was time for a peace offering. He thought for a moment, then went to find Pamir.

'Chicken Street first – the Chelsea Supermarket – then the Gandamack Lodge,' he said as they climbed into the Land Cruiser.

Chicken Street was heaving, people spilling from the pavement into the road, jostling in every direction and shouting loudly if they couldn't get to where they wanted to be. Bicycle bells and car horns added to the noise. Mac grimaced as the stink from a passing night-soil cart wound its way into his nostrils. A beggar shouted at a small boy who'd grabbed a couple of coins, but he soon vanished between the forest of legs on the pavement, and everyone else ignored the man's plight. Mac told Pamir to drive round the block – there was no chance of finding a parking space – and to pick him up in five minutes when he'd finished at the Chelsea.

The supermarket was busy, too. Most of its customers were westerners, but not all. Construction workers, journalists, NATO personnel and aid workers flocked here for home comforts, but for Afghan shoppers, it was an exotic paradise. Finest imported delicacies like Reese's Peanut Butter Cups, Marmite, Mars bars, Oreo cookies... But what would Baz like? He decided that maybe he should introduce her to the delights of McVities and picked up a packet of chocolate digestives, carefully checking the sell-by date before joining the queue to pay. He'd more than once come back from the Chelsea with items that were at least a year out of date.

It was almost dark by the time he came out of the shop. He scanned the road in both directions for the Land Cruiser, but the traffic was hardly moving, and the chances were that Pamir was gridlocked halfway around the block. There was an alleyway between two carpet shops that would bring him out on Sher Ali Khan Wat. It wasn't the sort of place he'd normally venture down, but it was short and if he could catch Pamir before he looped back around into Chicken Street, it would probably save them a good ten or fifteen minutes in a jam. He tried to use his phone to tell Pamir what he was doing, but Pamir didn't pick up and it was too noisy in the street to leave a message.

The alley was empty, and it stank of rubbish and sewage. Mac concentrated on where he was putting his feet – he didn't want to spend the next half hour in the car with the smell of shit coming off his boots. The recent rain had left puddles of now-stagnant water, and the overflowing rubbish from a nearby butcher's stall, blood-soaked and stinking, turned his stomach.

He didn't hear the footsteps coming up behind him until they were extremely close. He whipped around as soon as he did hear them, but by then the men were upon him. There were two of them, their faces hidden by *keffiyehs*, black-and-white desert scarves.

Mac had always had fast reaction times, and his fist smashed straight into the closest one's face. The man staggered back as

Mac went for his weapon. But the second man, a dark silhouette outlined against the light at the end of the alley, had his arm raised. As Mac spun towards him and attempted to crack a boot into the man's kneecap, a baton crashed down on his head, pain splintering across his skull. His legs went from under him, and he plunged onto the filthy ground. A rain of blows followed him down. He could see nothing but stars. It felt as if a thousand shards of glass had cut their way into his brain. The man bent over him and rifled his pockets, taking the folded twenty dollar bills he found.

Fuck him!

However, Mac had his hand on his pistol now and he rolled onto his side so that he could raise his arm.

The first man, now back on his feet, came at him to kick him in the guts, but on seeing the gun, gave a yelp of fear. He grabbed his partners' arm and they made off down the alley as fast as their legs could carry them. Their footsteps receded, deeper into the alley, leaving Mac alone, still struggling for breath and in no fit state to give chase. He half-heartedly fired off a couple of rounds after them, but with no real intention of hitting them. He just wanted to make sure they'd be too frightened to come at him again.

Then he took a deep breath and clambered to his feet. The air around him still stank, and now his clothes did too.

Chapter 23

Saturday, 13 December 2003

Should she have had that extra glass of wine with dinner? Probably not. But her mother wasn't here to tell her off and there were days when the stress just got to her. That, and Bob from the *Post*'s incessant prattle. Thankfully she'd grabbed a seat at the Italians' table this evening, so the whole meal had been a more civilised experience. All three were Romans and told her of their love for their home city as they flirted with her charmingly.

She climbed the stairs feeling a little buzzed, and laughed at herself as she nearly stumbled on the top step. A door slammed somewhere along the corridor. *Shit!* She didn't want to bump into anyone in this state. But the footsteps hurried away in the opposite direction. Not that it led anywhere, but then the chances were there was some bedroom-hopping going on. Nothing unusual. Nothing to see here.

She found her room key in the pocket of her jeans and fumbled for the lock. The floor swayed under her feet and she grabbed at the door handle to steady herself. The handle pressed down as she leant her weight on it. Then the door swung open and she fell into the room. That was odd, because she hadn't even got her key into the lock yet.

She sobered up fast.

She stood up and turned the light on. For a second, she thought she'd come into the wrong room. But the stuff that was strewn across the floor was her stuff. The case that was open and empty on the bed was her case. The make-up and perfume bottles lying scattered on the dressing table were hers. She ran to the bedside table and yanked open the drawer. Her passport was gone. So was the stash of US dollars. The lapis necklace she'd bought from Ghilji. The gold bracelet with the evil eye charm that her mother had given to her the night before she'd left for Kabul. And Davie Marshall's *drachm*.

'No, goddamn it!'

She sank down on the bed and then realised. The door she'd heard slamming must have been her own. Whoever had ransacked her room had only just left – and had run down a dead end. She got up and ran to the door, looking round in both directions. There was no sign of anyone. She went along the passage. It turned a corner, beyond which were two more rooms. And at the end, the fire escape door.

It was open, cold air streaming in. Baz ran towards it and looked out. There wasn't an actual fire escape. It simply gave access to a small sloping roof, from which a person could jump down onto the veranda. She stared out into the dark garden. The fairy lights were off – the restaurant was closed – and everything was swathed in the dark shadows of the shade trees.

Was that something – or someone – moving, over by the wall?

It was too dark to see. It could have been a cat. But it might have been the person who'd broken in to her room.

She went back down the corridor and examined her door. The lock had been forced and broken. She looked round the room again. There was something blue, glinting under the bed. She knelt down and felt with her hand. It was the lapis necklace, carelessly dropped on the floor, then maybe kicked out of sight. She looked round more carefully and found her bracelet and her passport. The wad of dollars that were secured in it with a rubber band was still there. But the *drachm* was definitely gone.

She hurried downstairs to tell Peter what had happened, and while he sent the male members of staff outside to search the garden, she called Mac. There was no point in calling the Afghan police – they wouldn't lift a goddamn finger unless she paid them – and it seemed likely this had something to do with the case he was investigating. What the hell had he got her mixed up in?

–

Within half an hour, the lock on her door was mended, her room was half-heartedly tidied, and she was sitting at the bar with Mac. He'd turned up a little shaky on his feet, with traces of dried blood along his hairline.

'You should have gone back to the medical centre rather than coming here,' she said, looking more closely at the gash on the side of his head. 'What if it's concussion? You should see a doctor.'

Mac sighed. 'I've had concussion enough times to know that this isn't it. Head wounds bleed a lot and look worse than they are. It's nothing but a wee scratch.'

His soft Scottish accent reminded her of afternoons watching *Brigadoon* with her father, him perplexed and her enchanted. She sipped her wine and then told him about the break-in.

'Are you sure you're okay?' he said, after she'd told him what had happened. She hadn't had the guts to mention the *drachm*, though she knew at some point she'd have to tell him that she'd persuaded the professor to give the coin back to her.

'It was just a shock, that's all. But what happened to you?'

'I went to Chicken Street for chocolate biscuits. I was mugged.'

He took more than a sip of the whisky she'd ordered for him.

She forced him to make eye contact. 'They got the biscuits?'

'They took some cash. That's all. But the biscuits were trodden on and kicked into a puddle, so I left them.'

She managed to keep her expression neutral. But there was no doubt in her mind now. The timing can't have been a coincidence.

'When did it happen?'

Mac sucked in a deep breath. 'Just after five, around dusk.'

A few hours earlier. It could have been the same guy. When he didn't get the amulet off Mac, he'd come looking for her. She still hadn't said anything to Mac about having, then losing, the *drachm*.

'Chicken Street's a dump – just being western makes you an automatic target.'

'I think the guy was looking for something.'

'Are you serious? After all, he couldn't have known you'd be in Chicken Street, could he?'

'He might have followed me. There was a kid hanging around watching my car earlier today, according to Jananga.'

'So? You can't be sure.'

'Maybe not.' He pulled something out of his pocket and handed it to her. A scrap of paper.

'*Ghwal ukhura*,' she read out loud. 'Where did it come from?'

'I found it in my pocket after the attack. What does it mean?'

'Eat shit.' She handed it back to him. 'I'm sorry.'

'Why? You didn't write it.'

'You're being warned off.' She finished her wine, knowing that she couldn't delay telling him the truth any longer.

Mac's phone buzzed on the bar in front of him. 'Sorry, I'd better take this.' He picked it up and pressed it to his ear, holding a hand to the other one to shut out the clatter of noise all around them.

'Jananga? Yes... yes... no, I'm at the Gandamack.' There was a pause. 'No, someone broke into Basima's room. I don't think they took much.' A longer pause. Baz signalled to the waiter to pour another wine for her and another whisky for Mac. 'What?' Mac was shaking his head. 'Say that again.' He was looking at Baz, his eyes narrow. 'Too bloody right I'll ask her.' He disconnected from the call with a face like thunder.

'What is it?'

'You.' Mac slammed his fist down on the bar. 'If you're not the solution, you're part of the problem.' He pushed his stool back and stood up.

'I don't understand.' She was playing for time. Had the man who broke into her room been one of Jananga's men? It didn't make sense, but how else could he know — and after all, what else could it be?

Mac stood above her, glowering. 'When were you going to tell me you had the *drachm*?'

'Jananga's got it now?'

Mac dropped back onto his bar stool. 'No. His men went to retrieve it from Paghahan, and the professor told them he'd given it back to you.'

'Oh, crap. I didn't mean to get Professor Paghahan into trouble.'

'That's not the fucking point, Baz. I trusted you. When were you going to tell me you had the *drachm*?'

Baz sighed and looked away. She should have told him as soon as he arrived here. 'I was going to—'

'Doesn't cut it. I assume that it went missing from your room?'

Baz nodded, biting her bottom lip.

'For fuck's sake.'

'I think we were both targeted.'

Mac rolled his eyes. 'What are you? A fucking rocket scientist. Of course we were both targeted. Whoever Marshall stole that *drachm* from clearly wanted it back. And you let them have it.'

Baz pursed her lips. How could she explain? 'I'm sorry. I wanted to take some pictures of it.'

'Why?'

'To send to my father. To see if he recognised it. He has an almost encyclopaedic knowledge of what was in the Kabul Museum, and a lot of other museums around the country.'

'You should have told me you had it.'

'But you would have taken it off me.'

Mac rapped his empty glass on the bar, his mouth compressed into a thin line. The barman filled his glass and offered more wine to Baz. She shook her head.

'I'm sorry,' she said, once the barman had disappeared to the other end of the bar. How many times was she going to have to apologise to him?

'Fuck,' said Mac, knocking back all the whisky in his glass. 'I'd better go.'

It was Baz's turn to frown. 'Come on, this has got to tell us something, right?'

'I don't see what.'

'The fact that we were both attacked on the same evening, and the *drachm* was the only thing taken.'

Mac looked up at her. 'How do you mean?'

'It must have been important to someone – to get it back. And that person must have known one of us had it.'

Mac looked thoughtful for a moment, his temper tantrum thankfully dissipated. 'Maybe. Marshall was wearing it round his neck when he died – but the killer didn't take it.'

'It was left on his body?'

'It was taken by the kids who found the body. They claim to have found it on the ground nearby, but I think they went through his clothes for cash.'

'You got it off the two boys?'

Mac nodded.

'Who knew that you had it?'

'Jananga. The kids and their father. Jananga's deputy. My boss, Ginger, Captain Holder…'

'It's not going to be Jananga or his deputy – they could have taken it off you before now.'

'The professor.' Mac paused. 'You.'

Baz blinked. 'You're kidding, right?'

'Did you tell anyone about it?'

'No.'

'Do you think the professor told anyone about it?'

'I totally trust the professor. One hundred per cent.'

'That's not my point. If you or he, or Jananga or I, told anyone, who knows who they might have told about it? Or what if you or me or someone was overheard talking about it?'

'Do you trust your driver?'

Mac shrugged. 'I would say yes – but someone knew to come looking for it, evidently.'

'So someone we've mentioned has a link to whoever killed Marshall?'

'Perhaps not directly, but you know what this city's like for connections. It's always someone's cousin, brother, uncle…'

'Tell me about it.' It was like that at home too, in Baltimore's small Afghan community.

'What about Logan?' said Mac. 'Is there any way he knew about it?'

'Logan? The American at the Lucky Star? I didn't tell him. And why would he want it?'

'For its value?'

Baz shook her head. 'It's not about money, or they would have taken my lapis necklace and my gold bracelet. Even my passport would be worth stealing if it was just about getting maximum bucks.'

'True.' Mac gestured for another whisky. 'Ghilji? I still don't get where he fits in this picture.'

'I think he just acts as an agent for the antiquities dealers. If he introduces a buyer, he'll get a cut of the profit.'

'He would know the value of the *drachm*.'

'We're going round in circles.'

Mac pulled the note out of his pocket again.

'We need to work out who wrote this…'

'Good luck with that.' She laughed as the mood lightened, and he grinned back at her. Their eyes met.

'How long have you been out here?'

'Four months,' she said. 'You?'

'About the same. Enjoying it?'

'I'd call it a learning experience.'

He nodded in agreement. 'It's interesting. Different to what I expected.'

'In what way?'

Mac thought for a moment. 'The people, mostly. I'd never met anyone from Afghanistan before I came out here. Now, I feel like I'm getting to know Major Jananga, getting to understand what he's been through and the issues he has to deal with. You must have come out here with more realistic expectations than me.'

'Maybe – but it's very different being a reporter out here than being a reporter back in America. You married?' She had no idea where that had come from, but it was out of her mouth before she could stop it.

Mac gave her a look, then finished his drink. 'Really, I'd better head off.'

Damnit – that was a conversation killer.

'Sorry. None of my business.'

'I need to be sure that you're going to be safe,' he said, changing the subject.

'Peter's sorting me another room,' she said.

'With a lock that's just as flimsy?'

Baz shrugged. 'I guess.'

'Have you got someone here who can act as protection? Your driver?'

'Seriously, that won't be necessary. They came and got what they wanted, didn't they?'

He conceded she was right and quickly took his leave. But after he'd gone, she went in search of Javid, knowing that she'd sleep much better if he was sitting outside her door with the Makarov on his lap.

Chapter 24

In his dream, Mac was running up a hill, somewhere near his parents' home in Argyll, and when he looked back at his footprints in the snow, he realised he was still a boy. But a boy wearing dark blue Kevlar body armour with POLICE stamped in white across the back, and carrying a Glock 19 pistol. And it wasn't a hill he was running up, but stairs, in a house that he recognised. Then he knew what was going to happen next. Every sinew tensed, ice-cold terror flooded through his body and panic gripped his chest, his throat, his heart.

No, not again. He had to wake himself up.

But he was awake, and he was running up those stairs for the thousandth time, knowing what was waiting for him at the top. It played out the same every time, even if he noticed different details. And every time he tried to stop and turn and go back down the stairs, to avoid the carnage behind the door at the top, but it never worked. His legs kept running up the stairs.

His voice kept yelling, 'Police, open up.'

The door never opened. He always kicked it in. But that wasn't what had happened in real life. In his dream he was alone. In reality, he'd been with his team. In his dream, he was the one who caught the blast, who was smashed back through the door, shredded by shrapnel, dead by the time he landed. In real life, that hadn't been him. It had been Lauren, his sergeant, ripped to pieces in front of his very eyes.

The boy kicked the door in, and now Mac was watching from above. Raising his pistol to shoulder level, the kid stepped

cautiously into the room just as the suicide bomber detonated her vest. The explosion sucked Mac back into his body,
smashed him to the ground and the last thing he saw was the
bomber's head, detached from her body by the blast, embedded
in the polystyrene ceiling tiles above him. Eyes open wide,
staring with a sneer on her face as the blood dripped from her
severed spinal cord.

Only it wasn't the bomber looking down at him.

It was Mairi. His fiancée. The girl who'd died in the car
accident ten years before the bomb blast that had ended his
career in the Met.

'*Why did you let me drive?*' she whispered from above.

—

Mac woke up with a throbbing head, and his heart pounding.
He was drenched in icy sweat. The dream. The fucking lucid
dream, again and again, mixing things up, mixing people up –
but always pointing the finger of blame.

Was it never going to leave him be?

He'd lost two members of his entry team that day in
Paddington, and it had been his fault. The surveillance had been
compromised and he should have cancelled the operation, but
he'd been so desperate to score a win that he hadn't put his
foot down when he should have. The Al-Qaida safe house was
supposed to have been empty. His DCI, Fletcher, had ordered
him to go ahead when he'd expressed reservations, and he'd
done it, when for the safety of his team, he should have refused.

Fletcher, that worthless piece of shit. In cahoots with the
chief super, Chris Joseph, who'd demanded his resignation. Not
that he'd have been able to carry on after that anyway…

He wrestled his breathing back under control and gingerly
felt the bump on the back of his head before opening his eyes.
Why had he thought whisky such a good idea after what had
happened in Chicken Street?

The container was freezing, and his hands were cold against his brow, which felt soothing. It was still dark outside, and he pulled his blankets further up – maybe he could just stay in bed for the rest of the day.

The next time he woke, his head still hurt, but he could see the dull outline of the window, which meant dawn was coming. He wasn't going to miss his daily sunrise ritual, so he pulled on a sweatshirt and went outside. The muezzin had started their calling but a bank of dark, low cloud meant that the mountains were out of sight and that the sunrise would be drab.

He went back into the container and put some water on to boil for coffee. He checked his head wound in the mirror – it didn't look too bad, and certainly didn't need stitches. A couple of Nurofen and a cup of coffee later and he started to feel part human again. He called Baz to check that she was okay – but she wasn't thrilled to be woken. Then he headed for his office via Ginger's for a couple of egg banjos. If anything could effect a recovery, it was egg banjos.

There was other work to be done, but all morning, the theft of the *drachm* played on his mind. He had no doubt that his mugging was connected with the robbery at the Gandamack. Someone was warning him off the case. He stared at the note on his desk. The cheap paper would be unlikely to give up prints or finger marks even if he had some decent kit and access to a forensic lab. The writing was in biro. Somehow it seemed unlikely that Jananga's department would run to a handwriting expert. He put the note in a polythene bag and locked it in his filing cabinet. He was going to take no chances with this piece of evidence.

His phone rang. It was Holder.

'Mac, Noddy here. Got a call booked later with a Sergeant Gordon at RAF Lyneham. You might want to join me for it.'

'On my way.' So they were on first name terms now? Seemed like Holder was willing to work with him, even though Mac would hardly consider him an ally.

Holder was waiting for him at the gate and escorted him through to the MP compound.

'I spoke to Mike Gordon of Lyneham's Special Investigations Branch unit less than twenty-four hours ago. Didn't really expect to hear back from him so quickly.'

They went into Holder's office, and he booted up his ancient, cranky desktop computer. The video screen finally opened and Mac found himself looking at the grainy image of a bulky RAF sergeant.

'Sergeant Gordon?' said Holder.

The man nodded.

'I'm Captain Holder and this is DI MacKenzie. Good of you to call – I assume you've got something for me?'

'Captain.' He glanced around as if worried that someone might be listening. Then he leaned in closer to the screen. 'I do have something... possibly.'

'Go ahead.'

'Last night we carried out a spot check on the loggys' lockers here.'

'And?'

'We came across this.' Gordon held up a package wrapped tightly in clingfilm.

'What's in it?' said Mac. It just looked dark and amorphous.

'Weed,' said Gordon. 'Half a k.'

'Whose locker?' said Holder.

'A private called Villiers.'

'What's his story?'

'Claims he's never seen it, doesn't know what it's doing in his locker.'

'Have you dusted it?' said Mac.

Gordon gave him a look that told him not to teach his grandmother to suck eggs. Or anything else for that matter.

'And?'

'A partial. Not Villiers', but that means nothing. These guys work wearing gloves. He could have retrieved, put it in a bag and got it back to base without leaving a print on it.'

'And the partial?'

'No match on our files.'

'Okay. Send us the partial and we'll see if it matches the victim. Or anyone else here.' Mac glanced at Holder to check that he wasn't stepping over the mark, but Noddy looked fine.

'And can you send us a copy of Villiers' work roster so we can check it against Marshall's?' added Holder. 'If they were in this together, it meant they had to be working the same planes.'

'Sure.'

'Thanks, Sergeant. You don't know what plane that came in on?'

Gordon shook his head. 'That depends on how long it was sitting in his locker for. No way of knowing – though you'd think he'd try to move it on as quickly as possible. We run spot checks with reasonable frequency. Anyway, let me know whether you get a match for that partial.'

'Will do. In the meantime, lean on Villiers, would you?' said Mac. 'He's gotta be involved somehow. See if you can get him to give up the rest of the crew.'

The screen fizzed and went black as Gordon disconnected the call.

Holder leaned back in his chair. 'Looks like we could be on to something,' he said. 'Moving drugs would be the most logical way for Marshall to pay off his gambling debt.'

'I'm not so sure,' said Mac. 'Half a kilo of weed? That isn't going to pay off anything fast. More like personal use, small-time dealing. But it does establish there's illicit traffic through Lyneham. And if heroin's being shipped through the same chan-nels, chances are it wouldn't spend time in any loggy's personal locker. They'd want to get that through and off site much faster.'

'What we need to know is how they work the system,' said Noddy. 'How did Marshall let Villiers know something was coming through? A coded message somehow? Directly or via a third party? Phone or email?'

'Ball's in your court on that one,' said Mac. 'I presume you can get access to Marshall's phone and email records?'

'His official ones, yes – already requested. But these boys would use private channels – burner phones and encryption.'

'There's a connection here somewhere and we'll need to dig until we find it. Look for a match in their duty rosters – when Villiers was on duty unloading planes from Kabul that Marshall loaded.'

Then he remembered what Dixon had said about robbing Peter to pay Paul.

'I wonder if Marshall was really that stupid. A stolen consignment of heroin might go a long way towards paying off his debts – but it would go a long way to getting him dead, too.'

Chapter 25

'I think you guys are in way over your heads.'

Mac took his mobile away from his ear and stared at it as he calculated how to respond to this outrageous suggestion.

Or was it so outrageous?

'Listen, chum, while I appreciate your concern, I've got a job to do. A British soldier was left bleeding out with his throat cut in the tank graveyard. So don't you go trying to tell me where to get off.'

'That ain't my intention at all,' said Logan at the other end of the line. 'But I just heard that Baz Khan's room at the G Lodge was turned over. She shouldn't be involved with this – and I feel partly responsible for putting her in a dangerous position by introducing her to you.'

'I think she was already doing a fine job of that, all by herself,' said Mac.

Logan let out an exasperated sigh. 'We have a shared interest.'

'Which is?'

'You have reason to suspect your guy was tangled up with the wrong people. People who hang out at the Lucky Star.'

'And your part in all this?'

'I see how these men treat Bao's girls. She doesn't like it and she wants them out of the place. If that's into police custody, so much the better.'

'But that doesn't tell me why you would get involved.'

There was a pause at the other end of the line. 'Look, let's just say I'm looking after my own.'

Mac wondered what to do. They might have a common goal, but he didn't think their working methods would be close to similar.

'Do you have a proposal for us?' he said. The sooner he could wrap this up, the sooner he'd escape working with Jananga – so he might as well see what Logan could bring to the party.

'I can probably help with whatever you're proposing to do.'

'Then we should all meet, and you can give us your thoughts.'

–

Half an hour later, Mac found himself in unknown territory. He'd taken a left at the end of Shahr-e Now Park as instructed, trying not to think of it as the place where the Taliban had built their gallows, where crowds of jeering spectators gathered to watch public executions. Then a right, and now he was parking the Land Cruiser in the small, crowded compound car park of the Global country HQ. The fact that it housed one of the city's busiest ex-pat bars had never drawn him there. Global was practically the largest PMC – private military contractor – in Afghanistan. Police, even ex-police, and mercenaries didn't make natural drinking buddies. The Global guys were mainly screwballs and nutjobs as far as Mac was concerned.

He'd called Baz and Jananga and they'd agreed to come. But the venue had been Logan's suggestion. And it came as no surprise to Mac that the Global bar was where the mercenary would feel most at home. If he didn't work *for* Global, the chances were he would work *with* them often enough.

It was almost dark, making the compound's garden into a maze of shadows – at least no one would see him coming in. Unlike his collaboration with Jananga, this little co-operative venture needed to stay strictly under the radar. Logan had a reputation and Mac knew Phelps wouldn't approve of joining forces with him. WTP guarded their squeaky-clean reputation assiduously.

He walked across the lawn, mud squelching under his desert boots. In six months' time, the grass would be brown, the ground stone-hard and cracked, the plants begging for water, but so far it had rained nearly every day in December. He wondered if the Afghans discussed the weather as often as the Scots. Steps led up onto a wide veranda – it was a similar set-up to the Gandamack. Beyond a plain wooden door, he could hear the clamour of voices, accompanied by loud and raucous laughter. Men using alcohol to release the pressure of a stressful posting.

He pushed through the door and stepped into a room that was warm and noisy and bright. It was cluttered, too, with people, tables, chairs, bottles, glasses, a forest of bamboo plants in rough, earthenware pots and a glass-topped bamboo bar with a tiki carving lording over one end of it. The air was heavy with tobacco smoke, and in one corner a green glow emanated from a couple of ancient PCs. The Global internet café.

Jazz music blasted out from a pair of speakers suspended above the bar, so loud that the clientele had to lean in close to each other to make themselves heard. It certainly wasn't a place where people on the next table could overhear your conversation. Logan looked round. A woman with an eyepatch was sharing a bottle of vodka with a small man wearing double denim. Three long-haired men sat round a table playing cards. They eyed each other suspiciously, an argument simmering just beneath the surface. Logan was leaning against the bar, talking in hurried whispers to a middle-aged Asian barman.

Mac muscled his way through a crowd of noisy Brits to come up next to him. He half stumbled over a random foot as he reached the bar, and his shoulder smacked into Logan's. The American's head whipped round with lightning speed, his hand dropping swiftly to his belt.

'Sorry,' said Mac.

Logan's expression relaxed.

'First to arrive,' he said with a grin. 'Beer or whisky?'

'Beer,' said Mac, heedful of the fact that he hadn't brought a driver.

The Asian barman nodded and reached for a glass from a shelf above the bar.

'Meet Ram,' said Logan. 'Ex-Gurkha legend.'

Mac got a quick handshake, but Ram was evidently more interested in doing his job than reliving his glory days.

Before he could say anything, a commotion at the entrance to the bar grabbed everyone's attention. A flash of yellow fur and a ferocious snarling caused heads to turn. A man coming through the door took the full weight of an infuriated Labrador against his legs, stumbling back against the woman coming in behind him. Mac saw that it was Jananga.

'*Boro goom shoo!*' shouted the major. Get the fuck off!

Behind him, Baz dropped to her knees, grinning wickedly. 'Timebomb, get down! Bad dog!' She grabbed the dog's collar and pulled it away from Jananga, giving it a hug. The dog barked and slobbered enthusiastically.

A man came towards them both from the other end of the bar. 'Sorry, mate,' he said to Jananga. 'The dog's racist. Nothing I can do to convince her otherwise. Come on, Timebomb.' He took the dog by the collar as Baz straightened up and kissed him on the cheek.

'Good to see you, John,' she said.

Jananga didn't look particularly amused by the incident, so Mac supressed his grin as the major and Baz came over to join them by the bar.

'You're a regular here?' he said, turning to Baz.

She shrugged. 'A lot of the press pack drink here – it's fun, relaxed… John's the Global country manager – ex-Australian Navy, a good guy and a good contact for me.'

Logan gestured to Ram.

'Beer, whisky?' he said, turning to the newcomers.

'Beer, please,' said Baz.

'Juice,' said Jananga. He still didn't look happy. Not surprising – he was the only Afghan in the place, and while the proprietor was turning a blind eye to his presence, plenty of people had noticed him.

'There's an empty table over in the corner,' said Baz. 'I'll grab it.'

It was a tight squeeze around the tiny table, and Mac found his thigh pressed tight against Baz's. He felt hot.

When they were all settled, he cleared his throat. 'I suggested meeting up like this because I think we all can help each other,' he said. 'There's something going on at the Lucky Star and whatever it is, I'm pretty sure it's linked to Marshall's death.'

Logan glanced around the table before speaking. 'I don't know who killed the soldier, or why, but I do know he was playing in a nest of vipers.'

'What do you mean?' said Baz.

'Bao's filled me in on what was going down. Marshall was in hock to some Chinese guys he played mah-jong with at the Lucky Star. They sold his debt to a man known as the Swede. He's a player and he's dangerous.' He turned to Baz. 'If you were supposed to be meeting an antiquities dealer with Ghilji, odds on that it was him.'

'He's a smuggler?' said Mac. He wondered if this was the big Viking he'd seen at the Lucky.

Logan nodded. 'But not just antiquities. He trades in drugs, weapons, even girls. And he acts as a money man for some anti-Karzai elements.'

'What's his name?' said Jananga.

'Olle Holmberg,' said Logan.

Jananga nodded. 'We know of him. My informant in District Four reports that he pays Sarwani regularly. A lot of dollars.'

'Sarwani?' said Baz.

'Colonel Sarwani, the chief of police in District Four,' said Mac.

'That's his official job,' said Jananga. He sounded bitter. 'Unofficially, he recruits and fundraises for Abdul Rashid Dostum.'

'And Dostum's a bastard,' said Logan. 'Guilty of more war crimes than you can shake a stick at.'

'What's Holmberg's reason for being in Kabul? Apart from the smuggling?' said Mac.

'He grew up in Cairo and around the Middle East,' said Logan. 'Now he works for a Swiss construction company called Stuessy GmbH – road building and infrastructure projects. Apparently.'

'How's that financed?'

'US and United Nations aid money. The small part of that which hasn't already been siphoned off to line government officials' pockets.'

Jananga scowled but it wasn't something he seemed prepared to argue with.

'What does he do for them?' said Mac.

'He's their chief of party, the overall country manager. It probably gives him the perfect cover for travelling round the country moving antiquities and whatever else he's trading in.'

'That would be ideal,' said Baz. 'He needs to be able to move his stock to wherever he can meet with buyers, and he also needs a way of being able to ship stuff abroad.'

'Which must be where Marshall fitted in,' said Mac.

'Have you got a picture of him?' said Jananga.

'No,' said Logan. 'But you can't miss him. About six-five, white-blond hair…'

'That was the bloke!' said Mac.

All three of them stared at him.

'He caught me snooping in the Lucky Star and looked properly pissed off about it.'

'Be careful,' said Jananga. 'He's a dangerous man. He'll want to know what you were up to, and if he was involved in Davie Marshall's death, he'll be watching you like a hawk.'

A sensation passed down the back of Mac's neck. He could still feel the Swede's eyes, pale and sharp as ice chips, boring through him.

'He uses Bao Liang's basement for storing things, but she wants him out – he mistreats her girls and seems to think a few dollars extra gives him the privilege.'

'And that's why you'll help us?' said Jananga. 'So we can solve your problem?'

The accusation didn't faze Logan. 'Sure. Like Mac said when we started, we've got interests in common.'

'Only if Holmberg's the killer,' said Mac.

Logan shrugged. 'That's up to you to find out, isn't it?'

Baz watched the men closely as they spoke, her gaze flitting from face to face. 'So…' she said as all three fell silent. 'What's the plan?'

Mac and Logan looked at her.

'Whatever it is, hen, it's not going to include you.'

'Swivel!' said Baz, raising her middle finger at Mac good-naturedly.

Logan laughed and waved a hand at Ram, indicating they were ready for another round.

'I'll have a whisky now,' said Jananga, *sotto voce* in Logan's direction. Then he looked at the other two. 'I think we need to discover what Holmberg's storing in Miss Liang's basement – and then if I need to, I can bring him in for questioning.'

Mac knew exactly how that would go. And for once he was glad.

Chapter 26

The wind threw daggers at Mac as he walked across the compound to the office he shared with Ginger. It would soon be dark, and although it wasn't raining, the gravel was wet underfoot and the clouds were oppressively low. It was eight days since Marshall's body had been found in the tank graveyard, and he didn't really feel as if they'd made much progress in finding out who might have killed him.

Jananga and Logan wanted to raid the Lucky Star, to see what Olle Holmberg was keeping there in the basement. But that wasn't going to help them identify Marshall's killer. He had no concrete evidence that Holmberg had been involved in the killing, and only Logan's word for it that Holmberg had taken over Marshall's debt. How much faith could he put in that? Logan had his own reasons for wanting Holmberg off the restaurant premises and into custody, so who knows what stories he might cook up to achieve that?

Mac took off his padded jacket as he came into his office and immediately regretted it. If anything, it seemed colder in here than it was outside. He fired up the gas heater, but it would take a while before it would make the room feel warm.

Ginger came through the door.

'Morning,' said Mac.

'Not until I've had coffee. Want one?'

'Does a bear…?'

Mac's email inbox was full of junk – notifications from head office in Washington about office safety regs that didn't apply here, and details of how to claim back for petrol that supposed you might actually get a receipt for your money. He scanned and deleted them rapidly, determined to keep his inbox clutter under control.

'Crap! Rubbish! Why do they bloody send me all this guff?' he said as Ginger came in and put a mug of coffee on the end of his desk.

'They want to make sure that your every waking moment is taken up with company business.'

'Too bloody right.'

But then he came across an email that looked more interesting. Forwarded by Holder, it was from Sergeant Mike Gordon at Lyneham, and it had a couple of attachments. He read the message – Gordon was sending a scan of the partial print he'd taken from the package of weed, Villiers' work roster for him to compare to Marshall's, and a recording of his interview with Villiers.

Mac played the recording.

> *Gordon: Come on, Private, the sooner you spill, the better things will go for you.*
>
> *(Noise of chair scraping floor.)*
>
> *Villiers: Sorry, sir. I don't know what you're referring to.*
>
> *Gordon: Don't call me sir – I fucking work for a living. And don't play the dunce with me, soldier.*
>
> *(Pause.)*
>
> *Gordon: This hash was found in your locker. If you don't tell us what was going on, you'll find yourself facing a court martial, time in Colchester, and no more career when you come out.*
>
> *(Pause.)*

Gordon: Listen, Mick – don't be an idiot. There are clearly others involved, and they'd rat you out straight off to save their own skin. Who was your contact at Souter?

Villiers: I never knew the bloke's name. It was all set up before I came on board.

Gordon: Set up? How did you communicate?

Villiers: Email accounts in false names.

(Background noise – shuffling of paper.)

Gordon: Write them down.

Villiers: Not sure I can remember them, sir.

Gordon: Your own will do – that'll lead us to the rest.

(Pause.)

Gordon: Good. Now, who recruited you in the first place?

(There was an even longer pause.)

Villiers: Corporal Broadley.

Gordon: Kevin Broadley? That makes sense. What else is the little shit smuggling in? Heroin?

Villiers: Not that I've ever seen.

Gordon: Just hash?

Villiers: Yeah, that's all. It's nothing really... just small amounts.

Gordon: Any amount is too much. What about other things? Ever seen any antiquities, pieces of art, coming in?

Villiers: No, sir. Nothing like that, sir.

Gordon had noted in his email that he didn't believe Villiers final answer – and Mac could understand why. The answer had come out rushed, almost garbled. As Mike Gordon put it, he was fooling no one. He knew something about the antiquities smuggling. Gordon had another interview scheduled with him later in the day, and this time he'd lean on him even harder.

'Watch this space…' muttered Mac, putting down his empty mug.

He turned his attention to the work roster. It wasn't only Villiers', but the whole of his troop's. Mac compared it to Marshall's schedule to see how often their work times overlapped. It wasn't uncommon for Villiers to be unloading planes that Marshall had loaded, but there were a couple of other loggies who synced with Marshall's hours equally often. He didn't necessarily think that Marshall was supplying drugs, but it certainly looked possible that there were regular consignments and that more than one person was involved at either end.

Mac fired a reply to Sergeant Gordon, copying in Holder and Jananga, asking him to look at the men he'd identified, particularly in reference to antiquities smuggling. Then he thought about what he had so far… The *drachm* that Marshall wore around his neck. The money he owed to the Chinese men, and now apparently to Holmberg. The scrap of hessian sacking in the boot of his car – could that have been wound around a statue or a ceremonial sword? Maybe it was beginning to add up into something.

He called Holder.

'Who's been put in charge of Marshall's troop?'

'Captain Khatri. He's in command of both his own and Captain Marshall's troop at the moment.'

'Thanks.'

Holder waited at the other end of the line while Mac cogitated.

Could they trust Khatri and bring him into their confidence? Or should they assume that all three loggy troops were tainted until they found out more precisely who was involved in secreting drugs or antiquities onto flights back home?

He mulled it over as the rain beat against the window.

'Mac?' said Holder, growing impatient.

'I've got an idea. Ginger's with me, and I'm putting you on speaker phone.'

Ginger sat down and rested his elbows on the far side of Mac's desk.

'Fire away,' said Holder.

'Would you be able to set up a series of spot checks over the next ten days or so? Look at flights about to go out, all three loggy troops. Only check them once they're fully loaded and ready to go.'

'What am I looking for?'

'Drugs – Sergeant Gordon found that weed, just enough for personal use, but he's of the opinion it had come out of Kabul.'

'Don't they check every flight coming in with dogs, anyway?' said Ginger.

He was right. With Afghanistan being the world's biggest producer of opium, there was plenty of scrutiny already in place.

'For sure,' said Holder. 'They check a lot of the flights.'

'So it's gotta be worth a lot to know in advance which flights are going to be checked, and which aren't. Everyone has their price.'

He heard Holder suck in air. Mac knew that was quite some accusation he was throwing around.

'But dogs don't sniff out antiquities,' continued Mac. 'That's the other thing we're after. They'll probably be hidden in crates, labelled as something else, underneath false bottoms, or in voids in vehicle bodywork…'

'This is to do with Marshall, right?'

'Yes. Looks like he was in hock to a bunch of smugglers.'

Holder cleared his throat.

'What is it?' said Mac.

'I don't know, but since Marshall's death, even if he was working in league with others, don't you think they'd stop for a bit? Till the investigation's finished and the noise has died down?'

He had a point.

'Can you check them anyway?' said Mac with a sigh. 'And let me know if you find anything.'

'I'll set it up.'

As soon as he disconnected, Mac's mobile buzzed but he didn't recognise the number of the incoming call.

'MacKenzie.'

'Logan here.'

Mac made a mental note to save the number in his contacts.

'What can I do for you?'

'You busy right now?'

'I'm in my office.'

'I didn't ask where you are. I asked if you're busy. Can you get away?'

'I could…' Mac needed to know why before he committed to anything.

'Because now we've got a perfect opportunity.'

Logan seemed to pause unnecessarily. Mac prompted him. 'For?'

'I've had a couple of guys watching the Lucky Star. They picked up the Swede and followed him. Apparently, he's heading out of town in the direction of Kalakan.'

'Kalakan? Why would he be going there?'

'Who knows? That's not the point. The point is, he's not at the Lucky. He won't be back for a bit. Now's our chance.'

'To do what?'

Logan sounded surprised that Mac had to ask.

'To take a look in Bao's basement, of course.'

Chapter 27

Mac parked on the street – in fact, two streets away from the Lucky Star. The Swede was miles away and it might seem like he was being over-cautious – after all, why would the bloke even be looking out for him or know what vehicle he drove? – but you could never be too careful.

His mind was racing as he approached the restaurant. He was on his way to search a premises without a warrant in a country where he had no jurisdiction anyway, in the company of a known mercenary. It was mad, but they had to find out what Holmberg was up to and how he might be linked to Marshall's murder. The end justified the means, he told himself, but he wasn't entirely sure anyone else would see it that way.

A sulky teenage guard pushed open the gate for him and he went into the compound without making eye contact. Logan was propping up the bar dressed in a black T-shirt and black jeans, two beers on the counter in front of him. He was talking animatedly to Bao Liang. When he said something and followed it with a bark of laughter, Mac saw Bao's face soften into a smile for the first time. She looked like a different woman – the severity he'd seen on his previous visit momentarily melted away.

She glanced up and, when she saw him looking at her, her expression changed instantly. Logan looked round.

'MacKenzie,' he said, beckoning Mac to join them.

'Mac is fine.'

Bao gave him a slight nod of recognition, then moved away from them to the other end of the bar. Logan's eyes trailed her as she retreated.

'Here,' said Logan, pointing at one of the beers. He lowered his voice. 'Cover – so it looks like you're just in for a drink.'

Mac took the stool next to him and put a hand around the glass. 'We need to be careful with our time.'

Bao Liang hovered at the other end of the bar, watching them both surreptitiously.

A young Chinese girl came in and waved at Logan.

'Hey, Xiaoli,' he said, raising his hand in return and watching her as she went over to Bao. 'Bao's daughter,' he said, turning to Mac.

'She doesn't work here?' She looked all of fifteen.

'Of course not. Nor will she. She's hoping to go to college in America.' Logan took a long drink of beer. 'We'd better get on.'

'What are we up against?' said Mac. 'Has Bao given you a key?'

The American shook his head. 'Holmberg rents the basement from her and he keeps it padlocked.'

Mac took a sip of his beer. 'I've got a lock pick set. If it's a straightforward padlock, it shouldn't present any problems.'

'Sounds better than bolt cutters.'

Mac laughed. 'I passed the breaking and entry course with flying colours. Knew it would come in useful someday.'

'That's a genuine police training course?'

'It is. We like to make sure our boys can go onto meaningful careers, once we ding them out.'

Logan laughed and finished his beer. Mac laughed too, but it was partly bravado. What they were about to do was strictly off the books and if word got back to Phelps, he could find himself deep in it. And the thought kept worming its way back in – could he really afford to trust Logan, or his motives?

'Let's get to it,' he said in a low voice.

Logan left the bar by the door at the rear that Mac had gone through on his previous visit. After a couple of minutes, Mac followed him. Past the stairs leading up to the first floor, and along past the toilets, Logan was standing by another door.

'It's down here,' he said, pushing the door open.

The staircase was small and narrow, lit by a weak bulb hanging from the ceiling at the top. By the time they reached the padlocked door at the bottom, the light was dingy and the air around them cold.

Mac inspected the padlock. It was a heavy-duty Abus, but not particularly complex.

'Do you think you can do it?' Logan peered over Mac's shoulder.

'No prob.' As long as he could remember what he'd learned on the course.

He took a small black plastic pouch from his pocket and unzipped it. Twenty tiny picks and two tension wrenches, all of which had never been used since he'd finished the course. He never really thought he'd have to. But he'd found them again, in the bottom of his duffle bag of miscellaneous unused kit that he'd brought with him just in case... In case of what, he didn't know, but at least the lockpick was coming in useful.

He pulled out one of the tiny wrenches first – hardly more than a strip of metal bent at a ninety-degree angle – and, holding the padlock in his left hand, he inserted it into the lock with his right. He pressed his left forefinger against it to apply tension to the inside of the barrel in order to create a shearline.

'Grab me that first pick, would you?' he said, handing the pouch to Logan.

Logan extricated the slim silver tool and passed it to him. It was a city rake and the end of it looked like a flat, very shallow key. Mac pushed it into the padlock and rocked it gently up and down to raise the pins, one by one, and edge them up to rest on the shearline. Each one made a satisfying clicking sound as he got it in position.

While he worked on it, Logan climbed silently to the top of the stairs to listen at the closed door. The Swede might be out of the building, but they didn't want anyone else to realise what they were up to either.

'How're you doing?' he said as he came back down.

Mac didn't answer. It was taking all his concentration to get the last pin into position to open the lock.

The sudden sharp buzz of Logan's phone made Mac's hand jerk and the city rake slipped out of the padlock and clattered to the floor.

'Shit!'

'Sorry,' said Logan. He pressed a key to accept the call and went back up the stairs for improved reception.

Mac bent down to pick up the pick and started over again.

What was the bloody problem? The practice locks on the course had all sprung open easily, within a couple of seconds.

He reapplied the tension inside the barrel of the lock using the tension wrench and then slipped in the city rake. Just as before, he managed to line up all the pins bar the last one. He rocked the pick up and down, minutely adjusting the tension of the wrench. Logan came down to watch him work, his bulk blocking the light. But it didn't matter. Picking a lock was about feeling, not seeing.

Finally, the last pin clicked into place and the padlock sprung open. With a grin of relief, Mac withdrew both the tools and quickly slid them back into the pouch. He put the open padlock down carefully on the floor so they could lock up quickly once they were out.

Logan stepped forward and pushed the handle down. The door swung open and they were into Olle Holmberg's private warehouse.

It was pitch black inside.

Mac felt around the wall by the side of the doorframe. A metal switch plate, a switch, a click and then they were bathed in light by another naked bulb, this one much brighter than the one that lit the stairs.

'Jesus H Christ, look at all this,' said Logan.

Wooden crates and metal boxes lined the walls, two deep in some places, reaching from the floor up to the ceiling. More were stacked in tiers in the centre of the room, which was itself not particularly small. Mac recognised some of the metal boxes – weapons and munitions. The wooden crates varied in shape, size and colour. Some were stamped with Arabic or Persian script, others were stickered and others were just plain wood. At a guess, they could have contained anything.

'Let's take a look,' said Mac.

'We need to be quick.'

Mac's head snapped round. 'What haven't you told me?'

'That call. It was my guys – Holmberg's on his way back.'

'Already?'

'He didn't go as far as Kalakan.'

'Fuck! How long have we got?'

Logan shrugged. 'They don't know if he's headed here or elsewhere in the city, so we'd better assume it's here.'

Mac didn't wait for more. What a cock-up. He went to the nearest tower of metal containers, but even if he could have reached up to lift the lid, it would be too high to see into. Logan went over to a block of wooden boxes in the centre of the room. One of them wasn't quite as high as the rest, enabling Logan to prise the lid off it and look inside.

He gasped.

Mac went over and stared into the crate. It wasn't big, but it was full, almost to the brim, with copper and silver *drachms*. Not individually wrapped or packaged, or numbered in any way – just heaped into the box.

'It's like *Treasure* fucking *Island*!'

Mac reached into the box and grabbed three or four coins. He wanted to compare them with the pictures he still had of the *drachm* Marshall had been wearing around his neck.

Logan meanwhile had gone round to the other side of the central stacks.

'Weapons, too,' he said. 'AK74s, brand new.'

'Going to whom?' said Mac.

'The highest bidder. Dostum. What's left of the Northern Alliance. Southern warlords. They're all still sniping at each other and they all need kit. But I'm pretty sure Holmberg has anti-Karzai contacts.'

Mac looked around nervously at the rest of the haul. They'd never hear a car being parked in the compound from down here in the basement. In one corner, there was a huge wooden crate, standing on its own. He went across to it. The lid was nailed down – they would need a crowbar to get into it. But there were a couple of small holes in the side. Mac pressed his face against the wood so he could look through. Of course, it was pitch black inside.

'Got a torch?'

'There's one here.' Logan took one from a nearby shelf.

'Shine it through that other hole.'

Mac put his eye back to the crate. The narrow beam of light from Logan's torch hit stone. Logan moved the angle of the torch up and down. The circle of light skidded across the surface of something sculpted.

'It's a Buddha,' said Mac. He had no idea how old it was, but he didn't think Holmberg had got it at the local garden centre.

'We'd better go.'

Logan took out his phone and took a couple of pictures of the contents of the boxes they'd opened.

'Come on.'

Mac waited for Logan to get through the door and then reapplied the padlock.

'Shit, we left the light on.' He reached into his pocket for his picks.

Logan peered down at him from the top of the stairs.

'No time for that. Come on. Holmberg will just think it was his own mistake. And he won't care – he doesn't pay the power charges here.'

Mac went back to the bar and asked for a couple of whiskies. He sunk his gratefully, a slight tremor in his hand as he put his empty glass back on the bar. As Logan reappeared, he heard a couple of cars pulling into the compound parking area outside.

A text buzzed on Logan's phone.

'That's them,' said Logan, checking the screen. 'Let me walk you out.'

They came face to face with Holmberg at the front door. He pushed past them, but not before his fierce blue eyes raked across Mac's face with recognition.

Mac had forgotten how tall the man was.

'You found the toilet okay this time, Mr MacKenzie?'

The Swede didn't hang around for an answer.

Shit.

Chapter 28

Wednesday, 17 December 2003

Fuck knows where Ginger had managed to get a real Christmas tree from, but he had. Mac sat in his office staring at the emaciated branches. It looked more like a tree at the end of its tenure than one just put up. Blue, yellow and red fairy lights twinkled on a rotation that matched his own thought pattern.

He had made a mistake – going into the basement. He had made a mistake – leaving the light on. He had made a mistake – running into Holmberg on the way out. He had made a mistake... He tore his eyes away from the lights.

But the Swede had made a mistake, too. He'd let slip that he knew his name. He'd bothered to find out about him, though that wouldn't have been too hard to do. In the tangle of overlapping spiders' webs that enmeshed the city, gossip slipped easily along the threads. Information could be converted into cold, hard cash, and was routinely traded.

But the fact that the Swede had known who he was, and would probably by now have realised they'd been in his storeroom, drew a line in the sand. They needed to move against him fast – faster than he expected. He informed Jananga of what he and Logan had seen at the Lucky Star, and the major had agreed with him that it was time to take action. Prostitution targeting westerners was something the Afghan police were prepared to turn a blind eye to, but if Holmberg was using the place for gunrunning for Dostum or his associates, that was a different matter.

Jananga decided it was time to raid the brothel. Mac told Phelps what was going to happen, and Phelps had been far from happy about the plan. 'You and Ginger can observe, but there's no need to get tangled up in a Kabul turf war,' he'd said, with a sigh of regret. *Observe.* Mac had decided to make his own interpretation of exactly what that would mean, and he spent the rest of the morning cleaning the police issue AK Jananga had provided.

—

There was no Christmas tree in the major's office when they gathered there after lunch – just the usual fug of green tea and wet wool. Mac, Ginger and Jananga had chairs pulled up round one end of the desk and were studying a roughly sketched floorplan of the Lucky Star. Baz was sitting at the other end, examining the *drachms* that Mac had liberated from Holmberg's stash – he wanted to get some idea from her of how valuable they were. Logan arrived. Mac had suggested bringing him on board as he had first-hand knowledge of the brothel's layout and who they might expect to find there.

'They're definitely very similar to the one Marshall had,' said Baz, putting down the magnifying glass she'd been using. 'His could have come from a different source, but given the connections… it probably came from the same cache.'

'Which could give us due cause to have Holmberg in for questioning,' said Mac.

'Leave the interrogation decisions to me, please,' said Jananga.

Logan drew a finger across his throat and made a gurgling sound, earning himself a filthy look from the major.

'Right,' said Mac, assuming control. 'Logan, talk us through the entry and exit points.'

'The Lucky's got the main gate at the front, which you know' – he pointed at the gates on his sketch – 'and a small pedestrian gate at the back, which is used by members of staff who don't live in the compound.'

'Who has the keys for that?' said Mac. Logan knew the building inside out and as an ex-Green Beret he had probably far more operational experience than anyone else at the table, so Mac wanted to get all he could out of him.

'I do,' said Logan, producing a set of keys from his pocket. 'But also five or six staff members. They come in at seven a.m., and most of them leave by sixteen hundred, apart from the two chefs and whichever barman is on duty for evening service.'

'We'll go in at twenty hundred,' said Jananga, 'so the day staff will be gone.'

'How many men will you have available?' said Logan.

'Sixteen. We'll take four vehicles.'

'Good,' said Mac. 'Let's put men on the back gate as our first move. We'll all park round the corner on Qalla-e-Fatullah Road. Logan, you take Jananga's sergeant and four of his men and place them on the gate, then go inside and give us the signal to move in from the front. That way, none of the staff or the girls will realise that you're part of the raid.'

'Apart from Bao,' said Baz. 'I assume you've warned her about this?'

'Yup – she knows what's happening,' said Logan, 'but none of the girls will be told in advance. We can't afford to have Sarwani and his goons getting wind of this. Anyway, when you get the signal from me at the back, you come in through the front gates and mop up.'

'What about your men, Jananga-jan?' said Mac. 'Can we trust them not to let their District Four colleagues know what's going on?'

Jananga shrugged. '*Insha'Alla* – but when I briefed them, I didn't tell them the address, or even the district, we're going to. And when we leave here, I'll confiscate all their mobiles.'

'Word will get out as soon as we hit the Lucky Star,' said Logan. 'We'll never get all the girls and all the johns corralled before one of them makes a call. But the most important thing is to secure Holmberg.'

'Where's he likely to be?' said Ginger.

'He'll either be in the restaurant, eating, or he'll be upstairs, here.' Logan put a finger on the diagram of the upper storey of the brothel, pointing to a large bedroom at the front of the building. 'He usually eats at about nineteen hundred and then takes two or three of the girls upstairs after that, which is why going in at twenty hundred makes sense.'

'That room's at the front,' said Mac. 'Doesn't that risk him seeing our arrival from his window?'

'It'll be dark by then and the curtains will be shut. As long as you maintain silence as you disarm the gate guards and cross the front of the compound, you should be okay. Once you're in, the team needs to split – a group to secure the restaurant, a group to head upstairs to secure Homberg, and men to corral the girls and their clients.'

'What will happen to the girls, Major?' said Baz, looking at Jananga. 'You're not going to charge them all, are you?'

Jananga exhaled noisily. 'I should, but... too much paper-work.'

Mac didn't like it. Even if it was unlikely, the chance that Holmberg might be looking out of the window just as they came in added an element they couldn't control. But there were always elements beyond control on an operation like this, and the key to good planning was to try and foresee as many of them as possible and build in contingencies. The 'what ifs', and how to deal with them.

'If he does see us, he'll head for the rear exit, right?'

'Exactly,' said Logan, 'and I'll be waiting. We'll hold anyone who tries to leave that way – johns, girls, staff.'

'Good,' said Jananga.

'What about the mah-jong players?' said Mac.

'They'll probably just carry on,' said Logan. 'They've lived through enough brothel raids over the years not to get excited about another one.'

'But we'll bring them in for questioning,' said Jananga.

Logan shrugged. 'That's up to you. You'll have to square all this with Sarwani afterwards – he gets paid plenty to protect the place, so he'll be coming at you. All I'm interested in is getting Holmberg out of there.'

Mac turned his attention back to the schematic of the building. 'Okay, let's put all the girls into this room here, and all the johns, including Holmberg, in here. Handcuff them, take their phones, get their names from any ID they're carrying. And, Major, make sure all your men are in body armour. Not everyone checks in their weapons at the door like they're supposed to.'

Jananga looked embarrassed. 'I don't have enough for all my men. Just for the first vehicle in.'

'Okay. It'll have to do.'

'We could probably bring some from WTP,' said Ginger.

'Good thought,' said Mac.

'I'll bring my own Kevlar vest,' said Baz.

The men looked at her in unison.

'You're joking, right?' said Mac.

'I'm not,' she said. 'I'm an accredited member of the press. I have a press card. This is a story I'm reporting.'

'But you can't be embedded for the raid,' said Mac.

'Either you take me in, or I'll just follow you in. I wouldn't miss this for the world.'

Chapter 29

A text from Bao Liang confirmed that Holmberg was in the building. Jananga confiscated his men's mobile phones, and they all piled into the vehicles, including Baz who'd promised Mac that she would stay out of the way and behind all of Jananga's men when they went inside.

For once, it wasn't raining. The sky above was clear and, as always, the multitude of stars visible in the velvety black reminded Mac of being home on his parents' farm near Oban. They might be in a city, but light pollution wasn't an issue in a place where there were no streetlamps. It was, however, bloody cold, and as they crept round the corner into Street 4, Mac wished he was wearing his fingerless gloves.

Logan's group had peeled away from them already to go in at the rear gate. Baz was with them, dressed in dark clothes, a black hijab and her own Kevlar vest. She wasn't armed, but was carrying a small digital camera so she could document what happened and what they would find in Holmberg's store.

Jananga led the rest of the team towards the main gate at the front of the compound. They walked on swift, silent feet, keeping close to the walls and fences of the other compounds on Street 4 so they remained bathed in shadow. Mac and Ginger were at Jananga's shoulder – and each of them had a team following behind.

Jananga's group had responsibility to remove and disarm the gate guards. When they were level with the next-door property,

Jananga stopped and held up a hand to halt the party. He was waiting for the signal from Logan. A silent minute seemed much longer, and Mac's nerves jangled. What if…? He tried to stop his mind from second guessing what was coming.

Then Jananga made a gesture beckoning two of his men forward. Both in uniform, they moved the fire selector on their AKs to single shot and walked up to the two guards. One of Jananga's men spoke quietly and showed them his police ID, while the other trained his weapon on them. Although they were young, they were sensible – neither of them tried to play the hero, and after a swiftly silenced word of protest, they handed over their weapons and accompanied the two policemen up the street to an unmarked van that had been parked there earlier. The guards would be held in the van until the raid was over, then transported, with others, to the Police HQ for processing and release.

As soon as the guards were out of the way, Jananga gave a hand signal, and the entire contingent followed him as he slipped through the gates into the compound. Weapons held ready, they streamed through the door into the brothel. The hall and locker room were deserted, but there was a low rumble of voices coming from the restaurant. Jananga whispered to one of his men, who took up position in the locker room.

'This is where all the customers' weapons are,' said Jananga. 'He will stay here and guard them.'

Then the major went through the door into the restaurant, flanked by two uniformed officers.

'Police,' he said in English. 'Put your hands behind your heads and kneel on the floor.'

His officers spread out through the restaurant, pointing their rifles at any of the bemused diners who were hesitant in following the instructions.

Mac looked around. There were probably ten or twelve men sitting at tables, and a handful of Chinese girls, some sitting with the men, others waiting tables. The girls were quicker to do what they were told – no doubt the brothel had been raided before – but some of the men started to protest.

'I'm not doing anything wrong. Just came here for dinner,' said an overweight man with a strong South African accent.

'Get down,' said Ginger, gesturing with his AK.

The man reluctantly obeyed him, while Mac carried on through to the other end of the dining room.

There was no sign of Holmberg and, filled with a sense of foreboding, Mac beckoned Ginger and his team, and headed towards the stairs at a trot.

The upstairs landing was empty, apart from one girl in a diaphanous robe. The smile on her painted face vanished as she realised Mac was carrying a weapon, and she gave a harsh little scream upon seeing the men streaming up behind him.

Mac put a finger to his lips, but it did no good. She started to shout in guttural Chinese, no doubt to warn the other girls what was happening. One of the uniformed police officers grabbed hold of her and slapped her cheek. The woman gasped. Mac frowned, but he didn't have time to deal with it. He went straight to the door of the room Holmberg used and tried the handle. It was locked.

'Police, open the door,' he called out, banging his fist on the flimsy wood.

There was no response.

'Police!'

Around him the Afghan officers were banging on other doors. Some had opened and western men and Chinese women were being separated and herded into the designated rooms according to plan. Other doors were being kicked open.

'Let me,' said a voice behind Mac.

It was Logan. He put the boot in and the door flew open. The room was dark, and Mac could see an unmade bed, but no people. Logan reached in and turned on the light. There was nothing – no sign of the tall Swede's presence, only a lingering smell of stale tobacco.

'Fuck!' said Mac.

Amid the chaos of bodies in the hall, they checked each of the other upstairs rooms. The police had eight punters held in a small back bedroom. They were busy cuffing them and searching them for ID. Some were in a state of semi-undress and had been interrupted in the middle of what they came to the Lucky Star to do. They were clutching clothes and backpacks, trying to dress themselves further before having their hands cuffed behind their backs made it impossible. Across the hall in another room, the Chinese girls clustered together, talking quickly and loudly, but generally co-operating. A further five bedrooms were empty, already cleared by Jananga's men.

Mac went back to the room where the punters were being held. One of the police officers was struggling to take a mobile phone from one of the men. Mac wondered who he'd alerted to what was going on. He wouldn't have been calling his wife, that much was for sure. Mac counted heads, but there was no sign of Holmberg.

'Where's Bao?' he said to Logan, who was emerging from one of the empty bedrooms.

'I told her to get out as soon as she'd texted me. She'll be round the corner somewhere in her car – I'll call her when it's safe for her to come back, and she'll sort out a lawyer for the girls.'

'She won't need to. It's not what Jananga's here for,' said Mac, heading towards the top of the stairs.

'You reckon?' said Logan. 'He'll want something to show his superiors, given that Holmberg's flown the coop.'

They were halfway down the stairs when a shot rang out. It sounded as if it had come from the restaurant.

'Damn!' said Ginger. 'It seemed to be going a little too well.'

They all paused at the bottom of the stairs.

'Cover me,' said Mac.

He darted out into the corridor, looking both ways. A police officer was coming towards him from the other exit at the back of the building, obviously having also heard the shot. Mac motioned with his palm and the man fell in behind him. They crept up the passage and Mac stopped at the door into the restaurant. He listened. He heard someone moaning loudly, voices talking in Dari. A raised voice, shouting something in Spanish.

'Stay down!' Jananga's voice rang loud and clear.

Mac went in.

There was a policeman struggling on the floor with a western man, one of the diners Mac had passed on his way to the stairs. Mac saw the glint of a pistol barrel between them. A few feet away, another policeman was sitting against the bar, blood pouring from a wound in his shoulder. The recipient of the shot.

Logan pushed past him.

'Let go of your gun, Luis, for God's sake.'

The westerner under the policeman blinked and looked round. His concentration momentarily broken, the policeman relieved him of a snub-nosed pistol, which he passed to one of his colleagues, before rolling the gasping man onto his front and applying a pair of handcuffs.

'Get off. Fuck's going on, Logan?' The words were slurred. The man was clearly drunk.

Jananga lowered his gun and turned to Mac and Logan. Baz burst through the door from the back and started taking pictures, ignoring Ginger's admonishments to wait.

'You have Holmberg?' said Jananga.

Mac shook his head.

'Not here,' said Logan.

'You think he knew?' said Mac.

'No fucking way. I would trust Bao with my life – she would never have told him.'

'So why would he have left?'

'It's one of the "What ifs…",' said Logan. 'I'll call Bao and see what happened.'

'What about Holmberg's storeroom?' said Baz. 'We need to catalogue what's in there as quickly as possible.'

'Come on,' said Mac. He led the way out of the restaurant to the back area of the brothel.

As Baz, Ginger and Logan followed him down the stairs, they heard the sound of a phone ringing beyond the locked door. This time Mac didn't bother to pick the lock. He set the AK for a single shot.

'Stand back.'

The crack of gunfire in the small space was deafening. The padlock flew off, hit the adjoining wall and fell to the ground. The door sprung open. The light was already on.

They stood on the threshold and stared.

The stacks of crates and boxes that had been in the centre of the room were gone, replaced by a single wooden chair. A woman was tied to the chair, her upper body slumped forward, her clothes drenched in blood. Long black hair formed a curtain across her face.

But they all knew who it was.

Chapter 30

'Bao!' Logan rushed forward. 'Bao!'

There was a mobile phone on the floor a couple of feet away. Mac bent down to pick it up. He switched off the ringtone and the silence was deafening.

Baz pushed past Mac and ran towards Logan. The big American was crouching in front of the chair. His hands were on Bao's shoulders, his forehead pressed against hers.

'Logan…' She didn't know what to say to him. Bao was dead. There was a gaping wound across the base of her throat – a wide, black smile of coagulated blood.

'Jesus,' said Ginger, turning his head away.

Mac stepped forward and put a hand on Logan's shoulder. 'I am so sorry.' He reached down and touched Bao's lifeless forearm. 'She's cold. She's been dead for several hours.'

Baz looked at him. 'Then who sent the text?'

Mac didn't answer. 'Take some pictures. This is a crime scene.'

Baz was torn. She couldn't take photos of Logan in this moment of unbearable pain, but it was her job to report on what had happened. There were days when being a journalist stank and being human had to take over. She quickly took some shots of the rest of the room and the remaining crates, conscious that Mac and Logan were watching her. Logan stood up. His cheeks were wet with tears, but his eyes spoke of nothing but hatred.

'Take the pictures, Baz. Holmberg is going to pay for this.'

A switch flicked inside her and Baz was back in work mode. Logan was right – this had to be documented. As she photographed the slumped body, there was the sound of a woman screaming from upstairs.

'What the fuck?' Mac raised his gun and went to the door. The cry was accompanied by more shouting and shrieking, and the sound of heavy boots on the wooden floors. He started up the stairs, then looked back. 'Baz, finish what you're doing. We'll check out what's happening.'

The three men disappeared. Baz waited, her heart pounding underneath the protection of her Kevlar vest. Alone, she took a few more photographs of Bao, but her concentration was shattered by the sound of footsteps, much closer this time. Someone was passing the top of the stairs.

Stashing the camera into the case hanging round her neck, she ventured to the bottom of the staircase. Step by agonising step, moving carefully so as not to make a sound, she started going up. This was madness. The screaming was sporadic now. She could hear people running backwards and forwards, and a man talking in Chinese. A woman crying.

She stood behind the door at the top, not knowing what to do. Should she stay here and wait, or venture out into the chaos?

The door burst open, practically jettisoning her back down the stairs. Struggling to keep her footing on the small landing area, she flattened herself against the wall. It was Mac.

'What's going on?' she said.

'All hell has broken loose. Come on – we need to get out of here.'

Mac peered around the door. It seemed all quiet on the corridor beyond him.

'Who was screaming?'

'The girls are terrified – and not without reason.'

He pulled open the door, looking carefully from side to side and listening. There was no one in sight.

'It's Sarwani – he's arrived with a team of men,' said Mac. 'The police chief of District Four. Someone must have tipped him off about what was going down. I can hear him arguing with Jananga in the restaurant.'

Baz darted past him and ran towards the restaurant door, taking the lens cap off her camera. If she could get some good shots...

'No!' said Mac, in a loud whisper, behind her.

The door was ajar by about an inch. Baz stood as close to it as she dared and put her eye to the gap. In the centre of the restaurant, Jananga stood face to face with a man in a blue Kabul police uniform. Gold flashes adorning his cap, collar, shoulder and cuffs served to broadcast his elevated rank and Baz guessed this must be Colonel Sarwani. Behind each of them, several of their own men stood with itchy fingers fidgeting on their weapons.

Jananga was talking in Dari with his voice raised. '...and I would remind you that I also have jurisdiction here.'

'But the brothels are my responsibility—'

'You mean you take their money—'

'You would if you could. But, please, remove your men. I will check what's going on here and take any necessary action, Major.' He was underlining the fact that he was the ranking officer.

'I'm here on a different matter. A British soldier has been murdered. This is part of my investigation.'

'It didn't happen here.'

'I would ask you to leave now, Colonel, so I can get on with my investigation.'

They were talking faster and faster, and Baz could tell that Jananga was only just managing to stay polite.

'No! You go!' shouted Sarwani, finally losing his rag.

A sergeant standing just to his left raised his AK.

Jananga stood his ground, glaring, but two of his men raised their weapons.

215

'Jesus,' breathed Baz.

Mac was craning his neck to see through the gap over her head. 'We need to get out,' he said.

The first shot definitely came from Sarwani's side, though Baz would be hard put to say which man fired. A man dropped, but by the time he reached the floor, gunfire had erupted from both sides and men were throwing themselves down or diving for the cover of doorways, tables and behind the bar.

'Run!' shouted Mac, grabbing her arm.

He ducked into a doorway and dragged her in too. Blinking, confused, she staggered inside, her foot landing on something and skidding out from under her.

'Umph!' She slid down the back of the door and landed on her arse, looking to one side to see what she'd tripped on. Scattered all across the floor were hundreds of small white rectangles, marked with red, green and blue pictograms. Mahjong tiles. There was an overturned table, and another table still laid out with a game. The mah-jong room. Was this where it had all begun?

'Damn!' said Mac. 'I thought there might be a way out to the back courtyard.'

But the room had no other door. They would have to venture back into the corridor.

'Where's Ginger?' said Baz.

'I sent him to scoop up all the weapons in the locker room and get them out of here.'

They waited, listening. Machine-gun fire peppered the air intermittently, backed by a chorus of shouts, screams and running feet. Baz got her breath back, wondering if she'd make it out of the building alive.

Mac opened the door a crack and peered out.

'Come on.'

They both slipped out into the corridor as quietly as they could. At that moment, the restaurant door at the end opened. Mac pushed Baz back into the doorway.

'It's Logan,' he said, and Baz breathed a sigh of relief. 'Come on, we need to get out.'

'I've got to get Bao,' said Logan, pushing past them towards the door to the cellar. His expression was bleak. Baz's heart went out to him – he'd engineered this raid to help her, and this had been the result.

'There's no time,' said Mac.

'You go ahead. I'm not leaving her body here with Sarwani's men. They won't treat her with respect.'

Mac looked infuriated but didn't argue.

He hurried Baz down the corridor towards the back entrance. There was a trail of blood smudged across the floor, and bloody footprints tracked in the direction of the back door.

She almost felt it before she heard it – a bullet whistled past her head and embedded itself into the wooden door frame in front of them. Mac grabbed the top of her arm and threw himself down on the floor. She crashed down after him, only just breaking her fall with her forearms, and slumping against his side. The camera case smashed into her chest as Mac rolled over on top of her to shield her from fire, and she was winded. But there was no time for recovery. A few seconds later, Mac shoved her forward as he sat up pointing his gun in the direction from which the bullet came.

As Mac opened fire, the door into the restaurant slammed shut and they were alone in the corridor.

'This way!'

He clambered to his feet first, grabbing her arm to pull her up. Together they ran up the staircase just opposite where they'd ducked down. Baz heard the restaurant door opening again and footsteps pounding down the passage. They rounded the corner of the stairs and practically flew up the second flight. Someone was coming after them.

'Stop!' shouted a man's voice, speaking Dari.

No damn way!

They ran along the upstairs landing. There were several of Jananga's officers, tasked with guarding the girls and their customers, standing at various doorways looking confused. One pointed an AK at them, until he recognised them from the drive across, and lowered his weapon.

'Tell them Sarwani's here,' said Mac, without stopping. 'Tell them they need to go down and help the major.'

Baz translated as quickly as she could, following Mac towards the furthest bedroom. He shoved the door open and they ran in.

'Stop!'

A young Chinese girl, barely in her teens, was holding a pistol with outstretched arms. Her hands were shaking, but she trained the gun on Mac as he walked towards her. He lowered his weapon and held out the other hand flat in a gesture that Baz supposed was meant to calm her.

'We're not here to hurt you. We're here to help,' he said.

She fired and Mac dropped to the floor.

Chapter 31

Wednesday, 17 December 2003

Fear froze Baz for a fraction of a second, then she lunged forward as anger took over. The girl tried to retrain her weapon on the new target, but Baz was moving too fast. She made a grab for the girl's wrist and slammed it against the edge of dressing table just behind her. The pistol scooted across the floor and Baz bent down to pick it up. By the time she had straightened herself, the girl was pushing past her out of the room.

'Fuck!' Baz tucked the gun into the back of her waistband. 'Mac, are you okay?'

Mac struggled to his feet. 'Clipped a wing,' he said, glancing down at a bloodied left arm.

'Jesus!'

'It's nothing... superficial,' he said. But the colour had drained from his face.

He went to the window and peered out.

'Right, we can get down here,' he said.

Baz joined him. The window overlooked a small area of flat roof where the mah-jong room extended out at the back of the building. Despite the wound in his arm, Mac was grappling to get the window open. Baz heard footsteps thudding down towards their room and helped him.

The window burst open and she climbed out onto the ledge.

'Go.'

'What about you?' She glanced at his arm.

'Really, it's fine. I'll come after you.'

'There's a man down there,' said Baz. A shadow had passed from one of the paths into the foliage. She blinked and recognised who it was – the big Hazara whom she'd met with Ghilji. What was he doing here? Suddenly he darted back towards the house, and when he reappeared, he was pulling a struggling girl by one arm. It was the girl who'd shot Mac. They scuffled – the girl was trying desperately to get away from him.

Holding onto the side of the window frame with one hand, she pulled the girl's pistol out of the back of her pants and watched. The bushes rustled in the strong wind. She stared out into the blackness, willing her eyes to become accustomed to the dark.

As they twisted and turned, Baz waited for her chance. Then she raised the pistol, put it ahead of his trajectory and pulled the trigger.

There was a yelp and the man stumbled to the ground. The girl broke free and ran off, disappearing down the side of the house. The man started crawling towards the back door, leaving a glistening trail of blood in his wake. Baz was glad he wasn't dead – she'd only aimed at his leg.

'Holy shit,' said Mac. 'You can shoot?'

Baz lowered herself onto the flat roof and turned back to him with a shrug. 'I'm American, aren't I?' It was the first time she'd ever fired a weapon outside a gun range.

She swung down from the roof into the courtyard at the back of the compound. Two of Jananga's men were standing at the back gate.

'Come on,' said one of them in Dari, beckoning her over.

Baz ran across the open space, half expecting a hail of gunfire from the back of the building. A solitary shot rang out, making the two policemen leap out of sight. Baz reached the safety of the gate and they hauled her through unceremoniously.

Crowded against the wall were a gaggle of Chinese girls, in various states of undress, most of them with their hands cuffed behind their backs. Two of them were crouched down, tending to a third, who appeared to have a gunshot wound in her lower leg. That explained the trail of blood along the corridor.

Nearby, Ginger was piling weapons into the back of one of the police Surfs, with assistance from one of Jananga's men.

Mac appeared through the gate a few seconds later.

'Why did Sarwani attack?' Baz thought about the wounded girl. Had she just been caught in the crossfire between the rival police teams?

Mac looked at the two officers. 'Tell them we need to get back to the police station.'

Baz translated and one of the officers explained that they would take the girls back to the vehicles parked around the corner and drive them to Police HQ.

'Go with them,' said Mac. 'Keep an eye on how they treat the girls.'

'What about you?'

'I'll liaise with Jananga and Logan. Tell them to keep a vehicle back for us.'

Chapter 32

It was a sight that Mac would never have wanted to witness and equally one that he would never forget.

Logan carrying Bao Liang's body up the steep steps from the basement, and on up the main staircase to her bedroom. He'd wrapped her in a clean white sheet, but it was smeared with blood, as were his hands and his face. Blood and tears.

Mac stepped forward once he reached the ground floor to try to help him, but Logan brushed him aside to continue up. Mac followed him quietly, holding open the door to Bao's room, and then sitting with him as he held vigil by the body.

Mac had seen grown men cry before – a dozen times or more – but he'd never been so affected as he was seeing Logan struggle with his feelings. What became painfully clear was that he had truly loved Bao Liang. It wasn't just the throwaway relationship of convenience that so many expat workers struck up on assignment to a new posting in a new city. Logan's heart was broken.

Mac felt like he was intruding.

Logan peeled back the sheet from Bao's face. He took a gold chain from her neck – Mac couldn't see what was hanging from it – and put it round his own neck. He kissed her on the forehead, and stroked her black hair until it was smooth and neat. Then he replaced the sheet.

'I was trying to persuade her to come back to America with me,' he said simply. 'I would have married her.'

He stood up and left the room.

Mac didn't go to church. He wasn't even sure he believed in God. But he made the sign of the cross against his chest before he followed Logan out.

—

By midnight, in Jananga's office, there was no sign of tears on Logan's taut features, but there were still traces of her blood in his beard and hair. Bao's body had been taken to the city morgue, and the girls and their johns had been processed into holding cells. Mac had received assurances from Jananga that they would all be turned loose without charge. Jananga was more concerned about the situation with Sarwani. The District Four police chief had killed one of his men. There were several injured officers on both sides. Two wounded prostitutes. Jananga's men had prevailed and he now held the colonel in custody. Apparently, it was not a situation his own superior, Colonel Badrashi, was particularly thrilled about.

'So District Four's not your jurisdiction?' said Baz. 'I just don't understand why one section of the city police would have opened fire on another section.'

'It is my jurisdiction,' said Jananga indignantly. 'All Kabul is my jurisdiction. But Colonel Sarwani is a higher-ranking officer than me and he's corrupt. He takes protection money from illegal businesses to guarantee no interference from the police.'

'But that's like the Wild West,' said Baz.

'Straight out of the O.K. Corral playbook,' said Logan.

Jananga shrugged. 'We're constantly in conflict with the different district forces, and the National Directorate of Security.'

'They should just let you get on with your job,' said Mac. He turned to Logan. 'Someone must have tipped Holmberg off about the raid, giving him enough time to get most of his stash out.' There had only been a fraction of what he and Logan had originally seen in the basement.

'Someone betrayed Bao and then killed her,' said Logan. 'I have a very good idea who.'

They waited for him to say more but his mouth set itself into a hard, thin line. His clothes were dark with his lover's dried blood and he stank of it.

'Whoever it was, they must have told Holmberg *and* Sarwani,' said Baz.

'Holmberg probably tipped Sarwani off,' said Logan. 'Those two are as thick as thieves.'

'More to the point,' said Mac, 'where's Holmberg now? Where's all the stuff he had in that storeroom? Someone at the Lucky Star must have seen him moving it out. We need answers.'

Jananga smiled grimly. 'If any of the girls or the restaurant staff know anything about it, they'll tell us.'

'What...' Baz paused. 'You mean you're going to hurt those girls more?'

'No one will get hurt if they tell us what they know.'

'I wish I could believe that, Jananga-jan.'

'Basima-jan, let me make you a promise. The girls will be fine, and when they've told me what I need to know, they can all go.'

'What will happen to them?' said Baz, turning her attention to Logan. She didn't look convinced by Jananga's words. Nor was Mac.

'Hell, I don't know. Assuming they're not deported' – he gave Jananga a meaningful look – 'and if the owner of the Lucky Star can get a replacement manager in quickly, they'll still have jobs. If not' – he shrugged – 'there are plenty of other brothels in the city.'

'God, it sounds bleak,' said Baz. 'Even if they make more money here, is it really better than where they come from?'

Logan looked exhausted. 'Bao Liang was a good woman, and she treated her girls well and paid them well. Don't judge the way other people live their lives by your own American standards, Baz. They don't have the same luxury of choice that you've grown up with.'

Mac stood up. 'I'd better go get this seen to,' he said, raising his right hand to his bloody left arm.

Logan followed suit. 'I've got to go back to the Lucky Star.'

'Why?' said Baz.

'I need to find Bao Liang's daughter, Xiaoli. I thought she'd be here with the girls, but she's not.'

'How old is she?' said Baz.

'Fourteen.' Logan clocked their horrified expressions. 'She doesn't work there. She lives with her mother. Lived.'

'Describe her,' said Baz.

'Long black hair, slim… she looks young for her age.'

'Sounds like the girl who shot you,' said Baz to Mac.

Mac nodded. 'Would she have the nerve to shoot someone?'

'Christ, yes,' said Logan. 'She was her mother's daughter and then some.'

'If it was her, she got away. The big Hazara was trying to take her, and she struggled free when I shot him.'

Logan's eyes widened. 'I've got to go find her.'

He left the room and the meeting broke up.

-

The doctor at the DK German Medical Clinic on Kolula Pushta Main Road examined Mac's arm. The small private medical centre was used by most of the expats in Kabul, who were happier to pay through the nose than take their luck in the municipal hospitals.

'It's not a scratch. It's a bloody gunshot wound, Mr MacKenzie.' Dr Muller wasn't impressed and he wasn't particularly sympathetic. He probably saw plenty of gunshot wounds, given where he worked. 'What have you been up to?'

Mac took it as a rhetorical question. He sat on the edge of a gurney in one of the medical centre's consulting rooms, while

Dr Muller cleaned and dressed the wound on his upper arm. It wasn't deep – cleaning and a couple of butterfly stitches were enough, ten minutes' work at most. But he wasn't thrilled at having been roused from his bed at one in the morning, even though he was the doctor on call.

'This linked to what happened in the Lucky Star restaurant?' said Muller, conversationally. 'I heard over the shortwave radio earlier that two police units were having a shootout in that area of the city.'

'I know nothing,' said Mac as the doctor finished patching him up. 'How much do I owe you?'

'See the receptionist on the way out. She works out the bill,' said Muller.

However much it would be, it would seem like too much, but Mac would have no problem charging this to the company. After all, it was Phelps's idea that he get mixed up with all this in the first place.

'All done,' said Muller, finishing off the bandaging.

'Thank you, Doctor,' said Mac. He slipped down off the gurney, and for a moment felt quite light-headed. Perhaps he'd lost more blood than he'd realised. 'Actually, can you bill WTP direct?'

'Get to bed, Mr MacKenzie,' said the doctor. 'I'll sort out the invoice in the morning.'

'Thanks.' He didn't think Phelps would be too thrilled by the bill, or exactly delighted to hear that two of his employees had been involved in a police-on-police fire fight. The chances are he'd want them off the case.

As Ginger drove him back to Julien, Mac stared out of the car window, thinking of a strategy to get Phelps to let them carry on with what they were doing. But then all thoughts vanished from his mind as sleep claimed him the moment his head hit the pillow.

Chapter 33

As well as a dull ache at the top of his left arm, Mac felt the grinding fatigue that always followed an extreme burst of adrenalin. The raid on the Lucky Star had been a clusterfuck. Holmberg had clearly got wind of it and had managed to remove most of his contraband from the basement. Bao Liang was dead and her daughter, Xiaoli, was missing. And they were nowhere near finding the key to Marshall's murder.

Phelps had demanded a full explanation from him after breakfast, had torn a strip off him and had issued an ultimatum: he was to continue working with Jananga, but could have nothing more to do with Basima Khan and Logan.

Mac had no intention of complying with this, and as soon as he escaped Phelps's office, he arranged to meet Baz at the Lucky Star. He wanted her opinion on the boxes of antiquities Holmberg had left behind – what their provenance might be and, more importantly, what markets they might be destined for.

The guards at the restaurant's gates were now Jananga's men, and although he was at Police HQ supervising the questioning of the witnesses, his deputy was there, in charge of recording the crime scene. The police team were particularly subdued – one of their colleagues had been shot dead, and several had been wounded. They'd taken photographs of the basement where Bao Liang had died and were happy to let Mac and Baz investigate the contents of the remaining crates.

Mac looked around the room. The blood-stained chair still stood in situ, the floor beneath it sticky with blood, which radiated out in footprints and smudges across the room. There was no sign of fingerprint dust, no numbered markers, no crime-scene tape. The only way they would know who had been responsible for slitting Bao's throat was from a witness statement or a confession – the first was unlikely and the second would be unreliable. Afghanistan was a country that couldn't afford the mechanisms of justice.

Baz stood by his side, contemplating the scene. She sniffed, then stepped forward, taking care not to tread in any of the dried blood.

'Let's get this done,' she said. It was horrible to think of what had happened there just twenty-four hours before.

There were rectangular crates, which Mac knew without needing to look would contain assault rifles, most likely AK74s. In addition, two large wooden crates remained in one corner. Baz went over to them and pulled a short crowbar from the side pocket of the cargo pants she was wearing. She prised the lid off one of them.

'Jeez, look at this!'

Mac went over and peered into the crate. Lying amid a nest of straw was a pale grey carving of a Buddha head. Baz lifted it carefully out of the box and handed it to Mac.

'Hold it,' she said.

She pulled back more straw with her hand to reveal a second, similar Buddha head.

'They're a pair,' she said.

'Where from?'

Baz raised the second sculpture and held it next to the one Mac had, comparing the two.

'I think they're from a ruined Buddhist monastery in what was known as the kingdom of Gandhara. But we need to get these to Professor Paghahan for proper authentication.'

'You'll need Jananga's permission to move them.'

Baz glanced towards the door. 'If they go to Police HQ, I doubt we'll ever see them again.'

She took her crowbar to the second box.

'This is ivory,' she said, reverently raising a small statuette of a voluptuous naked woman out of its straw bed. 'It would have come to Afghanistan from India, probably in about the first century AD. These items are priceless.'

Mac looked at the woman.

'It's not the sort of thing I'd expect to see in a Muslim country.'

'It predates Islam, but someone must have kept it well-hidden from the Taliban,' said Baz. 'They certainly would have destroyed it as a heretical piece.' She placed it gently back into its indent in the packaging. 'We need to get these out of here. They're worth a lot of money – Holmberg might come back for them. I need to phone the professor and get him here right now.'

She pulled her phone out of another pocket in her trousers and flipped it open.

'Damn! No signal down here. I'm going to call Professor Paghahan. He can take possession of the most valuable pieces on behalf of the museum.'

They replaced the lids on the cartons and made their way back up the stairs. Baz followed the signal towards the back door and went to stand outside in the courtyard. Mac went into the mah-jong room. It looked exactly as it had the night before, with mah-jong tiles scattered everywhere. He bent down and picked one up. The red pictogram on it looked like a dagger. For no reason whatsoever, he dropped it into his pocket and went out of the room.

'Mac, how you doing? How's that arm?' Logan was coming down the corridor towards him. Persona non grata number two, but Phelps would never know.

'The painkillers have kicked in, so not bad.' He paused. It felt awkward to ask how someone was the day after their partner had been murdered. How could anyone answer that? Close up, Logan's face looked drawn and hollowed out.

'Is Baz around?'

'She's just out back, making a call.'

'I need to talk to her about that guy she shot.'

Baz reappeared in the doorway. 'Professor Paghahan's coming down here. We can't let these things disappear again.'

Logan glanced towards the doorway leading down to the cellar.

'Come on,' said Mac, 'let's go and talk in the bar.' He wasn't that keen to bump into Paghahan after their last little altercation.

There were a couple of Jananga's men still searching the restaurant floor, but they ignored the arrival of the three of them. Even though it was only mid-morning, Logan went behind the bar and helped himself to a tumbler of bourbon. He tilted the bottle in their directions by turn, but both Baz and Mac declined. It was the last thing Mac needed on top of painkillers and very little sleep.

'Right,' said Logan, after downing half of his glass, 'I need you two to tell me everything that happened last night when you came across Xioali.' With his American accent, the name sounded like an off pronunciation of the name Julie.

'She was hiding in one of the upstairs bedrooms,' said Mac, 'if that was her. A teenager. Long hair. She was in a white dress – very pale and skinny.'

'That's her.'

'She's not… not your kid, is she?' said Baz.

Logan shook his head. 'No way. I've only known Bao just over a year. But I'm fond of her, and I want to find her, make sure she's okay.'

'So, she was there in this room when Baz and I went in. We were running from Sarwani's men.'

'She pulled a gun on us and shot at Mac,' said Baz. 'I took it off her and she ran away.'

It didn't sound great, being shot by a teenage girl. Mac didn't think this was a story he'd be recounting down the years. He wasn't even sure he was going to tell Ginger.

'But you saw her again, right?'

'We needed to escape out of the window onto the flat roof,' said Baz. 'I was on the window ledge and I saw her being tugged across the garden by this guy...'

'Describe the man,' said Logan.

'I knew him. I'd seen him before when I came here to meet Ghilji – he joined us. A big Hazara guy, really tall. Short hair. Mean sonofabitch, sort of leering.'

Logan's eyes lit up. 'That's Razul,' he said quietly.

'Who?' said Mac.

'Razul. He's Holmberg's henchman.'

'I shot him,' said Baz. 'I think I got him in the leg, and she got away from him.'

Logan frowned.

'So where is she now?' said Mac.

'I don't know. Razul's an animal and he does whatever Holmberg tells him to do. Holmberg has been sniffing around Xioali – that was one of the main reasons I wanted him out of the place. If Razul was trying to grab her, you can bet Holmberg was behind it.'

'Is there anyone she could have gone to, if she got out of the compound?' said Baz.

'I can't think of anyone,' said Logan. 'I was racking my brains all night, but they didn't have any relatives here. Bao's girls were like big sisters to Xioali, but they're all at Police HQ.'

'Oh God, I'm sorry I took the gun off her, Logan.'

'She was shooting at you – you had to.'

'But if she'd had it, she might have got away.'

'Maybe she did,' said Mac.

'The place was swarming with cops, there was a gunfight going on... and if she had got away, the only person she would have known to come to would have been me. And she hasn't shown up.'

'What happened to Razul?' said Baz.

'That's the worst of it.' Logan's voice was bleak. 'He's missing too.'

Chapter 34

'Razul Rahimi?' said Jananga. He shrugged. 'We don't have computer records like you do, and many of the police files were burned by the Taliban when they were in power.'

'So you have no way of looking him up then?' said Mac.

He'd come straight to Jananga's office once Professor Paghahan had arrived at the Lucky Star to look at the artefacts. Razul Rahimi was probably their best lead to Holmberg, and possibly to Xioali Liang as well.

'I have a way,' said Jananga. 'If he worked for Holmberg the way Logan says, then I think Sarwani or some of his men will know who he is.'

'And Sarwani's just gonna give you that information?'

Jananga wrinkled his nose. 'I think it better if we question his men. That way, we're not telling Sarwani what we're up to.'

'Until one of them tells him.'

'We can keep them locked up and separated for as long as we need to, see if their answers match.'

Mac raised an eyebrow but didn't comment. He had to let Jananga work things out by his own methods.

They went across to the cell block, but Mac elected to wait outside. He had a pretty good idea of what was going to happen next. Someone was going to take a beating. And he knew that if he saw anything, he should report it to the UN High Commission for Human Rights, for what good that would do. He felt like a shit, like someone driving past a road accident and not stopping. But a British soldier had been murdered. A teenage girl was missing. So if a crooked policeman was about to get a beating...

He paced the tarmac outside the cells, not at ease and wishing he was anywhere else.

It didn't take long. Information about Razul Rahimi wasn't a hill anyone would be willing to die on. Jananga reappeared after ten minutes. He didn't look the slightest bit dishevelled. However, his sergeant appeared behind him, ominously rubbing the knuckles of one hand.

'We have uncovered the address of a garage where Razul sometimes works,' said the major. 'We'll go there now, yes?'

'Yes.' It was unlikely Razul would be working there today, after being clipped by a bullet, but they might know where he lived.

Jananga called for his driver and they climbed into the back of the Toyota Surf. Mac was glad to leave the police compound.

'Where are we headed?'

'The Ziarat Motor Garage on Chilsitun Road,' said Jananga.

'Razul's a mechanic? Not just a paid thug?'

'This is our information.'

They turned from the police station onto the Asmayi Road that headed out to the south-west, passing through the narrow stretch at the base of TV Hill. Crowded with the hovels of a thousand internal refugees, it had the reputation of being the most landmined piece of real estate in the world. Mac was glad they didn't have any reason to stop there. They took a left turn onto the Darulaman Road. It was the same route he'd come with Baz when they visited the museum. That seemed a long time ago now. Jananga's rank and ID sped them through a couple of roadblocks and for once they didn't get tangled up in one of the city's interminable gridlocks. When they reached the Dar-ul-Aman Palace at the end of the long straight road, they took a sharp left.

'This is the Chilsitun Road,' said Jananga. 'The garage should be on the left, just before the Hanzala Mosque.' He spoke in

Dari to his driver. 'I've instructed him to park some way down the road, so we can approach on foot.'

The Surf pulled up by the curb and Mac got out. There was another exchange between Jananga and his driver, Wahid. Then they set off along the pavement.

Mac could see a sign with a picture of a tow truck a little way ahead and assumed this would be the place. There was a small forecourt, packed with a jumble of ancient vehicles, and beyond it, a workshop that looked not dissimilar to how his local village garage had looked some twenty years ago – oily and chaotic. That garage was shut now, and if his parents wanted anything done on their car, they had to go to the dealership on the edge of Oban, the nearest town.

Jananga wound his way through the cars towards the workshop, and a bearded man in an oil-stained shalwar kameez came out to greet them with a toothy smile.

'*Salaam alaikum*.'

Jananga flashed his ID at the man, who suddenly looked less thrilled as he realised they weren't potential customers.

Mac tried to follow the conversation in Dari, but he actually had no idea what was being said. There were a lot of arm gestures and frowning, their voices growing louder with each exchange.

Jananga turned to Mac. 'He says he doesn't really work here, and he doesn't know the other mechanics. He's minding it for the boss, who's gone to have tea with a customer. I've told him to call the boss back.'

The temporary custodian threw up his arms and retreated into the workshop. Jananga followed him, and Mac brought up the rear. The man went to the back of the space, where there was a bench piled up with old spare parts and tools that looked as if they'd seen better days. He plucked a dirty mobile phone from amid the carnage. Turning back to Jananga, he said something and threw the phone down.

'The phone has no charge,' muttered Jananga.

'Gulab!' the man said sharply.

A body slid out from under a car, and a teenage grease monkey stood up. He was duly instructed to fetch the garage owner from a nearby teahouse.

'This is all wasting time,' said Jananga as he finished translating for Mac.

They waited in silence for ten minutes, Jananga circling the workshop as if he was inspecting it, the man following his every move with nervous eyes. Mac went back out onto the forecourt to look at the cars, but they weren't really of interest. Ageing Toyotas with too many miles on the clock – probably just being harvested for parts, looking at the state of most of them.

Finally, a white-haired Hazara arrived in the company of Gulab. He was more deferential to Jananga than his deputy had been, and this time Mac heard the name Razul Rahimi mentioned in the conversation. The old man shook his head. Too vehemently, in Mac's opinion. An instant rebuttal of whatever Jananga had asked him. Like he hadn't even stopped to think or consider.

Mac reached into his pocket and brought out a roll of ten-dollar bills. Company money. He unspooled three of them and held them up in his other hand.

'You know Razul Rahimi?'

Jananga frowned at him, but he could see the old man's expression wavering, even as he continued to shake his head.

Mac added another bill to the clutch. 'We just need to ask him a couple of questions.'

Jananga said something – Mac assumed he was translating what he'd just said.

The old man nodded and talked for a couple of minutes, with Jananga interjecting frequent questions. Mac could only presume he was being given some useful information. Eventually the conversation drew to a close and, after Mac handed over the money, there was a formal leave-taking.

'*Tashakor. Khuda hafiz.*' Thank you. Goodbye. It was just about the first thing Mac had understood.

They went back out onto the pavement and turned to go up the street towards the Surf.

'You know, you didn't have to pay him your money to get answers.'

'Bribing him was quicker. And it wasn't my money. It was WTP's. So what did he say?'

'The garage owner says that he's occasionally used Razul, but only if his other mechanics are off. He hasn't seen him for several weeks, but thinks that he lives—'

Jananga's words were ripped from his mouth by a huge explosion thirty metres up the road, and both of them were thrown onto their backs by a rush of burning air.

Chapter 35

Mac opened his eyes and blinked furiously to clear the dust. The world still existed. He was lying on the pavement on Chilsitun Road. His ears were ringing. A bomb had gone off, somewhere nearby. His chest hurt and he was overcome by a coughing fit. He spat filthy phlegm onto the concrete and tried to clear his throat. Every muscle and bone of his body felt like it had been run over by a juggernaut.

'Jesus...'

What had he been doing here? He'd been with someone. Jananga.

He gingerly raised a hand to his face and rubbed his eyes. He struggled to sit up.

'Major?'

There was a loud groan from a few feet away.

A woman ran up to them, her hijab crooked and her clothes covered in dust. Tears ran down her cheeks, and she shouted something in Pashtun, and then started wailing.

Mac rubbed his face and made an attempt at standing up. It didn't work. One ankle buckled and his knee cracked down onto the pavement. He put out a hand to steady himself and turned to look round in the direction of the groan. Jananga was lying on the ground nearby. There was blood on his face, but he was moving.

'Are you okay, Major?'

'I'm alive,' said Jananga, and then swore in a stream of Dari.

238

The wailing woman meandered away from them and into the middle of the road – the traffic had ground to a standstill. In the distance, Mac heard a siren. He rubbed his eyes again and tried to assess what had happened.

He looked towards where the blast had come from. Thirty metres up the road, the tangled wreckage of a vehicle was ablaze. The cars that had been parked either side of it hadn't fared much better – their windows were blown out and the force of the blast had shunted them into the cars beyond that. Mac stared at the scene. He wasn't getting something. Then it came to him. That was where they'd parked. He looked harder at the vehicles. Where was the Surf? Had Jananga's driver moved it while they'd been talking in the garage? Why would he have done that?

He hadn't.

The twisted, burning wreck at the epicentre *was* the Surf.

'Shit!' This time when he scrambled to his feet, he managed to stay upright.

He turned to the major and held out a hand. Jananga raised his arm and Mac pulled him to his feet.

'That was your vehicle.'

'I know,' said Jananga, wiping blood from his forehead with his sleeve. 'My driver… we need to find Wahid.'

He set off at a trot towards the remains of the Surf. Heart racing, Mac followed him, still struggling to breathe as he coughed more dust out of his lungs. People were running up the pavement, away from the site, shouting and crying as they ran. Some had minor shrapnel wounds and most were coated with grey dust. Mac had to swerve to one side to get out of the way of two men who were carrying an injured woman between them. As the dust began to settle, the air was still thick with acrid, black smoke. On the other side of the road a small child stood howling, no parent in sight.

As they reached the Surf, the full horror of what had happened became clear. A few feet from the burning car, a mangled torso oozed black blood onto the pavement. Mac looked around – closer to the wreckage, just where the driver's door would have been, a solitary boot stood, soaked in blood, while beyond the body, he saw part of an arm. There was a stink like burnt meat. Bile rose in his throat, he could taste vomit, and he swallowed hard. His mouth filled with saliva and his eyes watered. He had to look away.

'Wahid!' Jananga's voice broke over the two syllables. When he repeated the name, it was almost a cry as he ran out into the middle of the road.

Mac followed him with his eyes. Jananga dropped to his knees in front of something.

Wahid's head.

Again, Mac looked away. What if that had been Ginger, or Ahmed or Pamir?

Fuck!

The driver must have left the car unattended. Surely, he would have known not to do that? Why hadn't they brought more men with them?

The local police arrived, blue lights flashing, siren blaring, and jumped out of their car. They barked instructions at the rubberneckers who were gathering to stare open-mouthed at the carnage. An ambulance drew up – too late for Wahid, but there were plenty of people with shrapnel wounds and a man with one side of his face and head badly burned.

Another car full of policemen arrived and Jananga instructed them to form a perimeter around the area, moving people on. Mac scanned the crowd. Was whoever planted the bomb still here, watching the fallout of their action?

He pulled his phone out of his trousers and, thankfully, the screen still came to life when he switched it on. He wanted to take some photos of the scene, just in case they could pick out a suspect in the small crowd of onlookers. The Afghan police couldn't be relied on when it came to forensics – and if this bomb had been targeting him and Jananga, he wanted to know who was responsible. He turned a slow circle, snapping pictures in the circumference of the blast – people helping the wounded, and others gawping at the carnage. Then he called Baz – this was certainly something she'd want to cover for the newspaper.

—

Baz arrived at the same time as the Explosive Ordnance Disposal technicians from Camp Souter. Bomb disposal was another area the Afghan police were lacking in, so any blasts in the city were attended by teams appointed by the multinational Internal Security Assistance Force. Mac watched Baz photographing the scene out of the corner of his eye, as the EOD technicians' Snatch and its accompanying armed Land Rover parked up. Jananga was arguing with the district police chief about the way to run the scene and three more ambulances blocked the road.

He caught Baz's eye.

'Sorry you have to see this – it's pretty grim.'

She lowered her camera and looked up at him. 'It's part of my job as a reporter to record events like this.'

'Thanks. I've taken some pictures already, but could you take more? They might prove useful in building a timeline of what happened.'

She gave him a mirthless smile. 'Anything I can do to help.'

Baz wasn't the only reporter jostling for pictures through the ranks of uniformed police.

'Can you all stay back, beyond the cordon?' Mac said to a clutch of men with cameras, but most of them ignored him, intent on getting a money shot they could sell to the newspapers and news channels back home.

Baz snapped a picture of the ambulance crew kneeling over Wahid's torso. 'Were you the target? You and Jananga?'

Mac glanced across to the EOD vehicle. The officer in charge was looking around expectantly.

He nodded, but said, 'I don't have time to go into the details with you now. Maybe later.'

He went over to the EOD Snatch and introduced himself. If the officer was surprised at Mac's unofficial status, he didn't let it show.

'I'm Captain Jardine of 11 EOD. Run through what happened.'

There wasn't much to tell, so they went across to the remains of the Surf. An ambulance crew had removed the bloody boot, but the ground on the driver's side of the car was awash with blood.

Mac grimaced. Less than an hour ago Wahid had been singing along to a tinny Bollywood pop song that was playing on the radio and Jananga had snapped at him to shut up. Jardine stood staring at the burnt-out Surf for several minutes. He beckoned one of his men over and instructed him to photograph the wreck from every angle. Then he turned to Mac.

'Hold on,' said Mac. He looked around for Jananga. 'Major? You'll probably want to hear this.'

Jananga came over to join them and Mac quickly made the introductions. The major was grim-faced, his forehead and cheeks still stained with blood from where he'd hit the pavement.

'We're looking at a small IED, improvised explosive device,' said Jardine. 'Only a couple of pounds maybe.' He pointed at tangled metal where the driver's door would have been. 'My suspicion is that it was attached magnetically, just underneath the driver's seat. We'll take a closer look underneath in a moment.'

'How would they have detonated it?' said Mac.

'The easiest – and therefore the most common – way to set one of these things off is with a mercury tilt switch.'

'Explain,' said Jananga.

'It's basically a glass tube with mercury at one end. When someone leans on the car or gets into it, the suspension moves and the tube gets tilted. The mercury runs down the tube where it completes an electrical circuit that detonates the bomb.'

Jardine glanced round. 'Looking at the distribution of the body parts, your driver was outside the vehicle when it went off – possibly he leant against the door, and that kicked it off.'

Jananga nodded. 'He wasn't allowed to smoke in the car.'

'Is there any reason why your car should have been targeted?' Jardine said to Jananga. 'Different groups have different signatures, and it might give us a hint as to what we're looking at.'

Jananga gave him a look that Mac had come to recognise, and then sighed. 'I'm head investigator for the city police. I have the police chief of District Four in my cells for murdering one of my officers. I'm investigating the death of a British soldier, the flight of a foreign national who smuggles guns and antiques, and the disappearance of a Chinese teenager. Also my cousin has declared a blood feud on my other cousin over a woman.'

Jardine's eyes widened steadily as Jananga spoke.

'Why would I not be a target?'

Chapter 36

Thursday, 18 December 2003

Baz wondered if Mac's punctuality was a Brit thing or down to him having been a policeman. Whichever it was, he was there when he said he would be, at a quarter past ten, sitting in the bar in the Gandamack Lodge before she came down – and she was dead on time. She looked him up and down. There was a certain drawn quality to his face, but the dust that had coated him from head to toe at the bombsite had been showered off. It was hardly surprising that he looked tired. He'd been shot at and blown up in the space of two days, and even for a man with his background, that was going some.

'Hey, good to see you,' she said.

'And you, Calamity.' He grinned at her.

He already had a beer in front of him, so she ordered a glass of white wine. It came from California, which seemed a long way for it to come – but that made it a little taste from home.

'Let's move elsewhere,' said Baz. The trouble with sitting at the bar was that there was always someone leaning over your shoulder, trying to get a drink. And invariably listening in on your conversation. She needed Mac to be able to talk freely about what had happened earlier.

She led the way to a small alcove in the corner of the room, filled by a slumping sofa and close to the small pot-bellied stove that kept the place cosy. Mac took a moment before sitting down to study a gun mounted on the wall nearby.

'Wow, a Boys Anti-Tank Rifle,' he said, tipping his glass in its direction. 'Commonly known as the elephant gun. Wonder where he got it...'

Baz found herself watching him as he appraised the weapon. He was fit, easy on the eye.

Mac sat down.

'Slange,' he said, raising his glass to her.

'That's Scottish for cheers, right?'

'Aye,' he said, hamming up his Scottish accent.

'Slange,' said Baz, taking a sip of her wine. 'Whereabouts in Scotland are you from?'

'Oban. Well, near Oban. My parents have a farm near a wee village called Ardshellach, about ten miles from Oban.'

'Oban's a city?'

Mac's burst of laughter took her by surprise. 'More like a small town. Or a glorified village.'

'I'd like to see it someday,' she said. Then, suddenly worried that she'd sounded a bit forward, she quickly changed the subject. 'How's your arm?'

His hand went to where the bullet had skimmed his bicep, but his face brightened. 'Could be worse, but it took another slight knock when the bomb blew me over.'

'Any clear ideas of who planted it yet?' she said.

'I'll have to wait to see what the IED expert says, though he was already of the view that it wasn't the Taliban. Not their style of bomb. But further than that... I think we'll just be looking closer at the most likely suspects.'

'Holmberg and his gang?'

'Or possibly one of Jananga's other enemies.'

'He's bound to have plenty of those given his job,' said Baz, taking a sip of her wine.

Mac filled her in on how they'd got the address of the garage where Razul worked from one of the District Four police officers. 'This information is strictly off the record, you realise?'

'All of it?' she said.

'At least for now. We spoke to the garage owner, another Hazara, and he admitted Razul had worked for him on occasion, but claimed he hadn't seen him for some time.'

'Did you believe him?'

'Good question,' said Mac. 'We paid for the information, but that doesn't make it reliable. However, it's probably the only answer he'd ever give, whether he'd seen him or not.'

'How long were you away from the car?'

'Fifteen, twenty minutes. Wahid was supposed to stay with it, but clearly he didn't. The bomb went off when he returned to the vehicle – just as we were making our way back to it too.'

'You were lucky.'

Mac shook his head. 'If Wahid had stayed by the Surf, there would have been no bomb at all – he'd still be alive, and we wouldn't have been blown over. That's what I would call being lucky.' He polished off the remains of his beer. 'Anyway, let's compare the pictures we took at the blast site.'

Mac got out his phone and opened his photos file, while Baz flipped open her laptop and brought up her portfolio to find the set of images from that afternoon. All the pictures showed carnage and chaos – men, women and children running in all directions, like grey, dusty ghosts – only someone had taken a brush laden with red paint and flicked it across the pictures like a spatter painting. Blood. A large quantity of it was Wahid's, but there were others with blast injuries, bleeding freely as people carried them to safety. Police and paramedics swarmed like black ants among the grey victims.

Mac scrolled through Baz's images. 'It takes guts to take pictures like these. Guts and a steady hand.'

'I didn't feel steady,' said Baz. She'd felt sick and shocked. It wasn't the first time she'd photographed the aftermath of a car bomb, but that didn't make it any less horrific.

Mac flicked back and forth between his own pictures and hers, then stopped on one particular image on his phone.

'Look at this,' he said, pointing at a doorway, several metres up the street from the main impact of the blast.

As Baz looked, he switched to another image – the same view, taken about fifteen seconds later, according to the timestamp on the picture.

'And this.' Another, more than a minute later.

Baz studied them. In each of the shots Mac had singled out, there was a shadow pressed against the near side of the doorway. A dark figure. A man.

'I think he's watching,' said Mac.

'You would watch, wouldn't you, if you lived nearby?' said Baz.

Mac shook his head. 'No, no one else in these pictures is just standing, watching. People are helping others, or trying to get away from the area. Let's check if he's in any of your pictures.'

Baz's images of the same spot had been taken some ten minutes later – and the shadowy figure had disappeared. They looked at her whole sequence of shots, eager to see if she'd caught him leaving so they'd know which direction he'd gone in – but he seemed to have vanished in a puff of smoke.

Baz scrutinised the figure again, but it was hard to make out his facial features. 'Who do you think it is?'

'I think,' said Mac slowly, 'it's someone who's interested in the outcome of what happened. Someone who wanted to know who had been killed and who had survived.'

Baz looked up and their eyes met.

'I think maybe it's Holmberg's henchman, Razul. You met him. What do you think?'

Baz thought about the tall Hazara she'd met with Ghilji at the Lucky Star. She compared the figure's height to the people passing nearby on the pavement. The man in the shadows was tall.

'I think you could be right.'

Chapter 37

Friday, 19 December 2003

Chicken Street. Totally unique, but always the same, always busy. Baz and Javid hurried past the Chelsea Supermarket and on towards Ghilji's antiquity shop. They were running late – the traffic had been the usual nightmare – and Baz had been subjected to twenty minutes of Javid's mounting disapproval which seemed to blossom exponentially with each expedition here.

'But Basima-jan,' he'd said for what must have been the tenth time, 'this place is dangerous. These are bad people you are mixing with.'

'I'm not mixing with them,' Baz had replied. 'I'm doing my job, Javid-jan, and you're not my *mahram*.'

Now she was purposefully striding ahead of him, lips pursed and ears deaf to his moaning. Baseer Ghilji had called her and said that his contact was at the shop and would wait there to talk to her if she could come right away. She couldn't afford to miss this chance – when she met Ghilji's contact, she'd be able to start joining the dots on how the stolen antiquities trade hung together and how Ghilji's shop was linked to the Lucky Star and Holmberg.

She tried Mac's phone again, but he wasn't picking up. She thought about leaving a message, but she didn't want him barging into the middle of things, so she left it.

'Wait out here, please, Javid-jan,' she said in a more conciliatory tone.

248

He frowned at her and patted the bulge in his shalwar kameez made by his pistol. 'Are you sure I shouldn't come in with you?'

'I'm sure.'

She pushed open the door to the shop and announced herself in the customary manner.

'*Salaam alaikum.*'

'*Alaikum a'salaam,*' said Ghilji, materialising from a small alcove on one side of the shop floor. 'It is good to see you again, Miss Khan. Are you well?'

'I am well, thank you. And you're well?'

He gave a small half bow to indicate that he was. 'And your mother, how is she?'

Baz allowed a flicker of pain to cross her features. 'It's a difficult time.'

Ghilji nodded dolefully as if he cared, and Baz's heart filled with hatred for the man.

'Your associate is still here?'

'Yes. Come through to the back.'

Baz had never seen the man who was waiting for them in Ghilji's inner sanctum, but she knew immediately that this was Olle Holmberg. The Swede. Immensely tall and rangy, with a cowlick of straw-coloured hair, an aquiline nose and crystalline blue eyes, it couldn't be anyone else. She just prayed that the recognition hadn't shown on her face.

He stood up when she came into the room, and extended a hand.

'This is Basima Khan,' said Ghilji.

Baz's heart was in her mouth as she stepped forward to greet him – until she worked out that he wouldn't necessarily know that she'd been at the raid on the Lucky Star. She swallowed and shook his hand. His grasp was firm, his hand warm and dry.

'Hi,' she said.

'I'm Olle Holmberg. Please, sit down.'

She took a place on a low sofa opposite the chair from which Holmberg had risen.

'Baseer tells me that you're looking to buy some Achaemenid coins.'

'I have a friend who collects them.'

'Interesting,' said Holmberg. 'What's your friend's name? Maybe I've done business with him before.'

'I don't think so,' said Baz.

Holmberg didn't look surprised that she was unwilling to share her friend's name.

Ghilji placed a brass tea tray on the low table between them, and poured three glasses of green tea from a small silver pot.

Holmberg picked up one of the glasses and drank. When he put it down, he fixed Baz with his sharp gaze.

'One of my contacts has come across a cache of Achaemenid coins. He's willing to sell them – for a price.'

'Of course,' said Baz. 'They're very valuable. Do you have them here for me to look at?'

'I've brought some with me. There are sixty-three coins in all. If the samples I've brought are what you're looking for, I can arrange for you to see the entire collection.'

'Thank you,' said Baz. She picked up a sugar cube, popped it in her mouth and sipped her tea through it in the traditional Afghan manner as she'd watched her parents do a thousand times.

Holmberg reached down and picked up a canvas bag that was on the floor next to his chair. He opened it on his lap, and pulled out a smaller bag. From this he withdrew two packages swathed in bubble wrap. He put them on the table and unfurled the plastic wrapping. As he did, Baz saw a glint of gold and then Holmberg placed two small, round coins in front of her.

She leaned forward and picked one of them up. She studied it carefully, turning it over in her hand, examining the details on either side. There was a kneeling man, with a crown and a staff on one side, an indistinct rectangular depression on the other. She assessed the weight of it and the thickness. Then she put it down and picked up the other one. It was similar, although the crowned figure on this one carried a spear in one hand and a bow in the other.

'Are they all like this?'

Holmberg nodded. 'All very similar, mostly silver, a handful of gold ones like these.'

'What price is your contact thinking of?'

'Are you interested in the whole hoard or just individual coins?'

'That will depend entirely on the price, and the quality of all the other coins. I assume you've brought the best examples to show me?'

Holmberg frowned. 'Like I said, they are all very similar. My friend is looking for two thousand dollars for each of the gold coins, and one hundred and forty dollars per silver coin.'

Baz looked at them for a few minutes longer.

'The prices seem a little high to me.'

'I think you will find that this price is a bargain, Miss Khan. You – or should I say, your friend – will be able to sell them on for substantially more when you get them to America.'

'At considerable risk,' said Baz.

Holmberg shrugged. 'I'm sure you will be able to find a way to smuggle them through customs.'

'I must think about it and talk to my friend.'

'Of course,' said Ghilji.

He clearly wanted the sale to go ahead. Baz wondered what his cut of it would be.

Baz carefully placed the two coins back into their bubble-wrap sleeves, taking the time to consider what she was about to say.

'However, I feel certain I can speak for my friend now. Two thousand dollars a piece is way too much to expect us to pay for coins that are obviously fake.'

Ghilji stood up abruptly, shaking the table as he knocked it with his knee.

'Basima-jan,' he said, 'you cannot mean what you are saying.'

'I'm afraid I do. These coins have sharp edges. Real Achaemenid coins date back to before the birth of Christ. They're fashioned from soft alloys – the edges are rounded and the faces worn. These have quite obviously been manufactured recently.'

Holmberg studied her with interest but said nothing.

Ghilji was showing signs of agitation. Of course – the deal was about to fall through and he wouldn't be getting his share.

'You're wrong, Basima. You are besmirching the honour of my friend. I cannot let you do this.'

Basima shrugged. 'Your friend shouldn't try to sell fake artefacts.'

'Tell her, Olle.'

But Olle Holmberg shook his head. 'No, Baseer, she's right. These aren't real Achaemenid coins. I was just testing her knowledge to see if she was a genuine buyer.'

'You were trying to rip me off,' said Baz.

'Well, if you'd been willing to pay that money for fakes, sure, I wouldn't have stopped you. But the purpose was to assess whether you knew what you were talking about. I do actually have a cache of real Achaemenid coins that I could sell to you – if you're still interested.'

'I'm interested, but no more bullshit, Mr Holmberg.'

Fast as a pouncing cobra, Holmberg grabbed hold of her wrist. He applied an intense pressure to the bones on either side and a sharp pain shot up Baz's arm.

'Don't ever speak to me like that again.'

His gaze seemed to cut right through her and for a moment Baz was scared. But just as suddenly, he let go and his face transformed to a friendly smile.

'It will be good, if we can do business together,' he said.

Baz nodded, not trusting herself to speak.

The Swede held out his hand once more. She shook it, but this time it made her flesh crawl. It would seem she really was dancing with the devil, and maybe Professor Paghahan and Javid were right – these were people she should steer clear of.

Chapter 38

'Screw you!' said Mac, but not before he was sure the call had disconnected.

Lambert had a nerve. He'd called demanding an update on the case as he felt he wasn't getting anything from Jananga. His assumption had been that because Marshall was a Brit and Mac was a Brit, that Mac would be a team player, on their side, presenting a united front against the corrupt Afghan administration.

'Major Lambert, I've seen no evidence of corruption on the part of Major Jananga. He's not covering anything up and we're doing our damnedest to find out what happened to Captain Marshall.'

Lambert hadn't been mollified. 'Your presence on this investigation is still questionable, so I would have thought it would behove you to co-operate with Captain Holder.'

'And I certainly have.'

Lambert grunted with disbelief. 'Listen, MacKenzie, it would only take a few words from me in the right ears to make your employment prospects in this country untenable for the foreseeable future.'

'Is that a threat, Major? Because it sure sounds like one to me – and I should warn you, I don't take well to being threatened.'

Lambert could go boil his head.

He called Pamir to bring the Land Cruiser round. He had a meeting with Captain Jardine at Police HQ.

Jananga was scanning a copy of Jardine's initial report into the IED when Mac arrived in his office. Mac took the other chair.

'So, Captain, what's your assessment?'

'We've seen a lot of IEDs like this recently. Mercury tilt switch, very basic components – something somebody could easily put together. Not sophisticated, but still effective.' At least he didn't seem to have caught Lambert's cynicism.

'Taliban?' said Mac.

Jardine shook his head. 'No, we don't think so. Taliban IEDs are slightly different. They don't tend to use mercury switches. They favour remote detonation, and build theirs out of Soviet ordnance. This one was built from scratch using plastic explosive – the analysis isn't back yet to tell us if it was PE4, Semtex or something similar, which makes it harder to ascribe to any particular group. However, there were traces of mercury in the wreckage – hence the switch.'

Jananga cleared his throat. 'Last night, my men rounded up and brought in a number of local informants. Under rigorous questioning it would appear that this attack had nothing to do with the Taliban.'

'You're sure?' said Mac.

'We keep a close watch on their activities. People know who they are, and they haven't forgotten what it was like when the Taliban ruled. Plenty are willing to talk to us.'

'That assessment gels with ours,' said Jardine. 'Did anyone know you were going to be at that address?'

'No.' Mac shook his head. 'We were given information by a man in custody and went straight there. Someone must have followed us.' He thought about their journey the previous day, but the only person who would have been looking in the rear-view mirror was no longer around to ask.

Once Jardine had left, he brought up the images on his phone.

'Look,' he said, tapping the screen. 'There's a man who stands watching. He doesn't help the injured, or talk to the police about what he's seen. Do you think it could be Razul?'

'If it is, the old man at the garage was lying,' said Jananga. 'I think we need to go and talk to him again.'

'I agree. Major, have you got a picture of Razul on file? We need to know we're going after the right man.'

Jananga looked affronted. 'I told you already – our files were mostly destroyed by the Taliban.'

Mac hadn't meant it as a dig. He wondered how long Jananga would continue to be prickly about almost everything.

'Okay, let's bring Logan with us. He knows what Razul looks like. All we know is that he's a tall Hazara – but Razul could walk past us on the street and we'd be none the wiser.'

Mac called Logan and arranged that they would pick him up from the Mustafa Hotel. Then he called Ginger to come and join them.

Eventually, after Logan and Pamir had nearly come to blows over whether it would be quicker to go down the Darulaman Road or take the more circuitous Chilsitun Road from Bagh Babur, they were once again parking up close to the garage where Razul supposedly worked. Jananga was waiting for them, leaning against an identical Toyota Surf to the one that had been blown up the day before. His new driver was sitting in the car – and no doubt would be under strict instructions to stay there.

Mac led the way into the garage and this time the old man was there, lecturing one of his boy mechanics in sharpish tones. His words evaporated on his tongue as the group of men blocked the sunlight streaming through the open garage door.

He shooed the boy away.

'*Salaam alaikum*,' he said, addressing Jananga first.

'*Alaikum a'salaam*,' Jananga replied, but that was about as polite as it got. After that the volume rose, and so did the tempo of the major's speech. Jananga was here to accuse the man of lying and though Mac couldn't understand what he was saying, it was clear he wasn't mincing his words.

The man protested in a whining voice, no doubt trying to make excuses, but this only served to make Jananga more severe. His sergeant, hovering at his shoulder, interjected fiercely and earned himself a withering glance from his superior.

Mac's phone buzzed and he surreptitiously slipped it from his pocket to look at the screen. It was Baz. Now wasn't the time, though, to take a call.

He looked up to see the sergeant take a step forward with his arm raised and his fist bunched.

'Whoa! Is that necessary?' he said. Jananga's sergeant was several decades younger and considerably more bulky than the old man who stood quaking before them.

Jananga's head whipped round. 'Please stay out of this, Mac. We are dealing with it. We don't need your dollars this time.'

Mac's phone buzzed again and Jananga glared at him, before he turned back to talk to the man.

Logan had watched the entire exchange in silence, and once Jananga's attention was back on the garage owner, he shook his head at Mac.

'Don't worry,' he said under his breath. 'The old guy will spill before they do any real damage to him.'

Logan was right. The threat of violence was enough to loosen the old man's tongue and within minutes it seemed he was all but telling them his life story. Mac waited patiently, wondering how much of the information the man was giving them would be relayed to him in English. Razul's name was mentioned several times and finally Jananga seemed satisfied that they'd got what they'd come for. He turned to Mac.

'There's a village, about an hour's drive from Kabul – to the north-west, Istalif. That's where Razul's family come from and apparently he's gone there to visit his mother.'

'So that can't have been Razul watching from the doorway?'

Jananga tilted his head from side to side. 'Maybe. He left late yesterday according to Haji here.'

'Did he see Razul yesterday?'

Jananga translated the question for the old man. His eyes darted from side to side as if he was looking for an escape route, or for someone to come and rescue him. Finally, he muttered something.

'Yes. No. He thinks maybe it was the day before.' Jananga looked exasperated and the sergeant loomed in closer to Haji.

Haji spoke again.

'Yes, he was around here yesterday, asking about shift work. He was limping – said he'd caught his leg on a piece of rusted metal.'

Where Baz's bullet had clipped him during the raid, thought Mac to himself.

'Ask him if he knows anything about the girl, Bao's daughter, Xiaoli.'

Jananga spoke to him again, and the old man shook his head.

'Nothing. He's never heard of her.'

'If Razul has her, he might have taken her to Istalif to hide her,' said Logan.

'Or he might have handed her over to Holmberg,' said Mac.

They left the garage.

'We know now where Razul is,' said Jananga. 'We can go and pick him up. But we don't know where Holmberg is.'

'But Razul might know. So tomorrow, we go to Istalif,' said Mac.

His phone buzzed once more, and then again when he ignored it.

'Damn – I'd better take this.' He put the phone to his ear. 'Hello.'

'It's me,' said Baz at the other end.

'Yeah?'

'I've just seen Holmberg. He tried to sell me fake antiquities.'

'Shit! Where is he?'

'I followed him when he left Ghilji's shop on Chicken Street but I just lost him.'

'Where are you?'

There was a moment's silence at the end of the line.

'Baz?'

'Shaheed Mazari Road. He turned off into a maze of tiny streets and we were too far back to see where he went.'

'What the hell were you playing at? He's a dangerous man.'

'My driver's armed.'

'He knew you were following him.'

'No way.'

'Classic evasion tactic… and now he'll come after you. You need to get the hell out of there.'

Chapter 39

Mac needed to see for himself that Baz was okay – and to make her understand exactly how dangerous it might have been for her to take on Holmberg single-handedly. A visit to Gandamack didn't count as part of the investigation, so there was no need to involve Ginger or Jananga. He would get Pamir to drive him over, check she was all right, and be back to Julien in time for an early night.

It was getting dark as they turned up Sulh Road and headed towards Shirpur Square. Baz had confirmed over the phone that she was back safely, adding that how she saw fit to do her job was none of his business. But when he'd suggested he come over for a drink, she'd sounded more friendly.

'Top-smelling cologne you have on, sir,' Pamir had commented with a grin as Mac had climbed into the front of the Land Cruiser.

Damn! He was fooling no one and now, the closer they got to the Gandamack, he was wondering whether he should simply order Pamir to turn around and go back to the camp.

But he didn't.

And he was glad he hadn't when he'd almost collided with Baz going into the bar, and she'd given him a wide grin as he let her go ahead. She looked relieved to see him. They sat in the same alcove as before, by the elephant gun, and Mac fetched a bottle of white wine from the bar before settling down on the sofa next to her.

'How the hell did you get an appointment to see Holmberg?' said Mac as soon as the wine was poured.

'I didn't know it was going to be Holmberg. Baseer Ghilji called me to come and meet a contact who could source Achaemenid coins for me.'

'And Holmberg showed up. How did you know it was him?'

'The hair. The eyes. Not exactly a local. But, also, he introduced himself.'

Why? Surely he'd be lying low after what happened at the Lucky Star.

'And did he have the coins?'

'He tried to palm off some fakes. Then, when I challenged him, he said he was testing my knowledge.'

'He knows who you are, that you're a journalist?'

'Baseer does,' she said with a shrug.

Mac took a sip of wine.

'You shouldn't have followed him. You should have called me or Jananga.'

'Duh – I tried but neither of you picked up.'

It was true – they'd just gone into the garage to question the Hazara when Baz's first call had come through. He wished he'd answered it, but it hadn't been the right thing to do at the time.

'It was dangerous.'

'If I'd waited for you to arrive, I would have lost him.'

'But what was your plan?'

'I was just going to see where he went – it might give us a lead on where he's taken the artefacts he removed from the Lucky Star.'

'Us? I'm not looking for stolen artefacts, Baz. I'm investigating a murder.'

'But the two are linked, I'm certain of it.'

She was probably right. They ordered another bottle of wine and some food, and settled into discussing how this might be the case.

Not very clever, given that Mac had dismissed Pamir with the intention of driving himself back to Julien. But then he'd only intended to have a glass or two.

\-

They talked into the small hours, about the case and about other things. After a while it became apparent that Baz was drunk. He knew he was too. So when she suggested it, he stayed the night.

Nothing had happened. He slept on the floor of Baz's room on a concoction of cushions, with a blanket, but it had been good, all the same. A hint of something to come, maybe, and a small snatch of intimacy that had been missing from his life for so long.

In the morning, he woke up early and allowed himself the luxury of watching her sleep for a few minutes. Then he tiptoed to the bathroom for a quick shower. When he emerged, Baz was still asleep. He picked up his jacket and his car keys and walked towards the door.

'Thanks.' She wasn't sleeping after all.

'For what?'

'Just for being around.' She pulled the covers up, almost over her head.

'You're welcome,' said Mac. But not until he was out in the corridor. 'See you soon.'

\-

Now he was running late for the planned departure to Istalif to pick up Razul. He and Ginger were supposed to liaise at Police HQ to pick up Jananga, with two vehicles of men, setting off for Istalif at 0800 in convoy. Logan was going to meet them at the police station and ride shotgun in the Land Cruiser. It made sense for him to come along – he knew what Razul looked like, and had more tactical experience than Mac. With his interest in retrieving Xiaoli, he would be an asset to the team.

Thanks to a roadblock between the Gandamack and Camp Julien, it was now a few minutes after seven and Mac needed to grab his gear and get out – no time for breakfast, and he was cursing himself for not setting the alarm on his phone for half an hour earlier. Not that that diminished the dumb grin pasted across his features as he quickly changed, grabbed his pack and his weapon and sprinted across the tarmac to where Ginger was leaning impatiently against the bonnet of the Land Cruiser, smoking a cigarette.

'Morning,' said Mac. He wasn't going to apologise or make excuses for running late.

'Morning,' said Ginger, grinding out the half-smoked cig under the heel of his boot. 'Of course I didn't notice that you weren't in your container last night, so I won't ask you where you were.'

'Good. Don't.' He knew his grin was probably a giveaway, but he wasn't going to name any names.

Thankfully, the journey across to Police HQ was delay-free, and within the hour they were heading up Sarak-E-Kabul Charikar Road out of Kabul. Pamir was driving, with Ginger next to him in the front, while Jananga, Mac and Logan sat in the back to enable them to discuss tactics. One of Jananga's police Surfs led the convoy, followed by the Land Cruiser, with another police vehicle bringing up the rear. As they drove north, the city gave way to the flat farmlands of the Shomali Plain – mostly dry brown fields at this time of year, punctuated by a few scrubby trees, bare of leaves, and strange dovecote-like structures that Jananga told him were used for drying grapes. The traffic was sparse outside the city – ancient Toyotas and the odd, even more elderly Mercedes, and the ubiquitous Afghan 'jingle' trucks that looked more like festival floats, intricately decorated in pink and red and green, shimmering with ribbons, carved flowers and bunting. The flat plains quickly crumpled into the rolling foothills that would eventually become the soaring mass of the Hindu Kush, but down here the hills were low and free from snow.

However, it wasn't a sight-seeing tour, and for most of the hour's drive, Mac, Logan and Jananga discussed their strategy for picking up Razul. Assuming he was still there. Jananga had spoken to the Istalif captain of police to establish that the Rahimi family did indeed have a compound there, and where exactly it was.

'He knew the family,' he reported. 'Razul's uncle is the oldest, then Razul's father, and two sisters. Each of them have children and grandchildren. The family lives in a compound on the south side of the river, just to the west of the village centre.'

'How will we know we have the right house?' said Mac.

'My information is that it's the third one after the street turns a sharp corner,' said Jananga.

'And the name of the street?'

'No name,' said Jananga with a shrug. 'He just explained to me how I get there from the ruins of the palace.' He looked out of the window and sighed. 'It used to be one of the most beautiful villages in all of Afghanistan, surrounded by orchards and vineyards, but the war... much of it has been destroyed. It was on the frontline between the Taliban and Masood's Northern Alliance. I fought here and good men died.'

'I'm sorry,' said Mac.

'This is where I lost one of my older brothers, Farhad. I'm still searching for the man that killed him.' Jananga's mouth set in a grim, hard line.

'You know who was responsible?'

Jananga nodded. 'Yes. It was a well-known Taliban commander. My brother was lying wounded on the ground. I saw the man walk up to him and shoot him in the head in cold blood.' He lowered his voice. 'When I find him, I will kill him.'

Mac wondered what it would be like to have a war in one's own country... if he had to defend Oban from foreign attackers or fight hand-to-hand combat through the tiny streets of Ardshellach. War was something always far from home for him. But Jananga had seen family members shot, and had no doubt shot men himself. How had that affected him?

They turned off the main highway onto a narrow road and Mac took careful note of the unfamiliar surroundings as they climbed away from the valley floor. As pre-arranged, the first police vehicle pulled over and let the Land Cruiser take the lead, so Jananga could direct them to the Rahimi house.

He started to see evidence of the fighting Jananga had talked about. On either side of the road, there were burnt-out buildings, crumbling walls without roofs, piles of rubble and stretches of land where nature was starting to encroach on what had once been farmed. Some houses had been entirely destroyed, while others appeared unscathed and still inhabited. Closer to the centre of the village, there was plenty of evidence of repair work and rebuilding going on – but it still looked like a place that had had the soul punched out of it.

A woman at the side of the road stared at them as they drove past her. A man tugged his donkey out of their path, naked fear written on his face. The heart of the village was busier. People were coming and going amid market stalls selling fresh produce and cheap household goods imported from China. One stretch of the main street was made up of a row of open-fronted shops, all selling blue glass and bright pottery – plates, jugs, vases – heavily decorated in turquoise and ochre. On the opposite side of the street, the land dropped away to a fast-flowing river.

Mac stared out of the window, but his mind was focused on what was about to happen. He was scanning the people, assessing whether any were armed, looking out for squirters – individuals taking flight at the sight of them – or dickers – people setting up an alert of their presence in the village.

Jananga directed Pamir through the side streets, and finally told him to pull over. The rest of the convoy stopped. They got out of the vehicles for the final briefing.

'The property we're looking for will be just around the next corner,' he said. He went over the details of the operation, in

Dari for his own men and in English for Mac, Ginger and Logan.

'Ready?' he said finally.

'Let's roll,' said Logan.

'Roger,' said Mac.

They were off.

Chapter 40

Three of Jananga's men set off immediately to position them-selves at the rear of the property. The local police captain had said there wasn't a rear exit to the compound, but if Razul made a run for it as they arrived, there was always the chance that he would clamber over the back wall and try to escape along the riverbank.

Once the men had radioed that they were in position, Jananga led the rest of the men, apart from the drivers who were to stay with their vehicles, towards the front of the prop-erty. Jananga stationed men at each of the front corners of the compound. In the centre of the wall was an old wooden door, badly warped and sitting crookedly in its frame. The lower third was scuffed with kick marks and the hinges were bent and buckled.

Jananga barked an order in Dari. 'Stand by,' he said in English as one of his men moved forward, pump-action shotgun raised to his shoulder. With two shots, he blasted away the hinges and then kicked the door inwards. With a loud creaking, the inner bolts gave way and the heavy wooden door crashed to the ground, throwing up a cloud of dust.

Leaving two men at the door to prevent unauthorised indi-viduals either leaving or entering the property during the oper-ation, Jananga led the rest of the men into the Rahimi family compound.

As the dust settled, Mac looked around. The bare earth courtyard was peppered with fig and other fruit trees. Directly

266

in front of them stood a sprawling, single-storey house, built of the same sand-coloured dried mud as the rest of the village. The windows were small, with polythene in place of glass, and there was a crude wooden roof that ran the entire length of the front of the house to give an area of shade, where there were chairs and a low table. To one side of the house there was a shambolic lean-to stable – Mac could see the hind quarters of a donkey inside it.

He, Jananga, Logan and Ginger ran to the front door as Jananga's men fanned out in the courtyard and went to check the sides of the building.

As Mac raised a fist to hammer, the door opened from the inside and an elderly man stepped forward, his eyes wide with fear. He started to shout.

'*Dur boro! Dur boro!*'

'Police,' said Mac firmly.

'*Man nakardam. Man… Hala inja nestand…*'

Jananga spoke to him, but through it all the man didn't stop shouting. Two younger men appeared at his shoulder. Jananga held up his gun and motioned them back inside. Mac followed them through the door into a large room – rough stone walls and a bare earth floor were in the most part hidden by carpets and tapestries, and in the centre there was a large, low table, surrounded by floor cushions.

Jananga shouted at the three men, directing them with a wave of his hand to stand against the rear wall. Ginger moved towards them, raising his rifle to stop them getting any ideas about making a break for it.

Jananga looked at Mac. 'They say he's not here.'

'Do you believe them?'

'Of course not. We'll search the house.'

The old man started talking again, gesticulating with both arms. Ginger trained his weapon on the man. 'Shut it!'

At that moment, a door on the left-hand side of the room opened. There was the flash of a face appearing, then disappearing just as quickly.

267

'Razul!' said Logan.

Mac was standing closest to the door and went after him just in time to see the silhouette of the Hazara disappearing through another door on the other side of a smaller room – a bedroom with sleeping mats on the floor. Mac stumbled over the corner of one of them, but managed to stay on his feet and kept running.

Down a corridor, through another bedroom. Footsteps and shouting behind him. Through another door. Women screaming. A girl covering her face with her hijab.

They had blundered into the women's quarters.

Mac carried on through – it was a part of the house where no men other than family members were ever allowed.

An elderly woman stepped into his path, trying to block the doorway through which Razul had disappeared. He shouldered her aside but she grabbed his arm, screeching words he didn't understand. One of the younger girls sprung up to help her.

'Let go!' He brandished his weapon at them, and they fell away, still shrieking.

By the time he made it through the door, Razul had disappeared. Mac found himself in a small bedroom. A young woman was feeding a baby and, with a terrified cry, tugged the child off her breast and hurried to cover herself. Mac carried on through the room, almost colliding with Logan in an empty hallway. There was an open door, leading outside.

'This way,' said Mac.

The outside area at the back of the house was similar to that at the front – bare ground, straggly trees. A dog ran towards him, teeth bared and snarling. Mac shouted at it, a harsh, guttural sound. The dog stopped in its tracks and stood its ground, still growling. Ahead, Razul had taken a running jump at the back wall and was scrabbling up it. Mac handed his gun to Logan and lunged after him, just grabbing hold of Razul's ankles as he pulled himself up to the top of the wall.

'Stop! Police!'

One of Jananga's men came to his aid, shouting in Dari. Together, they wrestled Razul off the wall and onto the ground. He struggled violently, but with three men bundling on top of him, they were able to subdue and secure him with plasticuffs just as Jananga appeared in the doorway.

Logan and Jananga's man stepped back as Mac pulled Razul to his feet. It was the first time Mac had really seen Razul's features, and Mac recognised his face. Razul was the man who'd been watching them with the boy prostitute in the tank graveyard.

The woman who'd tried to prevent Mac from catching him pushed past Jananga and came into the yard.

'Razul! Razul!' Tears ran down her cheeks and she started to wail. She ran up to Razul and threw herself at him. Mac stepped in to pull her off. The old man who'd opened the front door now came running up.

There was a crack of gunfire, and the three of them stumbled.

Mac looked round to see Jananga, his rifle pointing up to the sky. It had been a warning shot.

'Mac, let her go,' he said. 'Never lay hands on an Afghan woman.'

Mac stepped back as the old man pulled the woman into his arms. Everyone was talking at once, the woman still crying loudly and, of course, none of it made sense to Mac. One of Jananga's men guided the elderly couple to one side.

'They are his parents,' said Jananga, by way of explanation.

Razul was still talking, his voice high-pitched and whining. He lunged forward, but Mac grabbed his arm and held him still.

Jananga came right up to the Hazara and spoke to him harshly, practically spitting in his face.

'Come on,' said Mac. 'Let's get him out of here.'

They marched him back through the house, the cries of the old woman still echoing in their ears. Jananga sent for one of the police Surfs to be brought to the front gate. As they waited for the vehicle to arrive, Mac patted Razul down, immediately feeling a familiar shape in his trouser pocket. He dug his hand in and withdrew a pistol. He looked at it. It was horribly familiar.

A British Army-issue Browning Hi-Power.

He looked at the serial number. The last three digits matched the last three digits of Marshall's Browning.

Mac took a deep breath. Finally, he had his man.

'Razul Rahimi, I'm arresting you for the murder of Captain Davie Marshall—'

'No. You don't have that power.' Jananga glared at him.

'Well, you bloody do it then.'

Chapter 41

The gates swung open and the convoy drove into the Kabul Police Headquarters compound. Mac kept Ginger with him and told Pamir to wait in the car. He watched as Razul was manhandled out of the first of the two police Surfs and marched across to the cell block. Jananga was standing next to Logan, a look of grim satisfaction on his face.

'What happens now?' said Mac.

'We will question Razul about what he knows and how he came to have Davie Marshall's weapon.' He held out his hand for the Browning.

'I think the army will want this,' said Mac.

'It's evidence in my case.'

'They can have it checked for prints.'

'The prints will be Razul's.'

'There might be others that would be of interest.'

'*Nachair.*' Jananga shook his head vehemently. 'We have our killer, Mac. Don't try to complicate this.'

The major might be right, but then again he might not. However, Mac had come to understand that the law operated to a different level of proof in Afghanistan. He wasn't putting a case together for the CPS, so there was no point in arguing over it. He handed over the weapon.

'Thank you, Mac-jan,' said Jananga. 'I will talk to Razul now. Please to wait in my office.'

That suited Mac fine. He didn't want to have to witness Razul's questioning. Jananga's sergeant escorted them to the office, furnished them with glasses of tea, then disappeared.

Ginger frowned as he took a sip. 'Tastes like horse piss,' he muttered.

'You would know?' said Mac.

'Grew up on a farm,' said Ginger with a shrug.

Mac decided not to probe further, even though a bit of fun at Ginger's expense might have taken his mind off what was no doubt going on in the cell block across the compound. He found himself straining his ears, but came to the conclusion that he was really better off not hearing anything.

He watched the clock on Jananga's wall, next to the photo of Hamid Karzai. The hands didn't seem to move at all.

'Ginger, that clock broken?'

Ginger checked his watch. 'They're not on different time to us?'

'No, Ginger – we're working on Afghan time while we're here.'

'Looks like it's busted,' said Logan, looking at his own watch.

The silence stretched between them again. Mac's tea went cold.

Footsteps in the corridor made him jump. He looked at his watch – they'd been waiting for just over an hour.

Jananga's sergeant came in. He nodded at the three of them.

'The major asks you come with me,' he said, his English heavily accented.

'Of course,' said Mac, standing up. 'Come on.'

They went down the stairs – the lift was still out of order, naturally – and across the compound. In the cell block, the sergeant led them down a corridor. He stopped by a closed door.

'Wait here,' he said, then disappeared inside.

Mac had no desire to follow him.

'This isn't going to be pretty,' said Logan.

'Tell me something I don't know,' said Mac.

There was a harsh cracking noise from the other side of the door, followed by a high-pitched shriek of pain.

'*Bale, bale!*' Yes, yes.

Jananga's voice interrupted. There was another cracking sound, another cry of pain. Mac felt sick to his stomach.

Ginger took a few paces away from the door. 'For God's sake,' he said, his tone urgent, 'surely this is breaking international law?'

'Of course it is,' said Logan. 'But that's the way they do things here. It's what they've always done, and they're not going to change just because we don't have the stomach for it.'

Ginger looked at Mac.

'I know – I hate it as much as you do, but there's nothing I can do,' said Mac.

Ginger frowned. 'I'm going to wait outside.'

As he walked towards the exit, the door of the cell opened and Jananga appeared. His hair was damp with sweat, and his clothing was spattered with blood.

'Come inside,' he said. 'Razul has something he wants to say to you.'

Mac doubted this, but followed the major into the room. It was small, hot and claustrophobic. The concrete floor was cracked and stained, testament to God knows how many past sessions that had happened in here. He looked up. Razul Rahini was suspended by his wrists from the ceiling, at a height which meant that his toes just scraped the floor, barely supporting his weight. He was naked from the waist up, allowing Mac to see how his shoulders were practically dislocating. His head lolled to one side, and his face was bloody. His torso was covered in red welts, and there were deep red indents on either side of his nipples – from electrodes? The room stank of piss and there was a dark stain on his trousers.

'Jesus,' breathed Mac. 'This is inhuman.'

Jananga turned at his words. 'He's inhuman – he killed three people, and you expect me to be gentle with him?'

Mac didn't have an answer for this. For Jananga this was all in a day's work.

The sergeant reappeared, carrying a bucket of water. He threw it over Razul and the Hazara spluttered into consciousness. Jananga walked up to him and slapped his face – not hard, but enough to get Razul's attention. Razul tottered on tiptoes, losing his balance and grimacing as his arms took all of his weight. Jananga addressed him in Dari. Mac heard him mention Marshall's name. As he finished speaking, Jananga struck him across the side of his head. Razul's body jerked against his bonds as he let out a moan of pain.

Jananga stepped in closer and shouted directly into Razul's face.

His features contorted with agony and desperation, Razul nodded.

Jananga turned to face Mac and Logan. 'I just asked him if he was responsible for the death of Captain Marshall. You see he nodded?'

'He did,' said Mac, but he had no idea what Razul had been nodding to, or if he even comprehended what was being put to him.

Jananga continued to grill him, accompanying each question with a barrage of blows, as he mentioned Bao Liang and Wahid, the driver. Again, Razul appeared to be confirming what was put to him.

'He has confessed to all the killings,' said Jananga.

Feeling increasingly uncomfortable, Mac remembered that Logan spoke Dari, and turned towards him.

Logan nodded his head. 'He did.'

Mac turned back to Jananga. 'And did he tell you why he killed them?'

'What does it matter?' said Jananga with a shrug.

'Of course it matters. I don't suppose he was acting of his own volition. What will happen to him now?'

'He'll be charged with the murders and taken to Pul-e-Charkhi Prison.'

274

'Will there be a trial? You know the British Army will argue strongly for him to face trial in the UK.'

Jananga shrugged his shoulders, giving Mac a dismissive look. He had jurisdiction.

Chapter 42

'So what did you make of it, the confession?'

Baz was having coffee with Mac, but trying to get him to talk about what had just happened was like pulling teeth. He looked relieved when Logan called him and suggested he come over to the Mustafa.

'I'm coming with you,' said Baz.

'No way,' said Mac. 'This isn't something you want to hear about.'

'Of course I do. I need to do a follow-up story on the IED and the raid on the brothel.'

Mac paused for a moment too long.

'Come on, it's my job to write about these things.'

She made her point forcefully, and in the end Mac agreed.

'I want to hear your account of exactly what Razul confessed to and what he didn't,' said Mac to Logan as soon as they were all sitting around a table in the Mustafa bar, drinks in front of them. 'Much as I'd like to trust Jananga, it all seems a little too convenient. Even if Razul was guilty of one of the killings, I'm sure he's working for someone else, possibly Holmberg.'

'I think you're right,' said Logan. 'What motive would Razul Rahimi have for killing Bao?'

'So what did he say?' said Baz. 'Did he actually confess? Did he come up with any details that actually showed that he was guilty?'

'It was beaten out of him,' said Logan. 'But you know that.'

Mac frowned. 'You should have seen the state of him after-wards,' he said to Baz.

'Couldn't you have stopped them?' she said. Of course she knew that police violence and beatings were commonplace in Afghanistan, but she'd grown to like Jananga and it didn't sit comfortably with her.

Logan turned to look at her incredulously. 'How? It's the way they do things here, Baz.'

'I know, but... jeez.'

'There's nothing we could have done to stop it,' said Mac. He turned to Logan. 'You understood what was being said. How much of Razul's confession do you actually think was true?'

'Okay – this is my take on it. Razul planted the IED – he knew what sort of device it was, and claimed to have got it from his cousin, who had contacts with the Taliban, yada, yada...'

'But according to the EOD major, it wasn't a typical Taliban-style bomb,' said Mac.

Logan shrugged. 'Things change... different cells have different ways of doing things, and they use whatever kit's available at any given time. Anyway, the details Razul provided with regard to the bomb sounded genuine. What didn't sound so convincing was what he said about Bao Liang and Davie Marshall.' He paused and took a mouthful of coffee. 'It would suit Jananga to be able to pin their killings on Razul.'

'Why?' said Baz, fearing the worst.

'Gets them off his desk with a successful outcome.'

'So doesn't he care who actually did it? I honestly thought he was better than that.'

'He's working under pressure,' said Mac, 'with no resources and not many men. Lengthy homicide investigations are a luxury he can't afford. He needs to build public confidence in the police by being seen to solve cases.'

'Sad, but true,' said Baz. 'I suppose it's the world he lives in.' She could wish it was otherwise, but she'd known since childhood of the stark differences between the country she was born in and the country her parents came from.

'Basically, Razul didn't really seem to know how Marshall had died, and had to be led through it by Jananga,' said Logan. 'I don't believe he did it. I don't even believe he was there.'

'But he clearly knew of it – he was there watching us at the tank graveyard the next day when we came to remove the body,' said Mac.

'What about Bao Liang?' said Baz.

She saw a flicker of pain in Logan's eyes, and a muscle tightened in his cheek before he spoke.

'He knew how she'd died, and where, but again, the detailed information he gave didn't really ring true. He didn't mention anything about her being tied to a chair. He couldn't explain why he'd supposedly done it, or precisely when.'

'What about Xiaoli?' said Baz.

'She's with Holmberg, according to Razul.' Logan's voice was clipped with anger.

'Where?' said Mac.

'Nothing concrete. Holmberg clearly didn't share his plans with Razul.'

'Anything else?' said Mac.

Logan thought for a moment. 'There was one thing I couldn't make sense of. Razul mentioned an expert – as in "Holmberg and the expert", so not meaning Holmberg himself.'

'An expert in what?' said Mac.

Logan shrugged. 'It was near the end. Razul wasn't making much sense, just saying whatever he thought Jananga wanted to hear.'

They sat in silence for a couple of minutes, then all three spoke at once.

'If Holmberg's still in the city…' said Logan.

'Someone must know…' said Mac.

'Baseer Ghilji is setting…' said Baz.

Both men stared at Baz.

'What?' said Mac.

'Baseer Ghilji, the antiquities dealer. He set up my meeting with Holmberg – and we're supposed to be meeting again.'

'Holmberg's business partner? Could he be the expert?' said Logan.

'He's not that much of an expert,' said Baz. 'He didn't realise the coins that Holmberg showed me were fake.'

'Sure,' said Logan. 'But he probably looks like an expert to Razul.'

'Makes sense,' said Mac.

'Anyway, after what happened at the Lucky Star, I suspect Holmberg's plans have changed,' said Logan. 'Ghilji might know something.'

'It's worth a try,' said Mac. 'Can you give Ghilji a call?'

'I can go to his shop,' said Baz.

'It's a lead, and we should definitely follow up on it,' said Logan. 'But there's one other lead.'

'What?'

'Someone at the Lucky Star had to have betrayed Bao.'

'How do you mean?' said Baz.

'It must have been one of the girls. It's the only way Holmberg could have found out about the raid in advance.'

'Surely Bao wouldn't have told anyone?' said Mac. She'd known about the raid, as it was to have been her job to tip them off when Holmberg was there.

'No, but someone knew,' said Logan. 'The text we received telling us that Holmberg was there was actually sent after her time of death.'

'What? How come?' said Baz.

'Her body was cold when we found it, and that was only ten or fifteen minutes after we'd got that text.'

'So Holmberg knew,' said Mac. 'Do you think he might have paid one of his regular girls to spy on Bao?'

'I sure as hell do.'

'We need to find out which,' said Mac. 'Where are all the girls now?' Jananga had released them all from custody the day after the raid.

'Back at the Lucky. Apparently, the owner has appointed a new manager, who'll arrive in a couple of days.'

'Right, that's two possible leads to follow up on. Let's head to the Lucky Star now and, Baz, can you call Ghilji and push him for a meeting?'

Baz wasn't surprised when they found that the Lucky Star was closed. With no one at the helm until the new manager arrived, the gates were locked and would-be guests had to find their pleasures elsewhere. Luckily for them, Logan still had the key for the rear entrance.

Inside, the place was quiet. They walked down the corridor without speaking and Baz noticed that Logan turned his head away from the door to the basement as they passed it.

God, it must be tough coming back here.

The hubbub of the kitchen was missing, as were the clouds of steam laden with the smell of Chinese food. Instead, there was an almost overwhelming smell of bleach – and in the restaurant, a worn-out-looking girl was scrubbing the floor where Jananga's man had been shot.

'Huifang?' said Logan.

The girl looked up, her nose wrinkling in recognition of him.

'Huifang, is Mayleen still here?'

Mayleen, Logan had told them, was Holmberg's favourite.

Huifang's eyes widened as she clambered to her feet. 'Mayleen is too upset to work, Mr Logan.'

'Why's she upset?' said Logan.

'We're all upset. You too? So sorry for your loss.'

'Yes, I'm upset too, Huifang. But Mayleen didn't get on with Bao Liang, did she?'

'Why you need to see her?' Huifang seemed suddenly suspicious – maybe this was more than a courtesy call.

'Have you seen Xiaoli since last week?'

Huifang shook her head. 'She not here. She gone back to China, I think.'

'On her own?'

Huifang shrugged, and glanced back down at the floor.

'Sorry to interrupt you,' said Logan.

The conversation was over and Huifang looked relieved.

'Come on,' said Logan.

He led them back out of the restaurant and took the stairs two at a time to the first floor.

'Is he okay?' whispered Baz, as Logan turned the corner onto the landing ahead of them. She could feel him getting more and more tense with every minute that passed.

'I doubt it,' said Mac.

'This is Mayleen's room,' said Logan, indicating a door close to the top of the stairs.

He tried the handle without knocking, and walked into the room.

Baz heard a shrill, angry voice, but the words were Cantonese. As she followed Logan in, she saw a woman stand up from a small dressing table. It was draped in fabric and its surface was littered with make-up. There was a mottled mirror leaning against the wall – the woman had been doing her face, and was brandishing a mascara wand in one hand.

She lunged at Logan, leaving a streak of black make-up across his cheek.

Mac stepped forward, his hands raised, palms flat. 'Whoa, calm down. We're not here to hurt you.'

The woman, swathed in a fine silk kimono, practically snarled at him. 'He is,' she said.

Logan stepped menacingly towards her. 'What makes you think that, Mayleen? Your guilty conscience?'

Mayleen shook her head. 'I don't know what you talk about.'

'Where's your boyfriend?' said Logan.

The girl didn't answer, didn't even look at him. She glanced around the room and picked up a pair of navy cotton trousers from the bed. Ignoring the audience by the door, she pulled them on under her kimono.

'Where's Holmberg?' said Logan. He pushed her roughly backwards and she dropped to a sitting position on the edge of the bed. He towered over her. 'You were spying on Bao for him, weren't you?'

'No.' Mayleen shook her head. Her eyes flitted around the room. Baz wondered what she was looking for. She was starting to feel scared about what Logan might do to her.

'You heard something and you told him. That's why she's dead.'

Logan raised a hand.

'No, honest. Not me.' Mayleen was terrified.

'Leave it, chum,' said Mac, reaching out to grasp Logan's shoulder.

As Logan shook him off, Mayleen ducked around the other side of the bed. She grabbed a pair of dusty sneakers and thrust her feet into them.

'Goddamnit,' said Logan, all his anger directed at Mac now. 'If anyone knows where Holmberg is, it'll be Mayleen.' He started searching through Mayleen's dressing table.

Mac joined him, rifling through the few clothes in the wardrobe, checking for pockets. He looked inside two pairs of shoes, but there was nothing. Baz was stationed by the door and could see that Mayleen was slowly backing across the room towards her.

'What are we looking for?' said Mac.

'This,' said Logan. From underneath Mayleen's clutter of make-up he drew a square Chinese silk purse. It fastened with a zipper, which he undid to reveal a roll of banknotes. 'This is what I was looking for. This is a payoff. I guarantee it.'

He splayed out the notes. It had to be more than a thousand dollars.

'For what?' said Mac.

'For ratting out Bao Liang.'

Mayleen turned and ran headlong for the door. Logan went after her, colliding with Mac. Both men stumbled.

The girl flashed by, almost knocking her over. There was only one thing for it. Baz took off in hot pursuit.

Chapter 43

Sunday, 21 December 2003

Baz flew down the stairs, her heart pounding as she grabbed at the banister to stop herself tripping. At the bottom, she looked both ways. There was no sign of Mayleen. The back door and the door into the restaurant were both closed, and she couldn't hear the sound of footsteps. Of course not – Mayleen's sneakers wouldn't make a sound on the concrete floor.

She walked as quietly as she could along the empty corridor, listening at each door she came to. There would have been no point in Mayleen going down to the storeroom. It was a dead end. Baz opened the door to the large room where Bao Liang's customers had played mah-jong. The room was empty, tables still overturned from the raid of the previous week, mah-jong tiles still scattered on the floor.

She opened the door into the restaurant. The first thing she saw was Mayleen's bright blue silk kimono, carelessly draped over the back of a chair, but no sign of the girl. But she was here – a soft expiration of breath gave her away, and Baz looked around in a hurry. Movement flickered in her peripheral vision. There! Behind one of the tables, she saw the crouched figure of Mayleen. She was tying the laces of one of her sneakers. Then she rose up and lunged for the door that led out to the front hall.

Baz set off in pursuit. The front gates were locked. How was Mayleen planning to evade her? The front door slammed shut behind the Chinese girl and Baz struggled with the catch for a couple of seconds – valuable seconds – before she managed to pull it open. Mayleen was disappearing around a corner of the building. Baz ran after her. She was fit. She'd been a fast runner at school and college. Surely she'd be able to catch up with the skinny Chinese woman.

Rounding the corner, her feet skidded on gravel. She fought to stay upright as Mayleen sprinted across the barren earth towards the back gate. Powering herself forward, Baz began to make up ground as Mayleen struggled to get the gate open. But then she was through it, slamming it hard shut behind her. Baz could hear her footfall as she sprinted away down the small alley that gave rear access to the property.

She caught her breath as she pulled open the gate. Her phone was vibrating in her pocket, but now wasn't the time to answer it. She set off at a run – she could see Mayleen at the far end of the alley, leading onto Qalla-e-Fatullah Road. Mayleen turned right at the end. She was heading north. Once more, Baz felt as if she was gaining on her. She got to the corner and found herself on a busy pavement. The shops were open and the traffic was heavy. Car horns merged with Iranian pop music from tinny radios. She swerved round a beggar and slipped between two women who stood gossiping in her pathway.

'*Mazrat mechoham… motasefam*,' she called to them as she passed. Excuse me, I'm sorry.

One of the women shouted something after her in Pashtu but she ignored it. She had to concentrate to keep her eyes on Mayleen, darting between the stream of pedestrians, while also watching where she was going and avoiding getting tangled up with people coming in the other direction.

Her phone jangled insistently in her pocket.

With no warning, Mayleen flew out into the traffic to cross the road. A car slammed on its brakes to avoid her, but she didn't miss a step. Then Baz's view of her was obstructed by a lorry.

'Damn!'

She darted between the crawling cars, who sounded their horns at her, even though she hardly impeded their progress. A car coming in the opposite direction gunned its engine, so she waited between the two streams of traffic until it had passed, taking the moment to make sure her hijab was on securely. Further up the opposite pavement, she could see Mayleen, still running, though now it was more of a steady trot than a sprint. The gap had widened between them.

Once she was safely across, she sped up, once again having to dodge the other pavement users. A dog snarled at her as she flashed by, and a man shouted. Baz didn't know if he was addressing her or the dog. She ran on, but it was harder now. There was a searing pain in her chest and she could feel the burn of lactic acid in her leg muscles.

Her phone buzzed again.

'Goddamnit! Leave a message!'

Mayleen looked over her shoulder and, realising that Baz was still on her tail, she began to run faster again. Baz took a deep breath and forced herself to quicken her pace.

'*Mazrat mechoham, mazrat mechoham!*' She bundled her way through a gaggle of teenage boys, receiving a barrage of catcalls in return.

Where was Mayleen?

The pavement in front of her was empty – at least, she couldn't see the Chinese girl anywhere. She ran on, scouting from side to side, looking for the slim figure in her dark blue trousers and black kameez. Nowhere to be seen. She must have turned off – Baz was just coming to the junction of Qalla-e-Fatullah Road with Street 7. She stopped on the corner, panting, and stared down the side street. It was quieter than the main road, with hardly any people on the pavement, making it easier to see Mayleen jogging along on the north side.

She filled her lungs with air – she had to dig deep to keep running. Maybe she wasn't as fit as she'd thought. Where was Mayleen leading her? Along Street 7, into a narrow alley, out onto Street 8, past a small mosque where giant speakers at each corner of the building were blasting out the *Salat al-'asr*, the late afternoon call to prayer. Back towards Qalla-e-Fatullah, but then turning off up a street with a tight dog-leg corner, across Street 9 – she thought – but then she wondered if she'd lost count at some point. She certainly felt unsure of which direction they were running in.

Always ahead of her, she saw flashes of Mayleen – sprinting down a pavement, jogging across a road, looking round cautiously as she ducked down an alley.

Her phone rang. Again. She was too out of breath to be able to speak, so there would be no point in trying to answer it.

The shadows on the street were growing longer and the air was getting colder. Evening was on its way, and with no streetlights it was getting harder to see Mayleen as she slipped down shadowy pathways. Sound was her ally – the crunch of Mayleen's feet on a gravel surface, a laboured gasp as she pushed her way up a short incline. She must surely be as tired as Baz was herself.

The narrower the street, the darker it seemed, and where they were running now, the pavements were empty of people. There was very little traffic noise and only an occasional dog barking in the distance. When Mayleen turned into a tight crevice between two tall houses, it was almost pitch black. Baz had to slow down and feel her way along between two sheer walls. She was still panting loudly, her own breathing all she could hear. She wondered if Mayleen could hear it too.

The alley suddenly branched. In one direction it was completely dark, in the other there was a glow of light from beyond a corner. She had no idea which way Mayleen had gone. She stopped, held her breath and listened. There was nothing – no sound of running feet in the distance, just silence that was as oppressive as the darkness.

Baz stood still, trying to decide which way to go. If she picked the wrong way, she would lose the girl. Somewhere amid the buildings in front of her a door slammed, but she had no sense of the direction from which the sound came. The noise broke her sense of paralysis and she ran down the passageway that led towards the light.

She emerged seconds later into a long courtyard. The light came from a first-floor window, through gaps on either side of a flimsy, makeshift blind. Of course, there was no sign of Mayleen. A number of other alleyways led out of the rectangular space, all of them dark and uninviting. Baz had not only lost the girl, but she was herself lost in a part of the city unfamiliar to her.

She remembered her phone and pulled it from her pocket. Five missed calls from Mac. A text asking where the hell she was. And now, no signal. She couldn't ring him back and even if she could, she wouldn't be able to tell him where she was.

Damn!

She heard men's voices approaching between two of the buildings, laughing, speaking Pashtu — and then she saw them, before she'd had time to act on the thought that she should hide herself. Four men, three young, one older, appeared in the courtyard and started walking across it. Baz sank back against the nearest wall, hoping they wouldn't see her, or at least that they would ignore her if they did. She put a hand up to her hijab, partly to shield her face from them.

'*Spay bachai!*' said one of the younger ones, pointing at her and laughing. '*Kwassai!*' Pussy.

Fear coursed through her body, but Baz had nowhere to run.

Chapter 44

The older man told the young one to shut up, but not before the other two had shrieked with laughter.

Baz yanked off her hijab. 'Don't come any closer,' she said in English. 'I'm American.'

As if that would make any difference to them.

Even the old man laughed at this.

Baz looked frantically left and right as the men advanced towards her. All the doors were shut, all the windows bar one were dark. No one would see what was about to happen. And if they did, they'd sink into the shadows and stay silent. Who would try to defend an American girl who found herself out of her depth in a part of the city where foreigners had no business to be?

Maybe they'd just push her around a bit, give her a fright.

Maybe they'd do worse.

She didn't know what to do.

'Help! Somebody help me!'

One of the young men hung back, but the others laughed and kept coming.

'Please, somebody help me!' Baz's mouth was almost too dry for her to form the words.

There was the click of a latch to her left.

'Come here. Come quickly.' It was a woman's voice.

Baz's head whipped round, sending a sharp pain shooting across her right shoulder.

Three or four feet away, along the wall she was pressed against, a door had opened a slit. She dived for it as the first of her tormentors lunged at her, obviously realising she was about to make her escape. As she reached it, the door was pulled back to form a gap just wide enough for her to squeeze through. She shoved her way in and immediately the door was slammed shut. Heavy fists hammered and the men shouted for entry in Pashtu.

Baz bent forward, panting, and wondered if she was about to throw up. She was standing in semi-darkness on a tiled floor. The smell of home-cooking and spices hung in the air. She slowed her breathing and rubbed her face with her hands, before looking up to see who had come to her aid.

'Mayleen?'

Baz blinked a couple of times. Was it really the girl she'd spent the last twenty minutes chasing through the streets?

'Come,' said Mayleen, and led her towards the interior of the house.

'But why? I was chasing you. Why did you let me in?'

Mayleen looked back over her shoulder. 'Those men would have hurt you.'

Female solidarity from a girl who'd betrayed her female boss?

Mayleen opened a door and led her into a small room that appeared to double up as both kitchen and living room. She gestured for Baz to sit down on a grimy floor cushion and then fetched her a plastic cup of water from a bucket that stood on a low table by the wall.

Baz drank it greedily – she normally avoided well water, but right now she needed it. Although the fear that had flooded through her the minute before had subsided, her hands were still shaking and her legs felt like jelly from the prolonged running.

'Why did you come after me?' said Mayleen. 'What were you doing at the Lucky Star?' She spoke English with a faint American accent – picked up from the expat workers she entertained?

'Why did you run?' said Baz.

'I was scared. Logan' – she shook her head – 'he was going to hurt me.'

'He thinks you betrayed Bao Liang. He thinks you told Holmberg that we were coming.'

Mayleen shook her head harder. 'No. That's not true.'

'But you were Holmberg's girlfriend, right?'

'I hated him.' The vehemence in Mayleen's voice was shocking. 'He picked me to have sex with him whenever he came to the restaurant. Bao Liang had to give him what he wanted. He was great friend of the owner, and Bao Liang was scared of losing her job. She had no choice, but I no betray her.'

Baz thought for a moment.

'Did Holmberg see any of the other girls?'

'Yes, I saw him often with other girls. He was a pig and he always wanted new girls and younger girls.'

'Did he ask you to spy on Bao Liang?'

Mayleen shook her head. 'Not me. He knew stuff about Bao Liang, but he got it from other girls.'

Baz wondered if she was telling the truth, or just spinning a story that would show her in a better light.

'Can I have some more water?' She held out the cup.

Mayleen filled it from the bucket.

'Whose house is this?'

Mayleen glanced around. 'A good woman, Balbala, lives here. She worked for Bao Liang, cleaning the restaurant. When any of the girls were hurt, she would bring them here and nurse them.'

'Hurt? By who? The johns?'

Mayleen nodded. Then she turned her back on Baz and slowly raised her *kameez*. Baz watched as she revealed her naked back. It was covered in bright red scars, the welts of a severe beating. Or beatings – some of the marks looked fresher than others.

'Did Holmberg do that to you?'

'Yes,' said Mayleen, lowering her top and turning round again. 'But he wasn't the only one. Bao Liang tried to stop it, but she was a woman and the men did what they wanted.'

'Why did you stay?' Baz couldn't imagine enduring a life of forced sex and beatings.

'For my family. They need the money I send back to them.'

'Do you know who told Holmberg about the raid?'

Mayleen shook her head. Whether she knew or not, she wasn't saying.

Baz got out her phone. She needed to let Mac know she was safe, but there was still no signal.

'If you need to call, you can go on the roof,' said Mayleen.

She led Baz up a narrow stone staircase, along a hallway and then through a door that opened out onto a flat mud roof. Baz checked her phone and at last got a signal. Mayleen gave her the street address so Mac could come and collect her.

'The front of the house opens on Street 9. We can wait up here until we see him come, then you can go out to him.' Mayleen was not taking any chances of an encounter with the *gweilo*.

Half an hour later, Baz pulled open the door of Mac's Land Cruiser and climbed into the passenger seat.

'For fuck's sake, Baz – I've been driving all over the city looking for you.'

For a split second Baz was about to apologise. But then she thought better of it and said nothing.

'Why didn't you pick up your phone?'

'Because I was running. Because there was no signal. Because I couldn't talk.'

'You shouldn't have left the Lucky Star.' He started the engine. 'We came after you, but you'd already disappeared by the time we got outside. You could have been in danger.'

'I was in danger. But I spoke to Mayleen.'

She recounted all that had happened – the chase, the men in the courtyard and her unexpected saviour. Everything that Mayleen had said about Holmberg. Mac was sceptical.

'We found over a thousand dollars in her room. Whatever she says, that's more money than she could have earned as a prosi.'

'You don't know how long she was saving it for.'

'Come on, Baz. Girls like her don't save.'

'Girls like her? You know nothing about her life. Honestly, I don't believe she was lying when she said it wasn't her that told Holmberg. We're looking for someone else.'

'I doubt it.' Mac pulled up at the G Lodge gates. 'But I don't want to argue with you. I'm just relieved that you're safe.'

Baz's anger evaporated. She felt a little relieved that he'd been angry with her for putting herself in danger. After all, someone had to look out for her.

'Wanna come in for a drink?'

'I thought you'd never ask.'

Chapter 45

Jananga's call hardly came as a surprise to Mac. He'd been waiting for this particular bird to come home to roost since the day he arrived in Kabul.

'Mr MacKenzie, I need you to come to my office right now.'

No please, no explanation, and as the call was abruptly terminated, Mac noted that he'd gone from Mac-jan back to being Mr MacKenzie.

Damn!

He'd hoped to stay under the radar for a little longer than this.

Jananga's sergeant met him at the gate of Police HQ and showed him to Jananga's office. The major was sitting behind his desk and didn't get up when Mac came in. His face was grim, and he dismissed his sergeant in clipped tones.

Mac sat down opposite him without waiting to be invited and Jananga scowled.

'Mr MacKenzie, I've taken a phone call with Major Lambert. He had some disturbing news to tell me.'

Mac remained silent. It was obvious what was coming.

'Davie Marshall's commanding officer came to him and asked that you should be taken off the case.'

Mac could tell Jananga was stressed because his English wasn't as fluid as usual. 'Might I ask why?'

'I will tell you why. Colonel Tomlinson has made some enquiries about you with his friend Chief Superintendent Chris

Joseph of the Yard. Why did you not tell me that you had been dismissed from the London police?'

Fucking Joseph. Not content with forcing him to resign, the man was spreading it about that he'd been dismissed. It was going to lose him another job. How far away would be far enough from that bastard?

'Because it has nothing to do with this case.'

'That's not for you to judge.'

'But that wasn't a murder case – it was a counter-terrorism op that went wrong.' And it hadn't been his fault, but no one had listened to him since the day it had happened.

'From today, you and your assistant will no longer be working with the Afghan Central Police on the case of Davie Marshall's murder. I have informed Mr Phelps that your services are no longer necessary.'

'Fine.' Mac had heard enough. He stood up to leave.

Jananga got up too. A look of regret flashed across his face for a moment, but it clearly wasn't enough to change what he was doing. 'Goodbye, Mr MacKenzie.'

And that was that. Dinged off the case. And even worse, he'd spoken to Phelps. Although going back to the classroom was the last thing Mac wanted, he needed this job. If he had to go back home, his prospects for work would be even worse.

–

'The thing is,' said Mac to Logan in the Global bar later, 'Jananga thinks the case is done, because he managed to beat a confession out of Razul. But it's anything but done. Razul clearly wasn't working alone, and Razul is still the key to unlocking what happened.'

'Razul Rahimi is in a coma,' said Logan.

'What? How did that happen?'

'Jananga's sergeant took it upon himself to ask him some extra questions.'

Mac frowned. 'Without permission?'

'These things happen here. The guy probably wants a promotion and decided to show some initiative.'

'They haven't got a bloody clue,' said Mac. 'Will he recover?'

'*Insha'Allah* was all Jananga said when I asked the same. He is at the prison hospital.' Logan was clearly still inside the loop as far as Jananga was concerned.

Mac doubted the standard of care he was getting would be up to much. 'Did the sergeant gain any additional information from him?'

'Razul changed his story to claim that Holmberg killed Marshall.'

'Seriously? Do you think the Swede would really dirty his hands with that?'

Logan shrugged.

'Did Razul have any idea where Holmberg is now?' said Mac.

'He said Holmberg rented a place in Wazir Akbar Khan, but that he was preparing to leave the city.'

'That makes sense. The stuff he took from the storeroom in the Lucky Star is of high value, and he'll make far more if he sells it abroad.'

'I contacted the company he works for and blagged his street address in Wazir out of them. I am going there now. Do you want to come?'

'And do what?'

'Search the joint.'

'But I'm off the case.'

'And I'm hardly on it. But I still need to find Xiaoli. So, it's off the books, but I could use you.'

And why not? He was about to lose his job anyway, so he might as well throw in his lot with Logan.

They took Mac's Land Cruiser, with Pamir driving and Ginger riding shotgun. Ginger was happy to come along for the ride, even though he was off the case too. It beat demonstrating search techniques to a bunch of disinterested Afghan policemen who had their own way of doing things already.

Wazir Akbar Khan was the embassy district of the city – popular with expats whose employers would stump up for the inflated rents. Heavily guarded foreign enclaves rubbed shoulders with pastel-coloured 'poppy palaces', the huge mansions that were springing up on the proceeds of the opium trade and syphoned-off aid money. No wonder Holmberg felt at home here, Mac thought to himself as they drove through the wall-lined streets and a succession of security roadblocks.

Under Logan's direction, Pamir turned into a narrow street off Wazir Akbar Khan Road. They passed a couple of Eastern European embassies, before drawing up in front of a row of recently built villas.

'This is it,' said Logan, pointing at a pair of sturdy steel gates.

Mac instructed Pamir and Ginger to stay with the car as Logan pressed an intercom on one of the gate posts. Of course, if there was no one there, they'd have to find another way to gain entry, but Mac wasn't going to think about the implications of that.

Luckily someone answered, and Logan spoke in Dari, then Pashtu.

'*Polis. Drvaza kulava ka.*' He told whoever it was they were the police.

'*Sa?*'

'*Paregda ché zmm.*'

The gate was buzzed open. They walked into the walled compound, and Logan checked that the gate had closed properly behind them. Mac looked around. Someone, presumably not Holmberg, put in a lot of hours on the garden – apart from a paved driveway for parking at the front, the house was surrounded by lawn, a well-cared-for lawn despite the fact it was the middle of winter. Palm trees and shrubs, though bedraggled in the wet weather, would form an oasis in the warmer months and provide valuable shade in the heat of summer. The building itself wasn't huge – probably designed as a four-bedroom family home – but by Kabul standards, it was luxurious. Floor-to-ceiling windows looked out over the garden, and there were terraces and balconies for outdoor living. If Holmberg lived here on his own, the company that supposedly employed him certainly valued his services.

They walked across the paving to the front door. Logan's knock was answered by an old woman dressed in black.

'*Salaam alaikum.*'

'*Alaikum a'salaam,*' they both said in unison.

As Logan introduced them, Mac adjusted his impression – she wasn't an old woman, probably barely in her forties, despite a stooped back and slow movements. And she certainly wasn't born yesterday. She looked the two of them up and down and made a move to slam the door in their faces. Of course they didn't look like police to her – they were westerners.

Logan got a foot in the way and was easily strong enough to then push back. He barged into the property and Mac followed him into an octagonal entrance hall with a marble floor. He waited while she and Logan pursued a heated argument for several minutes. Finally, she ran out of steam and seemed to accept the fact that they were there and there was nothing she could do about it.

'She says that Holmberg does live here, but he's away travelling. I asked her when he would come back, but she doesn't know. He never tells her his schedule, but he travels a lot.' He asked another question and she answered. 'He usually telephones her a day or two before he returns so she can ready the house for him.'

'Can we take a look around?' said Mac.

'Of course we can,' said Logan, without consulting the woman.

Logan led the way out of the hall and into a spacious living room. The house seemed to have a more western layout than other houses Mac had visited in Kabul. Large windows overlooked the garden at the back, including a patio and a small rectangular pool with a fountain in the centre. It wasn't spouting water, no doubt turned off for the winter. Inside, the room was furnished with bland but expensive-looking leather sofas and armchairs. Afghan rugs covered the tiled floor, and a marble fireplace stood unused. In one corner, there was a large television, and on a cabinet opposite a state-of-the-art sound system. What little time Holmberg spent here was spent in comfort.

The woman frowned and said something. Logan replied sharply and she left the room. It was clear she wasn't happy about their incursion, but there was little she could do about it, having let them through the door.

They circled the room, opening drawers and inspecting the few personal belongings scattered about. On the coffee table was a pile of books – Afghan history, art books, and Nancy Hatch Dupree's celebrated guide to the country. Inside the front cover, Mac found a bundle of photographs. There were no people in any of them, just antiquities – a couple of Buddha statues and a Buddha head, some relief carvings with figures and animals, and some brass pots and ewers. But they found nothing that gave them any insight into Holmberg's work, or where he might have been planning to travel to, and no personal documents.

'Let's look upstairs,' said Mac.

The master bedroom yielded little. A wardrobe of clothes with a rack of shoes. A packet of pills in the bedside table drawer. The name meant nothing to Mac, so he dropped them into an evidence bag. Similarly, the en-suite told them nothing interesting about Holmberg. However, some of the toiletries suggested a woman's occasional presence in the house.

Logan pulled a cheap canvas grip bag from under the bed. They looked through it – some items of women's clothing, including a silk cheongsam dress. One of the girls from the Lucky Star had been here.

There were three further bedrooms that were furnished but evidently not used. And a fourth that was equipped as an office.

'This should be more interesting,' said Mac, sitting down at the desk.

There were charging cables for a laptop, which must have been with its owner, and an in-tray of papers. Mac lifted the pile of documents out and started flicking through them. Pay slips – Holmberg was paid royally by the construction company he worked for, Stuessy GmbH. Mac had heard of them and it tallied with the research on Holmberg that Baz had come up with. The company had infrastructure projects all over the country and were major contractors in the World Bank-funded regeneration programme. There were print-outs relating to projects Holmberg must have been working on, receipts for travel and hotels, a rental agreement for the house. Nothing that looked out of order. Nothing pertaining to illegal trading in antiquities or weapons. Of course not.

While Mac examined the papers on the desk, Logan opened the top drawer of a filing cabinet. He rifled through it quickly, but didn't draw anything out of the folders.

'It's just household stuff,' he said. He tried the second drawer and flicked through some more documents. 'Nothing of interest.'

Mac spent an hour going through Holmberg's paperwork, but found no clue as to where the man was now.

Once or twice the woman appeared in the doorway with a look of concern on her face, but each time Logan sent her away. He called Ginger every fifteen minutes to check they were okay out with the vehicle, and to let them know that he was still searching the house. When he finally finished, he felt they'd achieved nothing. Time wasted.

'Come on,' he said. 'Let's shift.'

They went down to the kitchen, where the woman was folding bed linen. Logan started talking to her – he'd said he would ask her to get in touch with them when she heard that Holmberg was returning, and he accompanied the request with a wad of dollars. Mac didn't have high expectations that

Holmberg would come back, not since he was a person of interest in two murders, but it was still worth asking her.

The kitchen was the only room they hadn't searched, so he took a moment to nose through the cupboards and drawers. A few contained kitchen equipment, most of which looked unused. The rest were empty. He went out into the hall and looked around.

Opposite the front door, between doorways leading to the living room and the kitchen, there was an ancient-looking painted chest that he hadn't registered when they'd first come in. He idly raised the lid, not in expectation of finding anything but simply to pass the time. But he did find something. Inside the rickety box was a steel strongbox, with two hefty padlocks securing it.

'Logan, here!'

Logan emerged from the kitchen quickly, the woman trailing after him, still speaking in rapid Pashtu. He shushed her as they both studied the box.

'A crowbar should do it,' said Mac.

Mac called Ginger to bring one in from the Land Cruiser, and a minute later they were staring into the strongbox full, almost to the brim, of cash. US dollars, in bundles and rolls, high denomination.

'Jesus,' said Mac.

Behind him, the woman was shouting. She pushed forward and tried to take the box from Mac's hands. Logan pulled her off and shoved her away.

'There's a note.' Mac plucked out a crumpled sheet of yellowing paper with a black handwritten scrawl. 'It says, "$20,000 now, more next month." And a name, Pahlawan. And a word, Junbish.'

Logan snatched it from him. 'Junbish is a political party – it represents the Uzbeks nominally, but really it's just a strong-arm organisation for Dostum.'

'What do we do with the money?'

'Leave it here. Stealing Junbish funds will unleash all manner of hell on us.'

'I wasn't thinking of stealing it – we should pass it on to the police.'

Logan gave a wry laugh. 'Like dropping it into a black hole.'

'Fair enough,' said Mac. He closed the strongbox and placed it back in the chest. 'Right, let's PUFO.'

'PUFO?' said Logan.

'Pack up and fuck off,' explained Ginger.

Ignoring the plaintive cries of the woman, now upset about the damage they'd done to the box, they headed out of the front door.

'So that's who he's sourcing weapons for,' said Mac. 'But it doesn't really help us find him.'

'Someone will know where he is hiding,' said Logan. 'I'll get onto my informants again.'

'You don't think the woman knew something she wasn't telling us?'

Logan shook his head. 'No. Women her age are wise enough not to wait to have their fingers broken. She would have told us anything she knew. And she won't steal his money – not if she values her children's lives.'

As they went towards the gate, Mac noticed a black rubbish bag to one side of it, waiting to be taken out. He bent down and ripped it open.

'Last chance,' he said.

He shoved a stinking chicken carcass to one side and rummaged through some food wrappings. There was a corner of white paper sticking up between them, so he gingerly pulled it out.

It was the top half of something, the bottom of which had been burned.

But there was no mistaking what it was.

A flight confirmation from UNHAS. The United Nations Humanitarian Air Service. A flight booked for two people. Date missing. Destination burned away.

Chapter 46

Logan took one look at the packet of drugs Mac had lifted from Holmberg's house and gave a wry laugh.

'Cialis,' he said. 'The American version of Viagra. Looks like Holmberg was reliant on the little blue pills.'

He handed them back to Mac, and Mac flicked them across the table to Ginger. 'There you go, mate.'

Ginger flicked them straight back at him with a laugh. 'These are for old timers like you, not someone of my age.' There was a three-year age difference between them.

They were having a late afternoon beer at the Mustafa, trying to work out their next course of action. The pills didn't add anything to the investigation.

'We need to track down the part-burned flight itinerary we found in Holmberg's rubbish,' said Mac. 'I'll try UNHAS.'

He got out his phone and dialled UNHAS, explaining what he needed to the woman who answered.

'Sorry, sir, but we can't give out that sort of information.' She was clearly a jobsworth.

'I'm investigating the murder of a British Army officer.'

'This organisation doesn't come under British jurisdiction, sir. I can't give out that information without a request through the official channels.'

'What official channels?'

'You can send a request in writing to our legal department.' She rattled off the Rome address of the World Food Programme who ran the air service. 'Or you could ask Interpol to intercede on your behalf.'

Mac disconnected.

'This is getting us nowhere. Doing it officially will take weeks.'

Ginger returned to the table with another round of beers.

'Man, don't waste your time on that,' said Logan. 'Maybe Jananga can winkle the information out of the local UNHAS office. I'll give him a call, tell him what we've found.'

'Rather you than me,' said Mac, remembering his last exchange with the major.

And that was that. They were at a dead end. Unless Jananga could come up with the flight information, Holmberg could be anywhere by now. Their last definite sighting of him had been the meeting with Baz. Three days had passed since then, and Baseer Ghilji had proved strangely reluctant to set up another meeting. Even if they did get the flight details, it would tell them nothing about his onward travel.

The thought of Holmberg getting away scot free with Marshall and Bao Liang's murders was fucking depressing. Whatever mess Davie Marshall had got himself into, surely he hadn't deserved to die for his sins?

—

When he and Ginger got back to Julien, Mac slunk off to his quarters and lay on his bunk, waiting for the inevitable summons to Phelps's office. It was cold and the wind whistled against the ridged metal sides of the container. But it was also a haven from the clatter and shouting, and the heavy sound of boots on concrete floors, and the smells of stale coffee, stale cooking and stale men. The small space gave him time to himself and respite. He should have been in his office, but he simply couldn't see the point when it was clear he was about to get his marching orders.

He didn't have to wait long.

Ginger knocked and stuck his head around the container door. 'Phelps wants to see you.'

'Here falleth the axe,' said Mac, sitting up to pull on his boots.

'Good luck, mate. Let me know how it goes.'

No kidding. Ginger knew exactly how it would go and so did he.

Phelps's eyes were already flashing with anger when Mac went into his office.

'What the fuck have you done, MacKenzie?' he stormed, before Mac had even had a chance to sit down. 'Major Jananga wants you off the case.'

'I know.'

'You know? And when were you going to get around to telling me?'

'I thought he would.'

'And he did, in no uncertain terms.'

Mac shrugged.

'Fuck's sake, MacKenzie. You've put the new contract in jeopardy – Jananga said you'd been forced to resign from the Met, and they couldn't have people like you working for the Afghan police. What the hell was he talking about?'

'Sorry, Egon. It's true. I was pressurised off the force when my DCI fucked up, and some arsehole colonel at Souter started digging around and discovered it. Because of course the army doesn't want me on the case. They've got a beef because it's out of their jurisdiction, so they're messing with Jananga.'

Phelps didn't look any less angry.

'But you never thought to mention it when you applied for this job?'

'I thought you'd find out through vetting, and when it wasn't brought up at interview, I wasn't exactly going to raise the subject.'

Phelps was silent for a moment, his hands steepled in front of him on the desk.

'Sure, the vetting process the company employs is pretty crap, almost non-existent,' he said after a while.

That explained a lot.

'So tell me about it.'

It wasn't something Mac really wanted to talk about, but he owed Phelps something. The guy hadn't been too bad to work with, and it wasn't as if anyone else was going to employ him at the point when he'd got the job with WTP.

'I was in charge of an SO15 raid on a terrorist safe house in Bermondsey – we had intel that it was being used by an AQ cell. The place was empty, and we had it under surveillance as part of the risk assessment. Two hours before we were due to go in, there was a snafu. The surveillance was compromised. I wanted to call it off. My DCI didn't, and he pulled rank. The operation went ahead and by the time we got there, there was a suicide bomber in situ. I lost two of my team, and my DCI lied about the lead-up to the op.'

Phelps stared at Mac. Mac didn't know what Phelps's background was, but he felt pretty sure it was managerial rather than operational – there was shock written all over his face. Then he recovered himself.

'So you were sacked? Without some sort of enquiry as to what had happened?'

'These things are pretty hush-hush. An enquiry would have drawn attention. The brass didn't want that. They tactfully suggested I resign – at least that meant I kept my pension.'

'Well, be that as it may, I'm afraid I'm going to have to let you go, Mac. Jananga's a man with influence and we can't jeopardise the contract.'

'I understand.' Mac wasn't lying when he said this, but it didn't make it okay. What the fuck was he going to do now?

'Take a week to clear yourself out of the container and find somewhere to go,' said Phelps, not meeting his eye. 'And, regardless of what's happened, I'll put in a good word for you if you find somewhere out here.'

'Thanks.' For nothing.

-

'These are some pretty spectacular pieces,' said Baz, leafing through the pile of photos.

Mac needed to take his mind off his immediate future, so he'd gone round to the Gandamack to show Baz the photos he'd found in the front of Holmberg's copy of Nancy Dupree. He'd called Logan to join them, but the American had yet to arrive.

'Look at this one – it looks like it could be a part of the Begram Ivories, or certainly from the same area and time period.'

'Elephants? In Afghanistan?'

Baz shook her head. 'No. Originally these pieces were made in India, in the first century. They would have been used to decorate furniture, which would have made its way to Afghanistan. And this statuette could be Bronze Age. I'd need to do some detailed research to tell you exactly what they are – but if Holmberg has all these, he's sitting on a goldmine.'

'Just because he's got the pictures, doesn't mean he owns the goods.'

'No one owns them,' said Baz sharply. 'They should be on display in the National Museum. And if he's intending to sell them abroad, then he's committing a major crime.'

'On top of murder, or conspiracy to murder.' Mac didn't want to lose the focus on the initial crime, even if the antiquities were Baz's main interest. Back when he'd been in the Met, he could never let go of a case and, in that respect, nothing had changed even if he no longer had an official role in the investigation.

Baz didn't answer, but sipped her coffee as she studied the pictures, one by one. She got out a notebook and jotted down a few details. Mac watched as she placed two pictures in particular away from the pile.

'What are they?' he said.

She held them out to him. 'Look at the background. Recognise anything?'

Mac studied the pictures. One was of a section of carved marble, with intricate geometric patterns standing out in relief. The other one was a bronze horse, two of its legs broken off and no tail, but still stunning. They were both positioned on the top of a low wall. Behind them, barren earth rising up to a boulder-strewn slope.

'Sure – I recognise that rock, just there,' he said.

'Don't be snarky,' said Baz with a grin.

'Well, seriously – they could be anywhere.'

'No, look closer. On the left-hand edge.'

He looked at them again. On the left margin of each picture a sliver of reddish-pink brickwork rose up from an area of flat ground behind the wall.

'Okay. A building. I still don't recognise it.'

'But I do,' said Baz. 'I think that might just be the Minaret of Jam.'

'Where's that?'

Baz rolled her eyes. 'You know nothing about this country, do you?'

'Sorry. I'm not here as a tourist, am I?'

'Sure. But if you're going to help Afghanistan thrive, you need to at least understand it.'

'That's a bit of a leap just because I don't instantly recognise some particular corner of brickwork.' There were times when Baz's proprietorial superiority jangled on his nerves. 'We're here on a very specific mission – not as general do-gooders.'

Baz frowned at him. 'The Minaret of Jam is one of Afghanistan's most important historic landmarks. It's in Ghor Province, about one hundred and seventy miles east of Herat.'

'Fine. Well spotted.' They wouldn't make any progress if they argued. 'So, is this where he would have acquired those artefacts?'

Baz shrugged. 'Some of them, maybe. There are a lot of illegal digs in the Shahrak district of Ghor and Jam is a World Heritage Site. There are plenty of cave systems too, which are remote and inaccessible. The sort of places where he could hide his stash. But the pictures don't tell us much… like exactly where those pieces are now.'

'Every bit of information has value,' said Mac. There was a noise behind him and he started to turn.

'Have I got some news for you two!' Logan slapped Mac on the back, almost making him spill his coffee.

Baz motioned to the barman to bring another round of coffees.

'What?' said Mac.

'I've just spoken to Jananga and he got the information we needed from the UNHAS office. Holmberg booked two seats on the Saturday flight to Herat.'

'Herat?' said Baz. 'There you go.'

'What?' asked Logan.

'Look.' Baz held out one of the pictures to him, pointing at the brickwork with her finger.

'Ah, Minaret Jam,' said Logan. 'Beautiful.'

'You know it, from just that corner of brickwork?' Mac couldn't believe what he was hearing.

'Sure. Didn't you?'

Mac shook his head, but at last, the pieces were falling into place.

'It might just be where Holmberg is headed now…'

Chapter 47

The Tuesday morning UNHAS flight to Herat was rammed – every seat taken, and Mac wouldn't have been surprised if there'd been people standing in the aisle. He settled into his window seat and did up his seat belt with a sigh of relief. It had been touch and go as to whether they would make the flight at all and in the last twenty-four hours sleep had been a luxury he'd had to forego.

Once it became clear that Holmberg had a reason to go to Jam, following him there seemed like the obvious course of action. Mac was now a free agent, so he didn't bother to get Phelps's approval for the trip, even though he used the remaining company dollars he had to pay for his and Ginger's flights. Ginger was sanguine about the risk he was taking – having been let go from the case, Phelps had given him a week's leave as his replacement was still in situ to cover the end of the current teaching module.

Logan had told Jananga what he was doing, without mentioning that Mac and Ginger were in on it – even when Jananga had elected to join the expedition. Arresting Holmberg for murder and whatever else he could pin on him would be a feather in his cap, so he wasn't going to miss out on the glory if Logan was doing all the leg work.

They wouldn't be able to take weapons with them on the UNHAS plane, but Logan had assured Mac that he had contacts in Herat who would be able to supply them with whatever they needed, while Jananga would be able to draw on arms from the local police.

Mac looked up and down the plane and spotted Jananga and his sergeant three rows in front and, two rows ahead of them, he could just see the back of Logan's head. Ginger was two rows behind him on the other side of the aisle. He wondered how Jananga would respond when he discovered that he and Ginger were part of the expedition.

The plane turned onto the runway and the engine tune changed from a hum to a roar. Mac gazed out of the window as the G-force of the take-off pushed him back in his seat. The northern outskirts of Kabul flashed past and then dropped away as the plane rose steeply, straining to gain enough height to make its turn to the west over the city's northern hills. The ordered grids of the city streets gave way to the shanty towns that were crawling higher and higher up the slopes – peace had brought its own problems to the capital. The population was rising faster than they could build houses.

Mac closed his eyes. The flight would be just over an hour and he intended to spend at least sixty minutes of it sleeping. The drone of the engines sang the perfect lullaby.

'*Mebakshed, fekr mekonom an jay-e man bashad…*'

The woman's voice cut through his brain-fog. He had no idea what she said, but for some reason the voice sounded familiar.

The man sitting next to him clearly wasn't impressed. His reply was aggressive.

'*Ne!*'

For the love of God.

Mac opened his eyes.

'Christ! What the hell are you doing here?'

'Asking this gentleman if he wouldn't mind swapping seats,' said Baz, grinning down at him from the aisle.

'No, I mean, what are you doing on this plane?'

Now it was the man's turn to look puzzled, and he interrupted with a stream of Dari.

Baz turned on the charm with him and the steward who came to find out what the commotion was, and two minutes later she was settling into the seat next to Mac.

'What in God's name are you playing at, Baz?' Mac was anything but happy to see her on the flight.

She finished buckling up her seatbelt and then turned to speak to him.

'Duh, I'm coming with you.'

'No way. You get off this plane in Herat and take the first one back again.'

Baz frowned. 'You're not the boss of me.'

'No, but I don't have to take you with me on a live operation, either. How did you even know we would be on this flight?'

'I checked with Logan.'

'Fuck's sake.' He looked out of the window, hunching up his shoulder as a barrier.

'Come on, Mac. I need to trace those artefacts. After all, if I hadn't spotted the minaret in those photos, you wouldn't even know where to look.'

She had a point, but Mac wasn't going to admit it.

'Listen, this could be dangerous. If we locate Holmberg, the chances are he'll be armed—'

'And you know I can handle a gun.'

'One lucky shot?'

'Goddamnit, there's no reason to think this will end in a shootout. You and Logan can find Xiaoli, Jananga can arrest Holmberg and I can retrieve and catalogue any antiquities we discover. Seriously, it makes sense for me to come along.'

'It so doesn't.'

She turned from him to take a bottle of mineral water from the steward. She took a second one and passed it to Mac.

'I thought you'd be pleased to see me.'

'I am – I just don't want to be responsible for taking you into a dangerous situation.'

'Like I said, you're not responsible for me.'

Sleep was out of the question now – Mac was too riled up. He stared out of the window at the extraordinary landscape they were flying over. It was unlike anything he was used to. It could have been the surface of Mars – a rocky wasteland of brown, ochre and gold. Range after range of jagged hills, crushed together by the movement of the earth's plates beneath, cut through by narrow, fast-flowing rivers of snow-melt. The patches of green were few and far between. Tiny, mud-coloured villages clung to the hillsides with the same tenacity that the people of this barren land clung to life itself.

As they started their descent to Herat, Mac's nerves started to jangle.

What would they find at the end of their journey?

Chapter 48

The plane touched down on the Herat runway at a quarter past one, and by twenty past one Jananga had spotted Mac and Ginger inside the small, stone terminal building. And he wasn't fooled for a minute.

'Mr MacKenzie, this is not a coincidence, I think,' he said, glaring at Mac through narrowed eyes. 'What are you doing here?'

Mac decided to try and break through the formal tone. 'Jananga-jan, you are, of course, completely right. But now that I'm out of a job, Logan asked me to help him locate Xiaoli. So it would seem that we'll be working together for a while longer.'

Baz was standing next to him, and she said to Jananga something in rapid Dari, finishing with an encouraging smile. He answered her without a smile, then looked back at Mac.

'Mac-jan, don't cross my path or get in my way.'

'Of course not.' Mac grinned – they were back on first name terms at least – and Jananga strode off to locate his sergeant.

'All okay?' said Logan, joining them.

'Anyone's guess,' said Mac.

'He's fine,' said Baz. 'He tries to look fierce, but really he's a pussycat.'

Mac wasn't so sure about that. After all, he'd seen Razul when Jananga had finished with him and Baz hadn't. But it seemed like they were still playing for the same side. For now.

The airport had been bombed by the Americans in 2001, and there was still evidence of the damage – one side of the terminal was a mess of rubble, letting the wind whistle through. The landing had been bumpy and Mac was relieved to have his feet on the ground. He looked round with interest as they waited for their baggage to be trolleyed in. From what he could see outside, the landscape was flatter and there was more greenery here than there was in Kabul.

Logan did a headcount of the group – Mac and Ginger, Jananga and his sergeant, Ardshir, and Baz.

'Come on,' he said. 'I've pulled in a favour – my contact, Commander Kourash, has sent transport for us. No point hanging around here.'

'To where?' said Baz.

'The citadel, where Ismail Khan's militia is based.'

He led the way out of the shed and, although the day was bright, a sharp northerly wind buffeted them as they walked across the dusty hardstanding in front of the airport. Two Toyota Surfs, one blue and one black, started their engines and pulled out of their parking spaces. Logan waved at them as they drew up by the group.

The passenger door of the front vehicle opened and a wiry man in camouflage fatigues and a black-and-white patterned *keffiyeh* sprung out. He had a full head of black hair, a glossy black beard and dark beady eyes. As soon as he'd picked out Logan from the group, a wide grin creased his features.

'Commander!' Logan held out his arms. '*Salam! Che hal dared?*'

'*Salam!* My old friend, it's good to see you.'

The two men embraced, kissed cheeks once, twice, thrice, and rattled off a stream of Dari that Mac didn't have a hope of following. Finally, as the excitement abated, Logan introduced the rest of the group.

Commander Kourash was serious and courteous, speaking English to them and putting out his hand to shake Mac's as

Logan said his name. He was equally polite to Ginger, which Mac liked to see. However, when it was Jananga's turn, the major scowled and didn't shake Kourash's hand.

'Major Jananga,' said Kourash, his grin reappearing. 'Welcome to my city. We are not monsters, you know.'

Jananga begrudgingly took his hand and shook it for the minimum time possible with a curt nod of his head. Mac knew he disapproved of the way Khan ran the city. The governor of Herat was a law unto himself, and though the city was safe and stable, even for western workers, he thumbed his nose at Kabul at every opportunity.

'This is Basima Khan,' said Logan.

Kourash had been eyeing her with puzzlement since he'd emerged from his vehicle.

'Pleased to meet you, Miss Khan.' He gave her a nod but no handshake.

Baz spoke to him in Dari, he answered, and they both smiled. The ice was broken and it was time to go. Logan, Mac and Baz got into the front vehicle with Kourash, while Ginger, Jananga and Ardshir got into the one behind.

'*Boro! Boro!*' said Kourash. Go! Go!

The driver revved his engine and accelerated out of the parking area onto the road. He continued to accelerate at every opportunity and seemed reluctant to ever apply the brakes. They sped along the highway, north towards the city, across a wide, flat river valley, scattered with fields and villages, until they reached the industrial outskirts of the city. Russian-built grain silos stood in sentinel rows along the side of the road, and Kourash proudly pointed out the rebuilt city bakery.

It was Mac's first visit to Herat – in fact, his first trip out of the environs of Kabul – and he looked out of the car window with interest.

Kourash's driver blared on the horn to get a slow-moving lorry to pull over. The commander wound down his window and shouted something at the unfortunate truck driver as they passed.

'Never get in the way of Ismail Khan's forces on the road,' said Logan with a laugh as they swerved around another crawling vehicle. 'I've seen them run other cars into ditches just for the sheer hell of it.'

'Only the cars of our enemies,' said Kourash, looking round at them with a sly smile.

Mac grinned back. He had a feeling, whatever the outcome, he was going to enjoy at least parts of the trip.

Baz, sitting in the centre of the back seat where there was no seatbelt, gripped Mac's arm with white knuckles to stop herself sliding across the seat into Logan.

They had to slow down a little as they came into the city centre, but the driver made good use of his horn to cut through the traffic, and within half an hour of leaving the airport, the citadel loomed up in front of them. Mac didn't need to be told that this was it – it was obvious. The huge golden structure was like a medieval crusaders' castle, rising above the city, walls crumbling, towers falling down, but with a bristle of modern weaponry visible over the ramparts. Whatever the situation now, he was beginning to realise that Afghanistan had an extraordinary history at the crossroads of some major civilisations – a role that even now was still being played out.

'We stop here tonight,' said Logan to Baz, 'and then head east to the Minaret of Jam in the morning.'

The minaret was an eight-hour drive in good conditions, longer if it rained or snowed, and while Mac had been all for driving through the night, Logan had counselled against it.

'We'll be driving through bandit country,' he'd said. 'They attack at night. Even Khan's militia will only travel in convoy during the day.'

The gates to Alexander the Great's fortress were more heavily guarded now than probably at any time over its two-thousand-year history. Armed militiamen manned a walled checkpoint, and once Kourash had got them through that, they drove up a steep incline to a pair of solid wooden gates in the original stone walls, where they were checked by more guards.

Finally, they got out of the Surfs in the large rectangular courtyard at the centre of the citadel, lined on one side by an arched walkway and on the other by the main structure of the building, punctuated by double doors and shuttered windows. The visitors were shown to the rooms they would use for the night. There was some consternation caused by Baz's unexpected arrival, but Kourash volunteered his quarters for her to ensure her privacy.

'*Tashakor*,' said Baz, bowing her head.

'*Kosh amaded*,' answered the commander, obviously charmed by his American guest.

The afternoon was spent preparing kit for the next day's journey. They would travel in five vehicles – two Surfs and three Toyota High Lux trucks – Kourash was taking ten men and there were six in the Kabul party, but as he explained, they always travelled with spare vehicle capacity in case of breakdowns or worse. There were more than enough weapons to go around – AK74s, Makarov pistols, PKM machine guns and RPG7s. From his time in anti-terrorism, Mac was familiar with them all, though his experience with Soviet-era ordnance was limited. Kourash showed them off proudly, recounting tales of derring-do during the Soviet occupation and after that under the rule of the Taliban. The weapons were allocated and loaded onto the vehicles, along with water and basic food supplies for four days – again more than they thought they'd need.

As the sun set, the convoy was declared packed and ready for their sunrise departure.

'Now, please take pleasure in our hospitality,' said the commander.

The Kabul party were shown through a heavy wooden door studded with iron into what must have been one of the great rooms of the ancient citadel. It was cavernous and bare, apart from the overlapping carpets that covered the floor. The ceiling was vaulted, and a series of high arched windows allowed the last rays of sunlight to carve amber patterns on the bare stone walls and worn carpets. Two teenage boys unfurled and spread out a rectangular stretch of oilcloth in the centre of the floor, while another lit braziers around the sides of the room.

Following Kourash's lead, Mac unlaced his boots and left them neatly by the door. As the others did the same, he found a place to sit down cross-legged at the edge of the oilcloth. Baz joined him on one side, and Jananga sat on the other. Ginger sat opposite, already making stilted conversation with Ardshir and one of Kourash's deputies. As everyone settled, one of the boys came round with a tray of glasses, followed by his companions offering drinks. Bottled water, green tea, a yogurt drink called *doogh*, or Zamzam. Mac helped himself to a bottle of Zamzam, an Iranian cola named after the water from the Holy Well in Mecca. It wasn't Coke, but it was infinitely better than green tea.

The food started to arrive. Huge platters of Kabuli *palaw*, a golden rice dish studded with raisins, grated carrot and huge chunks of steaming, fatty mutton. It was accompanied by *mâst*, a yogurt sauce that Mac knew was delicious but played havoc with his digestion, big bowls of brightly coloured salad and mountains of naan bread, which doubled up as plates. There was no cutlery, and Mac was careful to follow Kourash and his men, eating only with his right hand.

It was a feast. The stringy meat had the distinctive strong flavour that always transported Mac back to his grandmother's kitchen as she cooked mutton pies or Scotch broth. He ate till he was full, as did the others, but it seemed they made hardly a dent in the mountain of food before them.

Logan and Kourash spent the time trading war stories until the dishes were cleared and one of the boys came round with tea.

'So,' said Kourash, looking around to include Mac and Jananga in the conversation, 'the man you are hunting is travelling alone?'

'We don't know,' said Mac. 'We think he'll be collecting stolen artefacts at the minaret to take over the border, so my guess is he wouldn't attempt that without some fire power.'

Kourash nodded. 'Does he know you're coming after him?'

'He'll be expecting it.' Logan's mouth settled in a grim line.

'He's wanted for murder,' said Jananga.

'So you want to take him alive, Major?'

'*Insha' Allah.*'

Kourash called to one of his men to join them and there followed a heated discussion in Dari.

'What are they talking about?' whispered Mac to Logan.

'Final details for tomorrow.'

The conversation continued in a mixture of Dari and English as the plans were laid. Orders were issued, maps were consulted, details settled. Finally, Mac felt, they were ready for action – and he could already feel a charge of excitement tautening his muscles.

Eventually, the commander clambered to his feet, signalling an end to the evening.

'We leave at dawn. Time to sleep. May Allah grant you the dreams that you wish for.'

Chapter 49

Mac cursed silently into his pillow as the alarm went off. One minute Ginger had been snoring on the other side of the room, next the tinny digital alarm on his watch was hammering against his temple. He could have done with another few hours.

'You awake, boss?'

There was no shower, just a pitcher of cold water and a bowl, and Mac had to use his electric razor without the benefit of a mirror. Thankfully, he knew his own face well enough for it not to matter.

Ten minutes after the alarm had sounded, they were out in the courtyard. Mac blinked, still bleary eyed with sleep, but Baz was standing by the open boot of one of the Surfs, already in animated conversation with their host.

'Good morning, Mac-jan,' said Jananga, coming up behind him as he arrived with Ardshir. Mac noticed that Ardshir was carrying both of their backpacks. At least his bad mood seemed to have melted away.

'Morning, Major,' he said. 'Did you sleep well?'

He didn't really listen to the reply. He was too busy watching Baz.

After putting on a camouflaged ops vest, she took hold of the Makarov pistol Kourash held out to her, saying something in Dari as she measured the weight of it in her hand. The commander grinned and so did she. Then she expertly ejected the magazine, racked the slide back, caught the ejected round

321

neatly in her other hand and looked inside. Having viewed it to her satisfaction, she released the slide, fired off the action and inserted the magazine. She racked the slide back again to feed a round into the chamber, ejected the magazine and reloaded the round she still held in her hand. Finally, she inserted the magazine, applied the safety and tucked the pistol into the holster in her ops vest.

'Shut your mouth, Mac, you'll catch flies.' Logan could hardly suppress the laughter in his voice.

Mac shook his head. 'You're pretty nifty with that Makarov, Baz.'

'And why would that surprise you?'

'Just didn't realise you'd have much call for it, as a reporter.'

Baz laughed. 'True. My father taught me how to handle weapons a long time ago. But a spot of revision with Logan and it all came back to me.'

'Impressive,' said Ginger, grinning at Mac. 'Probably better than you, plod.'

Kourash's men were milling about the courtyard, carrying out last-minute checks on the vehicles and arguing about who was going to ride where. His number two was briefing the drivers and issuing handheld radios to the lead personnel in each of the trucks and Surfs. Kourash, Mac, Logan and Baz would be in the blue Surf, with a driver. Jananga, Ginger and Ardshir would be in the black Surf with Kourash's deputy. Kourash's ten men were divided across the Toyota trucks, two in each cab, with the rest in the open backs, armed with AK47s, RPGs and machine guns.

'Are we ready now?' said Mac.

Kourash nodded.

'Okay. Load up and let's head out.'

As soon as everyone was aboard their allotted vehicle, Kourash gave the order to move out over the radio.

'*Boro! Boro!*'

The heavy wooden gates opened, and the first of the trucks rolled forward. The two Surfs followed it out, with the other two trucks bringing up the rear. As soon as the first set of gates opened, the guards at the lower checkpoint opened their steel gates to let the convoy through.

It was barely light and the city was still sleeping. Most of the streets were empty of traffic and it only took them ten minutes to get onto the Martyr Alauddin Khan Boulevard. This took them east to the edge of the built-up area, where it became the A77, the main road between Herat and Kabul. Kourash spoke briefly with his driver, then turned to the passengers in the back.

'Mac-jan, if you are hungry, there is a bag with naan and fruit behind your seat.'

It was a basic breakfast, but despite the previous evening's feast, everyone had an appetite. By the time they'd eaten, they'd left the environs of the city behind them and were passing through the arable lands of the river valley. Small holdings with postage-stamp fields flashed past, though at this time of year nothing was growing in the brown earth.

Although it would take several hours to reach Jam, Mac was already feeling on edge with the prospect of what lay ahead.

'My informant came to me last night,' said Kourash. He spoke in English out of courtesy to Mac, even though Logan and Baz were both fluent Dari speakers. 'Holmberg stayed two nights in the city, at the Park Hotel, and left yesterday in a rented Land Cruiser.'

'Was he on his own?' said Logan, leaning forward in his seat.

'He had a woman with him, and two bodyguards, according to the hotel manager.'

'Maybe it's Xiaoli,' said Logan. 'Was she Chinese? Young?'

'Yes, Chinese,' said Kourash.

'His destination?' said Mac.

'They didn't share that with the hotel staff. But you are certain he had business in Jam?'

'We think he's storing stolen artefacts out by the minaret,' said Baz.

'Jam is a small village. We'll find out straightaway if he's been there, or if he's still in the area.'

About half an hour outside the city, the road forked. The North Circular Highway swung away north towards the border with Turkmenistan, while the A77 continued east in the direction of Jam and, ultimately, Kabul. After the split, the road they were travelling on went from tarmac to gravel. Rutted and with frequent potholes, their speed dropped significantly, and Mac suddenly wished the vehicle had better suspension. His teeth jarred and he grabbed hold of the handrail above the door to keep himself steady. But he didn't care – he was impatient to reach their destination, and they needed to gain ground on Holmberg.

—

The dirt road wound along the valley of the Harirud River. Sometimes they were passing through farmlands, but just as often all Mac could see were barren, rock-strewn hillsides, climbing on either side of the river. As the day wore on, the villages and cultivated areas became further between and the valley narrowed. The Harirud carried meltwaters from the mountains to the north of them, and he could clearly see the highwater marks of the spring torrents, but its winding course made the journey arduous and probably three times longer than the distance as the crow flies.

Baz slept part of the way, resting against his shoulder, occasionally softly snoring, causing him to exchange smiles with Logan across the top of her hijab. She smelled faintly of sandalwood and oranges.

Kourash checked in regularly with the other vehicles. The morning wore on, and Mac found himself dozing off too every now and again, until a particularly big pothole would jolt him awake.

The hills on either side of the road grew steeper, and there were glimpses of snow-topped mountains in the distance. Most

324

of the time, however, all he could see was ochre earth and blue sky, all filtered through the cloud of dust thrown up by the Hilux truck ahead of them. The men sitting in the back of it had wrapped their *keffiyehs* tightly around their faces and most of them wore sunglasses to keep the grit out of their eyes.

There was virtually no other traffic on the road – an occasional KAMAZ truck, liberated by the locals as the Soviets had withdrawn, one or two scooters, and a man with a donkey. The villages they drove through were like ghost towns. He heard a dog barking in one, and saw an old woman in another, but most of the time they could have been deserted. They also saw a couple of Kuchi nomad encampments by the side of the road, their sprawling tents the same colour as the dirt they were pitched in. Goats and camels roamed the camps, watched over by small boys, while grown men would stop their discussions and stare as the convoy passed by. It was as if they'd travelled back in time.

A couple of times they stopped and Kourash's deputy would talk hurriedly to one or two old men sitting outside their village mud huts.

'What's he doing?' said Mac, the first time it happened.

'He's asking if anyone's driven through recently,' said Kourash, watching the exchange closely.

The deputy walked back to his Surf, giving Kourash a nod as climbed back in. A moment later the radio crackled into life as he reported the conversation.

'Yes,' said Kourash, 'a blond westerner passed through here yesterday. Holmberg.'

Mac felt a surge of adrenalin. They would corner him at the minaret – the road effectively ended here as there was no way he would be able to ford the river in winter unless he was in a Soviet Kamaz ten-tonner, and they knew he wasn't.

They parked up at lunchtime to stretch their legs and eat. Ginger looked particularly pained as he clambered out of the second Surf.

'All right, chum?' said Mac as they hiked a small hillside by the road to take in the view.

Ginger shook his head. 'Just bored. The major and Ardshir haven't stopped talking the whole way – and I can't understand a bloody word of it.'

Mac laughed. 'At least you haven't had Baz snoring in your ear.'

They crunched down the slope to where Kourash's men were apportioning more naan and the leftover Kabuli *palaw* from the night before. Mac grabbed a bottle of water and drank greedily – the dusty air left him with a dry throat and gritty eyes.

Baz was talking to Kourash in Dari. He laughed, showing off a dazzling set of straight white teeth. For a moment, Mac didn't like him quite so much. Then Baz came over and pointed at the food.

'Dig in.'

They didn't stop for long, and ten minutes later, they were back in their vehicles, pulling out onto the road again.

'How much further, Commander?' said Mac.

'Two more hours,' he said. 'If the road stays good.'

If this was a good road, Mac didn't want to experience a bad one.

Mesmerised by the hum of the engines, he closed his eyes.

'Stop! *Estad shaw!*' It was Baz. 'Look!'

He opened his eyes and looked in the direction she was pointing. He could see nothing – just another empty slope.

Kourash started shouting instructions into his radio as the Hilux ahead of them screeched to a halt.

'What? What did you see?'

'There,' she said, pointing again. 'A man.'

Mac looked and this time he saw it – on the crest of the hill, a man on horseback, rifle raised and pointed in their direction.

He wasn't alone.

Chapter 50

A stream of automatic gunfire ripped through the silence as the vehicles stopped, and Baz heard the sharp crack of bullets piercing metal and pinging off stones. The windscreen of one of the trucks shattered and it skidded onto the gravel at the side of the road. She gasped – it was heading over the edge, towards the river. The men in the back dived out, clutching their weapons and shouting. Then it suddenly swerved. Someone had managed to grab the wheel and avert disaster.

She could breathe again.

Mac shouted something at her but his voice was drowned out by gunfire. She ducked her head down to her knees, feeling in her ops vest for the pistol Kourash had given her earlier. Mac was already cradling an AK47 between his legs. She heard return fire coming from the trucks behind them and twisted her head to see what had happened to the mounted gunman. The hillside was empty. Of course – he wasn't going to present himself as a sitting target, but she could see small puffs of smoke coming from behind a rocky outcrop. That's where they were firing from.

'Get out! Get out!' Mac yelled in her ear.

He had the door on his side open and pulled her roughly by the arm. Adrenalin flooded through her as they scrambled out and dropped down behind the cover of the Surf. Mac glanced around.

'Here,' he said, scurrying back from the Surf towards a pair of giant boulders.

Baz inched her way to the edge of the truck to peer around the side. It was all quiet at the rocks where their attackers were stationed. She could feel the pulse at the base of her throat going ballistic.

'For fuck's sake, Baz – you'll get yourself killed. Get over here and stay down.'

She scrambled low to the ground and joined Mac behind the first of the boulders. Logan, Ginger and Jananga were crouched behind the other, alternately reloading their weapons and firing.

Out of the corner of her eye, she could see Kourash. He was still sheltering behind their Surf, but he sent one of his men out towards the Hilux that had skidded off the road. Mac and Logan leaned around their rocks to give the militiaman covering fire. When he reached the truck, he snatched open the driver's door. The blood-covered driver slumped out and Baz could see a chunk missing from the side of his head. The soldier dragged him to the ground and then helped the passenger out – equally covered in blood, but still alive.

'I'll help him,' said Baz, making a move.

Mac grabbed her shoulder. 'No. Ginger, you go.'

Ginger scurried across the few feet of open ground to where the militiaman was supporting the injured occupant from the vehicle. The commander shouted at his troops – the gunfire went ballistic – and together Ginger and the militiaman lifted the wounded passenger and ran back to the boulders. He was moaning loudly and, from behind the rock, Baz could see a bullet wound in his upper right arm. Although it was bleeding profusely, most of the blood covering him was from when the driver's head had been blown apart – the bloodstains on his upper body carried fragments of bone and tissue that certainly weren't his.

Baz's stomach churned but she bit hard on her bottom lip, willing the pain to distract her from feeling sick. She felt a cold sweat on the back of her neck.

She crawled over to him and patted the pockets of her ops vest. One of them had a small medical kit – just a military field dressing comprising some tightly rolled bandages and wadding to minimise battlefield bleeding. She found it and started ripping off the wrappings.

Mac scrambled across and inspected the wound. He undid the man's ops vest and battledress.

'Give me a moment,' he said. 'There's a kit with some iodine in the back of the Surf. I'll get it.'

Baz nodded.

'Cover me!' Mac shouted to the rest of the team.

He was back in less than a minute with a small first aid kit that looked like it dated back to the Soviet occupation.

'It's a through and through,' said Mac as he cut away the man's sleeve.

'What do you mean?' said Baz.

'In one side, out the other. Got a tampon, Baz?'

She squinted at him. It seemed a weird thing to ask.

'I can use it to pack the wound.'

'Sure, of course.' She dug into her jacket's inside pocket, where she always stashed one or two. Mac took it from her, stripped off the wrapper and pushed it unceremoniously into the man's wound. He grunted with the sudden jab of pain, but he'd probably thank them for it later.

They worked together in silence, as sporadic shooting went on around them. With a clear task, Baz's nerves calmed down. She cleaned around the wound and then Mac helped her to bandage some more wadding in place. The man continued to moan. He'd need to be stitched up properly, but they'd certainly prevented a further loss of blood.

As they finished, Kourash came across to their boulder to thank them.

'His wife will see him again and he will father many more children, *insha'Allah*.'

Logan joined them.

'They've made a clusterfuck of this,' he said, tilting his gun up towards the bandits' emplacement.

'How so?' said Baz.

'One firing point only,' said Kourash. 'If they wanted to do real damage, they'd need to come at us from the front and the side at the same time.'

'How many are there?' said Mac.

'Five by my count,' said Logan.

The commander nodded in agreement. 'There were more, but I know we've hit two of them.'

Baz hoped they hadn't shot the horse.

'Ten minutes to finish them off?' said Logan.

Kourash laughed, rubbing his beard. 'I think five.'

He called to two of his men who were sheltering behind the third truck with machine guns.

'He's told them to start firing on his signal, and not to stop until he signals again,' said Baz, translating for Mac. 'Now he's telling these three here with the RPGs to use that cover to move into a position where they can see the PKM tracer fire going in.'

Kourash gave the signal with a raised arm, setting off a constant barrage from the machine guns that effectively stopped the bandits from returning fire. He let it go on for ten seconds, then gave the signal to stop.

It worked. One, two, three of the bandits raised their heads above cover to see what was going on. The men with the RPGs let rip, followed by the rest of the team, including Logan, Mac, Jananga, Ginger and Ardshir. Baz squinted around the edge of a rock and took a couple of shots with her Makarov, ready to prove her worth in a combat situation. There was no way she could tell where her rounds had gone. She hoped to God she hadn't killed anybody – putting them out of action was all she wanted to achieve.

The fire thundered out, glancing off stones and ricocheting in every direction, the roar so loud that Baz thought it would burst her eardrums.

Finally, Kourash raised his arm to stop the din. '*Estad shaw! Estad shaw!*'

Silence fell.

There was no response.

He shouted another command and three of his men scurried up the hill towards the rocky outcrop, the rest of the group standing ready to cover them. The men circled the rocks cautiously, weapons raised.

Then a shout went up. '*Hama morda!*'

'All dead,' said Baz.

There was more shouting.

'No, one's still alive apparently.'

Two of the men appeared from behind the rocks, supporting an injured man between them.

'We will question him,' said Kourash, going up the slope to meet his men.

'The commander was right,' said Logan. 'Less than five minutes to sort the jokers out.'

'He knew what he was doing,' said Ginger.

Logan laughed. 'So he should. That man has fought the Russians, the Afghan Communists, in the civil war, the Taliban – more action than you or I could see in ten lifetimes. You know what they say? Never underestimate an old man in a profession where they usually die young.'

Baz went to the Surf and grabbed some water bottles. The air smelled of burnt propellant, and brass cases littered the ground all around the vehicles and the rocks. She threw a bottle of water to Mac and then went over to listen to what the wounded man was telling Kourash.

'He paid you to ambush us?' the commander was saying.

'Yes, yes,' said the man.

'How much?'

'Not enough for my brothers to die for.' The man started to cry. 'But he scared us. I said we should have run when we saw five vehicles. We expected only one vehicle, two men. But my older brother was greedy. Now he's dead.'

Logan came over and gave the man a shot of morphine.

'We'll drop him off at the next village,' said Kourash. 'But now your Swede has a new enemy. Ismail Khan won't forgive him for using his people in this way.'

Chapter 51

They gained two vehicles from the tribesmen to replace the one that had been shot up. Neither had much petrol, or any contents that would be of use, but they picked up the weapons from around the dead bodies and stashed them in the back of one of the Toyotas. Mac helped to collect the bodies of the bandits and of their own driver who had been killed. His hands shook. It could easily have been him or Ginger, or Baz or Logan. It made him feel uneasy that it had been down to luck – but that's the way it was. He'd been lucky. They hadn't. The militiamen wrapped the bodies in their *keffiyehs* and loaded them onto the back of one of the captured vehicles. Kourash gave instructions to one of his drivers to take the wounded man and the bodies back to Herat, to ensure that the dead could be buried by nightfall, as was the Muslim custom.

Mac watched a pair of buzzards circling overhead. They would be out of luck this time.

The sun was low in the sky by the time they got going again. They'd had to transfer kit and equipment out of the damaged truck, and reallocate the men between the new vehicle, a Surf, and the two remaining trucks. Ginger, Jananga and Mac had taken the opportunity to drink some water and eat some naan, but Baz had declined. She went down to the river to wash the blood of the wounded men off her hands, and Mac sensed that she needed a few minutes alone.

'*Boro! Boro!*' came the familiar cry, and they all scurried back to the vehicles.

'All right?' said Mac to Baz as he waited to allow her to get into the middle seat.

'I was fine when it was happening,' said Baz, 'but now I feel a bit shaky.' She held out a hand for him to see. It was trembling.

'That's natural,' said Mac. 'Live action isn't something you want to get used to or blasé about.'

The road swung abruptly south and then after another ten miles they reached the turn off for Jam. Mac hadn't thought the road conditions could get any worse, but the track they pulled onto was narrower and bumpier than ever.

'How much further?' he said to Kourash.

'An hour and a half. Then we reach the village of Jam. The minaret is a few miles further on, to the north.'

As they got closer to their destination, Mac's stomach started churning. It would probably be dark by the time they arrived – and they had no idea where Holmberg would be. In the village or out at the minaret? The intention was to arrest him and bring him back to Herat, along with the stolen antiquities and Xiaoli, if it was indeed her.

Jam was a shabby, one-goat village – a collection of mud huts, bolstered by the nearby presence of a cluster of Aimaq nomad tents. There were no shops, or any other kind of business. A woman was walking along the side of the road, accompanied by two girls in bright green shalwars over red and orange kameez. They stopped in their tracks as the convoy rolled through, staring with wide, dark eyes and suspicious expressions.

'No point stopping here – let's keep straight on to the minaret,' said Logan. 'If we don't find him, we can come back to ask questions – if he's been here, they won't be able to keep their mouths shut.'

'Where else could he be?' said Baz.

Kourash shrugged. 'The road beyond the minaret crosses the Harirud and heads east towards Chagcharan and, after that, he could have followed a track towards the border with Turkmenistan. But at this time of year, the ford across the river is usually impassable and the country beyond it hostile. I think it more likely that he would have come back in this direction.'

'Meaning we could have missed him already,' said Mac. 'Fuck!' The little reception committee Holmberg had laid on for them had cost them valuable time.

They reached the minaret just as dusk was falling, which meant it was virtually dark in the steep-sided river valley. There was no sign of the Swede, but there were fresh tyre tracks in the gravel, suggesting someone had been here recently. Mac stared up at the ancient monument – an astonishing tower built of baked bricks and blue glazed tiles, and decorated all the way up with Kufic and Naskhi calligraphy. Almost a thousand years old, the sixty-five-metre minaret was the tallest in Afghanistan and marked the site of Firozkoh, the ancient capital of the Ghurid Dynasty. It was all that was left, a solitary reminder in a barren world.

Kourash pointed to a squat whitewashed building with blue window frames about a hundred yards away.

'That's where we sleep,' he said. 'The UNESCO guesthouse.'

Baz's eyes lit up. 'Civilisation! All the way out here.'

'Don't get excited, doll,' said Logan. 'Wait till you see inside.'

'You've been up here before?' said Mac.

'I have.' He turned away. He clearly wasn't going to say more.

Baz grabbed a torch from the back of the Surf and scouted around the base of the tower.

'Look!' she said. 'This is the bit that's in the photos. That means the antiquities were definitely here at some point.'

'But now?' said Mac.

Baz looked around and pointed in the direction of the river gorge. 'There are caves along the Harirud. Holmberg could use them to hide things. Or maybe they were never stored here at all, but just photographed passing through.' She shrugged.

'Well, we know he was coming this way, and it must have been for some reason.'

Ginger appeared at Mac's shoulder.

'Seems like the river's flowing too fast for vehicles to cross the ford. He must have gone back down to the main road.'

'But we would have seen him,' said Mac.

'Not if he was warned we were coming,' said Logan. 'He could have taken cover somewhere until we passed.'

'Damn!' said Mac. He caught up with Kourash, who was walking towards the guesthouse, shouting orders to his men. 'Listen, Commander. He's not here. If we stay for the night, he'll get an even bigger lead on us. Can't we get moving?'

Kourash's look mixed pity with exasperation. 'Mac-jan, what are you not understanding? We won't drive at night. We are Ismail Khan's best men, but we are not stupid. We stay here.'

Mac went back to the Surf to pick up his backpack. Baz joined him and together they walked across to the building where they were to spend the night.

'Feeling better now?' said Mac.

'I will be, when I get some food inside me.'

They went in through the painted wooden door and were assaulted by a strong smell of cooking, something rank and oily. Mac looked around – they were in a small reception area. There was a threadbare Persian rug on the tiled floor, but it was faded and sand-logged. Every step he took crunched, and the window on the far wall was too dirty to see out of. Baz wasn't going to find her creature comforts here.

Kourash and Jananga were deep in conversation with a white-haired man at the reception desk. No doubt wrangling over the room rate. Baz leaned in closer and Mac watched her expression change from polite interest to surprise.

'What?' mouthed Mac, cursing himself for not having made more of an effort to learn to speak Dari.

She beckoned him over.

'They're asking whether Holmberg's been up here.'

'We know he has,' said Mac.

Baz nodded and pulled a face at him. 'Sure. But the guy's telling them where he went.' She listened intently.

'And?'

Baz gasped.

'He paid the Aimaq for their camels, loaded them up yesterday morning and set off north, into the hills.'

'What the fuck?' said Mac under his breath. 'We need to go after him.'

Kourash turned to face him. 'We can't. By tomorrow he'll have a two-day start – we wouldn't be able to make up that time.'

'Shit!'

All this fucking way for nothing.

Chapter 52

Wednesday, 24 December 2003

The meal they sat down to at the UNESCO guesthouse shared some similarities with the meal they'd eaten in Herat the previous night – rice, stringy meat, naan – but couldn't have been more different. Mac thought he'd broken a tooth more than once on the gritty rice, and the age of the chicken that had been slung into the pot didn't bear thinking about, but it tasted like it had reached a ripe old age without the benefit of a fridge. He was already feeling pissed off before they sat down, and being offered a choice of green tea or green tea to drink didn't lighten his mood.

They'd been allocated bedrooms – the Kabul team sharing two to a room, while Kourash and his men would all bunk down in the dining room once the meal was over. Naturally, there'd been an assumption all round that he would share with Ginger, which would leave Baz sharing with Logan. He couldn't think of a reason to suggest swapping rooms, so now he was thoroughly out of sorts.

He chewed endlessly on the same piece of gristly meat, lost in thought about where the mission had gone wrong. When Ginger went outside for a cigarette after the meal, Mac followed him out.

'Bloody snafu, isn't it?' he said, taking the cigarette Ginger offered.

They made sure they were standing between the wall of the building and one of the Hilux trucks – they didn't need to offer themselves up as targets to whatever brigands roamed the area at night. Ginger had brought his rifle out with him. Just in case.

'Should have had eyes on him as soon as he arrived in Herat,' said Ginger.

'No fucking communication, no co-operation between the Kabul police and the Herat police.'

'Like they say, Afghanistan – parked diagonally in an alternate reality.'

They smoked in silence for a minute and Mac looked around. The dark shadows of the gorge loomed above them and the sky was as black as velvet, sprinkled with a billion stars that you would never see from the city. A few feet below them, the rush of the river was as noisy as traffic on a busy road, drowning out any other sounds they might have heard. It was cold, but there was no wind, and savouring the cigarette, Mac began to feel a little calmer.

'Hey, guys, where's the party – because it sure ain't here.' It was Logan.

'What I wouldn't give for a beer,' said Ginger, rolling his eyes.

'You did good today, Ginger,' said Logan. 'So did you, Mac. For a limey.'

Mac laughed.

'And a shower,' added Ginger. His fatigues were still stained with the blood of the injured man he'd helped, and like the rest of them, after a day's travel and a skirmish, he stank. However, the guesthouse didn't actually run to a bathroom – just a tap with ice cold water and a hole-in-the-ground toilet.

'You weren't so bad yourself, for a merc.'

'Ain't no shame in that, brother.'

Mac wondered idly if that was where his future now lay. But he'd already decided to put off serious thought about his prospects until the mission was over.

Jananga and Baz loomed out of the darkness, Jananga lighting up as they joined the huddle.

'No shame in what?' said Baz, catching the end of the sentence.

'Being a soldier of fortune,' said Logan. 'For example, I could use my contacts and dig this mission out of the hole it's in.'

'Out here?' said Mac. 'You know some local camel herders or something?'

'Not exactly,' said Logan. 'Just let me see what I can do.'

'Please to come inside now!' It was Kourash and he didn't sound happy.

Cigarettes stubbed out, they all trooped back into the entrance hall. Mac looked into the dining room, but the meal had been cleared and Kourash's men were already unrolling their bedding for the night.

He caught Logan's arm.

'What did you mean out there, about digging us out of a hole?'

'I've got an idea. Let me talk to the guy on the desk.'

The white-haired old man was fetched from his quarters by one of the militiamen. He came grumbling into the foyer rubbing his back, and took the only chair with a sour exhalation of breath. Logan squatted down in front of him and started talking to him in Dari.

Standing to one side, Baz whispered a running translation into Mac's ear.

'He's asking the man how many camels Holmberg took, and what provisions... and how many men he had with him... two men and a young girl...' Mac saw Logan wince. 'They have six camels, each with a boy... they loaded some with food and water... three of them with boxes and packages...'

'The artefacts?' said Mac.

'I think so,' said Baz. 'The old man says they took a local guide to show them the way through Jawand District and take them north to Jawand Bazaar, the district capital.'

The commander interrupted the man with a sharp exclamation.

'He says they're crazy to try that,' said Baz. 'One hundred miles of festering brigands who'll kill them for a pair of sunglasses... they won't make it.'

'And we can't follow them?' said Mac, stepping forward to address the group.

'One of my men is from Jawand,' said Kourash. He went to the dining room door and spoke to someone. The militiaman who had helped the injured passenger out of the car came and joined them. Even Mac could tell the Dari he spoke was strongly accented and Baz struggled to understand him. He talked for some minutes with the guesthouse keeper and then with his commander.

Kourash translated for them. 'He grew up in Jawand and he knows the guide who Holmberg is travelling with – his uncle's second wife's cousin – they grew up in the same village.'

It wasn't as far-fetched as it sounded. Mac had quickly come to realise that everyone in Afghanistan, especially outside Kabul, seemed in some way related to almost everyone else.

'He can guess the route they're taking. It will be governed by how far they can walk each day, and they'll need to find caravansaries for their overnight stops – to keep them safe and to ensure they have food and water.'

'So he could act as our guide?' Mac was determined they shouldn't just give up and go home.

There was more talk between Kourash, his man and the innkeeper.

'No. Not without camels or mules to carry provisions – and we have neither.'

'There might be a way,' said Logan.

'How?' said Jananga, who'd been surprisingly quiet up to now.

'Just gonna make a couple of calls,' said Logan. He had a Thuraya satellite phone with him and he went outside by himself to get the best signal.

Mac caught Baz's eye and she shrugged. He didn't want to get his hopes up. He paced around the reception area waiting

341

for Logan to come back and explain himself. He looked out of the door into the pitch black, but he couldn't hear anything. He peered around and saw a tiny glow of light in one of the vehicles. It came from Logan's phone. Mac went back inside.

'I'm gonna call it a night,' said Baz, stifling a yawn.

'You going to be okay?' said Mac. 'Sharing a room with him?'

'With Logan? Of course.' Then she laughed. 'Safer than with you, I think.'

Mac glanced round. The dining room door was shut. Ginger had gone to bed already. There was no one around, not even the guesthouse manager. He took a step towards her.

'I think you'd be safe with me.'

'Too bad you're sharing with Ginger.'

Being so close to her made him acutely aware of how much taller than her he was. And, despite the day, how good she smelled. And how awkward and difficult it was to work out whether he could kiss her.

She made the decision for him.

'Happy Christmas,' she said, leaning in. She kissed him on the cheek, then she was gone.

Chapter 53

Mac was dreaming. Snow was falling, silently at first, then with a soft thwap-thwapping noise as the flakes grew larger. Something was wrong. Snow didn't make that sound. And it was getting louder and louder...

He sat up and opened his eyes. He wasn't in his container. He was in a small room, somewhere east of Herat. Afghanistan. Light bled in at the edge of an ill-fitting blind. The blanket-covered form on the other side of the room was Ginger. But the sound of his snoring was rapidly drowned out by an insistent thwap-thwap-thwap somewhere outside the window.

It was coming closer.

He pulled off the rough cover he'd slept under and squinted out through the gap, but he could see nothing but one side of the ravine and the watery grey sky above it. The room was cold. A glance at his watch told him it was just before seven. Thwap-thwap-thwap.

'What the fuck?' He knew what it was now. 'Come on, Ginger. Up.'

He pulled on his trousers, shoved feet into his boots without bothering to do them up, and ran out into the foyer. He opened the door onto the gravel car park at the front of the guesthouse. Outside, the noise was practically deafening.

A helicopter, descending rapidly, blotted out the scrap of sky between the two sides of the gulley. Logan was waving it down to land on a flat gravel area just beyond the end of the guesthouse.

343

'What the fuck, Logan? How did you manage that?'

His words were whipped away in the downdraught and there was no chance of Logan hearing them.

As the aircraft settled onto the ground, Mac shielded his eyes from the whirlwind of dust.

'Christ,' said Ginger, from somewhere behind him.

Kourash and his men streamed out of the guesthouse, shouting excitedly, followed by Jananga and a very confused-looking Ardshir.

Mac rubbed his eyes and blinked. No, he wasn't still dreaming. The blades of an old Soviet Mil Mi-17 transport helicopter were still slowly turning as Logan ran up to greet the pilot.

Vertical Lift.

He knew the logo painted on the side of the plain grey chopper. Vertical Lift was a charter helicopter company used extensively by the UN and a lot of the NGOs. Mainly because it was the cheapest option. Shit, he hoped Logan wasn't expecting the Afghan police to foot the bill for this – there was no way Jananga could finance this type of op.

'*Privet*, Kolya!' shouted Logan above the dying noise of the chopper. 'Surprised to see this old crate still in the air.'

'Logan, my friend,' said the pilot as he dropped down onto the ground. 'Surprised to see nobody has shot you yet.' He spoke with a distinct Russian accent, and had pale skin and Slavic features. All of Vertical Lift's pilots and engineers were ex-Soviet air force or army who'd flown in Afghanistan during the occupation.

The two men laughed and hugged each other, before walking back towards the guesthouse. A second man came round from the other side of the helicopter and caught them up, giving Logan a hearty slap on the back.

'Pyotr, you dog. I thought you went to Dubai.'

Dark haired and dark skinned Pyotr shook his head and laughed. 'Too boring – the hotel to the airport. The airport to the hotel. Back and forth, all the day.' He spat in disgust on the ground.

'Logan, how the hell?' said Mac, stepping forward and snagging Logan's attention away from his reunion.

'My Christmas present to you,' said Logan, with a grin.

'Best stocking filler ever, pal,' said Mac. 'But seriously?'

'Let's just say these boys owe me a favour. A big favour.'

Mac raised his eyebrows.

'Another time, man.'

Somehow Mac doubted he'd ever hear the full story, and maybe he didn't want to.

'That's one fuck of a favour,' said Ginger in his ear.

'What's all the commotion?' Baz was the last one out of the guesthouse.

'Logan's Christmas present to us,' said Mac.

'A helicopter?' she said. 'I was hoping for camels.'

—

An hour later, Mac felt his stomach being left behind as they lifted off. Dust and gravel clouded underneath them, and the guesthouse became as small as a doll's house before they swept away over the top of the gorge.

He'd been surprised that they all fitted inside, but the Hip, to use the NATO name for the Mi-17, was a transport helicopter, designed for heavy payloads and up to twenty-four passengers. It wasn't comfortable inside, and it was bloody noisy, but it meant the mission was back on track, so Mac, for one, wasn't going to complain. One of Kourash's men was distributing naan and water. The commander and the militiaman with local knowledge were sitting up at the pilots' shoulders, while the rest of them sat on hard benches down either side of the fuselage. At least there were windows, so if they couldn't talk, they could look out over the extraordinary landscape.

Holmberg had a two-day start on them. As they'd boarded the chopper, there had been some debate as to how far he could have got in that time. According to Kourash's man, there were two routes he could have taken – due north towards Qeysar, or north-west in the direction of Qala-e-Naw. Both lay on the N Cir Highway, but the latter was nearer. From either of these he would be able to go on to the border with Turkmenistan.

'We'll try the trail that leads to Qala first,' said Logan. 'The terrain is easier and it's not so far to travel – it would be the logical choice. He'll do, say, fifteen, max twenty, miles a day. We'll drop down into the first village that might have been an overnight stop and find out if anyone's been through.'

Out of the window, the landscape was steeper and more spartan compared to that they'd flown over between Kabul and Herat – and they were flying much lower over it, at just a couple of hundred feet. The trail followed the rocky valley of the Harirud for a few miles west and then, where the river took a sharp bend south, struck north away from the water. The chopper climbed as the track curved up towards a shoulder on a low ridge. Over the other side, they swooped down and Mac felt his stomach flip as if they were on a roller coaster. They swung down towards a long valley. It was wider than the course of the Harirud, but there was no river at the bottom, just the mountain track, following the path of least resistance, used by traders on the Silk Road for more than a thousand years.

Cold air rushed through the cabin – one of Kourash's men was crouched by the open door, one arm hooked through a metal rail, the other holding binoculars to his eyes.

'What's he doing?' said Mac, leaning against Logan's shoulder to shout in his ear.

'Looking for camel dung.'

They lurched up again, the sides of the crags dropping away as the trail passed through a narrow buttress of rocks.

'Shit!'

Mac read Ginger's lips, rather than heard the word. He was looking positively green, slumped on the bench opposite with his head in his hands.

'Here you go, chum,' he said, leaning forward and tapping on Ginger's knee with a sick bag.

Ginger nodded, his mouth clamped tight shut. Mac turned back to looking out of the window – the last thing he needed to see was Ginger puking his guts out.

After another half hour of stomach-churning ups and downs, Kourash walked unsteadily down the swaying fuselage, hanging onto the guide rails.

'There's a village ahead – could have been their night stop. We're putting down,' he said.

Ginger looked overcome with relief – and then scrabbled to get the bag to his mouth before being volubly sick.

Mac couldn't get out of the Mi-17 fast enough – it stank of vomit. The ground seemed weirdly unstable for a couple of seconds, but once he'd got beyond the sound and the downdraught of the rotor blades, things started returning to normal. Ginger appeared to be somewhat shakier, but he managed a weak smile as he reached the patch of rocky ground the team were gathered on. Baz handed him a bottle of water and he rinsed his mouth out. The two pilots strode a bit further away and both lit cigarettes, laughing loudly at some private joke.

A hundred yards below them, Mac could see a small settlement – a handful of muddy brown dwellings, crudely built and without glass or even polythene in the small windows. There was a narrow stream and a patch of tended land, but it hardly looked like a place to subsist. A woman in brightly coloured tribal dress hurriedly herded two small children into one of the buildings.

'Stretch your legs for a minute,' said Logan. 'Kourash will take a couple of guys down to the village and ask if Holmberg came through.'

'I'll go with him,' said Jananga.

Logan shrugged. 'If you like.'

Mac was happy to let them go. He wouldn't have understood what was being said anyway. As he watched them walking down the hill, Baz came and joined him.

'Weirdest Christmas Day ever,' she said.

'Too true.' He took a swig of water. 'Do your family celebrate Christmas?'

'Not as such. But it's the holiday season in America, and I'm used to it. I love the Christmas lights and all the festive food. You missing it?'

'Christmas dinner, Mum's mince pies, sure. I think they miss having me home at Christmas, more than I miss the celebration itself. Hogmanay's more my thing. How are you doing, Ginger?'

Still looking green, Ginger had come over to where they were talking.

'I've felt better.'

Mac laughed. 'A fully paid-up member of the airborne brotherhood – and you puke your guts up on a short helicopter flight.'

Ginger managed a smile. 'Why d'you think I was so damn keen to jump out of the bloody things?'

Below them, a man emerged from the first of the homesteads. He was carrying a weapon and had a leather bandolier of rounds slung across his chest. Mac squinted and so did Ginger.

'Is that what I think it is?' said Ginger.

'A Lee Enfield No4.'

'He's had that a long time.'

'Must be sixty years old, if it's a day.'

'What?' said Baz.

'They were using those in the Second World War,' said Mac. 'It must have seen some action over the years.'

The man shouted something at the party going down the hill and raised his weapon. Shit – hopefully it wasn't about to add to its tally. Kourash shouted back at him. The man scowled, but he lowered the gun. As they got closer, the first man was joined by another, older man. They spoke for a minute and then Kourash led his men and Jananga back up the hill.

'No – no one's been through here since the summer,' said Kourash, confirming what Mac had suspected from the brevity of the conversation.

'We'll cut north-east, across to the Qeysar trail,' said Logan. 'All aboard.'

Another hour of flying, punctuated regularly by Ginger retching into a paper bag, and they picked up the other track. The way was steeper and the gulley narrower than the first route. The Mi-17 stayed just above the top of the crags on either side – smoother flying, at least for a while. Then the valley opened out and the chopper swooped down. Patches of vegetation became more common, close to the banks of a fast-flowing river, and at one point they passed half a dozen or so nomad tents.

Mac got up and picked his way precariously to where Logan was sitting with Kourash.

'Are we not going to stop and ask those tribesmen we just passed?'

Kourash grinned and then dragged a forefinger across his throat.

'They'd as soon shoot us as talk to us,' said Logan. 'They hate Ismail Khan, his men and anyone in uniform.'

Mac went back to his seat. Surely Holmberg couldn't have made it much further than this?

He didn't have to wait much longer.

Fifteen minutes later a cry went up from the front of the helicopter.

'*Shotor, shotor!*'

'Camels,' said Baz, wide-eyed with excitement. 'We've got him.'

349

Chapter 54

Thursday, 25 December 2003

Baz might have spoken too soon. The helicopter lurched to the side and then jerked upward. For a second Mac thought it was going to stall. Baz gasped and grabbed hold of the nearest thing, which was his arm. Pyotr and Kolya were cursing almost loud enough for him to hear them over the engine noise. A precipitous swoop to the right, and Mac realised what was happening – they were avoiding gunfire from the ground.

You couldn't sneak up on someone in a helicopter.

Kourash's men calmly readied their weapons for combat, while their commander, hanging onto one of the handrails with white knuckles, stood at the pilots' shoulders, assessing the situation on the ground below.

The plan was simple. Once they spotted the caravan train, they would land, arrest Holmberg and whoever else was with him, and rescue the girl. Of course, Mac had anticipated some resistance – but shooting at the chopper? This guy was taking no prisoners. If one bullet hit one rotor... He tried not to think about it, but there was nothing else to think about as they swung from side to side and lurched up and down. A sudden rush of acceleration took them out of range, then Mac felt the elevator-drop sensation of a fast landing.

As soon as the wheels had touched down on the uneven ground, the militiamen stormed out, dropping behind a ragged outcrop of rocks. The camel train was about two hundred yards further down the trail from them. Mac squinted out through one of the Mi-17's windows. Holmberg was also using boulders for cover. He watched as the three camel boys took off down the track the way they'd come, too terrified to try and retrieve their frightened animals.

'How many weapons does Holmberg have?' he enquired of Kourash, who was directing his troop from the open door.

'At least four men with AKs.'

'Including him?'

'Yes.'

Kourash barked a command in Dari, and four of his men broke cover from the rocks to move to a forward position. The remaining four gave them cover.

'Come on,' shouted Mac to Ginger and Logan.

They dived out of the chopper and took up the spaces behind the rock vacated by the men who moved forward. Ardshir and Baz crouched low behind them, while Jananga consulted with Kourash inside the fuselage. Kolya and Pyotr stayed in their craft, ready for a quick take-off when needed.

The shooting continued intermittently. Despite being outnumbered and with nowhere to go, Holmberg and his thugs were putting up a fight.

Baz bobbed up and took a shot at the rock Holmberg was sheltering behind. A second later Mac heard the crack of bullet against stone.

'Get down!' he shouted.

Incoming fire whistled past her, too close for comfort, and she dropped to the ground.

'Olle Holmberg!' Mac looked round. Kourash was just visible inside the Mi-17, holding a megaphone to his lips. 'Olle Holmberg, surrender now. Put down your weapons and come out with your hands raised.'

The commander's speech was drowned out in a hail of enemy fire.

Then silence. It lasted ten seconds, fifteen seconds…

Mac waited. Whoever broke cover first would get the first shot in, but would draw immediate fire.

'Stay down,' he said to Baz.

'So what happens now?' she said.

They could see the four men that had gone forward looking around for the next area of cover. They used hand signals to communicate with each other and Kourash, pointing to a low shoulder on the right-hand side of the gully where they would, if lying down, still be covered. Kourash nodded his agreement.

'Get ready to cover them.'

As soon as the first of the militiamen moved, Mac, Logan, Jananga and the rest of the men let rip with a blanket of fire. Holmberg's men returned fire. Despite the fact they were outnumbered and facing a hail of bullets, they still managed to get a hit. One of the militiamen let out a sharp cry and went down. Mac could see blood welling from his thigh. It didn't look good. He would need emergency treatment and they didn't have a medic with them. He carried on firing until the rest of the men reached the safety of the hillock.

'We need to work forward up the other side,' said Logan.

'With you.'

Bent low, Logan scurried to the furthest point of cover afforded by their current position. Mac followed him. Kourash nodded at them both, and instructed his men to give cover.

Logan pointed to a large boulder on the left-hand flank of the narrow valley. It was big enough for both of them to duck behind, but it was almost forty feet away.

'That's pushing it,' said Mac.

'Bob and weave,' said Logan.

Bob and weave. Mac knew the drill. Keep moving. Don't move straight. Stay small, stay low. Dive for cover.

'Go,' yelled Logan, waiting a second for the covering fire to initiate. Then he was off.

Mac followed him out from behind the rock, darting from side to side as he crossed the open ground. Bullets bounced off the dirt in front of him and whistled past his head. He was in their sights for less than six seconds but it seemed like forever.

Then he practically smashed into the rock and dropped to the ground next to Logan, panting loudly.

The shooting subsided.

Mac looked round the edge of the boulder. The shot militiaman was still lying in the open, not moving, not making a sound. Mac didn't rate his chances. A bullet glanced off the rock a couple of inches above his head, and he ducked back.

'One thing's for sure,' said Logan. 'If the guy's prepared to go down rather than be pulled in, he knows he's guilty as fuck.'

'Yes, he's guilty all right,' said Mac.

The team on the other side of the gully were preparing to move forward. As the gunfire started up again, Mac pushed his rifle barrel over the top of the rock. He sneaked a peek to get an aim on Holmberg's men – and that's when he saw Holmberg making his break.

'Fucker's running.'

Holmberg hardly had to break cover to dart up the steep, rock-strewn slope only a hundred or so metres from where they were.

'I'm going after him,' said Logan. 'I can't let him get away.'

'I'm coming with you,' said Mac. He turned back to where Kourash was watching from the chopper, and made some hand signals to him so he'd know what was going on.

Then they were off, skirting a small stream that ran down their side of the gorge, ducking and weaving to avoid fire, and keeping a constant eye on where Holmberg was headed. He disappeared over the top of the outcrop, about forty yards due north of where they had found cover.

Mac took in the lie of the land. If they dropped back a bit, they could take advantage of a low col and get out of the theatre of fire. Then they could track Holmberg in the open, which would make their progress much faster. He pointed out the route to Logan, who nodded.

Just ten yards of open ground, then over the top and down the other side. Just ten yards.

Logan went first and Mac ducked after him. It was steep, but it wasn't far. Mac thought they'd made it. He was ready to breathe a sigh of relief as he crested the ridge.

Logan was just ahead of him, a crouched silhouette against the blue sky.

There for a second and then gone as a bullet catapulted him down the other side.

Chapter 55

Mac charged down the slope towards where Logan had fallen. The American had rolled several feet, before coming to rest on his back on a flat ledge.

'Logan!'

'Fuck, that hurts...' He was alive. In agony, but fully conscious.

'Where did it get you?'

'Back, my shoulder...' Logan's face was already grey with pain.

'I'll get you back to the chopper.'

'No.' He winced and took a couple of deep breaths. 'Get Holmberg.'

Mac looked round. There was no sign of the Swede. But then he spotted him, galloping down towards the bottom of this new valley, where there was another track veering away to the north-east. Mac watched him for a couple of seconds, then raised his rifle and let off a volley of fire.

Holmberg looked round briefly but carried on running.

'I'll be fine,' said Logan. 'Go. Kill him if you need to.' This last was said through gritted teeth, and confirmed Mac's suspicions. Logan wanted revenge for Bao's death. That's why he'd come along – with the full intention of taking Holmberg out.

Mac traversed the slope in the direction the Swede had taken, making sure that he was always well under the level of the ridge.

He could still hear shooting in the neighbouring valley and he hoped like hell that Baz was keeping her head down. As Holmberg hit the trail at the bottom, Mac skidded on a patch of gravel and nearly lost his footing. He had to jump to stop himself stumbling over a rock – he was virtually out of control as the slope steepened.

Holmberg raised a pistol, a Beretta, and shot at him, then carried on running.

As Mac came onto steadier ground, he raised his AK and fired back.

'Stop, Holmberg. Give yourself up.'

The blond giant ignored him and kept running.

Mac reached the bottom. The track was flat, but by no means even, and he still had to keep an eye to the ground as he ran. Holmberg vanished round a bend – he had a lead of approximately twenty-five yards. Mac's chest felt tight with the exertion. How much further could he run? How much further could Holmberg run? His only hope would be to hide himself somewhere they couldn't find him – but there was nowhere here.

As he rounded the corner, Mac wasn't surprised to see that Holmberg was no longer on the track in front of him. He looked around. On the left-hand side of the trail the rocks were too steep to climb – at least not without leaving oneself a sitting duck. The slope on the other side was also fairly steep, but a narrow goat path wound up it. Holmberg wasn't on it.

Mac ran on, looking carefully from side to side. He was pressing against the wind, sharp as a blade against his cheeks, and the sky above was a flat, gun-metal grey. A damp flurry of snowflakes stung his eyes and made him blink.

'Holmberg, show yourself!'

There was a shot and a bullet ploughed into the sandy margin of the track. Mac veered to one side, looking for cover as he tried to work out where the shot had come from. Somewhere to the left, higher up. It didn't make sense – that was a sheer rockface. Wait, there was a cleft between two huge slabs. As Mac came level with it, he raised his weapon, ready to fire the moment he saw any sign of the man he was pursuing.

A small pathway disappeared between the rocks, sloping up into a dark canyon. Mac peered into the shadows and stepped back. He wouldn't see Holmberg, but Holmberg would see him against the bright light of the opening.

'Come out. You can't hide in there forever.'

But then he heard footsteps. Someone was on the main trail. He whipped round as another bullet just missed him. Holmberg was running again, Beretta in hand.

Jesus wept.

Mac broke into a run. He made up a few yards, then stopped to raise his rifle. Holmberg saw what he was doing and swerved from side to side. Mac lowered the weapon – there was no way he'd hit him. As he refocused his gaze and started to run again, he saw it.

At the edge of the path there was a small rock, about ten inches in diameter. One side was painted red, one side white. The side facing Mac was white. The side facing the part of the trail on which Holmberg was running was red. There was another similar stone on the other side of the path a few feet further on. He skidded to a halt. His blood froze in his veins.

Thank God he was still on the white side.

But Holmberg was on the red side.

'Minefield!' he shouted. 'Stop! Stop running!'

Holmberg stopped in his tracks. But then disbelief washed over his features and he took a step forward.

'Stop!' shouted Mac again. 'Look.' He pointed to the rocks.

Holmberg saw them. He knew what they meant. Everyone who lived in Afghanistan knew what they meant – walk where the locals walk. The warnings of a legacy minefield – probably left by the Russians, possibly by the Taliban or the Northern Alliance. But it didn't matter who – they were all lethal. The Swede froze. He'd run thirty yards into a minefield and survived. And now he was stuck. He was a sitting target.

Mac kept his rifle raised. Holmberg slowly raised his Beretta. But if he shot Mac, he'd still be stuck in the middle of a minefield and his chances of getting out alive would be even slimmer. Snow flurried around them both, but there was not enough on the ground for them to be able to see Holmberg's tracks. He was marooned, and he'd be a fool to move even an inch.

Mac lowered his weapon.

'Drop the gun,' he shouted at Holmberg, 'if you want help...'

'What can you do?' shouted Holmberg, his pistol still trained on Mac. His voice sounded shaky.

Mac didn't say anything. He was listening. The sound of gunfire in the other valley had faded away. But it was snowing heavily now and noises wouldn't travel so far. He thought quickly. There was only one way to get Holmberg safely out – with the chopper. For him to move would be suicide. So there was nothing stopping Mac from going back to help Logan. They could clear up, load up and pick up Holmberg last.

He looked back at the Swede. He was squatting now, but his feet were still in the same position. He would get tired and he would get cold, and eventually he'd need to sit. Even that was risky – there could be a mine within a centimetre or two of his boots, and there was no way of telling.

'I'll go for help,' said Mac, setting off back up the track. He didn't wait for Holmberg's answer. What was the point?

Exhausted as he was, he jogged along the flat bottom of the valley until he reached the slope where he'd come down. It was tougher climbing up than it had been skidding down, but the sight of Logan lying at the top spurred him on to go as quickly as he could.

'Logan? Talk to me.'

The body moved and let out a long groan of pain.

'Thank God.'

He squatted down next to the injured man. Logan was shivering, and the tunic he was wearing under his ops vest was soaked with blood around the area of his right shoulder.

'You a leftie?' said Mac, trying to remember which hand Logan favoured.

'Sure am.' His voice cracked through dry lips.

'You'll be okay then.' He would have punched his shoulder, but luckily thought better of it. 'I'm going for help – don't move.'

Logan's face twisted into what was almost a smile.

Mac crawled up to the ridge on his belly, feeling the snow soaking through his fatigues. There was definitely no sound of gunfire. He inched his head up just high enough to see over into the other valley. The mop-up operation was underway. Holmberg's thugs were cuffed and standing on their own, one of them sporting a slight flesh wound. Four of the militiamen were carrying their dead comrade, his head wrapped in a scarf, back towards the helicopter. Baz was talking earnestly to a young girl, presumably Xiaoli, though they were too far off for Mac to see if it actually was the girl who shot him. Kourash and Jananga were talking with the rest of the militiamen. Ginger glanced up in his direction and pointed – obviously telling the men where he and Logan had last been seen.

He raised an arm and shouted.

'I need help up here. Man down.'

Led by Ginger the men started up the hill immediately. Baz stopped talking to the girl and followed them at a run, a worried look on her face.

Mac stood up and beckoned them on. Baz's expression changed to a smile.

'God, you had me worried for a second there,' she gasped as she came level with him. 'You're okay?'

'I am. Bloody knackered, but okay.' Mac grinned back at her and, not caring what the others thought, swept her into a hug.

359

Chapter 56

They quickly patched up Logan using the first aid kit in the chopper. Mac gave him a dose of morphine to make him more comfortable, and once they had him wrapped in blankets, he dozed off. The taut pallor of his face looked a little less severe as his muscles relaxed.

Xiaoli sat shivering in the cold fuselage, watching them work. When they finished, she moved across to sit by Logan and took his hand.

Baz cleaned her hands with sanitising gel. 'We need to get him to a hospital,' she said. 'The sooner the better.'

'Okay, let's go,' said Mac to Kolya, who was at the controls.

The plan was to take the Mi-17 over the ridge to the next valley and pick up Holmberg. They would land first, at the edge of the minefield, and everyone but Kolya and Pyotr, and one of Kouresh's men to work the winch, would disembark. Then, hovering well above the danger zone, they would be able to lower the winch to the stranded man.

While Baz and Mac had attended to Logan, the camels had been rounded up. Ginger and a couple of the militiamen had loaded the packages they were carrying into the back of the fuselage, along with the dead body of their colleague.

'What'll happen to the camels?' said Baz.

Kourash laughed. 'Always so concerned for the animals, Basima-jan. The boys will come back to find them.'

Thankfully, it had stopped snowing, and once everyone was on board, the short hop to the adjacent gulley took less than a minute.

Mac disembarked quickly and went to the edge of the minefield. Holmberg was standing again, twisted around to watch the helicopter land – he still didn't dare to move his feet.

'Okay?' Mac shouted, as the noise of the rotors died away.

Holmberg glared at him. Of course he wasn't.

'We'll lower the winch and have you out in a jiffy.'

'But first a couple of questions, Mr Holmberg.' Mac turned to find Jananga at his shoulder.

Everyone was out of the chopper now and ready to watch the spectacle.

'Genius,' muttered Mac to Jananga.

'Make it quick,' said the Swede through gritted teeth. He looked wobbly on his feet.

'Tell me, Mr Holmberg, what are the goods your camels were carrying, and where exactly were you taking them?'

Holmberg bit his lip, clearly weighing up how he should answer. There was a veiled threat inherent in Jananga's questioning.

'We're waiting, Holmberg,' said Mac. 'And it's easier for us than it is for you.' He wanted to underline the threat.

The tension built and Ginger caught his eye. Mac shrugged. 'If he plays ball now, it might be easier for him back at Police HQ,' he said.

Holmberg cleared his throat.

'I have papers for all those items.'

'Where?'

'At my office in Kabul.'

Mac didn't believe him. If he was moving the artefacts legally, he'd have the papers with him to prove it, for when he reached the border.

Jananga snorted. 'If you are lying, you'll find yourself in Pul-e-Charkhi for an extended stay.'

But it wasn't the antiquities that concerned Mac.

'You knew Captain Davie Marshall, didn't you?'

Holmberg wasn't so slow to answer this time. 'Sure, I knew him. He played mah-jong at the Lucky Star. I saw him there from time to time.'

'He owed you money, didn't he?'

'He owed money to the men he played mah-jong with. We had a small agreement and I was helping him pay it off.'

'But he wasn't paying it off fast enough, was he? That's why you killed him.'

'I had nothing to do with his death.'

'I think you did.'

'I was out of the country the night he died.'

'Where?'

'Dubai.'

'We can check that.'

'Not while I'm standing in this bloody minefield.'

Mac paused.

Holmberg faced away from him and bent at the waist, his hands on his knees supporting him.

Mac wondered if he should say what he was about to say. He looked across at Xiaoli. Baz had found a spare fatigue jacket for her. It swamped the girl, making her look far younger than she was. Baz had an arm wrapped round her shoulders, but he could see that she was still shivering.

He swallowed, then spoke. 'You killed Bao Liang.'

'No.'

'We have a witness.' This was a lie, but Holmberg didn't know that.

Holmberg was silent. No more denial.

Behind him, Mac heard a scuffle.

'You killed my mother?' Xiaoli's pain sliced through the cold air.

Mac turned in slow motion to see Baz landing on the ground on her back. Xiaoli was holding Baz's pistol. She adopted a wide-legged stance and flicked off the safety. 'No...' yelled Mac. 'Get down! Everyone, get down!'

'I helped you and you killed my mother.' This time Xiaoli's screech wasn't a question.

She fired at Holmberg. There was the sound of an explosion. In the time it took Mac to turn his head, Holmberg was on the ground, several feet from where he'd originally been standing. A few feet from him, the tell-tale cloud of smoke from a detonated mine was rising into the air. The bullet had hit a mine. Holmberg sat up, blinking and rubbing dirt out of his eyes.

But Xiaoli still had the gun.

In blind panic, Mac lunged towards her, his hand outstretched to try to deflect the arm with which she was holding the gun.

She fired again, but this time there was only the click of the hammer falling on the empty chamber.

Then Mac made contact and they both fell to the ground. Ginger landed on top of them and Jananga removed the weapon from her hand.

Somebody started clapping slowly and Mac looked up. It was Kourash, his smile as wide as ever.

'Good save, Mr Mac-jan, good save.'

–

Jananga had handcuffed Xiaoli, who'd fought like a wildcat.

'What did she mean?' said Baz. 'I helped you and you killed my mother?'

Mac shrugged. 'It seems like maybe she wasn't with him under duress.'

'You think she ran away with him by choice?'

'She helped him... helped him in what way?'

'Of course she freaking did,' said Baz. 'It was her. She's just about the one person other than Bao who could have known about the raid in advance. Bao would have warned her – and she warned Holmberg.'

'Come on, she's a child,' said Mac.

'Yeah, it fits with what Mayleen said. He liked them young.'

'We'd better tell Logan.' It wasn't something Logan would want to hear. It could certainly wait until they got back to Kabul, until they'd had a chance to question Xiaoli about it.

Mac couldn't see charges being brought against her for what she'd attempted, but she'd definitely need to be restrained for the duration of the flight. The rest of them were waiting and watching as the rescue attempt got underway.

The helicopter was now hovering two hundred feet above the minefield – high enough up to prevent its downdraught from setting off a mine. Holmberg had very tentatively clambered to his feet in his new position. Mac could see that his trousers were stained with urine. The man had pissed himself, and Mac couldn't blame him, given the circumstances.

The winch was lowered slowly, and finally Holmberg was able to grab hold of it with a shaky hand. It took him a few minutes to attach it round his waist – he let go of it at one point and it swung away from him.

'Shit!' said Baz, next to him.

Mac held his breath as the Mi-17 was once again manoeuvred into a position where he could grasp it. But finally it seemed secure, and Holmberg gave the thumbs-up. As he was winched up to the cabin, the chopper swung rapidly away from the minefield, no doubt giving Holmberg the ride of his life.

He was handcuffed to one of the benches in the fuselage by the time they landed.

Ten minutes later the chopper was up in the air again. Four prisoners – Holmberg, Xiaoli, and his two thugs – one dead body, a consignment of retrieved antiquities. Xiaoli spat at Holmberg as she was bundled past him to her seat. They dropped off a couple of Kourash's guys at Jam to sort out the return of the vehicles, then they were on their way back to Herat, Pyotr and Kolya grinning about something at the controls.

'That must have been one fuck of a favour they owed you,' said Mac to Logan as the Mi-17 swept along the Harirud valley.

'It damn well was,' he said with a pained grin. 'Saved a man's life. An important man. But now I owe them in return — and believe me, they'll make sure I pay.'

Chapter 57

With Logan injured, a consignment of recovered antiquities and a prisoner who could be considered 'a person of interest' in the Davie Marshall murder, they needed to get back to Kabul as fast as possible. Luckily, Pyotr and Kolya's next job was out of Kabul, so after dropping Kourash and his men in Herat, and refuelling at their client's expense, they were quickly airborne again.

They took Logan straight to the German Medical Clinic, where he spent a day being patched up by an American doctor. The bullet was removed and he was all stitched up, though still moaning vociferously about the pain. Mac and Baz visited him and told them what they suspected about Xiaoli's involvement. He didn't seem surprised.

'That bastard had been sniffing around her for a while. That's why I wanted him out of the joint.'

Xiaoli hadn't left his side and hadn't stopped begging for his forgiveness. She'd had no idea when she left the Lucky Star with Holmberg that her mother was dead. It had all been a big adventure for her. But it turned out that her teenage ideas of a romance with Holmberg had already gone sour by the time they left Jam. Walking through the mountains in winter wasn't the elopement she'd expected. And then she'd discovered that her lover was responsible for her mother's death. It was no wonder she'd snapped, and tried to shoot him.

Holmberg was going to be charged with sex trafficking as well as all his other crimes, but that didn't answer the question of what was to become of Xiaoli. Jananga had been all for dumping her at the Chinese embassy, but Baz had taken her back to the Gandamack and said she'd reach out to some of the NGOs dealing with women's issues in the city. It was clear that Logan, fond of her as he was, was in no position to take on a teenage girl, and Baz didn't just want to send her back to the Lucky Star where she'd end up in a life of prostitution. She seemed bright and spoke several languages, so surely she could somehow claw her way into a better life.

For Baz, all the loose ends were starting to tie themselves up, but she knew Mac was frustrated.

'Holmberg's alibi for the night Davie Marshall was killed holds out,' he said, grim-faced behind the wheel as he drove her and the recovered consignment of artefacts to the museum. She and Professor Paghahan were going to unwrap them together and she was super excited to see what they would find.

'But surely you'd checked that already?'

Mac shrugged. 'He's got more than one passport. He was travelling on a different one.'

'Seriously?'

'It's not illegal. He's got dual nationality. He travels in the Middle East and visits Israel. A lot of people do it, but we hadn't picked up on it.'

'But he's still going down for Bao Liang's murder?'

'Definitely. And for owning a brothel – papers in his office show that he was actually the owner of the Lucky Star – plus sex trafficking a minor. That's all great. But it means I still don't know who killed Davie.' He banged the heel of his hand on the steering wheel in frustration.

Baz shrugged. 'Razul?'

Mac shook his head.

'One of Holmberg's other henchmen?'

'I suppose so. We'll probably never know.'

Baz was sympathetic, but nothing could dent her delight at being able to return Holmberg's stolen artefacts to the museum.

'You go in,' said Mac as he pulled up by the museum gates. 'I need to make a couple of calls. Then I'll bring the rest in.'

'Sure.'

Baz went to the trunk of the Land Cruiser and grabbed a plastic crate into which they'd stacked all the smaller packages. She hefted it out, gave Mac a wave and went up to the gate. It was still being manned by the same boy guards, and they opened it for her without question. Either Paghahan had warned them in advance, or they finally recognised her as someone who could go in unchallenged.

'Professor?' she called as she marched along the central corridor. 'I come bearing gifts.' It had been all she could do not to rip the packages open as soon as they were unloaded from the helicopter. But it had seemed right to wait until she got them here, so the professor could see them at the same time.

'Basima-jan,' said Paghahan, appearing from a side room. 'You are like the female version of Indiana Jones.'

Baz laughed as she followed him into his office. 'Not really, Professor.'

There was an awkward moment after she put the crate down on his desk. Baz went to hug him, he put out a hand to shake, and they ended up skirting round each other without doing either.

'You're well, Basima?' he asked.

'Yes, thank you.'

'And your parents?'

'Yes, indeed. You and your family are well too?'

'Yes, thank you. I think your father will be very proud of you.'

With the formal greetings out of the way, Baz lifted the lid of the crate. The professor peered in and then started to take out the wrapped items and put them on his desk.

'You have no idea what's inside these?' he said.

'No. Holmberg was heading for the border with Turk-menistan. I'm guessing his ultimate destination was Dubai or even Europe. He claimed that he had papers for them, but he hasn't been able to produce any.'

Paghahan took a pair of half-moon spectacles out of the pocket of the koti waistcoat he was wearing over his shalwar kameez.

'Let's take a look,' he said.

The packages were of varying size. Some were taped up in bubble wrap. Others were bundled in cloth and tied with string. Grey dust clung to all of them, suggesting to Baz that they had indeed been stored in a cave or had even been buried for a time. She wondered if Holmberg had more items hidden in the same place.

Paghahan picked up one of the cloth-swathed items. He took a pair of scissors and snipped through the string, then unfurled the rough cotton. Sand spilled out onto the desk and the floor as he revealed a small Buddha statue of carved clay.

'That's beautiful,' said Baz, hardly daring to breathe as he held it up.

The head piece was chipped and an arm was missing, but it was still an extraordinary piece.

'We have some like this,' said Paghahan. 'It looks as if it could have come from the Buddhist monasteries near Hadda, close to Jalalabad. I would have to compare them more closely, but the style is very similar.'

'How old would that make it?'

'Fourth to sixth century, I think.'

An unexpected wave of anger hit Baz. 'And Holmberg thought he could help himself to this stuff and take it out of the country?'

The professor shook his head sadly. 'It would have gone to the highest bidder and probably never be returned to its home.'

'These items are priceless.'

She picked up one of the bubble-wrapped objects and started to peel away the tape. Paghahan was unwrapping another Buddha statuette and carefully wiping dirt and sand from it.

Baz twisted the package in her hand, unspooling several layers until she revealed a small brass lozenge. A Paiza.

'Look, it's just like…' Baz's words died in her mouth, but the professor was engrossed in a close-up examination of the statue he was holding.

Baz turned the Paiza over, to be quite sure of what she was looking at.

She looked away from it, in the direction of the window. Where was Mac? Where the hell was Mac?

She looked at the Paiza again, up close. There was no mistaking it. *There was NO mistaking it*. There was the tiny groove at the top of the eyelet, the mark made by the constant wear of the thong or cord on which the Paiza had hung. The mark she'd noticed the last time she'd held this Paiza in her hand, here in the museum.

There seemed a sudden shortage of oxygen.

She blinked and stared at it. If this Paiza had been stolen from the museum, the professor would surely have said something.

But he hadn't mentioned it.

She looked up and her eyes met his. He knew exactly what she was thinking.

370

Chapter 58

The calls took forever – but even with a good word from Jananga, Phelps was adamant that his dismissal still stood. He updated Holder on the mission and got small thanks for his work. But finally Mac was done, climbed out of the Land Cruiser and headed into the museum. He was carrying two of the larger pieces they'd recovered, and they weighed a ton. As he used them to push open the main door, the top package started to slide and he had to push himself up against the doorframe to hold it in place.

'Shit!'

He couldn't risk dropping it – it was probably some priceless and irreplaceable artefact that was a thousand years old. As he struggled to get the packages balanced again, Professor Paghahan appeared from the bowels of the museum.

'Ah, Mr MacKenzie, let me help you.' He took the top piece and Mac was able to stand back from the wall.

'Thank you, Professor. I have a few more still in the car. Shall I bring them to your office?'

'Yes, please do.'

Mac put down the package he was carrying and rested it carefully against the reception desk. Then he went out to the car and brought in the rest of the artefacts. As he did this, Paghahan ferried them from the reception area to his office. It only took a few minutes, and Mac followed Paghahan down the corridor with the final item.

'Put it here, please,' said Paghahan, pointing to a corner of his office where there were more packages stacked up.

Mac looked around.

'Where's Baz? I thought she'd be in here, checking the artefacts.'

The professor gave a half smile and a half shrug. 'You missed her. She left just a few minutes before you arrived. I think she had a call from America.'

'Oh?' Mac thought for a moment. Sure, he'd been on the phone, and he'd been jotting things in his notebook, rather than looking around – but Baz wouldn't have left the museum and walked straight past his car. This didn't make sense. 'Are you sure, Professor? Maybe she's in the bathroom?'

The professor shook his head. 'No. She had to leave.'

There was something off about the way he spoke. Mac didn't believe him – but what the hell did that imply?

'But she never showed up at the car…'

It simply didn't make sense. He couldn't have missed her, unless she'd gone out by a different door, or somehow detoured as he'd been on his way in.

Professor Paghahan shrugged. 'She's not here.'

Mac shook his head in puzzlement. 'Okay, I'll go and check outside for her.'

A loud crash somewhere in the distance made the professor jump.

'What was that?' said Mac.

'I have some workmen here. They're clumsy fools.' The professor stepped forward with an arm outstretched to shepherd Mac towards the door. 'It would be better if you left now, so I can sort them out.'

Mac allowed himself to be escorted from the office but he had no intention of leaving the building. There was something fishy going on. What had happened to Baz? What had she seen or done? He made a move to go in the direction of the noise.

'Mr MacKenzie.' Paghahan's tone was sharp now.

372

'Professor, I think maybe Baz is still here. Perhaps she's with the workmen...' He realised that made no sense at all, but it gave him the excuse to stride away from the older man. He had no idea what was going on, but he was determined to find out. And to find Baz.

When he reached the end of the central corridor, he faced a choice. There was a suite of rooms off to his left, or a staircase to the first floor on his right. He replayed the sound in his mind. It had been on the ground floor, he felt almost sure. He turned to his left and went into the first room. It was virtually empty, bar a couple of display plinths with nothing on them. He stopped and listened. There were no sounds of any workmen in the building, but even stranger, he couldn't hear Paghahan coming after him. It was as if he was completely alone.

A creaking of floorboards in a room somewhere ahead of him reminded him that he wasn't. He walked slowly and quietly into the next space. It was also empty, so he carried on moving. The third room had a couple of statues in it, but after that his way was blocked by a locked door. He heard the screech of a piece of furniture being moved on the other side of it.

'Hello? Who's there?'

'You need to leave. This isn't your country. These things don't concern you.' Paghahan appeared from behind a screen on the other side of the room. There must have been a door beyond it. His expression was hostile, and one hand was pushed deep in his waistcoat pocket.

Mac tried the locked door again. There was definitely someone on the other side of it.

'Stop!'

He turned back to the professor. Paghahan was pointing a pistol at him. 'You should have left when I asked you to.'

'Where's Baz?'

Paghahan drew a set of keys out of a pocket in his shalwar. He gestured with his gun for Mac to step away from the door. Once it was unlocked, he flicked the gun barrel again to indicate that Mac should go inside.

'Baz! Thank God,' said Mac. She was tied to a chair in the centre of the room. Nearby, a statue lay on the floor, its head snapped off and in pieces. The source of the crash. 'What the hell is going on?'

'It was him,' said Baz. 'He sold the artefacts to Holmberg, I'm sure of it. I recognised one of the Paizas I had seen before.'

'Quiet,' snapped Paghahan. He hooked the leg of an empty chair with his foot and dragged it closer to Baz. 'Sit.'

Mac did what he was told, playing for time while he worked out his game plan. Of course Paghahan would put them close together, so he could cover them both with one weapon. But he wouldn't be able to tie his captive up without putting down the gun. So what was he intending to do? If he locked them both in, it would be the easiest thing in the world to untie Baz and he was sure they would be able to work out an escape.

So that wasn't what the professor intended. Where could he go from here?

Was he a man who was willing to kill rather than be exposed as corrupt?

Paghahan looked unsure of his next move. Was he?

'You killed Marshall, didn't you?' said Mac. 'He found out that you were supplying Holmberg and he threatened to expose you.'

'I passed the pieces on to him and Holmberg paid me.' Paghahan's mouth twisted into a demented smile. 'But Davie wasn't going to expose me. Your Captain Marshall didn't care one bit where the artefacts came from. He just wanted money. More and more money to keep his mouth shut. He was greedy. So I told him to meet me at the tank graveyard for a final pay off, a lot of money to buy his silence. He believed me, and I took my chance. I couldn't let him live – he would have just come back for more and drained me dry.'

Baz looked at him in disbelief. 'And what about you? Selling off our country's treasures to line your own pockets. You were just as greedy.'

Paghahan shook his head. 'No, Baz. You don't understand the politics here. Elections are coming and we cannot let Hamid Karzai win the presidency. We need money to beat him in the *loya jirga*.'

'Who's "we"?' said Mac.

'Junbish-e Milli.'

'But that's Dostum's party,' said Baz. 'You couldn't.' She looked over to Mac to explain. 'Abdul Rashid Dostum is a warlord who allies himself with whichever side seems most expedient at the time.'

Mac knew he'd been accused of committing war crimes.

'He's proved himself a strong leader against the Taliban. Karzai is weak,' said Paghahan. 'Our cause is important, and I had to sell off a few small pieces to pay for it.'

'But they weren't small pieces – they were some of the most valuable pieces the museum had. No doubt you'll simply claim they were stolen by the Taliban, if anyone ever comes asking.'

'I get it now,' said Mac. 'The connection with Holmberg – we have proof that he was receiving money for arms from one of Dostum's lieutenants.'

Paghahan's patience was wearing thin, which meant they were running out of time. With Baz tied up, it was all on Mac.

'Duck!' he shrieked to Baz, at the same moment as throwing himself at Paghahan's ankles. If he could make the professor fall backwards, any gunshot should hopefully end up in the ceiling. But the professor's reaction time was whip sharp. He attempted to side-step Mac, while lowering the gun. Mac crashed into one of his legs and Paghahan fell to the side. The gun went off and Baz screamed.

Mac got an arm around Paghahan's neck and wrenched it tight. They both lay on the floor, winded and struggling.

'You... okay... Baz?'

He heard her gasp. 'I think so.'

The gun had clattered to the floor, but Mac had no idea where it was. Paghahan was flailing around as if he was trying

375

to reach it. With a supreme effort, Mac twisted the older man away from whatever he was grabbing at. For a man of his years, Paghahan was still strong and Mac was having trouble overpowering him. They strained and grunted, each determined to come out on top. Feeling the broken statue against his back, Mac took a chance. He let go of the professor with one hand and felt around on the floor behind him. Paghahan sensed that his grip had weakened and went all out to push Mac away. As he skidded past the figurine, his fingers found what he was looking for. Part of the smashed head. It was heavy enough and it had sharp edges. He shifted his weight to give his arm the freedom he needed. He swung the piece in a wide arc and smashed the sharp edge into Paghahan's eye.

The professor's grip on him went slack.

Chapter 59

Mac climbed up the ladder and onto the top of his container at Camp Julien for one last time. The sun was a blood red orb in an amber sky, the spikey outline of TV Hill silhouetted against it. The muezzin were making the final call to prayer.

'*Allahu akbar... ashadu an la ilaha illa Llah...*'

He listened, as entranced as ever, watching the sun sink down as the air grew colder.

Even after the voices finished, he stayed sitting in his chair. He would miss this view. The room at the Le Monde guest house to which he'd transported his gear earlier in the day just overlooked a busy main road and an unremarkable building opposite blocked out any view of the Kush. And he probably wouldn't have time to sit around taking in the view anyway – he had to find another job.

Davie Marshall's case was closed, and even though he wasn't going to get any recognition for the part he'd played in it, he felt a grim satisfaction that justice had been served. Paghahan and Holmberg had been caught. And, somehow, Jananga managed to weave his way through the maze of corruption while still standing by his principles. Mac could bloody admire him for that, even if his methods were unorthodox compared to British police standards.

With a shiver, he climbed back down the ladder. He'd felt nervous when he accepted the job in Kabul, but now he was glad he was here. It was such an extraordinary place. And now a whole new chapter lay ahead of him.

Mac had spent the first half of the day with Jananga at a debriefing at Camp Souter. Lambert had insisted on a blow-by-blow — quite literally — account of the whole course of the investigation, and he'd written it out in triplicate on various official documents and forms. Paghahan was in Jananga's custody. The surgeons at the Afghan Apollo Indian Hospital on Salang Road had done all they could to save his eye, but apparently it was touch and go whether he'd see again on that side. Mac didn't give a shit. And he didn't really care how Jananga had extracted whatever information he needed to secure a conviction. Paghahan had as much as confessed to having killed Davie Marshall, and he would have killed him and Baz too.

Baz was shaken but unhurt, and as soon as he'd untied her from the chair, she'd hugged him as if she never wanted to let him go. That felt good. Then she'd kissed him, and it felt even better. He met her later that night, back at the Gandamack, and they sat in the bar, calming their nerves with a couple of bottles of wine.

'We did it, Khan,' said Mac. 'Solved the mystery and caught the villains.'

'Damn pesky kids!' said Baz, with a wide grin. 'It's going to be a great story to write up.'

'But you're going to leave out what happens next, aren't you?' He reached out a hand, intertwining his fingers with hers.

She nodded, still smiling. 'This bit will be on a strictly need-to-know basis, Mr Mac-jan.'

Now all the i's were dotted and the t's crossed, he could start to think about what he was going to do next. Logan had assured him there was plenty of work going in Kabul, depending on what one was willing to do, and the bar at the Mustafa was virtually an unofficial employment agency for businesses that wanted to keep their dealings under the radar.

It was time to go. He knocked on Ginger's door.

'Coming for a well-earned drink?'

'Wouldn't miss it, boss,' said Ginger, appearing on the threshold.

As Pamir dropped them outside the Mustafa, Mac saw Jananga coming down the pavement towards them. Mac raised a hand in an informal salute.

'*Salaam alaikum.*'

'*Alaikum a'salaam.* Mac-jan, how are you?' said Jananga, with a wide grin. 'It's good to see you.'

Mac held open the door into the hotel.

'Major Jananga. Or is it lieutenant colonel now after your great success?'

'I am certainly hoping not,' said Jananga following him inside.

'What?'

They headed for the bar.

'I am happy at my level. Being a major I'm safe and I know I will go home to my wife and children every day.'

'But being a lieutenant colonel is surely just as safe?'

'Not so. With every round of *padshahgardi*, the faithful servants of the old incumbent are assassinated...'

'*Padshahgardi?*' interrupted Ginger.

Jananga paused. 'How would you say... a change in power. The higher ranks are swept away – but as a lowly major, I'm safe. So I always say "No" when they offer me a promotion.'

Although he said it with a twinkle in his eye, Mac was sure it carried a grain of truth.

'Tell me, Mac-jan, how is your arm now?'

'On the mend,' said Mac.

Ginger clapped him on the back with a grin. 'Yes, Mac, you must tell me, does being shot by a little girl feel any different to being shot by a grown man?'

'Fuck you, Ginger,' said Mac. Now he'd never escape the story – Ginger would make sure of that.

They joined Logan and Baz in the bar. Logan had already lined up the drinks. Baz touched Mac's forearm and kissed him briefly on the cheek, going a pleasant shade of pink when Logan's eyebrows went up.

Mac pretended he hadn't noticed.

'What I find hard to believe,' he said, holding up his tumbler of malt to the light to appreciate the rich amber colour, 'is that you, Baz, purposely knocked over a priceless statue and smashed it to draw attention to yourself.'

Baz clinked her glass against his, and then against Logan's and Ginger's and, finally, against Jananga's. 'It was a fake. I wouldn't have damaged anything real.'

Logan laughed. 'So if it had been real? You would have sacrificed yourself to keep it in one piece?'

'No way. I just would have screamed really, really loud.'

Logan, freshly released from the clinic, had regained his colour but still had one arm in a sling. Now he was keen to hear how the investigation had ended.

'So if Marshall was sending antiques out of the country for Paghahan and Holmberg to pay his gambling debts, why did Paghahan slit his throat?'

'Because he got greedy,' said Mac. 'He was threatening to reveal what Paghahan was doing unless the professor paid him more money.'

'And are the Brits happy with the outcome?'

Mac shrugged. 'I think they would have liked to have got their hands on Paghahan, but being stuck in Pul-e-Charkhi is punishment enough.'

'Major Holder telephoned me,' said Jananga. 'They rounded up and arrested the men in the UK who were receiving the antiquities at Lyneham. He seemed satisfied.'

'Where's Holmberg?' said Mac.

'Also in Pul-e-Charkhi,' said Jananga, with a wry smile. 'The Swedish embassy are doing all they can to get him out, but we won't let go of him. Baseer Ghilji is in the next cell to him.'

'I told my father that last night,' said Baz. 'He sends you greetings and thanks, Jananga-jan. He's trying to persuade my mother to come back here, so he can take over the museum.'

'Seriously?' said Mac.

Baz laughed. 'It's not going to happen. Mom's been in America for nearly thirty years. She's too used to her air-conditioning and mod cons to come back here. But I think my father will visit.'

'What about Xiaoli?' said Mac.

'I've managed to get her a place on a woman's education programme,' said Baz. 'She's going to live with Mayleen, at Balbala's house. I should be able to get some financial support for them, until they find jobs for themselves. Neither of them want to go back to the Lucky Star.'

'I can't thank you enough,' said Logan. 'Xiaoli's been distraught over Bao's death, and the role she played in it. Thank God she's got Mayleen at her side.' His heartfelt tone made the mood suddenly more serious. 'It's Bao's funeral tomorrow. Baz, I wonder, would you come with me and Xiaoli?'

'Of course,' said Baz. 'Where will it take place?'

'At the British Cemetery, just up Shahid Road – about five minutes from the Gandamack.'

'I know it.'

'Ah, Kabre Gora,' said Jananga, using its Afghan name. 'She'll be at peace there amid the roses.'

Logan glanced down and remained silent. Baz briefly touched his hand. 'I'm so sorry,' she said. 'At least Holmberg will pay for his crime.'

More than pay, Mac thought to himself. His life inside Pul-e-Charkhi would be hell. He went to the bar for another round of whisky, but thought better of it and bought the whole bottle. When he returned to the table, the mood seemed lighter again. Jananga was telling Baz the names and ages of his children, counting them off on his fingers as he did.

'You've got six children?' said Baz.

'So far.'

'You're intending on having more?' Her eyebrows went even higher.

'Of course. I need to make sure there will be still some around to look after me when I'm too old to chase across the country after murderers with Mac and Logan.'

Mac opened the bottle and topped up their glasses. Even Jananga accepted another finger, shaking his head, but holding out his glass at the same time.

'Now,' said Mac, putting the stopper back into the bottle, 'I need to hear the story, Logan.'

'What story?'

'Whose life you saved that put Vertical Lift eternally in your debt.'

'Oh. That story.' He took a slug of whisky. 'It's long. Complicated.'

'And?' said Baz.

'Well, if you're all sitting comfortably...'

'Slange,' said Mac. The whisky tasted damn good.

Acknowledgements

Creating a novel is always a collaboration and we'd both like to thank all our accomplices in *Death in Kabul*.

Firstly, we're hugely grateful to our agent, Jenny Brown, for her help and encouragement along every step of the winding road to publication.

We also owe a debt of gratitude to our editor, Craig Lye at Canelo, for the faith he put in this book from the start and for his thoughtful input throughout the editorial process, resulting in the book we have today. Thanks too, to the rest of the team at Canelo, including Joanne Gledhill, Vicki Vrint, Francesca Riccardi, Claudine Sagoe, Thanhmai Bui-Van, Nicola Piggott, Elinor Fewster, Micaela Cavaletto and Iain Millar.

We are indebted to Tom Sanderson for his brilliant work on the cover, which we really love.

Thanks to our beta readers, Jennifer Hogan and Nellika Little.

Nick's acknowledgements

First and foremost, I'd like to thank my sister and co-author, Alison Belsham, for coming up with the idea for a murder mystery set in Afghanistan. Though this isn't strictly a murder mystery, it was originally.

I'd also like to further thank Nellika for teaching me so much about Afghanistan and the Afghans – I still remember sitting in the shade in Zinder Jan drinking tea and eating wild apricots with her and the village elders back in 2004.

I owe a great debt to many Afghan friends, in particular Baktash and Shariff.

And finally, I'd like to apologise to Manny and Rodney from Fred's Garage in Woodlawn just outside Baltimore. Guys, I wanted to put you in the book but until you open a branch in Kabul it just isn't happening!

Alison's acknowledgements

When the idea of writing a book with my brother first sprang to mind, I wondered if it could possibly work or if I'd taken leave of my senses... Well, thankfully it did work, and not only that – it was an incredibly enjoyable and satisfying experience. You may not believe it, but we actually didn't have a single argument or disagreement throughout the process.

Writing is a solitary pursuit (even when done in collaboration!) and every writer needs a support network. So thanks and respect to my partners in crime from the Edinburgh Writers' Forum, Jane Anderson and Kristin Pedroja, for their ongoing love, support and writerly chatter, particularly during the long and difficult months of lockdown. Our WhatsApp group is always busiest when we're supposed to be writing!

And finally, thanks to Mark, Rupert and Tim as always for being there.

A note from the authors

Nick fell in love with Afghanistan approximately twenty years ago. Alison fell in love with the country over the course of writing this book.

Since we started working on this project, Afghanistan has been overtaken by the most horrifying humanitarian crisis in its history. It's heart-breaking to watch the events that are unfolding there.

There is little practical we can do to help, but we are pledging to donate 10 per cent of the author royalties of *Death in Kabul* to Afghanaid.

Afghanaid is a British humanitarian and development organisation that has worked in Afghanistan for nearly forty years, building basic services, improving livelihoods, strengthening the rights of woman and children, helping communities and responding to humanitarian emergencies. With years of experience, their majority Afghan team has a deep understanding of local, cultural and ethnic issues, and they have earned trust and respect among the communities they serve. Their work is now more critical than ever before.